"I thought perhaps we had met before,"

Leighton said.

"I assure you, my lord, that if we have, I cannot recall the incident," Melissa said stiffly.

Leighton shrugged slightly, as if in puzzlement. "You must excuse me." He looked straight at her, his eyes sparkling. "I assumed that I had done something to merit the foul reception you are giving me."

Melissa, who was in the midst of snapping her fan in irritation, actually felt her jaw drop open at his words. Her surprise quickly gave way to anger, and she felt her blood rise to a boil. To stand here and be insulted . . . and by someone she had never spoken to before in her life. It was truly beyond anything!

"Or do you greet everyone with such dreadful malice in those lovely eyes?"

Melissa, now utterly flabbergasted, was speechless.

"Good," Leighton said with a nod. "I see that I have vexed you beyond words. Therefore, when I ask you to dance, you will be unable to deny me."

Dear Reader,

This July, Harlequin Historicals brings you four titles that you won't want to miss.

Texas Healer from Ruth Langan is the long-awaited sequel to *Texas Heart.* After years of study in the East, Dr. Dan Conway finally returns home to Texas . . . as a wanted man.

With *Temptation's Price,* contemporary author Dallas Schulze has turned her talented pen to writing a historical. Matt Prescott married young Liberty Ballard for the sole reason of preserving her good name, and promptly left town. But five years of haunted dreams have got Matt wondering whether life without Liberty is really worth living.

In Deborah Simmons's *Fortune Hunter,* set against the backdrop of Regency London, a viscount looking for a rich woman and an heiress looking for a title discover that they've both been had.

Dangerous Charade by Madeline Harper is the story of a prince who is unaware of his royal heritage and the headstrong woman who convinces him to rescue his birthright.

We hope you enjoy this month's selection.

Sincerely,

Tracy Farrell
Senior Editor

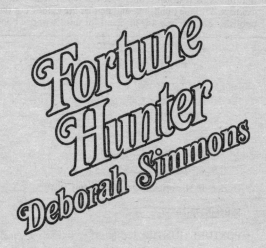

Harlequin Books

TORONTO • NEW YORK • LONDON
AMSTERDAM • PARIS • SYDNEY • HAMBURG
STOCKHOLM • ATHENS • TOKYO • MILAN
MADRID • WARSAW • BUDAPEST • AUCKLAND

Harlequin Historicals first edition July 1992

ISBN 0-373-28732-1

FORTUNE HUNTER

DEBORAH SIMMONS

grew up with a love of reading and writing instilled in her by her mother, an English teacher and closet poetry writer. After a brief stint in advertising, Deborah wrote for a newspaper for several years. She turned to fiction writing after the birth of her first child, when more time at home gave her the opportunity to tackle her pet project: a historical romance. A fan of the genre for many years, she longed to create her own and was lucky enough to see that first work published in 1989. She lives in rural Morrow County, Ohio, where she divides her time between her young family and writing.

For my friend Kim Lindsey

Chapter One

Leighton Somerset, Viscount Sheffield, frowned slightly as he leafed through some papers. Poised behind an elegant Louis XV desk, he leaned back in his chair and crossed his long legs at the ankles. London's late-afternoon sun shone vividly through the windows, lighting a desktop strewn with bills and casting a warm glow over Leighton's blond hair, recently ruffled by an absent stroke of his hand. With a sigh of disgust, he cast down the papers he held, which joined the others scattered in front of him, and rang for his secretary.

A trim, middle-aged man of good countenance appeared soon after the summons. His hair was a dusty brown, and he stood at average height, his head cocked slightly forward as he looked at Leighton. "Yes, my lord?"

"Mr. Parker," Leighton said, "prepare me a list of the most eligible young women of substance."

"My lord?" Leland Parker's eyebrows traveled up his forehead questioningly.

"We are going heiress-hunting, Parker," Leighton said, a crooked smile playing over his face.

"If I may inquire, my lord?" Parker's voice was laced with disapproval.

"Yes?"

"To what purpose will we be pursuing the, ah . . . females in question?"

"Why, Parker, I am shocked at your insinuation," Leighton said, feigning effrontery. "Nothing but marriage, I assure you!"

Parker's features immediately softened from an expression of distaste to one of gentle concern. "Has it come to that, my lord?"

Leighton frowned again. "I'm afraid so," he answered, a sweep of his hand taking in all the bills littering the desk. "Father's latest spree at Brighton has done us up."

"Surely the earl has not indulged in gambling again?" Parker asked, his voice betraying the answer to his own question.

"Mr. Parker, with my father, gambling is not an indulgence, it is a predilection, along with brandy and opera dancers half his age," Leighton said, a tinge of bitterness seeping into his voice. With a movement of his wide shoulders, he tried to shrug it off. "I gather he lost all but Greyhaven itself to Lord Braxton, leaving nothing with which to pay these creditors—who are already losing their patience." He frowned at the desk's burden, then looked up at Parker, who appeared too distressed to speak.

"Cheer up, Parker! It is high time I wed, is it not?" Leighton said, straightening up in his chair. When his secretary only looked glumly at the floor, Leighton smiled. "Run along now, and let us see what treasures of womanhood you can find for me. And tell Morgan that I will be dressing to go out this evening," he instructed. "I'll be looking in at White's and then ... I've a desire to visit Almack's."

The shocked look that appeared on his secretary's face in reaction to his intention to visit those particular assembly rooms, notorious for being a center for the marriage-minded, sent Leighton rocking back in his chair with a soft peal of laughter.

Despite his seeming disapproval, Parker presented a list to Leighton as he was dressing for the evening. His neckcloth dangling carelessly, Leighton walked through the dressing room to the bedroom, where rose-colored tapestries lined the walls surrounding an enormous bed draped in red velvet. Leighton dropped into a chair, crossed his feet on a delicately embroidered footstool and began to read.

"Emily Farnsworth," he said, choking out the name that topped the list. His eyes shot to Parker, who stood stiffly at his side as Leighton voiced his objection. "She resembles a giant toad."

"Quite so, my lord," Parker answered stoically, while Mr. Morgan, Leighton's long-suffering valet, tried to salvage the master's neckcloth. He was waved away silently as Leighton continued reading.

"Caroline Bridgebody...hmmm," Leighton said softly, raising one lean finger to his lips.

"Ahem." Parker cleared his throat, and Leighton looked up at him, a frown marring his features.

"Yes, speak up, Parker, before you burst."

"Miss Bridgebody, though she has never married, is rumored to be...quite free with her favors," Parker said, his disapproval apparent.

"I see." Leighton nodded, as though casting the name aside, and returned his eyes to the paper, slowly tapping his finger against his chin.

"Ann Worthington! Oh, really, Parker... She must have twoscore years on me!"

Parker shrugged. "She is an heiress, sir, and certainly...available."

"Arabella Russell!"

"A lovely girl, and quite well-mannered, I am told," Parker put in.

"And equipped with a giggle that sets my hair on end," Leighton said irritably. This business was not going at all as he had planned, and he was beginning to suspect that Parker was enjoying his employer's discomfiture. "Melissa Hampton... Hmmm..."

"My lord, she—" Parker began, only to be silenced by Leighton, who held up his hand to signal a halt. Parker opened his mouth and shut it again at the firm set of his master's features. For a moment, no one spoke. Leighton stared at his secretary, as though daring him to voice his objections. The only sound was from Morgan's quiet movements as he went about his duties.

"Very well, Parker, if you must speak, then do so. But watch what you say," Leighton threatened. His lips curved into a smile. "For you are talking about my future bride!" With those words, he jumped up from his seat, tossed the list casually onto the bed and proceeded to tie his neck-cloth.

Parker shook his head, leaving unvoiced whatever objections he might have had.

Leighton's club, White's, was crowded, and he ignored the stares as he walked through the room. He had not gone far when he saw Sir Charles Waverly—looking as though he had lost a relative—and Robert Smythe, who was far too sophisticated to show his concern, but surged forward to greet Leighton with a studied nonchalance.

"Sheffield!" Robert said with a grin. Tall, handsome, and dressed with understated elegance in midnight blue, Robert stood apart in a crowd, yet the attention he drew tonight was due only to his choice of company. It was Leighton who interested the other men in the room, and they watched him intently.

Conscious of the unwanted scrutiny, Robert leaned closer, whispering softly for his friend's ears only, "The whole place is talking about it, of course."

Charles was not so subtle. "Is it as bad as they're saying, Leighton?" he asked, his round face pink with distress.

Robert frowned down at his portly companion and glanced back to Leighton. "Braxton's been here, making more of it, I'm sure."

"What are you to do, Leighton?" Charles whined. "Why, the thought of someone else in Greyhaven, it's . . . it's preposterous."

Leighton flashed his usual smile, not only at the friends who pressed him, but also toward those others in the room who glanced unobtrusively his way or eyed him with open curiosity. Most looked away once they saw his carefree demeanor, some shaking their heads with amazement to see that the Greyhavens were going to scrape their way out of this one—or so it appeared, by Leighton's casual attitude. One by one the eyes dropped, a few with more than a little disappointment, for, like vultures at a kill, they had scented blood and were ready to move in to strip the carcass.

The Greyhavens were an old family, founded by Greyson Somerset, who had received the title in 1623. Although the boisterous old earl was friendly to a fault and Leighton himself was quite popular, there were always those who were ready to take advantage of another's misfortune, whether by gossiping cruelly or by taking a vacated place in the social sphere, and some minds were already working on how they could profit from the family's downfall. Perhaps some land or other holdings were to be had cheaply. . . .

"Gentlemen, please," Leighton said firmly. He extended his arms casually to his friends, and, with his hands resting lightly on their backs, steered them toward an uncrowded corner of the room. "The earl has not lost Greyhaven, and I intend to make certain that he never does," he said as they walked.

"And how are you to do that, short of locking the old man up in his room?" Robert asked acidly while Leighton calmly took a seat.

"But, but, but . . . Braxton," Charles spluttered, looking red-faced down at Leighton, who appeared not to have a care in the world.

"Ah, yes, Lord Braxton," Leighton said. Folding his hands together, he looked questioningly at Robert, who sat down beside him. "So he was here?"

"That obnoxious buffoon," Robert said coolly. "He's to blame for all the attention," he noted with a nod toward the other men in the room. Engaged once again in their own conversations, they appeared to have lost interest in Leighton's troubles for the moment. "He breezed in early, bragging of his winnings from the earl, and everyone knows—" Robert broke off.

"Everyone knows that my father can ill afford any new debt," Leighton finished with a slight grimace.

"Well, you still have many friends, for there were quite a few who refused to listen to the braying ass, and old Lord Montebank chastened him soundly," Robert said with a smile.

"Oh, you should have seen it, Leighton!" Charles cut in, finally sitting down with a gasp. "The old codger brandished his cane and took Braxton to task right in front of his fellows. 'What an accomplishment,' Montebank says. 'Why, winning money from Cubby Somerset is akin to taking sweets from an infant—it's easy, but mean-spirited.' Then he yells, 'Do you take pride in that, man?' Of course, he's nearly deaf," Charles explained, chuckling merrily at the anecdote until he caught Robert's frosty glare.

Robert's look was enough to flush his cheeks red with embarrassment up to the roots of his treasured brown curls. "Well, ah, not the sort of thing to repeat, I imagine," Charles mumbled, glancing sheepishly at Leighton.

"It's all right, Charles," Leighton said softly, shrugging slightly. "I have become quite used to tales of my father's doings."

Charles breathed a sigh of relief and returned Robert's glower. "Well, I would think so, especially after that episode last year with the blonde from Covent Garden."

"The earl's an easy prey for gossips," Robert broke in matter-of-factly, shifting in his seat. "I think he enjoys the fuss he stirs up."

"Oh, undoubtedly," Leighton agreed with a smile. "That is half of the fun for him. Unfortunately, his increasing efforts to top himself are leading him—and, consequently, me—to ruin.''

''What's to be done?'' Robert asked, his lips set tightly.

''You can't lose Greyhaven!'' Charles moaned. His thoughts, which had been momentarily diverted to the amusing and fun-loving earl, returned again to the enormity of the situation.

''As I said, I have no intention of forfeiting Greyhaven,'' Leighton said softly but firmly.

''You have a plan!'' Charles gasped, his face transformed immediately from glumness to glee.

''What?'' asked Robert skeptically.

''I, my friends,'' Leighton said, leaning back in his chair to watch their faces, ''am getting married.''

''No!'' Charles shrieked.

''Oh, my God,'' said Robert quietly. ''You mean it.''

''Of course I mean it,'' Leighton said. ''And why should I not wed? I am more than of age, my dear Robert. It is time I got some heirs.''

''From your smirk, I imagine the poor wench is comely,'' Robert said. ''Who is she?''

''Someone with lots of money,'' Charles said, smiling blissfully.

''Yes,'' Leighton said, ''my future bride is blessed not only with beauty, but with a fortune, too.''

''Good Lord, man, not Caroline Bridgebody,'' Robert said, starting forward in his seat.

''No.''

''Arabella Russell,'' Charles stated with certainty. ''What a sweet little thing for our Leighton!'' he added, nearly clapping his hands with delight.

''No,'' Leighton said. ''You are both wrong. Where are your eyes, fellows?'' He smiled. ''I speak of none but Melissa Hampton.''

Charles's hopeful face returned to its former forlorn expression, while Robert laughed scornfully. ''The Lady Disdain?'' Robert asked, shaking his head. ''If that's your

scheme, Leighton, you might as well put up the estate.
You'll get nowhere with that one.''

"Why?"

"Because," Charles twittered testily, "she has turned
down half the fortune hunters in town, and scared away the
rest with her vile tongue. The creature's a termagant!"

"As though you would know," said Robert with a scowl.
"I cannot personally vouch for the lady's disposition, but
she has not received the title 'Lady Disdain' for her
warmth."

Leighton, far from looking crestfallen at this news,
seemed slightly amused. "How intriguing," he whispered,
raising a forefinger to rub thoughtfully against his chin.

"You can take that smug grin from your charming features, Sheffield," Robert gibed. "A beauty she may be, but
the Lady Disdain is one female you will fail to win, I'll bet."

"Would you, now?" Leighton said, his hazel eyes taking
on a soft light that Robert recognized.

"Oh, no!" Robert protested, shaking his head and moving restlessly in his seat. "How can I rob you of funds you
do not have?"

Leighton laughed aloud, one of his famous dimples
making an appearance as he did so.

"*I'll* wager!" cried Charles.

"Remember, Charles," Leighton warned with a smile,
"unlike my father, I never make a bet unless I am certain of
the outcome."

"Humph!" snorted Charles. "So you may think. I say
you will never have the lady's affections."

"And what if I wed her?" Leighton asked.

"The Greyhaven earldom is an old and honored title,"
Robert mused, taunting Charles. "Perhaps the lady's family will snap it up, whether Miss Hampton says yea or nay."

"Humph!" Charles grunted again, undaunted. "I did not
say I would wager against the marriage. It is the lady's heart
you must win," he said slyly, "if she has one."

"Well, Leighton?" Robert said, looking from one man to the other.

"Bring on the betting book!" Leighton said with confidence. "But hurry, my friends. My God, look at the time! I must rush if I am to make Almack's before they close the doors."

"Almack's?" Charles squeaked in distressed tones.

"Why, naturally, dear Charles. Where else am I to be introduced my future bride?"

Melissa Hampton raised her head at the knock on her door. Frowning at the intrusion, she silently closed the novel that had held her attention and slipped it under a cushion. "Yes," she called softly, suddenly aware that she was still seated at the dressing table where the finishing touches had been put to her glossy, dark hair a good half hour before.

At her word, one of the new maids, Ann, entered and bobbed her head. "Pardon me, miss, but your mother wants you in the green drawing room," she said.

"Tell her I will be down shortly," Melissa answered, carefully hiding her irritation at her mother's summons.

"Pardon me, miss," Ann repeated nervously, her hands pulling at her skirts, "but she told me not to come back without you."

Melissa promptly squelched the temper that flared at this announcement. The maid's downcast eyes showed her embarrassment at her task and made it painfully obvious that she was new to the Hamptons' London household.

She would get used to these episodes soon enough, Melissa thought. It wouldn't be long before she joined the other servants in complaining of her overbearing employer, Gloriana Hampton, but for now the girl was shy and confused. Having no desire to make her life more difficult, Melissa set the maid at ease with a smile of acquiescence and rose to go with her.

They left Melissa's rooms and walked along the upper gallery, past her mother's newly purchased paintings, a motley group of lifeless landscapes and still lifes that appeared to have been chosen for their delicate nature rather than their artistry. Each time Melissa passed by, she missed her father's fine collection—including her favorite Vermeer—which had been sold after her father's death.

The inferior artwork only heightened Melissa's annoyance with her mother. Really, it was beyond vexation to be dragged about like a child by a servant. If her father could only see her now!

The thought brought a smile to her lips, for Melissa realized that, if summoned by Gloriana, her father would simply have gone to the top of the stairs—probably without his neckcloth, or in some other state of undress—and good-naturedly shouted down that he would be along in his own good time. His behavior, unseemly by Gloriana's standards, would have distressed her so that she would dare not utter another peep!

Yes, that was the late Harlan Hampton, Melissa mused. He had handled Gloriana with ease, ignoring her dictates. Melissa, on the other hand, was taught to obey but rebelled, and mother and daughter seemed always at odds.

Although Melissa had no desire to start an argument over this evening's order, she did not appreciate being led about the house like a schoolroom babe, and eighteen years of experience had taught her that it was best to nip this situation in the bud now. Otherwise, Gloriana would make a habit of sending the servants to escort her daughter wherever and whenever she liked.

Determined to relay her outrage, Melissa started down the steps, only to stop short when she caught sight of her mother. Gloriana was not in the drawing room, but was standing in the hall, attended by several servants.

"Ah, there you are, my dear," Gloriana said, slipping on her gloves as Melissa approached. A small, trim woman, Harlan Hampton's widow managed to mask her innate strength with a fragile femininity. Her short, dark hair, shot through with touches of gray, framed her face in tight curls, and her lips were more than lightly rouged.

She usually swathed herself in laces and ribbons, and tonight was no exception, Melissa noted. She frowned at the mass of white ruffles that stretched from Gloriana's neck to her waist and trailed down her back, and at the large bows that adorned the short, puffed sleeves of the jonquil-yellow gown. Melissa decided that her mother resembled nothing more than a giant daffodil sprung to life.

In contrast, Melissa's own ice-blue gown, with a single bright ribbon around its high waist, looked positively austere. Gloriana hated it.

"Not that blue again," Gloriana said. "You look like a simple serving maid. Doesn't she, Mary?" she asked of the maid who hovered nearby. Without waiting for an answer, Gloriana scowled at her daughter and sighed. "Naturally, it's too late for you to change now."

Melissa tried not to smile smugly over her small victory. There was still the matter of the summons, and Melissa realized that, unfortunately, that particular discussion would have to wait. Gloriana was ringed by servants.

Brown, the butler, was standing rigidly midway between his mistress and the door, where a footman stood at the ready. The housekeeper and Gloriana's personal maid were milling about, their only function, as far as Melissa could tell, being to provide their presence. She strongly suspected that Gloriana kept them at hand to prevent Melissa from complaining of her ill-treatment, for Gloriana never argued or discussed personal matters in front of the servants.

Since her mother usually managed to surround herself with a retinue of employees, this left little chance for Melissa to do either. *One day,* she promised herself, grinding her teeth in frustration, *One day, I will make an unholy scene in front of the entire staff.* She restrained herself tonight, however, and waited until she was alone with her mother in the coach before expressing her displeasure.

"Mother, I do not think it was at all considerate to send Ann after me, as though I were a child," she said, keeping her voice even.

"Well, my dear, if you did not act like one, perhaps I would not treat you as such." Gloriana's voice, too, was level as she reprimanded her daughter. Her face was composed, and her hands slowly moved to open her reticule.

"A young lady does not keep others waiting while she dawdles over her toilette," Gloriana said. Without even glancing at her daughter, she pulled out a handkerchief. "And we would not wish to be late for Almack's, my dear."

"Why not?" Melissa asked testily, smarting from her mother's barbs. "We have been there constantly since you obtained the vouchers, and it has changed little."

"I do not expect nor desire change because I find it most enjoyable as it is," Gloriana said, her gaze drifting out the window into the darkness.

"But I do not," Melissa said. "Oh, Mother, why must we keep going there night after night when it is plain—" She stopped short of saying the words that leapt to mind—that they simply didn't fit in—she had no desire to wound her mother. She only wanted to dissuade her from her course. "It is plain that we are not the same sort of people," she said instead.

"The only thing we lack is a grandiose title, and we shall have one," Gloriana said with a quiet vehemence as she finally turned to look at her daughter. "Your father's wealth will see to that, provided you put forth some effort to secure a husband."

It was an old quarrel between them, and Melissa fell easily into her usual arguments. "But what do we need with a title or a husband who is bought and paid for?" she asked earnestly. "We have more than enough money for our needs. We can enjoy our own household. We could take a house in Bath. You used to enjoy visiting there." This was a new suggestion, and Melissa held her breath with the hope that it might meet with Gloriana's approval.

"Your father did not work for his money only to have us retire to Bath as nobodies!" Gloriana said sharply. "Now, please, Melissa," she said, her voice suddenly soft once more, "you know how I dislike your constant arguing." With a sigh, she raised the handkerchief to her throat as though she would swoon from distress.

Melissa knew how very unlikely that possibility was, but she promptly closed her mouth, resigned to another night at the Marriage Mart.

Alighting from the coach in the soft glow of evening, she glanced with loathing at the plain brickwork of the building. Inside, she caught sight of a new face—some young thing from the country, no doubt, who stood enraptured by the tedious proceedings. Bad food, bad dancing and bad company, Melissa thought as she made her way through the crowd. Then she mentally chided herself for being so petty.

"Miss Hampton, how lovely to see you." A low voice sounded at her elbow, and she turned her chilliest smile—if, indeed, it could be called such—on one of her so-called suitors, Lord Richard Grimley. The second son of the Marquis of Trewesbury, Richard Grimley could boast of impeccable bloodlines dating back to the fifteenth century, and was related in some way to half the noble houses in Europe.

He was, however, only a second son, and, having no desire to live in reduced circumstances, or be anything other than a man of leisure, he was, as everyone was aware, searching for a rich wife. Had she the nerve, Melissa could have told him that he was wasting his time with her, for Gloriana had her mind set on a title, and nothing less. But Lord Grimley was far too full of himself to conceive of such a notion, so he condescended to speak with her, never dreaming that she hated every moment they spent together as much as he did.

Melissa answered his greeting with a stiff nod. "Lord Grimley." She decided as she watched him that his posture and scowl suggested someone who was confronting a fish in a condition of advanced decay. Perhaps it was the way he held his nostrils. . . .

"Would you care for some refreshment?" he asked. Melissa shook her head, knowing full well that he would certainly fetch nothing himself, but would collar some crony of lesser rank or a toady to slavishly do his bidding. Experience told her that he would not even hand it to her, and Melissa suddenly realized that in their several encounters he had never touched her.

The revelation was not really that surprising, since he seemed to view her as a leper of some sort. And yet he sought her out, presumably with marriage in mind. Melissa shook her head at the thought of spending a lifetime with such a man. She certainly held no girlish notions about love matches, but even members of the ton strove for amiable alliances. Not Lord Grimley, apparently. She could guess what would be in store for her with him: she would be installed at some ancient, crumbling and probably isolated mansion while he returned to London to squander his newly acquired fortune.

As Melissa pictured the scene, she silently thanked Betsy Belmont, as she often did, for imparting some knowledge of the world to her. As one of the older girls at Miss Hempford's School for Young Ladies, Betsy had taken the young and dewy-eyed Melissa under her wing and removed some of the stardust from her dreams. What illusions Betsy had not dispelled with her honesty. . . well, they had disappeared long ago.

With a sigh, Melissa returned her wandering thoughts to the present and Lord Grimley's perusal. Perhaps it was the argument with her mother, or her general annoyance with Almack's, or simply her unexplainable sour spirits, but Melissa's patience with his posturing was wearing thin. His ill-disguised look of distaste suddenly irritated her to the point of speech. "It is not catching, my lord," she said, snapping open her fan.

"Eh?"

"It cannot be passed from one person to another like a plague," she answered, fanning herself in short bursts.

"What's that?" Richard asked, looking peevish.

"Why, the taint of business, my lord," Melissa said, "or money made from trade."

Lord Grimley's mouth opened dully as he paused to digest this bit of information. Good Lord, Melissa thought. Too much inbreeding in these nobles has reduced their intelligence to the level of a lapdog's. Then she watched his chin twitch as he began to grasp her meaning.

"I'm afraid I don't follow you, Miss Hampton. You will excuse me." He barely nodded her way; he was already moving across the floor toward a young blonde who had been making eyes at him.

Good riddance, Melissa thought, pleased at having delivered herself so easily from his company. There was nothing like honesty to drive these aristocrats away, she noted wryly. Unfortunately, the exchange, repeated and distorted, would probably find its way back to her mother, and her momentary victory would only result in another battle at home.

Frowning at the thought of the inevitable quarrel, Melissa turned toward the entrance and began watching the new arrivals. It was a small game she played with herself, making mental notes on the illustrious, the grand, and the overblown as they came in. And it helped to pass the time.

Her eyes lighted immediately on Mr. Van Heusen, and her lips softened ever so slightly. Now there was a fellow after her heart, a nice old gentleman who made a point of dancing with all the young ladies, no matter how plain or how unpopular. Melissa included herself in both groups. As she watched, he stopped to speak with the Granger girls—tall, bony females who must surely find it difficult to sell themselves as future brides.

Melissa felt sorry for the Grangers, though she knew her sympathy would not be welcomed. If she were to approach either one, their large, horselike mouths would curve in contempt, for, despite their homely appearance and their less-than-ample dowries, the Grangers could boast of good lineage and a father, Lord Graham Granger, who had never lifted his finger in aught but leisure.

Melissa's father, on the other hand, had delved into trade to improve his lot, if not his social standing. A younger son of a younger son, he had provided amply for his family, and had cared not one fig for those who looked down their noses at such business dealings.

Although Melissa tried valiantly to be just as careless, she was finding the behavior of the Grangers and the Grimleys increasingly hard to stomach. Gloriana, apparently blessed with a hide as hard as nails, blithely ignored such snubs, declared Melissa too sensitive or too imaginative and plunged on into society.

"Miss Hampton..." Melissa felt a chill at the back of her neck; it was her usual reaction to Lord Bainbridge, a gouty old creature who considered himself one of her suitors. Unfortunately, he was an earl, and that found him some favor with Gloriana.

"Good evening, my lord," Melissa said levelly as she looked down at the man, who was several inches shorter than herself. She wondered, not for the first time, if what graced his head was some sort of false hair, or just the strangest-looking coiffure she had ever seen.

There was a furor at the door, thankfully drawing away Lord Bainbridge's attention, and Melissa glanced over the crowd. Lord, there's another one, she thought as she took in the general flurry that greeted the arrival of Leighton Somerset, Viscount Sheffield. The mamas were pushing their daughters forward, while the older ladies, married and unmarried alike, smiled and preened and cast sly glances his way.

It's positively sickening, Melissa mused. And the man has nothing to recommend him but a dusty old title and a head of golden hair. Why, he wasn't even that handsome, and his father, the Earl of Greyhaven, had a horrible reputation as a rake and a gambler.

"Humph! He's looking right cheerful for someone who's done up," Lord Bainbridge muttered.

"What?" Melissa asked, her eyes lingering on the viscount.

"The earl just lost this one's inheritance," Lord Bainbridge said. "There will be no more high living for him unless he has a scheme to right things."

Melissa did not answer, but watched the viscount now with curiosity. He was a little above medium height, a young man, probably in his late twenties, but he held himself with confidence, moving smoothly through the crowd as though he hadn't a care in the world. It was hard to believe that anything was threatening his life of luxury and, she assumed, excess.

He was wearing a claret coat over wide shoulders, and buff pantaloons that hugged a fine pair of legs, but that certainly was not enough to recommend him to her. While she watched, the viscount leaned forward slightly to speak to a dark-haired woman. Then, as if suddenly aware of Melissa's scrutiny, he paused and looked up. Across the room, through the press of people, he gazed directly at her and smiled.

Melissa immediately dropped her eyes and colored with embarrassment at having been caught staring. She glanced quickly at Lord Bainbridge, whose eyes seemed fixed on the viscount, then down at her feet, until the high-pitched cackle of Bainbridge's laughter made her raise her eyes again.

"Well, my dear, I think I know how he plans to extricate himself from his financial problems," Bainbridge said, and Melissa caught her breath in annoyance. The viscount was heading straight for her.

Chapter Two

❦

Bainbridge's laughter trailed off into disgusted snorts when he realized that the handsome and charismatic young Sheffield could give him quite a bit of competition for the lady by his side. As the only one of Miss Hampton's suitors to possess a title, Bainbridge had considered himself ahead of the pack, despite the chilly reception she had given him thus far.

His hopes rested not with the girl herself, but rather with her mother, for if what he had heard about Gloriana Hampton was true, she would happily exchange her daughter for a title. And Bainbridge was willing to oblige. He liked the thought of a luscious young wife. Plus, there was something about the girl's coolness that attracted him.

Perhaps it was the idea of warming her up, but her famous disdain did little to discourage him. And, although not desperate for funds, he could put the chit's fortune to good use. After all, he was maintaining three residences, two mistresses and one of the finest stables in England and the costs of all of them were rising a good bit.

So it was a less-than-enthusiastic eye that he turned to Sheffield, who now obviously was going to beg him for an introduction. The cheek of the stupid beggar! Bainbridge glared at the young man in an attempt to ward him off.

"Ah, Bainbridge! Where have you been keeping yourself?" Leighton asked, flashing a smile that was lost on his lordship.

"Right where I should be," Bainbridge grunted, hoping that his lack of cordiality would drive the viscount away. On the contrary—and to Bainbridge's extreme annoyance—Leighton smiled in genuine amusement and casually moved closer to Miss Hampton.

"Well, it is good to see you so well...and chipper," Leighton said. "And your lovely companion—I don't believe I know her...." Leighton said, looking the girl up and down.

"This is Melissa Hampton. Miss Hampton, Viscount Sheffield," Bainbridge murmured brusquely, noting with some degree of satisfaction that Miss Hampton looked as pained as he felt.

Melissa did feel put upon, for she was certainly not enjoying the exchange. She could conjure up nothing but disgust for this new fortune hunter.

Oh, he was handsome enough, she supposed, now that she could see him more closely. He was of medium build and sported dusty blond locks that presumably were trained to perfection into one of the latest modes. What were they calling it now? The Tousle? The Grecian? She had little interest in the fashion foibles of her own sex, let alone those practiced by these preening dandies, so she could not name the style.

Whatever it was called, the hair suited him nicely, so Melissa decided that she could not really take exception to his looks. His background, however, was another matter. He was a spoiled brat of the ton, she presumed, who ran through money like water.

As the saying went, like father, like son. His manners and morals must be deplorable if they matched those of his sire, and the way he was eyeing her now seemed to bear out that theory. As for his bold begging of an introduction, she was surprised that he did not just send for her at the gaming tables—or wherever his father had lost the money—and save himself the trouble of a visit to Almack's!

The thought made her lips curl slightly in contempt as he bowed over her hand. "Ah, Miss Hampton," he said, in a low but mellow voice.

The disdain fled from her smile, for when his fingers took her own, Melissa felt the warmth of his touch all the way down to her toes. The odd sensation threw her off balance, and she stepped back a pace, as if the very earth were subject to strange fluctuations. Then she stood her ground, waiting for him to kiss her hand, but instead his eyes—hazel, were they?—darted up at her, holding a question in their golden depths.

"Have we met before?" he asked.

"No," she managed to answer, and, gathering her resources, she looked pointedly at the fingers that still grasped her own. What ploy was this?

"Oh." Leighton released her hand and straightened. "I thought perhaps we had met before," he said, his mouth curving upward in a quirky smile.

"I assure you, my lord, that if we have, I cannot recall the incident," Melissa said stiffly, glad to be free of his touch. The warmth lingered in her hand, however, and if truth be told, the very air between them seemed to sizzle. Ridiculous, she told herself. Her back straight and her head high, she took her customary combative stance against the enemy—the ton—and their usual weapons of snobbery and deceit.

Leighton shrugged slightly, as if in puzzlement. "You must excuse me," he said softly. Then he looked straight at her, his eyes sparkling. "I assumed that I had done something to merit the foul reception you are giving me."

Melissa, who was in the midst of snapping her fan in irritation, actually felt her jaw drop open at his words. Although she had heard of such a reaction, she had never experienced it herself, and, hoping that she did not look as idiotic as she felt, she quickly closed her lips.

Her surprise at his words quickly gave way to anger, and she felt her blood rise to a boil. It was bad enough listening to Lord Grimley's condescending twaddle and then having to bear the company of Bainbridge, but to stand here and be insulted . . . and by someone she had never spoken to before in her life. It was truly beyond anything! She had just about had enough of Almack's and its precious patronage.

As though to rub salt into the wound his words had left, the fellow actually had the audacity to chuckle at her reaction—and he was not finished yet. "Or do you greet everyone with such dreadful malice in those lovely eyes?" he asked.

Melissa, now utterly flabbergasted, was speechless. "Good," Leighton said with a nod. "I see that I have vexed you beyond words. Therefore, when I ask you to dance, you will be unable to deny me," he said. With that, he tilted his head toward her and gave her a smile so disarming that it astounded her.

Melissa felt her temperature drop a degree, and she nearly had to shake herself in an effort to return to her senses. She realized, abruptly, just what made this man so popular. The viscount, it seemed, could ooze charm from every pore of his body when he was so inclined.

Melissa, however, was not a noble lady only too eager for a tumble, nor was she a green girl ready to faint at the sight of a handsome visage. She set her jaw, filled with an icy determination to take the viscount down a peg, though not quite certain how to go about it.

She swallowed the snappy retort that sprang to her lips, for she did not want to anger such a powerful person. Yet she had no intention of indulging his request—until events forced her to do otherwise.

"Sorry, Sheffield, but Miss Hampton is promised to me," Bainbridge growled suddenly, causing Melissa to glance down at him in mild surprise. She had forgotten his presence, so completely had the viscount occupied her attention.

Next to Leighton, the little man looked even more grotesque than usual, and she was annoyed by his expression—that of a boy gloating over a prize already won. As for dancing with him . . . the thought of bearing his touch made her skin crawl. And so she found herself in a quandary.

"Really, Bainbridge, you can't expect to hoard this beautiful creature all to yourself," Leighton said lightly. "That would be most unfair." He turned to Melissa. "You do not wish to be unfair, do you, Miss Hampton?"

"No, my lord," Melissa said dryly.

"Good, then it is settled. You will dance with me—the only just solution to our frightful dilemma," Leighton said with a mock gravity that Melissa found maddening.

"And thank you, Bainbridge. You have been most gracious," he added. The words were polite but dismissive, and Melissa could not help glancing back at Bainbridge as Leighton led her away. The look on the old earl's face was anything but pleasant, and it gave her an odd chill before the viscount once again demanded her attention.

"I've always wondered if that is his real hair," Leighton said. The statement was made so quietly and so quickly that it caught Melissa off guard, and she laughed out loud.

"That's better," Leighton said. His hazel eyes moved over her features familiarly, and when he took her hand to begin the dance she felt an almost overpowering heat. It would be best to cool things down a bit, Melissa decided, and the smile left her face as easily as he had drawn it out.

"Uh-oh. The chill has returned. Tell me, my dear Miss Hampton, what I have done to earn your enmity?"

Melissa eyed him appraisingly, debating her answer. Unlike most others she met, he seemed to have a predilection for the truth, so why not give it to him? *Because he can ruin you socially,* a tiny voice whispered, but Melissa would not heed it.

"I hold you in no more or less contempt than the rest of your class, a group of worthless, ill-bred, spendthrift popinjays who drink and carouse their lives away while holding themselves above all others," she finished in a rush. Then, aware that her cheeks were flushing pink, she clamped her mouth shut.

Leighton looked at her for what seemed like an eternity, which allowed the most alarming conclusions to run rampant in her thoughts. She had been too outspoken. Oh, how could she have been so foolish? She would lose her vouchers, would be shunned more than she was already, and her mother—Gloriana would have her head!

Just as the horror of Gloriana's reaction was insinuating itself into her mind, Leighton laughed. Melissa was surprised by the sound. For no reason at all, his mirth seemed to make her heart lighter, and she could not help but smile up at him.

"Well, I'm afraid you have me where my birth is concerned," Leighton admitted. "But, as to the other charges... I believe my mother would have argued with you over the ill breeding—she did try her best, you know. And I am as far from a spendthrift as you will find, my dear. My father may agree with you that I am worthless when he's tipped too much brandy, but, in fact, it takes a good head to manage our investments. My deft juggling of our accounts should qualify me for any financial position in the nation," he said with a wry smile.

"Certainly you have drawn a picture of some of my acquaintances, who, I agree, are a blight upon society, but your self-righteousness puzzles me, my dear—" Leighton leaned his blond head toward her "—for there are those who would certainly question your breeding and your extravagances. I don't feel the need to toss unflattering adjectives your way, but what, really, have you accomplished lately? You are a lovely ornament, I'll grant, but what else?"

Melissa could not move her lips in response. She could not even gasp. She was so appalled that she nearly halted her dance steps, and only a pointed glance from her partner urged her feet into motion again. For the second time this evening, the viscount had insulted her, so abruptly and completely that her composure was very nearly undone. Again, it took only a moment before surprise gave way to anger.

"Yes, flash those lovely dark eyes at me," Leighton whispered, leaning close. "They are a beautiful color."

This was too much. Melissa had thought herself inured to the contempt of the ton, but the viscount's personal attacks were simply too vicious. What kind of man would stoop so low as to ridicule her looks? Thank God the dance was nearly ended, for she would stand no more of this. When she could finally breathe again, she took in a slow, easy breath and arranged her features in what she hoped was her haughtiest expression.

"Well?" Leighton said softly. "Are you mulling over your accomplishments, or have I struck you dumb again?" When Melissa refused to speak, or even look at him, he chuckled. "You give up much too easily, my lovely. Well, then, let me help you. I should guess that you have plied a needle this week—sewn some embroidery, or perhaps simply a fine seam?" Although Melissa ignored him, Leighton blithely continued on.

Melissa kept her eyes firmly fixed on his cravat, which she imagined was tied in the most fashionable of knots, and refused to speak. It did little to discourage him.

Leighton leaned his blond head close to her dark one; she could feel his breath warm against her forehead. "Come now, Miss Hampton, let us both acknowledge we are not perfect, and have done with it," he said. His soft voice was cajoling, but Melissa was spared the effort of an answer, as the waltz, mercifully, was at an end. With a frosty glare, she stepped away from his arms.

"My dear Miss Hampton—" he began, holding his hands up in supplication.

"My lord, if you will please excuse me," Melissa said, "I have a headache." She stepped past him, her head held high, but he appeared neither hurt nor offended by her blatant effort to escape him. Rather, he gave her a bold look, and she could have sworn that those hazel eyes were twinkling. She was suddenly struck by a strong desire to slap the smile off Lord Sheffield's famous features.

"Perhaps the exertion of the dance has taxed you," Leighton said. "If you sit quietly, you may be recovered." He made as though to lead her to a quiet resting spot, but Melissa moved away in annoyance, her composure cracked at last.

"I am not taxed, I am beset!" she snapped, jerking away from the arm he presented to her and drawing a chuckle from the object of her irritation. "If you would release me from your...company, I will find my mother and be gone!"

To her further dismay, he simply laughed at her outrage. "All right, Miss Hampton," he said finally. "I will return you to your mother." He escorted her the few steps to a waiting Gloriana, and then bowed gently, though none too seriously, as he took her hand.

"Goodbye, for tonight," he whispered. He pressed a kiss to her skin that sent heat rushing up her arm, then moved off into the crowd.

For a moment, Melissa simply stood where he had left her, astounded by the man. In the span of only a few minutes, he had made her laugh, hurt her feelings, sent her temper soaring, and goaded her nearly to physical violence. And there was the small matter of the heat that he seemed to be able to wield like a lightning bolt.

He was obviously a very dangerous man.

Such a man could threaten her well-being in any number of ways, Melissa thought with a shiver, and anyone as cool and levelheaded as she should most certainly steer clear of him. She lifted her chin high, shook off the memory of her disturbing encounter with Viscount Sheffield, and turned to her mother.

"My dear child," Gloriana said, touching a cold hand to her daughter's cheek. "Are you well?"

"No, Mother, I am not. I have a headache," Melissa answered testily. "Let us go home at once."

"Surely it is not as serious as that," Gloriana said softly, taking Melissa's hand. "Come. A drink of water and you will soon be feeling yourself."

"No, Mother," Melissa said, pulling her fingers away. "I'm leaving."

"Melissa."

The rebuke in Gloriana's voice stopped her daughter in her tracks. "What is it, Mother?" Melissa asked, exasperation creeping into her tone.

"We will procure you a drink of water, and then we will return to the dance floor," Gloriana answered. The dark eyes staring into her daughter's made it clear that she would brook no resistance.

"As you wish, Mother," Melissa said with a sigh. She wondered idly what new transgression had vexed Gloriana. Perhaps it was her rude remark to Lord Grimley.... Melissa shifted her feet restlessly, anxious for her mother to move, but Gloriana remained where she was.

"Well?" Melissa asked impatiently, but her mother did not answer. She was staring across the room with a ridiculous smile on her face. At least Melissa thought it ridiculous, for she knew that the dainty smiles that so often graced Gloriana's face were there strictly for their effect on others.

With growing trepidation, Melissa followed her mother's gaze. As she had suspected, it led to the viscount, who was watching them through the crowd. When he caught her glance, Leighton nodded, and Melissa felt a childish urge to stick out her tongue in his direction. She restrained herself only through Herculean effort.

"Come, Mother, you promised me some water, and I need it," Melissa said.

"Don't be in such a rush, dear," Gloriana said, turning to her daughter.

"Mother," Melissa urged, but Gloriana did not budge until Leighton's attention was claimed by someone else.

"Well, I hope you are satisfied," Gloriana said, pulling herself up to her fullest height and moving in her most dignified manner as they repaired to the refreshments. "I'm sure I don't know what is the matter with you, Melissa. Finally, we see a suitor worthy of you, a young man with a distinguished name, heir to a fine and honored title. *Finally,* such a man pays you court, and you behave like a guttersnipe," Gloriana admonished in a deadly quiet voice. The words were meant for Melissa's ears alone, of course, and even she had to strain to hear them. To the rest of the fashionable gathering, Gloriana showed only her smile, pasted on to mask the scolding she was giving her daughter. "And in public," she added.

"He's not my suitor!" Melissa hissed, but her mother ignored her.

"I can only hope that no one else noticed your unladylike behavior," Gloriana said as she took a glass of lemonade. "Let us pray that I was the only one to see you snatch your arm away from the viscount as though he were a common villain and not a distinguished member of the nobility. Your appalling lack of self-control has been of constant concern to me, but I expected you at the very least to behave in a cordial manner at a social function."

"The man was rude and insulting," Melissa said from over her glass.

"Nonsense," Gloriana said, without even glancing at her daughter. Her eyes roamed the room, and she nodded slightly to an acquaintance. "You are constantly imagining slights."

"And you are always ignoring them!"

"Hush," Gloriana ordered, still looking away. "We will continue this conversation when we are home."

"Fine," Melissa said, her eyes blazing fire. "But you will not change my opinion of the man."

Gloriana very slowly put down her glass and looked at her daughter. Her dark eyes, cold as ice, bored into Melissa's, and then she tilted her head ever so slightly, as though in acquiescence.

"Very well, Melissa," Gloriana said. "If you prefer the attentions of Lord Bainbridge, we will leave it at that."

After a brief conversation with the daughter of a friend, Leighton looked back at his quarry. A quirky little smile appeared on his face when he spied her dark head and lovely profile, and then he strode away from the dance floor, humming softly to himself as he savored their encounter.

She was bright, too. How delightful! Bright and sparkling, like a fine diamond. He liked her. Of course, he had picked her from Parker's list for that very reason. Although they had never been formally introduced, he had seen Miss Hampton on occasion, and he had remembered her well.

The first time he had noticed her, she had been staring Lord Barnstable, a powerful and noble idiot, out of countenance for making an impudent remark about her father's source of income. The man had been induced to make a stammering, red-faced exit, and Leighton had been impressed.

Although they did not move in quite the same circles, he had seen her again at a large dinner party, where she had very nicely listened to the wearisome stories of an extremely old and verbose dinner partner. He had concluded that she was both courageous and kind, a rare combination—especially among the women he met.

Later, he had caught her standing in rapt appreciation in front of a marvelous Vermeer, while all those around her flitted and flirted. And that was what had lodged her in his memory, for Leighton had a genuine love of fine art.

Of course, the lady herself was a beautiful work, though some might argue the point with him. It seemed that blondes were in style this season—fragile-looking creatures with blue eyes and pale curls—and those who simply spouted the latest dictates of fashion would say nay to the dark beauty of Miss Hampton.

Leighton knew his own mind, however, and he had a discriminating eye. He preferred Melissa, with her pile of glistening mahogany hair and her huge dark eyes that sparked with the fire of a gemstone. Lady Disdain, indeed. Anyone with the least amount of sense could see that the lady was not cool at all, but blazing hot! Luckily, few men saw farther than their own noses, or his diamond would have been wed long ago.

Let those other idiots choose the delicate fair-haired flowers and the giggling gooses unable to carry on a conversation. Perhaps such fellows were content to closet their wives away at a country house or live as strangers with their spouses, each dallying with their string of lovers, but such schemes held no appeal for Leighton.

He planned to maintain a cordial relationship with his wife, so it was necessary to choose a lady he liked. He selected his lovers with care; although his choices were more limited, why should he not pick his wife just as carefully?

Leighton's parents had enjoyed not only a friendship, but also one of the most loving marriages he had ever seen, before his mother's tragic death had ended it. But he had given up harboring hopes for such a match for himself long ago. Besides, his duty lay elsewhere, in saving Greyhaven. And that would take money, the kind of money that precious few brides could bring. Miss Hampton, thanks to her father's businesses, was one of those whose fortunes would easily pay the debts and still provide a more-than-lavish income.

Satisfied with the course he had chosen, Leighton headed toward the door. He was still musing over his good fortune when the sound of someone calling him broke his reverie.

"Leighton ... Leighton!"

"Duncan! Good Lord, what are you doing here?" Leighton asked at the sight of his tall, thin cousin.

"Looking for you, dear boy," Duncan answered snappishly, a dark shock of hair that defied grooming falling into his eyes. "And you?" he said, with a nod toward Miss Hampton. "Have you found yourself a rich one?"

Leighton's eyes narrowed. It was true, of course. He was courting a fortune, but somehow he took offense at the idea of Melissa being referred to so dismissively. The comment was typical of Duncan, however, so he shrugged it off. "You were looking for me?"

Duncan's eyes widened momentarily; he was apparently surprised that Leighton had failed to answer his question. He recovered quickly, however, and smiled tightly. "Yes, it took some time for your man to convince me you were actually...here," he said, with palpable distaste.

Leighton chuckled. "And you wished to see me so desperately that you defied your long-standing oath never to darken the door of this establishment?"

"Something like that," Duncan answered brittlely, his face showing his disgust.

Leighton laughed softly. "Well, I am at your disposal," he said with a grin. "What is so important that it drew you through these doors?"

"I heard about your dear papa," Duncan said.

The smile left Leighton's face, and he shrugged again. "So has everyone."

"Well, dear boy, I thought I might be able to help."

"There's nothing left for you to salvage," Leighton said evenly.

"Greyhaven," Duncan said, his voice dropping low.

"No. Greyhaven is not for sale—not even to you, cousin," Leighton said softly. Suddenly he grinned again and reached out a hand to rest on Duncan's back conspiratorially as he led him to the door. "But there is something you can do to help."

"Just tell me what, dear boy, and I will be only too glad to do my bit for the family honor," Duncan said, falling in beside Leighton.

"Oh, it's nothing as dramatic as all that," Leighton said. "I was wondering if I could persuade you to make a small trip to the Continent."

Duncan stopped and looked keenly at his cousin. "I assume I am to fund the excursion," he said dryly.

"Why, of course. You're the only one in the family with any money," Leighton said with a laugh.

"My father, bless his soul, had a head for finances."

"And an aversion to gambling," Leighton put in as he continued toward the doors.

"Oh, I wouldn't say an aversion. He simply was not interested in losing money," Duncan said, moving with him. "Is there a purpose to my trip, or would you just rather see less of me?"

"Well, I was hoping you would take Father with you."

Duncan stopped and looked at Leighton with a jaundiced eye. "So I'm to be an unpaid nursemaid to the earl?"

Leighton flashed one of his famous smiles and reached out a hand to rest on Duncan's shoulder. "Think of it as spending precious time with your family, an opportunity to learn about your heritage, and—"

"And keep your father away from the tables," Duncan finished with a scowl.

"Right! A matter of family honor, just as you said," Leighton said, a little too lightly. They had reached the door, and he extended his arm with a flourish, gesturing for Duncan to precede him.

"And how long am I to hold your sire at bay?" Duncan asked when they both stood outside.

"Just until the wedding."

Duncan's step faltered for a moment as he looked sharply at Leighton. "So, you do intend to snare the Hampton heiress," he said softly.

"Oh, most definitely, but I imagine my suit would proceed better without any assistance from the earl," Leighton said with a short laugh.

"Ah, yes, he might prove a hindrance to negotiations," Duncan whispered. His eyes, unseen, looked straight ahead in the darkness.

"And, to be frank, cousin, I can ill afford any further debts. If he should go on another spree..."

"Yes, I imagine you will be hard-pressed simply to carry on until the marriage can be arranged," Duncan said thoughtfully. "Of course, as soon as the banns are posted, you should receive plenty of credit. Well, you may count on me as always, dear boy," he said, his voice suddenly brisk. "I shall spirit the earl away to the Continent until such time as your marriage plans are completed, and I will do my utmost to make sure he stays out of trouble."

Leighton sighed in relief. "Thank you, Duncan. I knew I could count on your help," he said, shaking his cousin's hand with sincere gratitude.

Now, if he could just talk the earl into the trip...

"Why on earth should I visit the Continent?" the Earl of Greyhaven testily asked his son as he poured himself a brandy from a crystal decanter. "Just where am I to go, with that cutthroat Napoleon on the loose? And traveling with your cousin Duncan... Why, I can think of nothing more tiresome. You must be balmy!"

"What?" Leighton asked. His attention had slipped as his eyes wandered lovingly about the painted salon, his favorite room at Greyhaven. The walls and ceiling were decorated with paintings by Antonio Verrio. Cherubs floated among the clouds, while deities dispensed justice from Mount Olympus, and on the earthly carpet below, gilt couches with smooth lines fitted into the classical scheme.

Verrio had painted several other rooms at Greyhaven, but this one was the most outstanding, and it never failed to remind him of his mother, who had shared his love of the arts. He could almost see her standing in the doorway. "And just what are you two up to?" she would ask, her hands on her hips, pretending to scold, when she caught them drinking up the best brandy. Then she would laugh and demand just a sip for herself and perch on the edge of that red velvet couch....

"Balmy! Batty. Dotty. Round the bend," the earl said, returning the decanter to its place on the sideboard.

His words were lost on Leighton, who was remembering his mother with a fond smile on his face. She had always seemed so very young, so full of life; in an instant, she would throw her arms around the earl or her son in an impulsive hug, before taking off again like quicksilver down some new avenue.

"Pah!" The earl choked on a swallow of brandy, his hefty middle jiggling. "I swear Kendall has been watering this stuff!"

"What's that, Father?" Leighton asked. He leaned back on a sky-blue couch, crossing his legs at the ankles in a casual movement.

"Good God, boy, are you listening to me, or am I simply airing my lungs?" he said with a snort, turning to look at his son. Meeting Leighton's mild gaze with a frown, he walked to the couch opposite his son and sat down.

Leighton chuckled as he watched his sire drink the brandy. Of course, it was watered. He had ordered it done, for he was trying everything to cut down the old fellow's drinking. Leighton smiled at his father, whose blue eyes twinkled above the pink cheeks that dimpled endearingly whenever one had the desire to scold him.

Although his fine head of blond hair and his large mustache was now tinged with gray and he carried far more pounds than in his youth, the earl was still a handsome man. Too handsome, Leighton thought, for his own good.

"Gad, I swear I've been locked up here for a century," the earl said, resting one foot on a gilt footstool. "Let's go back to London."

"You used to like it here," Leighton said softly.

"Yes, well, it's too quiet now...." The earl eyed his drink, then looked up at his son. "I heard there's a traveling theater troupe presenting a play in Haven's End. What say you and I take in the thing, then invite the actors back here. The whole damn troupe!"

Leighton laughed, shaking his head in genuine amusement. "Lord, Father, that's just what we need. I imagine they could strip the house bare of furnishings in record time."

"Ah, well, yes, I suppose so," the earl grumbled. "Well, not the whole troupe then, but only the female members. We could find two of the loveliest and invite them back for a private supper," he suggested with a wicked grin.

Leighton smiled, the odd juxtaposition of their roles striking him, as it sometimes did. Leighton, by all rights, was a young buck. He had a fine hand with the horses, was able to hold the obligatory amount of liquor, and could manage well enough at the tables, yet he was not out carousing—Melissa's accusation notwithstanding. Instead, he was trying to rein in his father, the infamous Cubby.

"One of these days you're going to come up with the pox, Father," he warned.

"Oh, a pox on you!" the earl said, rising from his couch and slamming his glass down on the sideboard. The glass decanter tinkled in the quiet.

Leighton frowned. "What is it, Father?" he asked softly.

"Pah! It's this place—it gives me the dithers. For God's sake, let's get up a house party . . . or, better yet, go back to town."

"Or, better yet, take a trip to the Continent."

"Gad, not that again," the earl moaned, turning around to glare at his son. Leighton relaxed casually on the couch, unmoved by his father's heated glance. "Why are you forcing this heinous trip on me?"

"Because I need some time, Father," Leighton said. "I need some time to mop up the mess with Braxton."

"Ah, yes." The earl's eyes dropped to the floor. "Well, that was a trifle expensive, but I'm sure you'll take care of it, eh?" he asked, clearing his throat and straightening. "Perhaps . . . well, hell, I suppose I could stand Duncan for a few weeks," he allowed. "We could go to Greece."

"Good. Perhaps you can bring back some sculptures. That should take a few months, not weeks," Leighton said with a smile.

"Pah," the earl groaned. He took a large swallow from his glass and winced. "I suppose I shall have to, or I shall have no end of it."

"You are right, of course," Leighton said. The two, so alike, smiled at each other, the dimples peeking through their cheeks. "To Greece," Leighton said, raising his glass.

"To Greece," the earl echoed. "And to whatever scheme you are hatching, my boy." He laughed at Leighton's look of innocent denial. "You obviously don't want to tell me, and I don't want to know. Just as long as it keeps us out of debtor's prison—or any other jail—I will cooperate."

Leighton laughed, but his smile faded a little too quickly when his father turned back to the sideboard. He had a sinking feeling that the earl, despite his words, would definitely not approve of his son's plans for a marriage of convenience.

Chapter Three

Melissa spent the days following her introduction to the viscount in a state of dread that they would meet again. She knew Gloriana would greet Lord Sheffield eagerly—even if the man sprouted two heads—and would push her to encourage him.

Melissa, however, had no intention of listening to her mother, despite the underlying threat that if she refused the viscount she would be forced to marry Lord Bainbridge. She would worry about Bainbridge later. Just now, Sheffield was her concern, and she hoped never to see him again.

The first day she complained of a headache and stayed in her room, fearful that he would come calling. What if he asked her to go for a drive or invited her on some other dreadful excursion that would force her to endure his company? She did not really relax until she was safely abed that night.

The second day she ventured from her room, but still claimed she was too ill to see visitors. That allowed her, thankfully, to escape Lord Bainbridge's call and an unexpected visit from Harry Morrison, a sharp young fortune hunter who did not find favor with anyone. There were no other callers.

On the third day she began to hope that she had naught to fear. Even if the viscount were hunting for a wealthy wife, he could choose from quite a few other ladies, some of whom were far more suitable than she. She had made it quite clear at Almack's that she was not interested in furthering their acquaintance. Perhaps he possessed the good sense to move on to a more agreeable party.

She was sitting in the main drawing room, trying to convince herself that this was the case, when one of the maids brought in some flowers. "For you, Miss Hampton," the girl said, a little breathless.

"What?" Melissa asked, turning her thoughts away from the viscount.

"The flowers, miss. They are for you," she said, holding them out for Melissa's inspection. "Shall I arrange them in a vase?" she asked.

"Well, yes, certainly," Melissa answered, putting down her embroidery. "Who sent them?"

"That I can't tell you, miss." The maid smiled broadly and looked pointedly at a sliver of paper atop the bouquet. "They were delivered by a servant, who would not name his master."

"I see," said Melissa, realizing that the pink-cheeked girl thought the mysterious posies the very height of romance. She gave them a cursory glance and decided they were a mixed bunch, rather nondescript. The choice showed a lack of imagination, she told herself, and therefore reflected sadly on the sender.

With a studied coolness, she took the note and dismissed the girl, who appeared quite disappointed with her reaction. Then she sat looking down at the paper in her hand, reluctant to open it.

"Well?" asked Gloriana. Melissa nearly started, for she had not heard her mother enter the room. Of course, Gloriana knew everything that went on in her household, so Melissa was not surprised to see her. She was just annoyed at how quickly her mother had heard of the flowers and come to investigate.

Melissa arranged her features impassively, but she could not stop her heart from beating just a little bit faster as she opened the missive. She broke open the seal with care and slowly unfolded it, her eyes running down to the bottom, where she hoped to find a signature.

Once she saw the name, all else was superfluous. Some prose, intended to flatter her, prefaced the signature. She shrugged in indifference.

"Well?" Gloriana asked again.

"Harry Morrison," Melissa said flatly. Why did she feel so disappointed?

"Ah," Gloriana said disapprovingly. "I thought it was made most plain to the young man that he was not welcome here. I see I shall have to write him a note, making my position clearer. I had hoped they were from Lord Bainbridge," she said as she walked past her daughter to stand by the windows.

"Since he is the only one of your suitors who is at all eligible, I feel we must do all we can to encourage him. After all, you are in your second season now, and we cannot hope to interest many others," she concluded.

Melissa nearly winced at her mother's words, which were plainer than usual. She had long suspected that Gloriana thought of her as a commodity to be bargained away for the highest title, but she did not like hearing her worth discussed so baldly.

"I don't think you need worry about Viscount Sheffield. It appears your behavior the other night repulsed him." Gloriana's voice was even as she turned to look at Melissa. "As I'm sure it would anyone. I heard today that he has joined his father at Greyhaven for an indefinite stay. Mrs. Marchant was most insistent that I be notified at once of his movements."

So that was what this was all about. Obviously, one of Gloriana's "friends" had made it a point to dash her hopes of a match. Good heavens, how foolish, Melissa thought, unable to stop the flood of resentment that washed over her. Why were Gloriana's pretentious acquaintances more important to her than her own daughter?

Melissa shook her head. "I'm sorry that you are disappointed, Mother, but I can't pretend that I am. Now, if you will excuse me, I think I will lie down before dinner."

Gloriana did not argue or try to stop her, but she did play one last card. "Remember what I said about Lord Bainbridge," she warned. "The next time he calls, I expect you to be more gracious."

All right, Mother. I'll be just about as gracious as I was to the viscount, Melissa thought as she passed silently by Gloriana. Let us hope Bainbridge gets the message as easily.

As Melissa mounted the steps to her rooms, she tried to tell herself that the news about the viscount was most welcome. Was it not just what she had wanted to hear? She no longer need worry about him calling or forcing his company on her, or about the implicit threat of being forced to marry him.

Reaching her own rooms, she closed the door behind her and asked herself why she didn't feel relieved. She dug her book out from under the pillow and stretched out comfortably, determined to forcibly eject the viscount from her thoughts, but she could not concentrate on her reading.

Her heart was still heavy with the sense of impending doom that she had come to associate with the obnoxious nobleman. Finally, she tossed down the book and turned onto her back to stare at the bed hangings over her head. She told herself sharply that she had no desire to be courted by the viscount. Although he was tolerably handsome and he did have a certain ability to affect her, he was much too thoughtless and rude. And he had made that sarcastic remark about her beauty.

Her beauty! Melissa hopped off the bed and went to sit in front of the mirror. A pale face dominated by enormous brown eyes stared gloomily back at her.

"Yes, flash those lovely dark eyes at me," he had said. Lovely? Melissa found nothing appealing in the muddy color. Anyone can have brown eyes, she thought. How boring! She also dismissed the long, thick lashes that ringed them.

She frowned into the reflection, finding fault, too, with lips that were not Cupid's-bow perfect. They were too large. Not horribly thick—just big, she thought. To Melissa, they were not fashionable and thus another example of how she would never fit in.

Her hair was not quite the thing, either, and she again wondered whether to cut the thick brown-black tresses arranged so smoothly atop her head. But closely cropped curls were the rage, and she doubted that her hair could be forced to curl, even by the most torturous of vanity-indulging devices.

A fairly sorry inventory, Melissa thought as she turned away from the mirror. Her assessment made the viscount's remarks seem doubly cruel. For perhaps the thousandth time, she assured herself that she had no desire to see the man again. Then why wasn't she heartened by the news that he had gone away, proving that he had no interest in her?

It was only then that she realized the problem lay not in the viscount's whereabouts, but in the assumption her mother had made concerning his intentions. She was certain Mrs. Marchant was correct in reporting he was at Gracehaven or Greenhaven, or whatever monstrosity his family had mortgaged to the hilt, but she did not believe that meant he would not be back for her.

Melissa simply could not shake the feeling that she had not seen the last of Leighton Somerset.

"Her lips were made to be kissed," Leighton said. With the earl safely entrusted to Duncan, Leighton had returned to London. When his friends accosted him at a large dinner party, he was duly called upon to report his progress with the Lady Disdain.

"I am sorry to disappoint you, gentlemen—and I do use the term loosely—but the lady is not made of ice. This legendary disdain is simply that—a legend—probably concocted by some rejected suitor to explain his own failure.'' Leighton shrugged. ''I can find no fault with Miss Hampton.''

''Careful now, Leighton, or you shall be the smitten one, and we will have to lay bets upon your battered heart,'' said Charles. He laughed so hard at his own witticism that the watch chain on his waistcoat jangled.

Robert Smythe and Lord Cameron Wolsey joined in, and Leighton himself chuckled, shaking his head in denial. The four were standing together companionably in a crowded reception room at Wolsey House. They formed a tightly knit group, not easily interrupted, but above the din of talk and movement and music they heard a voice that brought the conversation to a halt. ''My, my, you gentlemen are enjoying yourselves,'' it purred softly, and all eyes turned to appreciate Cecile, Duchess of Pontabeigh.

She was always adorned to perfection, and tonight was no exception. A luminous scarf, sparkling with tiny gems, draped tantalizingly over a bosom that nearly burst from her golden gown. Diamonds twinkled around her throat and down her slender arms. Her blond hair curled about her face in the most fashionable style, and her cheeks, perhaps aided by a little paint, were a luscious pink under eyes the color of aquamarine.

She fanned herself expertly and looked slowly and serenely over the group with seductive eyes, her rosebud lips curled into the slightest of smiles. ''Who is the butt of your humor tonight?''

''Leighton!'' Charles piped up. The blue-green eyes turned to him, and he luxuriated in the attention of one of the ton's most beautiful women. ''He's getting married,'' he added to prolong the moment.

Cecile's fan stilled momentarily at the announcement, but her gaze never wavered. ''He is, is he?''

''If he can convince the chit,'' Wolsey said with a laugh.

''Really?'' Cecile asked, one thin eyebrow raised questioningly. ''That shouldn't be too difficult.'' She ran her eyes over the viscount, her gaze lingering in just the right places, and elicited a laugh from everyone, including Leighton.

"It is when the female in question is the Lady Disdain," said Charles, longing for the smoldering gaze to return to him.

"Who?" Cecile asked, the brow rising again.

"No one you would know, Cecile," Leighton said.

"Oh?" she inquired, the single word conveying a wealth of contempt for anyone with whom she was not acquainted. "Well, gentlemen, I hate to sound slow-witted, but why not simply offer for her?" she asked, spreading her fan to gently caress the air nearest her swelling bosom.

"Oh, no! Can't do that. He has a bet to win," Charles said, too enthralled by Cecile to see Robert send him a quelling glance.

"A joke," Robert put in. "Come, Charles, I see your latest amour," he said, turning to lead his friend away. He was stopped by a fan, closed and hard. It whacked him none too playfully across the arm.

"Now, Robert, don't drag Charles away," Cecile said, her voice low but insistent. "I wish to hear all about this bet."

Charles, red-faced and looking like a ferret caught in a trap, glanced from Robert's smooth features to the blond beauty of Cecile. He was no match for the heat of that blue-green gaze.

"Well, well, there's not much to tell," he babbled. "A silly thing, really. I told Leighton he could not charm the Lady Disdain, and he wagered that he would win her. Not just her hand, mind you, but her heart, as well," Charles explained. "He'll lose this time, though. Even Leighton won't dazzle this one."

"Really? How very amusing," Cecile said, snapping the fan open again and moving it rhythmically. "But I think you are the fool, Charles, to have so little faith in the Sheffield charm. It is, I can assure you, quite devastating," she said, smiling at Leighton.

Leighton returned the smile, his eyes twinkling affectionately, and she abruptly snapped her fan closed again. She turned back to Charles and leaned so close to him that her bosom was but a hairsbreadth from his chest. "And to prove just how serious I am," she whispered, "I will sweeten the pot."

Charles watched numbly as Cecile pressed her fan intimately against his cheek and purred softly in his ear. "Fifty pounds on Leighton," she said before slipping away amid chuckles of admiration.

"God, she is amazing," Wolsey breathed, turning to watch her figure as she moved to another gathering across the room.

"Yes," agreed Robert. His eyes, too, followed the duchess, but he was not smiling, and the appreciative gleam so apparent on the features of Charles and Wolsey was absent from his serious face. He watched Cecile until she disappeared in the crowd. Then he turned to the viscount. "If I were you, Leighton, I would cry off this wager," he said.

"What?" Charles whined. "Why?"

"Because," Robert said, glaring at his corpulent friend, "Leighton couldn't make even the most agreeable girl fall for him if she's aware that you are betting on it. I say you've taken unfair advantage by spreading the story, and that's cause enough for canceling the wager."

"Why, why, that's preposterous!" Charles sputtered. "You've just been against the whole thing from the start. The duchess is not going to spread the story. You heard her yourself," he said. "She bet fifty pounds on Leighton."

"Don't get excited, Charles," Leighton said, holding up his hands to call a halt before his friend became further outraged at the suggestion. "I'm not crying off the wager." Charles, pink-cheeked with indignation—and perhaps a little guilt—appeared mollified.

Robert did not. He shook his head with a look of disgust that surprised the viscount. "Robert, Cecile wouldn't know Melissa Hampton if she bit her," Leighton said.

"You can be damn sure she will make it her business to know all about her now," Robert said dryly.

"Perhaps, but what of it?"

Although Robert said nothing, he shot Leighton one of his famous looks, known to make even the most educated and powerful men feel witless. Leighton, who considered himself immune to these withering gazes, felt himself look the fool, and it was not to his liking. He opened his mouth to argue, then promptly closed it again. Robert remained silent.

"I'll talk to her." Leighton inclined his head in the direction Cecile had gone. Robert eyed him skeptically. "Ah, Robert," Leighton said with a smile. "You are much too suspicious." He tapped his friend's arm affectionately, but Robert remained unmoved.

"And you, Sheffield, are too good-natured for your own good," he said.

Leighton chuckled, excused himself from the group and inched his way through the crowd in search of the duchess. He was stopped twice by solicitous acquaintances who inquired about his father, and was nearly trapped into a conversation with one of the most boring fellows he knew, before he finally spotted a golden head glittering with diamonds.

She knew he was coming. Cecile had long ago perfected the art of keeping her eyes open while supposedly deep in conversation, and her eyes roamed the room under half-closed lids, taking note of all those who entered her domain. Perhaps she even felt his presence before her gaze actually touched him. She was not quite sure, for with Leighton she could almost sense his approach. She had been thinking about him, of course, even as she sat on a small divan and listened to Lady Thornton.

He was getting closer, and now was standing beside her. She broke off her discussion with Lady Thornton to acknowledge him. He looked down at her with a warm smile, his hazel eyes sparkling with affection, and she nearly flinched.

It was an expression that never failed to hurt her.

The sight of that...fondness on his face always gave her pause. In other former lovers, she could bear hatred or bitterness or indifference, but that hideous fondness was nearly more than she could endure.

Cecile was haunted by the memory of a far more exciting emotion gracing those features, for she remembered when that face had been alive with love—love for her—the kind of passionate, desperate love that one finds only in the young. And, God, they had been young then. Cecile suddenly felt ancient and weary.

"Well, well, if it isn't the groom-to-be," she said softly.

"Hello, Cecile."

His voice was soft and gentle. Too gentle. Lady Thornton made a great show of giving up her seat on the divan and moving off in a rustle of stiff skirts, and Cecile patted the vacated place invitingly.

"How have you been faring?" Leighton asked sincerely as he sat down.

"Never better, my dear Leighton," she answered lightly. "And you? I heard about your father. I am sorry. The dear old fool."

Leighton shrugged. "He certainly keeps me busy. He said he saw you at the Montagues'. Thank you for keeping an eye on him, as I'm sure you did."

"It was no chore," she said. "He is most amusing company."

"He says the same of you," Leighton said with a smile.

The words, so well-intentioned, bothered her, as did the odd bond that existed between the earl and herself, a bond she had discovered at the Montagues' when she had sat up drinking with him into the wee hours.

She did not know whether it was a love of Leighton that cemented their kinship or something far more disquieting...a joint sorrow, perhaps, or a shared disappointment with life. No, the love of a good party, she told herself firmly. That was all. They both loved fine things, a good bottle and good company and . . .

"How is Henry?"

Cecile stiffened at the mention of her husband. "His gout has been troubling him, you know," she answered with an air of dismissal. "He rarely travels from the Devonshire estate." She began fanning herself and looking about as though the conversation bored her.

"That is too bad," Leighton said. He paused to admire her still-lovely profile. "Cecile, about the wager . . . I would ask you please not to mention it to anyone."

"Good heavens, Leighton, you actually don't mean to marry this . . . nobody, do you?" she asked.

"Yes." He raised his eyes to hers, as if daring her to argue with his decision. When hazel locked with aquamarine, she looked away. "I know I may count on you to be discreet about it," he said.

Cecile turned her head sharply to face him again. "I'm sure I've forgotten about the entire matter already, Leighton dear. Don't worry your pretty head about it. Now, if you will excuse yourself, I see someone who would like your seat."

Count Viscali, a swarthy Italian with whom Cecile's name had been linked, towered over them. It was rumored that he was her slave, but Leighton guessed that the penniless nobleman had his own reasons for linking up with the duchess. "Good night, Cecile," Leighton said, rising. "Give my best to Henry."

The fan stopped. The eyebrow rose. And the mouth thinned perceptibly. "Goodbye, Leighton." she said.

Melissa sported a light step as she walked to the entrance of the Hampton town house. The passage of another week had done much to relieve her mind on the question of the Viscount Sheffield, and she had decided that she had little chance of suffering his attentions again.

The day was warm and breezy and perfectly suited for her outing to the bookstore, and Melissa was well pleased with her purchases. A few steps behind her, a maid carried a package containing Virgil's *Aeneid,* as well as the latest Gothic, *Roderick and Camille,* neither of which would receive Gloriana's approval, for Gloriana rarely read anything more than the fashion magazines that piled high in her drawing room.

Melissa adored her books, entering fully into the realms that existed in the pages and finding there the friends and family that were lacking in her life. Her family consisted of Gloriana, who had dismissed her friends from school as being below her station. The bluebloods Gloriana claimed would make appropriate companions gave Melissa the snub more often than not.

Eager to begin reading her new volumes, Melissa had a smile for the footman who opened the door, but the greeting faded from her lips when she spied her mother exiting the green drawing room to call her name.

"Melissa," Gloriana said crisply, taking a stand just outside the room's doorway.

Melissa turned to her maid. "Clarisse, take the books to my room and unwrap them, please," she said before walking toward her mother. What now? she thought irritably, running over in her mind any transgressions she could possibly have committed.

With a frown, Melissa walked past her mother into Gloriana's domain, the green drawing room. She had never cared for the pea-green silk that hung on the walls, nor for the elaborately carved furniture, and the artwork could only be described as atrocious. Gloriana's taste was execrable, but she decorated to her exact specifications and would allow no other opinions. Melissa nearly shook her head in disgust as she perched on a massive couch and waited for her rebuke.

"Melissa," Gloriana said. Her voice sounded even, but her cheeks were flushed, and her eyes were bright with excitement.

"What is it?" Melissa asked, suddenly concerned.

"Melissa, we have been invited to Eudora Beauchamp's soirée," Gloriana said, her bosom rising and falling rapidly as she spoke.

"What?" Melissa felt like a prisoner waiting for the guillotine to drop, only to be granted a final reprieve.

"The Duchess of Baldwin! One of the most powerful and socially prominent noblewomen," Gloriana said, her voice rising just a little.

"How nice," Melissa said flatly, unable to drum up any excitement over a party invitation.

"Her grace has honored us," Gloriana said, pulling her hand from behind her back to brandish the priceless missive. "You could show a little enthusiasm." Her daughter only shrugged.

"Melissa, please do not adopt such common gestures," Gloriana scolded, but she was already looking away, her mind elsewhere. "We will need new gowns, of course," she said softly, putting her hand to her lips and starting to pace toward the windows.

"Of course," Melissa echoed, trying her best to subdue the giggle that threatened to rise in her throat at the absurdity of the situation. To get so excited over a soirée! Gloriana stopped suddenly and turned to look at her daughter absently.

"Something blush for you, perhaps, and with some trimming."

Melissa did not comment, knowing better than to begin an argument with her mother over fashion. She watched Gloriana grip the paper with an amusing possessiveness, and then something struck her. Why?

Why had the duchess invited them? They certainly did not move in the same circles. It was hard even to imagine them having a mutual friend. At that thought, Melissa's eyes narrowed, and a suspicion took root. "To what do we owe this honor?" she asked.

"What?" Gloriana asked.

"This invitation is most unexpected, isn't it?" Melissa asked. "After all, we don't know the duchess."

"Of course I know the duchess. Everyone knows who she is, and I believe I have been introduced to her. Yes, I'm almost certain of it," Gloriana said, seating herself gracefully in a large, ornate Tudor chair. "She undoubtedly remembered me and wished to further our acquaintance."

"Undoubtedly," Melissa agreed, with just a trace of sarcasm.

Gloriana put down the invitation and glanced coolly at her daughter. "And why should she not?" she asked.

Melissa declined to answer, although several reasons occurred to her. In the main, she could not understand why such a famous and powerful woman would take a sudden interest in virtual nobodies, especially when the nobodies in question were looked down upon as being in trade.

"Well?" Gloriana asked, folding her hands neatly in her lap. "I assume you know another reason why we were invited. Would you care to share it with me?"

Melissa had an idea, all right, but she definitely did not want to tell her mother. She did not believe for a minute that the duchess knew Gloriana from a hop toad. No, she suspected another's fine hand in this.

Someone else was responsible for the duchess's desire for their company, and Melissa could think of only one new acquaintance who had the influence to obtain an invitation for them from her grace.

Melissa said not a word to her mother, but she had that odd feeling again...the presentiment that Viscount Sheffield was not done with her yet, not by half.

Gloriana's excitement over the soirée had not dimmed by the night of the event, and she appeared to be nearly in awe of Lehigh, the duchess's famous town house. Recently re-

modeled and decorated in the Chinese manner, it had earned
the approval of the prince regent, whose own Marine Pavilion at Brighton had inspired the style.

Melissa was unimpressed. The abundance of sculpture
and statuary, including two enormous brass dragons flank-
ing the doorway, seemed quite overdone to her. She ignored the trappings that dazzled her mother and instead
scanned the small group of guests for a certain blond head.

Although Melissa, too, felt a small twinge of anticipa-
tion, it was not the party itself that intrigued her. She was
interested solely in the person behind it, for she could not rid
herself of the notion that Leighton Somerset was responsible.

Melissa barely listened to her mother's whispered comments as they were ushered from the hall into a room decorated so completely in red that it seemed to glow like an
ember. Gloriana was admiring a dreadful chandelier, but
Melissa hardly glanced at it. She was too busy eyeing the
other guests in search of the viscount—strictly to prove her
theory, of course.

They were greeted by the duchess herself, a lovely woman
with graying hair, sharp dark eyes and an infectious smile,
and Melissa felt her suspicions reluctantly slip away.

"Mrs. Hampton. I am so glad you could come to my little gathering," the duchess said, in a voice that was soft, yet
rich with authority.

"It is our pleasure, Your Grace," Gloriana said. She was
holding her own—cool, calm, yet definitely pleased. As
Melissa watched the two, she tried to suppress an unexpected burst of disappointment. She must have been wrong,
and her mother must have been right. Perhaps Gloriana had
met her grace and—

Then she spied him. His hair perfectly tousled, his dimpled grin perfectly charming, he was wearing a dark green
coat over smooth shoulders, and pantaloons in the palest of
willow. They fit him to perfection.

"Miss Hampton! What a pleasure it is to see you again," said Viscount Sheffield, bending over her hand.

"And such a coincidence, too, my lord," Melissa said. She caught a glimpse of her mother's reproving eye, but the viscount only laughed softly and took her hand.

"Come," he said, urging her away from Gloriana. "I have something to show you."

Melissa followed him, well aware that her mother's gaze was upon her, but she snatched her hand from his and gave him one of her most quelling looks at the first opportunity. Although such glances usually froze overzealous admirers in their tracks, the viscount only chuckled and smiled as though she tickled his fancy.

Melissa's back went up again at his response. The man was so frustrating! He never reacted in the way she expected. He was not condescending or snobbish. In fact, he let her say outrageous things, and apparently found them amusing. He ignored her coldness and her disdain with equal nonchalance, and yet he had said vile things to her at Almack's.

She eyed him warily, and did not return the grin, but she couldn't help notice how the candlelight glowed golden on his hair.

He led her into an adjoining room, where a couple of elderly gentlemen were ensconced at a chessboard. She could hear their grumbling, and the quiet hum of voices not far away, but a hush seemed to fall around her as they walked silently along the Axminster carpet.

"This is what I wanted you to see," Leighton said in a whisper as he raised a hand in a gesture that encompassed the room. Melissa turned slowly, her eyes moving along the walls and up to the ceiling, then tilted her head back to gaze, lovingly, above. Behind the divans and the tables and rising above the Oriental cabinets was a lovely painting that encompassed the entire room.

It had a classical theme, a temple with people—perhaps Plato and his students. The colors were vivid, the representation was striking, and the artistry compelling. It was a fine work that contrasted sharply with the garish Chinese decor of the room.

"It's beautiful," Melissa breathed, stepping forward. She walked to the far wall, where the view of the painting was unobstructed, and reached out a hand to touch one of the figures, larger than life.

Leighton came to stand next to her. "Antonio Verrio," he said softly. "He did some rooms at Greyhaven. When I was younger, I used to beg the duchess to sell me Lehigh simply to have this room. Luckily, I amused her, so she did not boot me out," Leighton recalled fondly. "I think she keeps the painting now only as a concession to me."

"You mean someone would actually paint over this?" Melissa was aghast.

Leighton shrugged. "On to the latest fashion."

Melissa looked around her. "It doesn't fit in with the rest of the furnishings, does it?" she said tactfully.

"No," Leighton said with a laugh. He leaned close. "Some of the greatest treasures are found in the oddest places," he whispered, and Melissa was suddenly acutely aware of his breath upon her neck. She stepped back abruptly.

"Oh, there you go again," Leighton said, shaking his head with mock seriousness.

"What?"

"You're retreating."

"I'm sure I don't know what you mean, my lord," Melissa answered formally, straightening her back and pursing her lips.

Leighton shook his head. "They call you Lady Disdain, you know," he said softly.

Melissa wanted to wince at the name. She had heard it before. "Let them call me whatever they like," she said coldly, turning to go.

"But it's a misnomer, isn't it?" Leighton asked, placing a long leg in her path. Melissa stopped and looked pointedly down at the elegantly shod foot that halted her exit. Then she looked up into those hazel eyes, soft and glowing in the candlelight, and she felt her guard slip.

"You remind me more of a turtle, Miss Hampton," Leighton said, reaching out a hand to lift her chin. "A turtle moving back into its shell."

Melissa ignored the comment, her attention focused more on the face before her. Viewed this closely, the man was much handsomer than she had thought.

"Don't go. Stay with me a while, Melissa," Leighton said, his voice soft and compelling in the quiet. Suddenly the air seemed to press upon her, and Melissa felt an overpowering heat envelop her. His face was moving nearer as his finger gently nudged her chin upward, but she was rooted to the spot, unable to move.

Melissa knew she was out of her element for none of her suitors had ever really tried to seduce her. Oh, she had endured a clumsy fondling here and there, or a whispered entreaty, and, of course, there had been Bertie, but this... She and the viscount were out of sight, all but alone in the dimly lit room, and that smooth face was moving downward, closer to her own.

"Really, my lord," Melissa said, stepping backward, "I've never heard such nonsense." Her brisk tone belied her nervous state, but her hands, clasped tightly in front of her, gave her away.

"Please call me Leighton," he urged softly, and Melissa noticed just how the green of his coat was picked up in the tiny flecks of his eyes. She did not mention it.

"My lord," she said firmly instead, "if you will excuse me, I should return to the soirée." She waited stiffly for Leighton to move his foot. He did finally, reluctantly, but not before giving her a smile.

And what a smile it was. He flashed those famous Sheffield dimples, and even Melissa was momentarily dazzled. Despite Leighton's claim to have a head for finance, Melissa decided then and there that he had another vocation—

the business of Viscount Sheffield was charming everyone and everything.

But Melissa was not fooled. This man had one thing on his mind, and one thing only. Money.

Chapter Four

"I'll escort you back," Leighton said.

Rather than argue, Melissa fell in beside him. The less time spent with the viscount the better, she resolved. Turtle, indeed! Well, if she was a turtle, he was a snake, she thought bitterly, glancing surreptitiously at his profile. Unfortunately for her, he did not at all resemble any reptile.

They passed the chess players, who were still grumbling at each other, and entered the more brightly lit card room.

"Ah, there you are, my dear." A mellifluous voice sounded in her direction, and Melissa turned in surprise to find the Duchess of Baldwin addressing her. "I suppose Leighton forced you to admire the Verrio," her grace said with a smile.

Melissa nodded mutely. Despite her disdain for the ton, she was slightly in awe of the famous lady who was speaking so naturally to her.

"I'm surprised he doesn't drag in a pallet and sleep there," the duchess added with a world-weary sigh.

Melissa laughed uncertainly, not quite sure what to make of this unexpected friendliness from such an unlikely source.

"I would, if I thought you would let me," Leighton answered, but the duchess only shook her head in mock exasperation.

"The boy is always jesting," she warned Melissa. "Well, if you can tear yourself away from the Verrio long enough,

I had hoped to make up a four for whist. Do you play?" she asked Melissa.

"A little," Melissa answered. Although her father had taught her years before, Melissa rarely played, because Gloriana did not really approve of card games. "I'm afraid I don't play very often or very well," she admitted. "I'm sure you would prefer to find another fourth."

"Nonsense, child," said the duchess. "We'll put you with Leighton. He's far too good for the rest of us."

So it was that Melissa found herself seated cozily across from the viscount, with the duchess on her left and a middle-aged knight named Sir Percival Paddington on her right. Far from escaping from Leighton, she was now partnered with him, and her lack of skill at cards made her ill-prepared for serious play. She had tried her best to demur, but the duchess would have none of it, and who could refuse the Duchess of Baldwin?

At first Melissa was concentrating so hard on the game that she could spare little interest for conversation. She barely listened as the duchess and Leighton exchanged chit-chat. She concentrated on the cards, deciding which to play and remembering those that had already been played. Try to keep track...

"Shot some grouse."

The statement, uttered suddenly and without preamble by Sir Percival, managed to draw even Melissa's attention.

"Really, Percy?" the duchess asked.

"Yes, lovely pair. Dogs scared them up. Damn fine dogs," he said. Melissa dared to take a moment from her hand and looked up at Sir Percival. He appeared to be speaking to no one in particular, for his gaze was fixed solely on his cards.

"Would this be recently, Percy?" Leighton asked, and Melissa caught a muffled sound from the duchess that resembled nothing so much as a stifled giggle. Now they had her full attention.

"Last week," Sir Percival answered, his eyes never leaving his hand. "Spent the fortnight at my lodge. Damn fine hunting."

Melissa glanced across the table at Leighton. Those hazel eyes seemed to sparkle in the soft light as he smiled at her, showing just a hint of his dimples. The gaze was too intimate, as if he were sharing a bit of whimsy with her. Unnerved, she looked down at her cards again.

"Oh, Percy, you are a dear," the duchess exclaimed as she and Sir Percival won the hand. Melissa waited for him to return the compliment and perhaps call the duchess a "damn fine woman," but no comment was forthcoming. Percy had apparently spent his conversation for the time being.

"Well, I was in the country myself this past week," the duchess said. She regaled them with tales of a visit to one of her estates, where an argument with the chief gardener had resulted in the butchery of a pair of prize bushes. Painstakingly trimmed by the volatile artist to resemble two giant swans, the shrubs had been beheaded by the man in a fit of pique.

Melissa, used to maintaining a chilly reserve around others, found it difficult to unbend, but the duchess was so amusing she could not help giggling. Laughing out loud at the thought of the indignant lady confronting her greenery, Melissa decided that she might have to reverse her judgment.

Perhaps she should not condemn all of London society simply because some of the ton were boorish snobs. The duchess was friendly and funny, and perhaps there were a few others like her—people so comfortable with themselves that they felt no need to belittle or condemn others.

Melissa stole a look across the table at the viscount. Perhaps he was not so bad after all. He was nothing but warm and witty now. He had not even commented on her play, which was very definitely lacking.

"I saw your father the other day," Sir Percival announced to the table at large.

"Not mine, certainly," the duchess said. "Is your father living, dear?" she asked Melissa.

"No, Your Grace."

"Well, then, that narrows the field considerably. Percy, you must have seen Leighton's father."

"Naturally. The earl. Who else?" he said, and Melissa looked up just in time to see the duchess's face disappear behind her cards.

"Fine hands. The man has fine hands. A real goer," Sir Percival said, his gaze remaining fixed on his cards. "He was racing those chestnuts. Dashed lively pair they are. Love to have them if you sell 'em." He made his play smoothly, without a glance at the others, as if capping off his monologue with the movement.

Melissa glanced over at Leighton. His carefree face showed no concern at the oblique reference to his financial difficulties. "Sorry, old boy, they're already gone," he said lightly.

"What? Don't tell me Braxton has them?"

Melissa thought she caught a glimpse of anger, but no. Leighton only smiled. "I'm afraid so. Perhaps he would sell them to you."

"A damn shame, boy. It's a damn shame." This time there was no mistaking the small muscle in Leighton's jaw that gave away his tension. The viscount, it seemed, was not as untroubled as he would have others believe.

"Percy! You are a dear," cried the duchess as she and her partner won another hand.

"Sorry, my lord," Melissa said. She was suddenly aware that Leighton was losing more money, although the stakes were sociably low, and that she was to blame.

"No matter," Leighton said with a shrug and a smile. Did he care or didn't he? Melissa could only guess that he did not have a passion for gambling, for he appeared unconcerned. If he did follow in his father's footsteps, he must reserve his zeal for much deeper play than this, she concluded.

"I am not a gambler, Miss Hampton," Leighton said softly, as if reading her mind. Melissa felt herself color slightly. She looked down at her cards, embarrassed at his perceptiveness, yet feeling some measure of relief that he was not his father's son.

But why should she care? Why should she worry if another worthless lord fell prey to the lure of the games? Fortunes were regularly won and lost on the turn of a card, and she certainly had felt no distress over the habits of any other nobleman.

Because you might just end up married to this man, she answered herself. Melissa's hand stopped in midmovement as the thought flashed across her mind, and she blushed a deeper hue.

She struggled to continue with her cards. Then, from under lowered lashes, she stole a glance at him again. Him. Viscount Sheffield, who appeared to be pursuing her with an eye to her father's fortune. As the future Earl of Greyhaven, he would have Gloriana's blessing if he but said the word. *Say that word, Leighton, and I just might have to marry you.*

He was lounging back a little, relaxed, the candlelight gleaming on his jaw, his hazel eyes hooded as he looked down at his cards, held negligently by long, slim fingers. Good God, Melissa, don't even think of it, she cautioned herself, suddenly feeling warm all over.

Leighton saw her eyeing him and wondered what the girl was thinking as she blushed a furious red. It must be something concerning him, for she was peeping at him still. He was enjoying the glances immensely, for he liked the way the pink rose in her cheeks and the way those long, dark lashes rested against her cheeks. And that mouth. It was infinitely kissable.

He had never intended to taste it yet, but tonight, in the Verrio room, he had been sorely tempted. She was very desirable, yet had little notion of her own power, a combination that he found uniquely appealing. An innocent would be a refreshing change from some of the rather jaded ladies he had chosen of late.

"Unless you intend to start a conflagration from across the table, I suggest you return that smoldering gaze to your cards," the duchess said. Leighton looked up, surprised to find the others waiting for his play. Sir Percy appeared unconcerned, of course, but Melissa, the poor child, turned a deeper shade of pink at the duchess's comment.

The duchess did not miss it, either, for she turned to call softly to a servant. "Randolph, give the young lady a glass of ice, please," she said, directing the fellow to Melissa. "If you turn any redder, my dear, you will be ablaze."

Melissa rode home in silence, her emotions in a state of confusion concerning the viscount. On the one hand, she had enjoyed herself this evening. She had endured no insults, no snubs, and no condescension. In fact, by the close of the soirée, she had felt perfectly at ease with a group of people, laughing and speaking openly for the first time since her days at Miss Hempford's School for Young Ladies.

It had been wonderful.

The duchess had been kind and Sir Percy had been amusing and the viscount... The viscount had been warm, witty and attentive—maybe a little too attentive. And there was the rub. How much of her enjoyment was predicated on Leighton? And how could she tell whether his behavior was sincere when he was practically a professional charmer?

Certainly his interest in her stemmed solely from her fortune, but Melissa was used to that. She was an heiress and, therefore, would never know the luxury of being accepted on her own merit. She could not expect otherwise.

Still, there were fortune hunters and there were fortune hunters. Compared to most, Leighton was like a breath of fresh air, but Melissa was too smart to be swept away by a sweet breeze. The viscount might very well be the personable fellow he seemed tonight, enjoyable to be around, polite and cordial—or he might be a master of deceit. Would the warm and witty Leighton turn cold and cruel once he had his hands on her money?

Against her will, her mind traveled back to another man and another deceit—to a time when she had listened and believed.... But then she had been young and foolish, so foolish as to believe in love, of all things! Now she was older and wiser; she knew no such thing existed, and she could see through any man. Or could she?

With an impatient groan, Melissa looked down, only to find her hands clasping and unclasping themselves in an old habit. She carefully placed them, one upon the other, in her lap, and glanced over at her mother. Gloriana usually noticed the nervous gesture before Melissa did and bade her daughter cease in no uncertain terms.

Tonight, however, Gloriana, too, seemed lost in thought, and Melissa realized her mother had been unusually quiet during the ride home. One look at that determined visage told her that Gloriana was busy pondering something, and it more than likely involved her.

Melissa did not ask, for she really had no desire to hear her mother's plans this night. She remained quiet as they left the coach and walked into the house. She was not to be spared a discussion, though, for upon entering the hallway, Gloriana said, "Melissa, I would like to talk to you, in the green drawing room, please."

"Mother, it's late, and I am tired," Melissa replied.

"Now, please," Gloriana insisted as she preceded her daughter to the doors of her domain. With a sigh, Melissa followed, shutting the doors behind her.

Pulling off her gloves, Gloriana stared off into the distance. "I believe this evening was arranged by the Viscount Sheffield," she said as she began her walk to the windows.

No jest, Melissa thought as she perched on an ornate chair. Out loud, she managed a fairly civil "So?"

"He wants to marry you, I'm sure of it," Gloriana said.

"Oh?" Melissa asked, trying to keep the panic from her voice as she frantically reviewed the evening in her mind. Had Leighton and Gloriana ever been alone? Had they spoken, and, if so, had they spoken of marriage?

"Yes," Gloriana said. "I see no reason for him to go to the trouble of arranging a meeting if he were not interested."

Melissa quietly breathed a sigh of relief. Only skewed logic had made Gloriana reach this conclusion. Leighton had said nothing, thank heavens.

Gloriana turned to look at her daughter, and Melissa was hard-pressed not to shrink under that appraising eye. "I wish we could do something with your hair," Gloriana said, lifting a stray lock from Melissa's head, as if it were a piece of furniture to be rearranged.

"Mother, please."

"Well, we will just have to make do," Gloriana said briskly. "Perhaps some new gowns are in order—something a little more ladylike."

"No," Melissa countered firmly, feeling resentment swell within her.

"All right," Gloriana said, pursing her lips. "You dress as you please, within limits, but I want you to encourage the viscount. I would hate to see you wed to Bainbridge."

That's something you will never see, Melissa swore silently. As for the viscount...she was not sure what to make of him, but she had the feeling that he needed no encouragement.

The night brought Melissa no answers and little sleep. She dragged herself through her morning toilette, her thoughts on the viscount instead of her gown, and was three minutes late for breakfast, tardiness which earned her a reproving glance from Gloriana.

"Punctuality is essential in creating a positive impression," Gloriana intoned from across the table as Melissa took her seat, too disgruntled to argue. "I wish to finish my meal promptly, as I have an appointment, and you, I'm sure, would like to be ready in case the viscount should call upon you this afternoon."

Melissa frowned down at some chopped eggs, her appetite fleeing at the reminder of her supposed suitor. She had never dreamed of such a dilemma. A few weeks ago, she had hardly noticed Viscount Sheffield, had never even been introduced to him, and now she was worried about having to marry him!

Marriage. Long ago, the word had embodied all her girlhood dreams of love, but then . . . Well, the specter of a forced union had haunted her since she had first made her debut, for she had always suspected Gloriana would buy and sell her for a title. Thankfully, her suitors had been few in number, and most she had sent running with a few cold glances.

The lack of any suitable prospects had lulled Melissa into a false sense of security, she realized now. She had expected to continue unmarried, while each day spent in that state made her more ineligible, until finally she would be declared a spinster and could spend her remaining days peacefully enjoying her own pursuits, perhaps at some lovely seaside spot.

Now those hopes and plans were teetering on the brink of disaster because of the viscount. Melissa dismissed Bainbridge, certain that her mother was using him only as a threat to get Melissa to do her bidding and accept Leighton. Curse the man, anyway! And Gloriana, too, for her social ambitions.

Melissa hid her panic behind a facade of bored indifference. "I hardly think the man is going to propose today," she said, picking at her eggs.

"One never knows, does one?" Gloriana said, with something akin to a real smile, and Melissa felt her panic rise. Gloriana obviously was already counting her chickens, preening at the thought of the envy of all her friends because she had secured a title for her daughter.

And then what? It was hard to picture her mother alone, without a daughter to direct and scold, her life's ambition completed. Gloriana had even seemed to resent the brief moments Melissa spent with her school friends, and she suspected that was one of the reasons they had been declared unsuitable companions. What would she do when Melissa was gone, pursuing her own life? Melissa eyed her mother suddenly with consideration. "If I did marry, what would you do?" she asked.

"Why, I—" Gloriana looked up, as if momentarily thrown off balance by the question, her fork suspended over her poached herring. "Why, I would entertain, of course," she said, looking down at her plate. "As the mother of a viscountess and future countess, I would have entrée almost everywhere."

Melissa was not so sure of that. Yes, Gloriana might be invited to some functions because of her daughter's new status, but she would hardly move into higher circles herself.

"You can entertain more right now," Melissa urged. "You don't need my marriage to do so. You could easily host a more lavish party than the duchess's soirée."

"Please, Melissa," Gloriana said. "I would like to finish my breakfast. Mr. Hornsby is calling," she added, dropping her voice as though the name were a foul word.

"Really?" Melissa asked, momentarily diverted. "Why?"

"It is his annual visit to discuss the situation."

Melissa smiled at her mother's distaste. Malcolm Hornsby was her late father's partner, and "the situation" was the financial status of the businesses they had shared, which continued to prosper under Hornsby's management. The very thing that kept Gloriana in fine clothes and all the other accoutrements of wealth was treated with all the contempt she could muster.

Melissa found the attitude puzzling. "You really should take more of an interest in Father's affairs," she said. "Mr.

Hornsby should be reporting to you every month, not once a year. If you find it unpleasant to meet with him, I would be happy to talk to him in your stead," Melissa volunteered, only too eager to learn more about her father's pursuits.

"Certainly not," Gloriana said, her lips pursing with disapproval. "A lady does not interest herself in business."

"Nonsense, Mother," Melissa said daringly. "Look at the Duchess of Baldwin. She handles enormous holdings without batting an eyelash."

"That is enough," Gloriana stated coldly, putting down her fork and knife. "I find it impossible to eat with this constant chatter. What the duchess wishes to do is her own concern. Nonetheless, a gentlewoman does not interest herself in such matters. It is unseemly." Drawing herself up to her fullest height, she left the table.

Melissa wished, not for the first time, that she was in control of her father's money. Then she would not have to worry about marriage, to the viscount or anyone else. She pushed aside her plate and daydreamed for a moment of the freedom such riches would provide, and of the chance to learn about her father's businesses. She would not waste her time deciding which hat to choose, but would concern herself with which factory to buy and which holdings to sell. Oh, it would be truly glorious!

With a sigh, she stopped her dreaming and, taking along a book, repaired to a position near the green drawing room in the hopes of running into Mr. Hornsby. She did not have long to wait, for she soon heard a knock on the door, but Brown rushed the man in to see Gloriana so quickly that Melissa reached the hallway only to see his back as Brown closed the door to Gloriana's sanctum.

Melissa returned to her reading, but shortly she heard the door open again. She pricked up her ears in surprise, amazed that her mother was getting rid of her visitor already, for the meeting had certainly been very brief to contain a year's worth of business dealings.

Melissa could only shake her head at Gloriana's notions concerning femininity. Although ladies were not encouraged to achieve, there were always those who succeeded—the women behind the men, ladies who wielded influence in their own right, reformers, authors... Why, the volume she held in her hand had been written by a woman. With an admiring smile for that lady, Melissa put it down for the moment and slipped into the hall.

"Mr. Hornsby, how nice to see you," she said, blithely ignoring her mother's disapproving gaze.

"Miss Hampton, how delightful." The old gentleman stopped to adjust his spectacles, as though to get a better look at her. Slight, slender, and not by any means handsome, Hornsby nonetheless had a certain bookish charm about him. "Harlan's little girl. How lovely you look," he mused, screwing up his face in an odd manner.

"Melissa is a young lady now," Gloriana said. "I've received several offers for her hand."

"Already? But she is just a child."

"This is her second season," Gloriana replied. "As I said, she has had offers, but one must be selective."

"By all means, by all means," Hornsby said. "A lady in your position must be ever vigilant for the rogue who would take advantage of your financial security."

"Too true," Gloriana said, her lips pursed tightly, as though the topic were drifting too close to business for her comfort.

"I want you to feel free to contact me if you should have any questions about a gentleman who is addressing your daughter," Hornsby suggested. "I'm sure you have those you consult in these matters, but as Harlan's partner, I feel an obligation to his interests."

"Thank you, Mr. Hornsby. I will do that," Gloriana assured him in a voice that said she would do no such thing.

"Of course, there is no need to rush into these things. No need at all. There is plenty of time. Miss Hampton is still young," he added.

"Of course," Gloriana said coolly. "Thank you for your time, Mr. Hornsby."

"Yes, of course." Hornsby shifted his burden of papers. "How lovely to see you both again."

Melissa sighed softly as she watched Hornsby leave without exchanging anything with her but the barest of greetings. So much for her hopes of learning anything about the family's financial dealings; Gloriana and Hornsby had stood discussing her as though she were a piece of real estate they had cautiously placed on the market.

"Melissa," Gloriana snapped, and her daughter glanced at her curiously. "A gentlewoman does not linger idly about the hall." Gloriana turned on her heels and walked back into the green drawing room without another glance. Obviously nothing would be learned from her concerning the meeting, either.

"Drat," Melissa said to no one in particular as she, too, left the hall and returned to her book.

Hornsby's visit, the family's businesses and all other concerns were eclipsed a few days later when Gloriana received an invitation to the Montagues' ball. The marquis and his wife had a vast fortune, moved in the first circles, and were famous for their entertainments, invitations to which were prized by anyone aspiring to be in the center of the social whirl.

The evening promised to be quite a crush, for the Hampton vehicle was held up a block from the Montagues' residence. The street teemed with fancy carriages filled with the elite. Gloriana had been lording the invitation over her friends since its arrival, however, and was not about to spend her time in the coach. To Melissa's surprise, she directed her to disembark, and they joined others who had decided to make their way on foot.

Melissa enjoyed the walk, but her steps lagged as they neared their destination. She could not share her mother's enthusiasm for such nonsense, and she was not eager for

another evening with the troublesome viscount. She was
certain this time that he was responsible for their presence,
and she was concerned about his continuing interest in her.
Oh, why couldn't he just leave her alone?

Once inside the hallowed doors of Montague House,
Gloriana began pointing out all the "important" people she
recognized in hushed tones. Melissa hardly listened, for she
cared little about who was escorting whom. She was looking for one particular face in the crowd, one that she did not
see.

Melissa was relieved when Gloriana's attention was diverted by an old acquaintance, leaving her free to keep an
eye on the main entrance to the ballroom. She took up her
old habit of watching the arrivals, but this time her interest
was more personal. She was waiting for the viscount.

While the music and voices swelled around her, Melissa
saw this one and that one, the famous and the infamous.
Confident noblemen, aloof ladies, young bucks and sweet
young things flittered through the doorway until her attention was caught by a blond head.

He moved with confidence. And why not? Those about
him surged forward like moths drawn to a flame. With mild
surprise, Melissa realized that although there were handsomer men present and others who received more deference, most heads turned when Viscount Sheffield entered
the room.

He had that indefinable something that made men nod in
greeting, young girls blush and flutter and mature women
smile. Unlike some of the nobles present—indeed, some of
the royalty—he seemed to be genuinely liked, for the grins
that greeted him were not simply pasted on. In fact, many
of those gracing female forms seemed overly friendly, Melissa thought in disgust.

Melissa shook her head. Of all the people who might
pursue her, why must it be this charmer? She watched as a
powerful duke raised his hand, motioning Leighton over. A
number of ladies were also vying for the viscount's atten-

tion. The man definitely had something . . . a warmth that seemed to radiate from within and envelop everyone in its glow.

Even now that warmth was reaching across the room to Melissa, making her want to be near him, to share his softly spoken humor and watch the slow smile that revealed those engaging dimples. She frowned at the feeling. It unnerved her, and Melissa did not like being unnerved.

As she watched, the viscount stopped to take the hand of a ravishing redhead. He lingered over her fingers, saying something that Melissa could not decipher, and the lady smiled in a manner that even at a distance appeared quite provocative.

Melissa felt a sharp stab of annoyance that further disturbed her. What did she care if he pawed every female in the place? She raised her chin, put on her coolest expression and turned her back on the scene—and nearly walked head-on into Lord Richard Grimley.

"Miss Hampton? How fortunate to see you," he said. "Are you enjoying the evening?" he asked, looking as though he couldn't have cared less about her answer.

Melissa was tempted to respond with a no, but instead smiled coolly. "Yes, indeed, my lord. And you?"

"Oh, the orchestra is most tiresome," he complained in bored tones. "Would you care for some refreshment? Some champagne, perhaps?"

"No, thank you, my lord," Melissa replied, as usual. Then she stopped herself. "No. I mean, yes, I think I would like some champagne. Yes, thank you, my lord."

Grimley appeared to take little note of her indecision. She doubted he remembered that she had never accepted champagne before, and she knew he was not aware of Gloriana's views on too much wine. "Ah, Claude," he called as he held up his finger to a young man nearby. "Would you be so kind as to fetch some champagne for Miss Hampton?"

"Certainly, my lord," Claude said, as though the directive was thrilling.

While the man sought to do his bidding, Lord Grimley gazed arrogantly over the crowd. "What a crush," he said. "But the Montagues are letting just anyone come these days. I expect to see the man who runs the Cluck and Clock next—or perhaps my climbing boy!"

He waited expectantly, and Melissa imagined that he had repeated the supposed witticism before. She could not muster up even a giggle, however, for to her it was simply not funny. Indeed, she could take it as a personal insult if she were so inclined, but she decided to let it go. Out of the corner of her eye she saw Claude returning with her champagne.

"Here you are, Miss Hampton," he said.

Melissa gave him a smile and a thank-you, then watched Lord Grimley dismiss him with a gesture. Raising the glass to her lips, she glanced back over the crowd, telling herself that she was *not* looking for the viscount.

"As you might have guessed, I've decided to forgive you for the other night," Lord Grimley said pompously.

"What?" Melissa asked, nearly choking on her wine. She eyed him incredulously.

"I've decided to overlook your tasteless remark," he explained, his eyes roving about the room in a bored fashion. "But let's not have any more such comments, please."

Melissa swallowed deeply and tried to catch her breath. Of all the arrogant, petty— She took another drink to stop herself from saying something she might regret later.

"I can only assume that you thought you were making a jest, but in the future, please refrain from such humor."

"Miss Hampton." Melissa was still struggling with her anger when she heard the warm, even tones of his voice, and, without a second thought, she whirled to greet the Viscount Sheffield.

To Melissa's surprise, everyone's favorite charmer looked irritated. His brows were drawn together slightly, and his mouth could not be described as smiling. He was not frowning, but he was definitely not grinning, either.

"Grimley," the viscount said with a nod.

"Sheffield," Lord Grimley replied.

"If you will excuse us, I believe Miss Hampton and I were to dance," Leighton said, reaching for her hand.

Rejecting any thought of refusing, Melissa drained her glass and moved along with him, as he seemed in a hurry. Lord Grimley, obviously not disappointed at her departure, nodded his assent, then turned away.

Leighton paused just long enough for Melissa to deposit her empty glass on a table before taking her in his arms, yet Melissa felt no cause for complaint. Confused by her reactions to the man—and the pleasure that surged through her at his touch—Melissa was not sure whether she wanted any conversation at all. Better to keep quiet and not look into his eyes, she decided.

Despite Lord Grimley's grousing, Melissa thought the orchestra wonderful, and the sound seemed to move through her from top to toe as she followed the viscount's steps. His hand in her own was warm and firm, and the hand on her waist felt so...

"Why do you let him talk to you like that?" Leighton suddenly demanded.

With an effort, Melissa drifted back from a glorious world of music and movement to reply. "He's the son of a marquis," she said. "What am I supposed to do?"

"You're supposed to stand up for yourself," Leighton said. "Good God, you gave me the deuce when we met, and I hadn't even done anything!"

"That was different," Melissa mumbled.

"Why? Did I look like I enjoyed being lambasted? As I recall, you called me little better than a pampered, witless dog."

"You were more blunt to begin with," Melissa said.

"More blunt? You could hardly get more blunt than Grimley. I would have thought you his serving girl." He hesitated. "By the way, what was this remark you made?"

Melissa smiled innocently up at him. "I simply told Lord Grimley that the taint of trade was not a disease, in hopes that he would stop treating me like a leper."

Leighton laughed aloud, showing both dimples in a delighted smile. "Now, that's my girl," he said softly. "You can't let them tread all over you, or they won't respect you," he advised, apparently mollified.

Although she nodded mutely, Melissa was no longer really listening. She was too busy mulling over the implications of his earlier words. Leighton, Viscount Sheffield, had called her his girl. What did that mean, and, more important, why couldn't she stop her heart from beating wildly at the phrase?

Chapter Five

Leighton's gaze roved over his partner's smooth, pale skin in appreciation. She was looking away, watching the other dancers, and he admired the thick, black lashes over the enormous eyes that he wished would turn his way. They reminded him of a forest pool, dark and mysterious, with unknown depths. They were a reflection of Melissa, who was so much more than the cool silence she so often presented to the world.

Poor Melissa, who, despite her wealth, had to listen to idiots like Grimley. Leighton wanted to kick the man for speaking to her so rudely. No wonder she had become the Lady Disdain, if that was the kind of treatment she had been receiving.

Perhaps Melissa was right in calling him pampered and spoiled. As the heir to an earldom, he expected respect, if not deference, and had received it all of his life. Even his enemies gave him a token civility. He had spent so much time repairing the damage to the family fortune wrought by his father that he sometimes failed to appreciate the benefits of his position.

How different it would be to travel through life without the subtle advantages that his title brought him and to suffer ill treatment with no recourse. He silently cursed Grimley again.

Ignore it, Leighton, he told himself. When Melissa is your wife, she won't have to listen to the likes of Grimley anymore. The very thought melted away his uncharacteristic annoyance, for he found himself looking forward to that day. He liked the way she felt in his arms; she was an excellent dancer and moved smoothly along with him.

Unfortunately, she still wasn't looking at him. She had on her Lady Disdain mask and steadfastly refused to glance his way, instead looking intently upon the other dancers or, more ludicrously, his cravat. This simply would not do.

"I can teach you how to tie it," he said.

She lifted her head, and he got his wish—her great brown eyes looked up at him. For a moment he saw a longing that startled him with its intensity; then it was gone, so quickly that he doubted his own powers of perception. He had been right about one thing, though. There was much more to her than even he could guess at.

"I beg your pardon?" she asked, raising her chin a notch higher, as though preparing for battle.

"I was offering to teach you how to tie my cravat, since you seemed so interested in it," Leighton replied with a grin. "Have you made a study of men's neckcloths, or is it only mine that has caught your attention?"

He watched her eyes widen in surprise, then narrow in irritation in just the manner he had come to expect. She was such a treat to tease—rather as a sister would be, he thought idly as her full mouth formed a stern line.

No. He was wrong on both counts. Those luscious lips could not look stern, and he definitely could not treat her as a sister. This last decision was made very firmly as the desire to kiss her struck him most forcefully. She was just too tempting. A dark-eyed confection. A rich dessert that was simply waiting for a true connoisseur, Leighton thought.

Luckily, Melissa did not know what he was thinking; she was already angry enough. "Grimley is positively polite in comparison to you!" she said, glaring at him. "Why do you persist in seeking me out, only to insult me?"

"I protest," Leighton, his eyebrows rising innocently. "I would never insult you." The words, spoken softly and sincerely, made Melissa drop her eyes and sent a rush of warmth surging through her.

"Well, you certainly aren't complimenting me," Melissa managed to say rather stiffly, although her cheeks were growing pink and she was acutely aware of her hand lying in his.

Leighton chuckled softly. "My dear Melissa, you do not seem to be the sort of female who is moved by flowery flattery. I can heap compliments upon you by the handfuls if you so desire—God knows you deserve them—but I rather like dragging you out of your shell, and to do that I have to annoy you."

"Oh, what drivel!" Melissa said in disgust, but he only laughed softly in return. She tried to give him one of her chilliest set-downs, yet when she glanced up at him she felt an overpowering heat instead.

No one had ever looked at her that way. She couldn't explain it, for she couldn't understand how a pair of orbs could have such power. One moment she was her usual self, cool and collected, and the next she was on fire, simply because of some subtle change in that hazel gaze.

He was smiling. Melissa could tell because of the tiny lines forming at the corners of his eyes, yet the look in those eyes was not humorous. It was intimate, and it made her heart beat so fast and so loud she thought she would surely burst.

Her breath lodged in her throat until she finally tore her gaze from his, glad the dance was ending. Although exhilarating, the viscount's effect on her was unnerving and, she suspected, quite dangerous.

Melissa was not to escape, though, for his fingers pressed her hand as they stepped apart. "Come, you must see the Montague collection," he said, inclining his head toward the ballroom's south doors. Although she pulled her burning fingers from his, Melissa nodded her assent. She had heard

too much about Lord Montague's famous artworks to forgo
such an opportunity.

Leighton led her through the ballroom into the east gallery, then on to a great hall lined from one end to the other
with paintings. Melissa drew in her breath at the size and
scope of the collection that stretched onward along either
side of her. The works varied in size and subject and history, but all shared the same high quality. Certainly all were
valuable, and some were undoubtedly worth a fortune.

"The picture gallery," Leighton said with a wave of his
hand.

Melissa was too engrossed in the sight to speak. Glancing at one wall, then the other, up to a giant portrait or
down to the delicate rendering of a simple vase of flowers,
she tried to take it all in. She stopped here and there, finally
raising a hand to reverently touch the frame of a glorious
Rubens.

"Beautiful, isn't it?" Leighton said, so wistfully that she
turned to glance at him. He smiled and shrugged. "Marl-
borough just received *Venus and Adonis* as a gift for the
gallery at Blenheim. Now that is a present I would gladly
accept," he said with a chuckle.

Melissa nodded in acknowledgment of his words, but remained silent, moving slowly along the hall until she finally
stopped before a Rembrandt. "The master," she breathed,
shaking her head in wonder.

"The master of light and shadow, to be sure," Leighton
said. "Your personal favorite?" he asked softly.

Melissa hesitated a moment before replying. "No, but it
is certainly no fault of his own that I prefer another."

Leighton smiled in the soft light of the candles. "Come,
I know where your heart is."

Melissa followed, dragging her footsteps reluctantly. "I
would wish for a day here—or more—to appreciate each
work, instead of a few stolen moments," she complained.
"Oh, my lord, just think of what I have missed! If only the
gallery could be open to everyone."

"Perhaps one day," he answered absently as he led her nearly to the end of the hallway. "Now, turn around," he said, watching her features as she whirled to face the Vermeer.

"Oh," she whispered, as if the painting took her very breath. Leighton saw the great eyes open wide in wonder and the full lips relax into a smile, and he felt a lurch in his chest that had nothing to do with the masterpiece.

"Look at the light, the light through the window. It is so beautiful, it is almost heartbreaking," Melissa said. Then, suddenly, she turned to Leighton. "But how did you know it would be my favorite?"

"I saw you admiring Waterbury's Vermeer. You were the only person there who seemed to appreciate it, including Waterbury, who wouldn't even know what piece to buy without the benefit of fifteen advisers to explain it to him," Leighton said.

She nodded, then looked up at him in open gratitude, all the disdain and distance banished for once from her features. "Thank you," she whispered. Her face, upturned in the gentle glow of the gallery, was itself a work of art, haunting and exquisite, Leighton thought. He wanted to hold her.

"Here," he said, taking her hand and leading her into the statuary room. She pulled her fingers free again as if scorched by his touch, and he was surprised by the distress on her features. He could have kicked himself for causing it.

Why shouldn't she be leery of him? The room was feebly lit by one candelabra and looked to be just the sort of place a disreputable roué would lure a young girl. Once married, a lady could do what she liked, engendering scandal after scandal with little censure, but until those vows were spoken she must follow the strictest codes of conduct. These rules happened to preclude unchaperoned trysts with men, no matter how noble their intentions, Leighton thought with chagrin.

Turn around now and leave, Leighton, he told himself, but this night had a magical quality that he had not experienced in a long time, and he did not want to end it. He felt an affinity with the girl who now stood nervously clasping her hands and glancing around the room. They had shared something in the gallery, something that he hadn't even realized was missing from his life. Fine and noble arguments all, Leighton thought, when all he really suffered from was a simple desire to take her in his arms.

Even though she was looking away, Leighton could feel the sparks between them, and as his eyes traveled over her luscious curves, his decision was made. He couldn't go—not yet, anyway. He told his conscience that they would soon be wed, and stepped toward her.

"This is Montague's prize treasure," he said, his hand moving toward the Botticelli figure that graced the center of the room. But his voice trailed off and he dropped his hand to his side in a lame gesture as she turned and met his gaze, for they both knew the sculpture was not the reason they were there.

"She is perfect, isn't she?" Melissa asked, tearing her eyes from his to glance at the marble, but the words stuck as she spoke. Her heart was beating so wildly it threatened to leap up into her throat, a very real impediment to conversation.

"Not as beautiful as you are," Leighton said softly.

His voice was gentle, his face genuine, but Melissa did not believe the words for a moment. "Oh, don't be absurd," she said, turning on her heel, but he would not let her go. His hands found her shoulders, and the heat she had been fighting returned in waves.

It was positively palpable, and she knew he felt it, too, because he had the oddest expression on his face. No, it wasn't odd, just unusually intense for the carefree viscount, she decided in a lucid moment before his hand cupped her cheek. His fingers were smooth and warm, but it was his gaze, more than his hand, that held her.

"You are beautiful," he whispered as he looked into her eyes. "How can you not see it?"

Her lucidity melted away, for suddenly, with the most amazing leap of faith, she believed him, or at least believed him to be sincere. Perhaps he was blind, but Leighton thought she was beautiful, and that was enough. More than enough, actually.

She could not reply to his question; her voice was again caught in its passageway, yet it did not matter. She gave him an answer in her gaze as his head bent, moving so close that she could see the dark lashes lowering over the deep golden-green eyes, the smooth skin of his cheek, the curve of his lips.

His mouth met hers with a gentle persuasion, softly taking her upper lip, then her lower, then touching the corner of her mouth, the momentum building until she was gasping for air. Their breath entwined as he pulled her close. She had been kissed before, but never like this.... Perhaps she had never really been kissed at all. This was not kissing, she thought fleetingly, it was madness, a madness that leapt through her blood and made her press against him.

Leighton's body was lean and muscular against hers, and when she moved closer she felt his arms tighten around her. Gone was the gentle persuader as his lips took hers with a searing strength and his tongue explored her mouth expertly. One of his hands traveled up to the back of her neck, where the chills it sent through her intermingled with the heat that rampaged elsewhere.

He kissed her, and she returned his kiss, unable to deny herself. She raised a hand to grasp his neck and slipped her fingers into the tousled golden locks, a soft sigh of pure pleasure escaping her lips. She found herself gripped even tighter as Leighton pressed her to his hard length. His mouth moved over her cheek and along her ear and trailed down her neck.

"My God, Melly," he whispered as they both took in a breath.

It was then that they heard it: the soft whisper of laughter. It drifted in from the gallery; then a woman's voice was raised, followed again by the echoes of laughter.

"Damn." Leighton swore softly as they broke apart, running a hand through his hair and his eyes over Melissa. She was scarlet, he was sure of it, but, he hoped, the light was too scant in the gallery to notice. Her eyes downcast, she nervously put a hand to her hair.

"You look fine," Leighton reassured her softly. "Quickly now," he urged, taking her arm. "Be a brave girl, and let's go out to the Vermeer. We've been nowhere else," he whispered.

Melissa did not feel up to it, but she followed his lead, moving silently into the gallery to stand in front of the masterpiece. She stared at the painting that had meant so much to her only a few minutes before, trying to concentrate on its beauty instead of her whirling emotions. Beside her, Leighton was speaking, smoothly relating a brief history of the Montague collection in his usual charming manner, while she struggled to regulate her breathing.

The main thing, Melissa told herself, was to calm down and not imagine the possible consequences of her foolishness—a reputation in tatters, total ostracism, Gloriana's contempt.... Now, standing where she was, attempting not to shake like a leaf, she wondered how on earth a normally coolheaded girl had gotten into this situation.

It was the champagne, she decided. She had drunk it too quickly and it had gone to her head, making her more susceptible to the appeal of a man for whom she appeared to have a strong physical attraction. Now that was an understatement, she thought ruefully. The man made her burn with a desire so intense she could not even bear to remember it!

The voices broke into her thoughts. They were louder now, and she heard a woman's softer cadences intermingled with deep male tones. Short bursts of laughter were followed by footsteps, and Leighton turned, placing a hand on the small of her back to nudge her along with him.

Melissa was surprised to see how far away the people were. In the adjoining room—and even here—the sounds, magnified by the huge gallery, seemed so close that she fully expected the group to be nearly upon them, when they were actually standing quite a distance down the hall. Melissa forced her lips into a smile as they approached.

A woman led, while three men arrayed themselves around her. The lady's bearing bespoke a title, and when they neared, Melissa could tell she was definitely a person of consequence. A beautiful blonde, she was dressed in a shimmering deep green gown that barely covered her luscious curves. Diamonds sparkled at her ears, wrists and throat, and she had the look of someone used to deference.

She stopped before them, and the three men grouped themselves around her like slavish admirers waiting breathlessly for her next word or move. She smiled slowly, her eyes upon the viscount, then expertly snapped open a fan and gently began to move it.

"Why, Leighton, giving a private...showing, are we?" she asked.

Melissa felt herself go cold at the insinuation, her gaze flying to her companion, but Leighton merely chuckled and shrugged casually. "You know my love for the Montague collection, Cecile," he said.

"Yes, of course. And who is your protégée?" the lady asked. Melissa stiffened, her nervousness and bewilderment disappearing under that contemptuous gaze. Although she never knew what to expect from the viscount, this was an attitude she recognized. She was familiar with the blue-blooded disdain in the voice and the unfriendly smile on the face of the lady standing before her.

Melissa responded in kind. She raised her chin, straightened her shoulders and looked coldly back at the blonde, who was eyeing her from head to toe as though she were a troublesome piece of lint.

"Your Grace, may I present Melissa Hampton," Leighton said. "Miss Hampton, this lovely lady is Cecile, Duchess of Pontabeigh." Melissa curtsied gracefully, her features revealing nothing but a chilly politeness. "And I don't believe I'm acquainted with your entire entourage," Leighton said.

Cecile laughed, a sultry sound that set her three attendants to chuckling in unison. "Sir Snavely," she said, directing her fan to the tall man at her right. "Mr. Maplethorpe," she said, snapping the fan at the short fellow to her left. "And I'm certain you know Lord Hawthorne." A dark man appeared from behind Maplethorpe and nodded his head.

The duchess paused, her fan finally stilled, before introducing Leighton. "Viscount Sheffield," she said, purring the name.

The men all uttered cordial greetings as if on cue, and Melissa was reminded of a puppet show she had once seen at a fair. In this case, it was the duchess who pulled the strings, and her three woodenheaded dolls, large as life, responded accordingly. Melissa half expected them to do a little dance at any moment. Well, let them all act as doltish as they wish, Melissa thought, only too glad that the duchess's attention had shifted from herself.

Melissa's reprieve was brief, for she soon was receiving the attention of a pair of blue-green eyes that had all the warmth of an iceberg. "Ah, Miss Hampton, I've heard so much about you. It is a treat to meet you." The duchess's voice was silky and her smile showed even white teeth, but something lingered in her tone that made Melissa doubt her sincerity.

"Leighton, run and get us some champagne, please," Cecile said, bestowing one of her slow, sultry smiles on him. Melissa watched him hesitate a moment, as if he would deny the request, but then he smiled crookedly and bowed in acquiescence.

Melissa imagined that very few people refused the duchess anything, but she sensed that Leighton was not happy about the order. It seemed to her that the bow he gave was slightly exaggerated, and apparently the duchess thought so, too, for she did not look at all pleased as she watched him move down the hallway.

The duchess took it out on her minions, dismissing them with a wave of her hand that revealed her irritation. Although their protest seemed to lift her mood a little, she would not relent. "I must get to know this young lady," she said by way of explanation, and turned to eye Melissa as she might have a choice morsel.

Melissa watched the men depart with a mixture of relief and trepidation, for although she was heartily sick of them, she was now alone with a woman who made her extremely uncomfortable. Melissa tried to mask her uneasiness with a cloak of composure and nodded politely when Cecile gestured to the chairs that lined the walls at intervals.

The duchess chose an imposing Jacobean seat, and Melissa sat down next to her. Her back straight, she folded her hands together in her lap and turned to face blue-green eyes that revealed nothing of the duchess's thoughts. It was just as well, for had Melissa known what was going on behind those aquamarine pools she might not have been able to maintain her calm demeanor.

Cecile was not pleased, for the evening was not going at all as she had planned. She had seen Leighton disappear into the gallery with a pretty young thing, and had followed, hoping to catch the two in the kind of scandalous situation that might cast a chill on his wedding plans. Intent on creating an interesting evening and stirring up a little trouble into the bargain, she had never dreamed that the girl with him was his intended.

Cecile had discreetly sought a little information on the Nobody, as she thought of the girl Leighton intended to marry, and had discovered she was one of the richest ladies on the market, which explained Leighton's sudden desire to marry her. The girl was not at all what Cecile expected, however. Not by any means.

Cecile ran her eyes over her companion again with displeasure. With lustrous dark hair, huge dark eyes and the kinds of lips that men liked, the girl was far too pretty to be an heiress. Women with money should either have the grace to be as ugly as Emily Farnsworth or have some other annoying habit, like that creature who giggles incessantly, Cecile thought bitterly.

The Nobody appeared to have a peculiar effect on Leighton, too, for he was acting oddly, and Cecile did not care for that, either. His behavior when she had sent him for champagne had irritated her, even though she knew the reason for it. With his overdone bow, Leighton had conveyed the message that he would not be treated like the fops who were flocking around her, eager to be at her beck and call.

But then, she already knew that Leighton did not like to be treated cavalierly. How well she knew. Unlike most of his peers, Leighton had an odd streak of morality—or was it loyalty? Whatever it was, it certainly ran deep. Perhaps that explained his rush to defend the girl when Cecile had nearly caught them alone in the statuary room.

Cecile had been forced to abandon her original scheme anyway, once she had discovered the girl's identity. Any scandal involving Leighton and his heiress might force them even closer together. That would not do, for Cecile certainly wanted no hand in promoting this marriage. On the contrary, tonight's events had made her decide that it would not be at all the thing for Leighton to wed this Nobody.

The girl was prattling on about art, for God's sake, so Cecile forced herself to take a token glance around the gallery. When she did, her contempt drained away, and her eyes stopped dead. Directly in front of her, on the opposite wall, hung the Rubens.

Cecile thought back to the last time she had been at Greyhaven. Certainly it was not that long ago. Two years? Three? It was all a bit foggy, but one thing was certain. The

Rubens, Leighton's favorite, was staring back at her, and the last time she had seen it, it had been gracing the Painted Hall at Greyhaven.

The heart she had thought well-hardened by the world trembled at the thought of Leighton's loss. Foolish though it seemed to her, he had always loved art with a passion, a passion equaled only by his love for Greyhaven itself. The Rubens, his favorite, had been in the family for years.

Damn! Cecile was surprised at the wave of guilt that rushed over her. She darted a look at the girl beside her, who was pointing to a nearby work and blabbering about light and shadow. Whatever Cecile's personal feelings about her, the Nobody had the power to save Greyhaven.

Cecile sighed softly and leaned back against her chair, all her elaborate schemes for breaking Leighton's engagement unraveling before they were sewn. There was no point in pursuing any of her plans now, for her heart was no longer in it. She remained silent, letting the young girl beside her talk, haltingly at first, then smoothly as she warmed to her subject.

Cecile was still leaning back in her chair when she sensed Leighton returning. She slowly straightened into her most elegant posture, her face naturally seeking the most flattering light and her fan at the ready.

"Your Grace," Leighton said, bowing mischievously as he handed her the champagne. "Miss Hampton," he added with a nod, giving her a glass, too. Then he turned to look at them both. "Have you ladies been having a nice chat?"

Cecile smiled in genuine amusement. "Why, yes, of course, Leighton, dear. Your protégée has been instructing me in the appreciation of these great works."

Leighton looked annoyed, while the Nobody simply turned away and sipped her champagne. Then she stood up and put the glass down. "Your Grace, my lord, I beg your pardon, but I really must be getting back to my mother."

"I'll escort you," Leighton said, cocking an arm for the girl to take. She nodded after the briefest hesitation, and

Cecile wondered if all was as it should be between the two. Perhaps all her ruminations had been for naught, and there would be no wedding after all. She smiled.

"Cecile?" Leighton said, extending his other arm to her. Cecile looked at him, one eyebrow rising at the absurdity of his offer. When she walked with a man, she did not share him with another woman.

"No, thank you, Leighton," she said smoothly. "I think I will just sit here for a moment and enjoy the collection." She ignored the amused look on his face, and waved her hand airily in dismissal. "Begone with you, you wastrel, before I change my mind—about everything."

Melissa watched the odd exchange with interest. She could have sworn there was some other meaning to the duchess's words, yet Leighton's indifference seemed to belie her suspicions. He turned to go, and Melissa joined him, though as they walked away she shot a glance at the duchess.

The beautiful blonde was leaning back in her chair and laughing softly to herself. Melissa wondered if the woman might not be just a little mad. Their little "chat" certainly ranked as one of the strangest encounters Melissa had ever had. Nevertheless, the ton was rife with odd characters, and she was becoming accustomed to all sorts of eccentric behavior.

With a sigh of bewilderment, Melissa put the duchess out of her head, returning her thoughts to the man beside her, a far more troublesome topic. Now that her fear of discovery was gone and her attention was no longer focused on the duchess, Melissa found herself furious with the viscount. How could he lure her into a private room on the pretext of admiring art and then try to seduce her?

She glared at him, but he was looking away, and his nonchalant behavior irked her still further. What had happened between them had reduced her to a distraught wreck, while he seemed totally unaffected. Presumably, handsome charmers such as the viscount made such a habit out of seducing young ladies that the encounters were as quickly forgotten as a hand of cards—and just as meaningless.

They walked along silently, Leighton apparently lost in thought, until Melissa thought she would surely scream if he did not say something soon. She wanted to shout at him, but the desire was frustrated by his calm quiet. Finally, the sounds of the ball became louder, breaking the silence, as they reached the east gallery and came upon some other guests.

Leighton appeared to catch the eye of a man standing near the entrance to the ballroom, and he slowed his pace. "Melly, I have some business to take care of, so I'll have to return you to your mother," he said, without even glancing in her direction.

"Really?" Melissa asked through clenched teeth.

"Yes," he said distractedly. "I'm sorry, but you'll have to manage without me for the rest of the evening."

"What a disappointment for me, my lord," Melissa whispered sweetly, smiling up at him. "However, I will endeavor to survive without your presence, thank you."

Her acid comment finally caught Leighton's attention, and he turned to look at her, his head cocked to the side, then laughed out loud, both of his dimples making an appearance. "My dear girl, are you trying to tell me that you have not enjoyed my company this evening?" he asked.

"I'm trying to tell you that I have not enjoyed your company any evening!" Melissa answered.

Leighton only chuckled and put a finger to his chin in mock pensiveness. "But I seem to recall a few moments tonight when you seemed very taken with me," he said. "If you dislike me so, you certainly have an odd way of showing it."

Melissa's hand itched to slap his face. She actually had to clench her fingers into a fist to stop herself from taking that grin off his face—dimples and all. Once again he had rendered her speechless with fury.

"Ah, there you are, Melissa, dear." Melissa straightened her fingers and relaxed her jaw automatically, rather like a schoolgirl caught misbehaving by her governess, at the sound of her mother's autocratic tones.

"Mrs. Hampton," Leighton said warmly. He bowed low over Gloriana's hand and was rewarded with one of her ingratiating, if stilted, smiles. "I must apologize for engaging so much of your daughter's time, but she is so beautiful and charming that I am loath to share her presence."

Melissa tried to keep from choking on that one. Even Gloriana looked a little skeptical.

"I was hoping that you and your daughter could join me at Vauxhall—perhaps Friday," Leighton said.

"That would be lovely, my lord," Gloriana said before Melissa could speak. "We would be honored to enjoy your company." She appeared quite pleased with the invitation, and Leighton bowed over her hand again.

"Thank you," he said. "I must excuse myself now, but I look forward to seeing you." He took Melissa's hand, too, though she glared at him under lowered lids.

He gazed at her wickedly as he held her fingers, then pressed a kiss against her skin that sent heat pulsating up her arm into her chest, where it robbed her of breath. And when he raised his eyes again to hers, they burned with the same fire she had seen when he had held her close, bringing back the hot, vivid memory of when she had returned his kisses with a mad passion.

"Miss Hampton," Leighton said softly, and then he was gone. Melissa stood gazing after him dully, her fury replaced by a desire for the man that eclipsed all else.

"Well?" asked Gloriana.

"He called me Melly," Melissa said stupidly.

"Melly? How improper!" Gloriana said in a disgusted voice. "No one has ever called you Melly."

"I know," Melissa said. And somehow, in spite of everything, her lips curved into a slow smile.

Chapter Six

Melissa stood at the window, looking out into the dusk, hoping the viscount had forgotten about this evening's planned trip to Vauxhall. She did not want to go to Vauxhall with the viscount.

In fact, Melissa did not want to go anywhere with him, least of all to Vauxhall, with its darkened pathways, notorious as a setting for lovers' trysts. She was still fuming over his unconscionable behavior at the Montagues' ball. How could he seduce her, then act as if nothing had occurred, and finally force this new invitation on her by going through her mother?

She had considered him different from his fellows, but now she was not so sure.... Well, in all honesty, he *was* different, Melissa conceded, but she was beginning to believe that the difference did not constitute an improvement. She twisted her hands in frustration, unable to stop the torrent of feelings the viscount seemed to provoke.

"Come away from the window, Melissa," Gloriana demanded, breaking into Melissa's thoughts as she swept into the room. "Ladies do not exhibit themselves to the public. And stop wringing your hands. Good heavens, what is the matter with you tonight? The viscount should be here any moment, and I am certain you would not want him to think you are anxious."

Gloriana followed her sharp words with the most graceful of movements as she sat daintily on the edge of a chair. Fingering the enormous pink feathers on her hat, she looked for all the world as though she were as sweet and helpless as a kitten. "I wonder who else will be included in the viscount's party tonight," she said in a softer tone.

I don't care, as long as there are plenty of them, Melissa thought, wishing for dozens of other guests to take the viscount's attention away from her. Then it would be easy to avoid his attentions, even if he touched her. Melissa shivered at the memory of his warm hands on her shoulders, of his body wrapped up with her own, and frowned. She could not, would not, let that kind of madness occur again, for the sake of her reputation—and her sanity.

Gloriana had harbored hopes of joining a small party of a dozen or two of the ton's smartest set, so she was sadly disappointed to discover that only one other man was included in their group. Her expectations were further dampened by the man himself. Presumably invited to keep her company, the other guest most assuredly would not have been her choice for an evening's companion.

He was a rather odd-looking fellow with great, bushy gray eyebrows over eyes that never seemed to have their sights on anything in particular. It was a trait that Gloriana found most annoying. More important, she had never heard his name before, and she could only assume that, as a mere knight, he was not a person of consequence. She rejected him—without quite cutting him—and gazed about for a familiar face.

Melissa was even more disappointed than her mother by the small size of the party, because, as one of four, she could hardly escape attention. And she certainly couldn't count on Leighton's guest, pleasant though he might be, for diversion. If she waited for Sir Percival Paddington to speak, she would have a long night of it.

Sir Percival. Melissa glanced over at him, walking straight and stiff beside her mother as they made their way along the Grand Walk, and she felt a giggle rise into her throat. What an unusual pairing that was. Her amusement died when she realized that Gloriana was studiously ignoring the poor man. She would have to put a stop to that.

"How is the Duchess of Baldwin, Sir Percival?" Melissa asked, smiling when she was rewarded by her mother's immediate attention. Gloriana's head turned so quickly at the mention of one of society's most prominent ladies that the pink feathers on her hat threatened to take flight.

"Fine. Fine lady, her grace," Sir Percival stated unhelpfully.

"You are her preferred partner at whist, aren't you? Now, don't be modest," Melissa said, trying her best to draw him out.

"Fine player, her grace. Damn fine player," Sir Percival said. His salt-and-pepper hair bobbed as he nodded his head for emphasis and gazed at the elm trees lining the avenue.

Melissa felt like giving up, for, instead of making points with her mother, Sir Percival's comments only caused Gloriana to frown in distaste at the foul word uttered in her presence. The whole situation struck Melissa as so silly that she felt the giggle threatening again, and the more she tried to swallow it, the worse it became. Finally, she hid her face behind her hand and covered the escaping laughter with a cough.

"Why, Miss Hampton, that is a bad cough," Leighton said. Melissa found his overly solicitous tone extremely suspicious, and she refused to look at him, for she imagined that those hazel eyes were twinkling with mischief. "I do hope you aren't coming down with a chill," he said.

"No, no. I'm fine, my lord," Melissa choked out, unable to look at her mother, either, for she was certain that Gloriana was eyeing her questioningly.

She took a deep breath and dared a peep at the viscount. As she had guessed, he was grinning outrageously. She scowled at him in return. After all, Sir Percival was his guest; he ought to be lending a hand, instead of impeding her efforts to include the knight in the conversation.

The strains of Haydn grew louder as they approached the Grove, where the orchestra was playing, and Melissa took the opportunity to scold her companion. Stepping closer to Leighton, she whispered, "You could help me out."

"What's that, Miss Hampton? I didn't quite hear you over the music," he said, smiling wickedly.

Realizing she would receive no assistance from that quarter, Melissa glared at him from behind her fan and took matters firmly in hand. Obviously, subtlety was lost on Gloriana, so she was going to have to tell her in plain English to stop ignoring Sir Percival. "Excuse me, my lord," Melissa said to Leighton. Leaving his side, she walked over to Gloriana. "Mother, do you perchance have a handkerchief?" she asked sweetly.

"Certainly, dear," Gloriana said, smiling at the viscount as he and Sir Percival walked a few steps ahead. When Gloriana reached into her reticule, Melissa leaned close and whispered into her ear.

"You ought not to slight Sir Percival, Mother. He is one of the duchess's favorites," she said.

Gloriana clicked her tongue in disbelief. "I can't trust anyone who will not look me in the eye," she declared.

"Oh, heavens," said Melissa, earning a frown from her mother. "You are just miffed because he's not admiring your new gown—and how well you look in it."

"I am not so frivolous," Gloriana said, pursing her lips at the accusation. She handed her daughter the handkerchief and sighed like a true martyr. "Very well," she said grudgingly. "There must be something to recommend him, if her grace is so fond of him, but I cannot condone cursing in my presence," she warned.

Melissa held up the handkerchief to disguise the smile her mother's words engendered. She knew very well that Gloriana's rules of conduct varied according to a person's rank.

If Sir Percival were a duke or an earl, she would undoubtedly be a little more forgiving about his shortcomings.

As she walked beside her mother for a few steps before catching up with the others, Melissa took the opportunity to admire the viscount. He was talking to Sir Percival, so Melissa let her eyes leisurely take in his frame. Tall, wide-shouldered but lean, he moved with grace and assurance, and from his broad shoulders to his firm calves he filled out his clothes quite nicely.

This observation accelerated her heartbeat alarmingly, and she took a deep breath just as he turned to look at her. She didn't know whether he divined her thoughts or was just pleased to see her again at his side, but he smiled so slowly and so warmly that she felt her resolve to remain aloof slip down a notch.

"Walk with me?" he asked.

It took all of Melissa's strength to disregard her pounding heart and shake her head. "But, my lord, we simply must stay and enjoy the concert," she said with a cool smile. Although he looked slightly amused by her refusal, Leighton nodded his assent. Pleased to have triumphed so easily, Melissa turned her attention to the Haydn and tried to keep it there.

It was a struggle. Try as she might, Melissa could not immerse herself in the symphony as she would have liked, for she was acutely aware of the man beside her. She fought a dreadful desire to peek at him, and instead glanced at her mother. Gloriana, who did not care a fig for music, was fanning herself prettily, but looked dreadfully bored.

Sir Percival appeared to be the only one enjoying himself, for his gray-and-white head of hair bounced up and down jauntily as he eyed the musicians.

"How do you find the orchestra tonight, Sir Percival?" Melissa asked.

"Looking fine, I'd say," he said.

"Are you a music lover?" Melissa persisted.

"Tin ear," Sir Percy said, shaking his head. "Don't mind watching the fellows, though."

Melissa coughed softly, her handkerchief again covering the small gurgle of laughter that escaped her. Despite her determination to ignore the viscount, she could not help herself. Slowly and surreptitiously, she slid her eyes over to Leighton to gauge his response to Sir Percival's latest comment. She was surprised to find that his cheeks were not creased into their dimples and no wicked smile tugged at his mouth; he was looking ahead, apparently concentrating on the orchestra.

To her immense annoyance, Melissa realized that *Leighton* was the only one enjoying himself. He had not heard Sir Percival, or anything else except the symphony. With a disgruntled frown, Melissa returned her gaze to the violinists and forced herself to appreciate their work.

By the time the bell rang signaling the end of the first act, Melissa was heartily sick of sounds that would normally have enthralled her, and Gloriana looked as peeved as was possible for one in the company of a titled gentleman of good standing. Sir Percival...well, Melissa found it hard to decide exactly what the good knight thought about anything.

Leighton finally turned to her, a look of amused surprise his response to her grim visage. Slowly he took her hand and leaned over it. "Could I interest you in a stroll now?" he asked, his voice as silky as the night. Melissa pulled away her burning fingers and refused to look into his eyes.

"If it is a stroll to a supper box, my lord," she said stiffly. "I simply adore the ham. Don't you mother?" The smile she pasted on her face seemed as silly as Gloriana's, and Melissa felt a glum disappointment with the entire evening.

"Yes. Let us do have some refreshments." Gloriana looked relieved at the prospect of escaping from the concert.

A box was duly obtained by the viscount, who then personally presented Melissa with a plate piled high with

Vauxhall's famous wafer-thin slices. "Your ham, Miss Hampton," he said softly, a smile tugging at the corners of his mouth.

Annoyed at his manner, Melissa took the plate with an ungrateful frown. "Are you perpetually amused, my lord?" she muttered.

Leighton laughed aloud. "Not usually, Miss Hampton, but I find your company so delightful that I can't help myself." He chuckled again at the scowl she sent him, causing Gloriana to look up from her food with a questioning eye.

Leighton leaned back against a wall as he surveyed the group. Melissa's dark head was bent over her plate; her thick, nearly black hair was so glossy that he ached to run his fingers through the softness. Oblivious to his lustful gaze, she was staring at the mountain of ham he had given her as though her stomach were heaving at the sight of it.

In the opposite corner of the box, her mother was picking at her food delicately and sending the odd smile, while Sir Percy was attacking a tiny chicken with gusto.

"Careful, Percy," Leighton warned him. "Don't eat with such relish, or Miss Hampton will scold you for enjoying yourself."

His words did not bring on the heated outburst he expected, for, instead of raging at him, Melissa looked positively mortified. Her eyes flew to her mother, then back to her plate as Leighton watched the interchange curiously.

Leighton looked on, astounded, as she bent over her food like a cowed servant—when only a few minutes before she had chewed him to pieces. Her voice, wafting up from under her bent head, was hardly recognizable. "My lord teases me," she said in little more than a whisper.

Racking his brain for a reason for Melissa's sudden change in behavior, Leighton could only blame it on the presence of her mother. He realized that the banter with Melly he so enjoyed had been exchanged privately or in front of Eudora and Percy, but never within hearing of Gloriana Hampton.

A tiny, dainty woman with graceful movements and horrid taste in hats, Gloriana seemed rather frivolous, so Leighton had never given her much thought. His eyes flicked across the box to her, catching a cold look of disapproval on the lady's face, and he decided that a reassessment was in order.

"If I do tease, it is only because I enjoy seeing you blush so prettily," he said softly, turning his attention back to Melissa. "She does blush prettily, doesn't she, Percy?"

"Fine girl," Sir Percival agreed with a nod, still grappling with his chicken. "Nice manners. Very pretty." He hesitated a moment, a meaty leg brandished in the air. "Not very good at whist, though," he declared before taking another bite.

Melissa looked up at Percy and smiled, and Gloriana seemed to relax a little. "And how do you find Vauxhall this evening, Mrs. Hampton?" Leighton asked her.

"Oh, I find it most pleasant, my lord," she began, before launching into a recitation of who she had seen with whom during the concert. Apparently Gloriana had spent more time watching the crowd than the musicians. Leighton feigned interest with a nod; this was just the sort of gossip that bored him into oblivion.

Leighton listened patiently while Gloriana droned on. Sir Percy was ignoring the conversation to tackle another chicken, and Leighton assumed that Melissa was either applying herself to her ham or glaring at him as she had been most of the evening. When he glanced her way, he found to his astonishment that her full lips were curved into a beautiful, warm smile directed at him and her dark eyes were shining with gratitude.

He wanted to take her in his arms then and there, but Gloriana was still talking and Sir Percy was still eating. By the time they had all finished and he had coaxed them out into the crowd again, it was as though an eternity had passed. Impatient with the delay, he was determined to persuade Melissa to walk with him as soon as possible. Now that she was pleased with him, all the better for his purpose, he thought with a grin.

Melissa watched Leighton's carefree smile with foreboding. Although she was grateful that he had dropped the verbal swordplay in front of Gloriana, she still had no intention of joining him on one of Vauxhall's dark and secluded walkways. Despite her two refusals, she was certain he would ask her again, and she was even more certain that tonight's invitation had been issued for the sole purpose of completing the aborted seduction he had begun at the Montagues'.

Seeking to avoid a final reckoning on the matter, she had lingered over the ham until she was positively stuffed, and had dawdled still further with her ice cream. She had expected Leighton to lose patience with her at any moment, but he had only given her that dry, humorous look, as though he was amused by her tactics.

He did not appear to be entertained, however, by Gloriana's gossip. In fact, Leighton seemed as bored as she was by the comings and goings of the titled thickwits whose names meant so much to her mother. After he sent her several agonized looks, Melissa finally took pity on him and agreed to leave the supper box.

She regretted the decision immediately, for they ran into a group of her mother's snobbish friends as soon as they began walking. Naturally, Gloriana was delighted, revelling in the opportunity to introduce the viscount to Mrs. Marchant. Then they had to listen again to Gloriana's litany of who was where and with whom. Leighton still had little to add to her comments, and even this idle conversation died after a while.

They all stood together a bit awkwardly until Mrs. Marchant's group decided to go meet someone's new beau. Nothing would do but that Gloriana must join them, and Melissa felt her heart sink as her mother abandoned her to the company of Sir Percy and the viscount.

Of course, they continued on only a few paces before Sir Percy found he had a pressing errand, too, and Melissa was alone with Leighton. Although they were surrounded by others on the Grand Cross Walk and Melissa knew even the viscount could hardly drag her off to the Lovers Walk against her will, she didn't trust him—or herself. She was stricken again by that feeling she so often had about him, the feeling that Leighton would have his way no matter what she might decide.

"Walk with me?" The soft request intruded on her thoughts.

"I am, my lord," Melissa answered, a bit peevishly. She heard his soft chuckle, but refused to look at him, glancing down instead at her feet.

"Are you afraid of me?" he asked.

The question put her back up, and Melissa turned to glare at him. "Certainly not!"

He smiled at her in an infuriating way, as though her denial were a lie. "You've been shying away from me all evening like a frightened colt."

"So now I'm a colt, am I?" Melissa snapped. "Does that mean I'm no longer a turtle? I'm not quite sure which is preferable, to be compared to a lizard or to a horse!"

"A turtle is not a lizard."

"And I am not afraid of you," Melissa said heatedly.

"Good," Leighton answered lightly. "Then you'll walk with me?"

Melissa realized she was caught in a challenge, but she could not easily extricate herself. She sighed heavily. "Yes, my lord, I would simply love to stroll with you, wherever you wish to go," she said in sarcastic tones.

"Now that is a very promising attitude," Leighton said, smiling so broadly that both his dimples appeared.

Melissa was not softened by his grin, and she had no intention of letting his charm lure her into another intimate situation. She put on her coldest expression and walked stiffly beside him, determined to keep her mind focused on her footsteps and not on the man beside her.

She succeeded very well until they turned onto the Lovers Walk. "What a surprising choice, my lord," Melissa said snidely. "I would never have guessed that you would choose this path."

"I'm glad to see you've returned to your usual acid-tongued self, Melly, love," Leighton said dryly. "I was worried about you in the supper box. For a moment, I feared you might become agreeable."

The comment reminded Melissa of how deftly he had solved the problem with Gloriana, and she felt a mild twinge of guilt. "Yes, well, my mother does not appreciate my acid tongue," she mumbled.

Leighton stopped in the shadow of a stately elm and turned to face her. He reached out his hands to take hers and held them lightly in his own. "Then she is surely missing out on some of the wittiest repartee to be had in all of London," he said. His words and his smile, soft and sincere, melted away her chill in the span of a heartbeat.

Melissa dropped her head, suddenly aware that they were alone in the darkness and his fingers were warm and alive. All her fine resolve dissolved into the night as he lifted her hands to his lips. He placed a kiss on each knuckle and then pulled her toward him.

A sliver of moonlight slid over his features, softly lighting his eyes and mouth, while the rest of him disappeared into the night. The trees rustled softly above her, and the distant sounds of gaiety drifted on the breeze, but Melissa was silent, as was Leighton.

The heat between them seemed to grow in the quiet until it surrounded them like an unseen smoke. For a long moment, they stood still in the shadows, as though daring a blaze to ignite; then, suddenly, Melissa saw an urgency in his features and he bent his head. She was prepared to burn in his arms, but he merely whispered into her ear.

"Marry me," he urged.

Melissa felt her heart lurch in surprise at the words. Although she had been expecting—even dreading—them for some time, she was still not prepared to hear them. Like a dose of reality intruding on an idyllic dream, they doused the fires that had kindled so quickly.

It took her a moment to recover herself. When she did, she responded lightly, playfully pulling her hands away. "And why should I?"

"Ah," said Leighton, leaning his head to one side and grinning. "Because I am far superior to Bainbridge."

"Ha! You are too full of yourself," Melissa said, turning away so that he would be unable to see her face. Too often he had seemed to read her easily, and she did not want to give anything away. Unsure herself of just how she felt, she did not want him watching her struggle to maintain an air of detachment while she sorted out her myriad responses to his proposal.

"All right," said Leighton, coming to stand behind her and enfolding her in his arms. "Then marry me because I am inferior to Bainbridge, and therefore pitiable."

Melissa smiled in spite of herself, but it was a sad smile. He was so glib and so charming that she could never really be sure of his sincerity. The question that lurked at the back of her mind whenever she was with him stepped forward, refusing to be ignored. Exactly how much of the viscount's behavior was studied charm, guaranteed to dazzle the most jaded miss, and how much was the real Leighton?

Melissa was grateful for the darkness that hid her confusion. "Why me?" she asked. Although her voice was still light, the question meant far more to her than she would have cared to admit, even to herself.

"Because you are beautiful and witty and wise," Leighton answered, his breath warm against her ear. His voice was soft and smooth and oh, so romantic, and his arms around her felt so strong and vital. Better to avoid his touch entirely, Melissa decided. Stepping out of his embrace, she turned to face him.

"And rich," she said, watching for his reaction.

"And rich," Leighton repeated, without a pause. "I assume you've heard about my father?" When Melissa nodded, he shrugged casually. "Let me assure you that not all the stories you've heard are true. Only some of them," he added dryly.

Leighton clasped his hands behind his back and took a step along the path, as though considering his words. "The earl has the same faults that we all do. It's just that in him they seem to have grown larger than life." He stopped walking and frowned down at the ground. "He mismanaged his inheritance, then gambled away the rest, but he is still my father, and he is still a man well worth knowing." Leighton glanced up at her quickly, and Melissa could see that he meant what he said.

"Despite his excesses, the earl has held on to a few things. And one of them is Greyhaven," Leighton said, looking off into the darkness with a faraway expression on his features. His face was serious and his cheeks were taut, yet his eyes, caught by the moonlight, were passionately alive.

"Greyhaven is my home. It's my heritage," Leighton said. He was silent for a moment; then he turned to look at her and she could see the fierce, possessive love he harbored for the place. "And I intend to keep it." He made the statement with a calm determination that left no doubt in Melissa's mind that he was equal to the task.

"So, you are right," he admitted with a quirky smile. "I must marry for money." He stepped closer, and she could see the fine print of one dimple as he grinned. "So, why not let it be you?"

Why not, indeed? Melissa thought to herself as she let her eyes range over him. Leighton was everything a marriage-minded miss could want. Her gaze took in his broad shoulders, trim waist and finely muscled legs, and she realized that from the top of his tousled golden hair to the tips of his perfectly polished boots, he was well made.

He was young, witty, handsome and titled—a future earl. What more could a girl desire? Melissa felt herself weakening. They were alone among the trees, drenched in moonlight. A dusky, woodsy scent was in the air, the gentle sway of the leaves the only sound, and Melissa could feel the attraction between them as if it were something real. How could she refuse?

Just as she asked herself that question, Leighton spoke, and his words broke the spell that had held her. "I think we deal well together, don't you?" he asked.

Deal well together.

The words hung in the air, and Melissa closed her eyes against the tears that threatened to well up behind her lids. So much for magic and romance! It would be a fitting end to all her childhood dreams if she married someone because they dealt well together.

Melissa struggled against burgeoning depression. After all, she had abandoned her dreams of love long ago. Love was a fantasy, confined to books; real people did not fall in love, and they certainly did not marry based on such delusions. And it was not as though she harbored any tender feelings for Leighton. On the contrary, the man seemed always to antagonize her.

As though growing impatient with her silence, the subject of her musings took matters into his own hands. "And then there is always this..." His voice seemed to deepen, and Melissa warily watched his features soften as he moved nearer. He cupped her chin with his hand, his thumb stroking her cheek, and the now-familiar heat rushed through her.

"There *is* something between us, Melly," Leighton said. "You can't deny it." He placed a kiss at the corner of her cheek, and another along her hairline. "Marry me," he whispered into her ear.

Melissa stood stock-still, unable to answer, as his tongue caressed each curve and crevice and his hand moved down to her waist. When he found her tender lobe, she gasped softly, and he asked again. "Marry me," he urged.

Then his lips trailed down her neck, sending hot tendrils of flame shooting throughout her body, until he reached the top of the sleeve of her gown. There he paused but a moment to slip the offending garment off her shoulder so that he could move his mouth to where it had rested. "Marry me," he whispered against her shoulder.

Melissa said nothing. She couldn't speak. She couldn't move. She felt limp from her struggle against the burning heat besieging her body, but at the same time more alive than she had ever been. When she said nothing, Leighton continued pressing kisses against her skin. From her shoulder he moved downward, along the curve of her breast, and Melissa thought she would surely scream at the slow, pure pleasure of it. She tried vainly to raise her hands against him, but they only slipped onto his firm shoulders as she leaned her head back, abandoning the struggle. "Marry me," he whispered again.

He slid a finger under the curve of her gown, and Melissa felt it slip from its place, baring her breasts, and still his mouth continued downward, making lazy circles across each breast and finally closing around a nipple. Melissa gasped as the feverish feelings overwhelmed her. Her hands tightened around his neck, her body aching to be closer to his. His name ran through her head over and over as her hand moved through his silken hair.

"Marry me," she heard him demand huskily, and she could stand it no more. Whatever she longed for, she knew that only Leighton could provide it. Whatever he desired, she desired, too, but, most of all, she wanted him and she wanted this wild inferno to continue.

"Yes," Melissa finally gasped.

And then it stopped. Leighton stopped, lifting his lips from her skin and slipping away from her. Her hand trembled in his hair and her brain whirled with confusion as her body tried to adjust to the shock of the loss. He raised his head slowly, and she could hear his shallow breathing. His eyes, heavy with heat, met her own.

"Couldn't you have held out just a little longer?" he asked, his lips curving gently. For a moment, Melissa could only stare at him in bewilderment, and then she laughed, releasing some of the tension that still enveloped them. Leighton chuckled, too, and Melissa dropped her head against his chest.

He was right, of course. They could not go on. As much as she wanted to continue, she knew with some semblance of sanity that they could not, and she was grateful for his decision.

When she rested her cheek against him, she felt the ties between them as firmly as if they were connected. She had agreed to marry him. Perhaps it was just as well. She had the feeling that their wedding had been ordained from the moment she had watched him approach her purposefully at Almack's, and that all her anger, confusion and worry had been for naught.

Melissa laughed again, this time at the warm feeling of pleasure that rose in her chest, overwhelming all her misgivings. It felt so right, deep down inside, that she simply enjoyed a moment of delight at the notion of marrying this man. She heard the hammering of his heart over their laughter, affirming her suspicion that he had found it just as difficult to call a halt to their heated embrace as she had.

The discovery made her smile to herself, yet something tugged at her happiness. She raised her head and leaned back to look at his face. She saw a beautiful visage, caressed by the moonlight. Eyelashes shadowed his eyes, but his mouth was curved at the corners, one dimple peeping out of its cheek as he looked down at her with warm affection.

Melissa felt a sharp stab of disappointment. She realized with sudden clarity that warm affection was not really what she wanted from this man. She had seen something else in his eyes, and now that she knew he was capable of so much more, how could she settle for less? With a piercing longing, Melissa wanted to see on Leighton's face the same passionate possessiveness that he felt for Greyhaven.

Chapter Seven

Melissa fidgeted where she stood and stared morosely at the copy of the *Times* that lay on her writing table. She was poised in her rooms, waiting patiently for her maid to adjust the pleats that ran down the back of her elegant white satin gown, but she couldn't stop staring at the newspaper. In it was the announcement of her engagement.

After she had accepted Leighton's proposal, he had met with Gloriana, the arrangements had been completed, and the banns had been posted in the following Monday's paper—today's paper. It had all happened so fast that Melissa's head was spinning. Had she done the right thing?

Gloriana was in transports, but Melissa was less than enthusiastic about her impending nuptials. Although she had consented to the marriage, she was still not sure she knew the real Leighton, the man underneath the gloss of charm, and the idea of risking the rest of her life on such an unknown quantity made her feel like the gambler with the most to lose in this game.

Melissa was so lost in her own worries that she nearly jumped at the sound of her mother's voice. "The white satin again," Gloriana said, her voice dripping disapproval at the sight of one of Melissa's favorite dresses. "It makes you look so pale. Oh, Melissa," Gloriana said with a sigh, "please wear a hat and not that strand of pearls through your hair. They are so plain-looking, people will think we aren't worthy of a title," she complained. "I have a white hat with purple plumes that would be perfect. You need some color."

"No, thank you, Mother," Melissa said evenly. As she watched Gloriana frown, Melissa thought that perhaps she had done the right thing in accepting the viscount's proposal. She could escape her stifling existence with her mother and embrace a new freedom in Leighton's household, where she could wear what she wanted, read what she wanted, say what she wanted and even prop her elbows on the dining table if she felt so inclined.

The very idea made her giddy, but then she began to worry anew. What if Leighton objected to such things? Well, she thought firmly, he would just have to get used to her, for she would have her way. What was the point of marrying if she couldn't get the independence she so desperately desired?

"I suppose it's your own choice if you refuse to look fashionable," Gloriana said with an air of dismissal. "Come along, then, let us not be late for the party. I'm sure your engagement will be the talk of the evening!"

That's just what I'm afraid of, Melissa thought as she followed her mother from the suite. Although used to the censure of the ton, Melissa found herself dreading tonight's gathering more than usual. Would they look even further down their noses at her now that she was promised to one of them?

Melissa entered the ballroom with trepidation, covering her fears with the appearance of cool composure, and, to her surprise, found that now that she was linked to Leighton her social standing had improved. She could see the change immediately, for those who had previously ignored her as though she were a stick of furniture now spoke to her with some semblance of pleasantness.

When the Granger sisters came up to congratulate her on her engagement, Melissa thought she might faint from shock. She smiled politely instead, noting cynically just how shallow these people were. Titles, lineage and connections were all that mattered.

And then he arrived. Melissa looked up to see him enter, noting idly how the dark brown of his jacket contrasted nicely with his blond hair. Viscount Sheffield was greeted with even more than the usual furor as people rushed forward to give him their congratulations. He handled the crush with aplomb, smiling and moving smoothly through the crowd toward her, his eyes looking past the others to send her a smoldering gaze that made her heart skip a beat.

He was at her side in but a few minutes, including her in all the salutations he received, his hand possessively on her back as the well-wishers came and went. When they were finally left alone for a moment, he leaned close. "How are you?" he whispered, and suddenly she felt shy and awkward. "You look beautiful," he added.

He meant it. Leighton thought she looked like a glorious sculpture, dressed as she was all in white, her enormous dark eyes and the light blush of her cheeks adding life to the work. Her satin gown was cut low, giving him such a delightful view of her smooth, full breasts that he ached to touch them. The pearls that wound through her hair were so simple, yet so sensual that he longed to bury his hands in her dark, glossy locks, freeing them from their beaded prison.

"You shouldn't wear such a revealing gown, my love. It makes me long to tear it from your body," he said softly, and saw her start at the words. Her eyes flew up to his, her face coloring brightly, and then she looked down at the floor. "I'd like to take down your hair, too, and run my hands through it. I want to see it fall loose," he added huskily.

She made a small choking sound, her head bent and her cheeks scarlet. She refused to look at him. Leighton chuckled and let his hand slip an inch or so down her back, then watched her wriggle away in response. "Leighton!" she said, turning to him, aghast, and he realized it was the first time he had heard his name on her lips. He liked it.

"Say it again," he said with a smile.

"What?" she asked angrily.

"My name. Say it again."

She snapped her fan. "Really, my lord, do you want everyone talking about us?" she asked.

"They already are," Leighton answered easily. "And you know you don't care a fig what they say." She smiled at that, her dark eyes revealing that she was not really too upset at his whispered words. "Come, since you won't let me tease you, I'll take you to meet some of my friends." He took her arm in his, satisfying himself with a brief caress of his hand against hers as he led her toward the refreshments, certain that he would find Charles somewhere in the vicinity of the food.

"For God's sake, let me compose myself," Melissa whispered.

Leighton laughed aloud. "You don't have to be composed in front of these fellows."

Apparently she did not agree, for when next he glanced over at her, the warmth had disappeared from her face, to be replaced by the cool facade she normally presented to the world. Perhaps when she met them she would unbend, he thought, for he found himself longing for his friends to see her as he did, beautifully vibrant and alive.

He saw Charles first, popping comfits into his mouth with one chubby hand while he held a plateful of the treats with the other. Robert stood by, looking elegant and occasionally quizzing the crowd. Leighton hailed them both, wishing suddenly that they would find Melissa as wonderful as he did.

His hopes were dashed the moment Charles opened his mouth.

"So this is the famous Lady Disdain," he said, and Leighton could have kicked him. Robert looked as though he might cheerfully smash his companion's face into his plate of sweetmeats.

Charles was oblivious to their glares, however, for his eyes remained on Leighton's bride-to-be. He thought she looked like an icicle, all white and cold, and he couldn't, for the life of him, imagine what Leighton saw in her. Nor could he understand how Leighton had managed to secure her hand—and in such a short time, too. Wasn't it only a few weeks ago that they had made the bet?

The bet. If truth be told, Charles was a bit out of sorts over the whole thing, for if Leighton had already won the lady's hand, perhaps he might win the wager, too. That idea made him most disgruntled, for he wanted to get the best of Leighton for once. He was brought out of his musings by a firm grip on his shoulder.

"Don't pay any attention to him," Robert said to Melissa.

"Ouch!" grunted Charles, trying to shrug off Leighton's hand.

"If I recall, they used to call him Cheltenham Charles at school," Robert said. "His penchant for drama, you know. In fact, I believe there was a little ditty they used to sing—"

"Robert!" Charles snapped. He scowled at his two friends while they laughed uproariously. "Well, I, for one, wish to congratulate you, Miss Hampton," he said, with as much dignity he could muster ignoring Robert and Leighton. She nodded in acknowledgment, a chill smile gracing her features.

"Shall I get you some comfits, Melissa?" Leighton asked, still chuckling at Charles.

"That would be nice," she said, nodding. She tried not to look at Charles, who was staring at her rudely. Instead, she let her eyes follow her husband-to-be as he walked away. He really did have such a nice pair of legs, so strong-looking....

"I must say I was surprised at the wedding date," Charles said, and Melissa was forced to glance at him. He was eyeing her rather warily now. "That you're to be married so soon, I mean."

"If you feel the engagement is too brief, you'll have to take it up with the viscount," Melissa said. "He set the date." She wished that Leighton would return and wondered, uncomfortably, if this fellow was going to continue asking such personal questions.

"Really, Charles," said Robert. "I hardly think it's any of your business."

Melissa concurred, but she said nothing. Far from appearing chagrined, Charles looked a little pleased, his face relaxing into a friendly smile. "Ah," he said, as if he hadn't even heard his friend. "Leighton must be held up at the refreshments. Would you care for one of mine?"

Melissa chose a comfit from the wide array on Charles's plate and looked around for Leighton, for she wished now that he had never left her side. Charles chuckled softly and shook his head, as if at his own foolishness. "I thought for a moment that he had swept you off your feet, and you wanted to be married immediately," he said.

"No," Melissa answered coolly. "I think he just wants to take care of his debts as soon as possible." To her amazement, relief flooded the man's features. He then broke into an enormous grin, and just as she took a bite of her sweetmeat, he slapped her on the back so heartily that she nearly choked on a piece of walnut.

"There you go! I knew you weren't one of those silly, romantic wenches," he said.

"Charles!" Robert groaned.

Melissa swallowed abruptly. Had she been given a compliment? No matter, she sent the man one of her chilliest looks anyway. Good God, if this was what it was like to be a favorite with the gentlemen, she would rather remain an outsider! And where was Leighton?

"I believe I see my mother," Melissa said. It was a lie. "You will excuse me, please, won't you gentlemen?"

"Certainly," Charles answered, beaming at her.

"Of course," Robert said, glaring at Charles as though her quick departure was his fault.

It was. Melissa couldn't wait to escape from her odd encounter with the man. Pretending to head toward her mother, she instead went looking for Leighton. How was she going to refuse to visit with his friends again? The tall fellow wasn't bad, but that Charles!

"I imagine that congratulations are in order."

Melissa turned to see Lord Richard Grimley looking down his long, aristocratic nose at her. His attitude toward her certainly hadn't improved. "Thank you, my lord," she said, hoping to make a quick escape from him, too, but Grimley was not finished yet. The man actually raised his quizzing glass and turned it upon her.

"One must congratulate Sheffield, too," he said. "One would assume that his financial situation will markedly improve."

"I'll convey your good wishes to him," Melissa answered tartly, and was pleased to note the grimace on Grimley's face. Dare he give her another lecture on proper respect for her betters? Not this time, for his ruminations were interrupted by another.

"Grimley, did I hear you congratulate me?" Leighton said, suddenly appearing at Melissa's side. "How kind of you, but I must forbid you to speak with my future bride," he added. "I'm insanely jealous, you know, and won't allow her to talk to any of her former suitors." One of Leighton's best smiles, both dimples showing, accompanied the words, making it difficult to tell whether he jested or spoke the truth—as unbelievable as that might seem.

Melissa, standing silently by the viscount, could see that Grimley was discomfited by Leighton's words, and she hid her amusement behind her usual cool facade. When Grimley looked her way, she smiled apologetically and shrugged her shoulders, as though to say that Leighton's behavior was beyond her control.

"I just wanted to warn you," Leighton said, leaning slightly toward Grimley as he spoke, "so you'll understand when she cuts you dead next time she sees you." With that parting shot, Leighton nodded, smiled, and, taking Melissa by the elbow, moved past an astounded Grimley, who was left standing alone, a throbbing muscle in his jaw the only testament to his outrage.

Leighton led her decorously out of the crowded room, but once they were in the hallway, he grabbed her arm and dragged a bemused Melissa toward a deserted area near the kitchens, pulled her into a pantry and shut the door. As soon as they heard the door close, they looked at each other and burst out laughing. Melissa raised both hands to her face as she eyed Leighton, who was nearly bent double, he was guffawing so hard.

"I can't believe it," Melissa choked between spasms of laughter. "I can't believe you did that—said that!" She laughed until she cried, and, through her tears, she saw more than a handsome man laughing along with her.

By God, she thought dizzily, he was surely her knight in shining armor, for hadn't he just slain the dragon for her? It was so foolish, so idiotic, to be touched by his simple act of giving Grimley a good set-down, but Melissa couldn't help it. She smiled tremulously, and then, without further ado, she threw her arms around him and kissed him.

It was meant to be nothing more than a fleeting touch of the lips, but Leighton had other ideas. Although he was still chuckling when she suddenly moved toward him, his amusement died when those soft lips found his own. They pressed against his briefly, but he would not let them go; he gently prodded her mouth open, seeking her tongue. Tasting her sweetness, he pulled her closer, reveling in her soft curves.

"Kiss me," he whispered against her mouth. "Kiss me like this." He probed her warmth with his tongue, inviting her to do the same, and rewarded her first tentative efforts by grasping her tighter. "Yes," he said. "God, Melly." And Melissa nearly swooned at the sound of his words, soft and husky, in her ear.

She wanted to hear more, and do more, and feel more, so she pressed herself against his lean muscles and tousled his hair with her fingers. It felt wonderful. She rained tiny kisses all over the fine lines of his face and his jawline until he whispered, "Melly... Mel," against her dark locks and took her mouth with his own.

His fingers were smooth against her skin as they trailed down her neck and slipped down beneath her gown to caress her breasts. His hands worked magic with her flesh, cupping and curving, the thumbs riding her nipples until she pulled at his shoulders, arching against him.

She was leaning back against a barrel, and she gasped when she felt his hand slip up underneath the fabric of her dress to slide along her leg. He smothered her cry with a kiss so searing that she could not protest when he cupped her derriere, nudging her closer to his own hardness. Instead, she squirmed and wiggled against him until she heard his voice, soft and raspy. "Mel, Mel. God, Mel, don't do that."

Leighton was certain she had no idea just how far she was taking things, so it was up to him to assume control of the situation. Unfortunately, he had no desire to do so. His desire was focused solely on the incredibly hot creature in his arms.

He realized that she probably had no notion of just how she was affecting him when she wriggled against him so provocatively or threw her dark mane back to expose her slim white throat or pulled at his shirt with those dainty fingers. She probably didn't realize that the sound of those breathless gasps made him want to bury himself in her here and now....

God, she made him burn like fire with her smooth skin, her silky, rich hair, her creamy breasts.... Leighton shook his head and tried to slow his rapid breathing. He had never before found himself in the unusual position of wanting a woman so desperately that he could barely think clearly.

The fact that the woman in question was soon to be his wife appeared to have no bearing on the matter. He wanted her now, so very much so that only the lurking suspicion that one shouldn't deflower one's bride on the floor of someone's pantry kept him from taking her silent urging to its natural conclusion.

"Mel, Mel, Mel," he whispered, shaking his head at the passion between them. "We're in the pantry, for God's sake." With incredible force of will, Leighton removed his hands from their cozy positions on his fiancée's pale flesh and stood up. He practically had to pry her hands loose from around his neck. That made him want to kiss her again, and he leaned down, caught in the spell, for one more taste.

"Ah, Mel," he said, tearing himself away at last. "You are so beautiful, so utterly fantastic, that it dazzles my mind," he said with a quirky grin.

Melissa, slower to recover from the heat of the moment, leaned against his arm and smiled back at him, wide-eyed, full of wonderment at the passion that had raged between them and at the things he could make her feel. She placed a hand on his chest and looked up at him. Leighton, Viscount Sheffield, her soon-to-be husband.

Melissa could feel his heart racing under her fingers, and she tried to straighten the line of his waistcoat, which was askew. She heard him chuckle and glanced up to see hazel eyes sparkling with humor and fire. Her eyes wandered with affection over the handsome lines of his face to his dusty blond hair, which was looking far too tousled at the moment to be fashionable. She raised a hand to run her fingers through the locks, but he caught her wrist and pressed a soft kiss to the inner pulse beat.

In that instant, all her misgivings were discarded, and Melissa decided that marriage to this man was a good idea. In fact, she realized, she was looking forward to the wedding. She rested her head against his chest and laughed softly. Oh, hell, why not admit it? She was looking forward to the wedding *night*.

* * *

Melissa actually became impatient. She longed for the ceremony to take place, if only so that the flurry of festivities would end. Each week brought an endless round of social functions, many in honor of the engagement, and Gloriana was pushing her to attend every one. As if that weren't bad enough, it seemed to Melissa that she never got a chance to be alone with her intended.

Now that Gloriana had snared her prize, she became a more vigilant chaperon, keeping track of both of them as if guarding against anything that would upset her plans. And in those instances when Gloriana was not lingering near, someone else was, for they were inundated with well-wishers.

Melissa, her eyes on her impending freedom, gritted her teeth during another interminable evening spent with Gloriana, who was throwing a dinner party to show off the viscount to a few close friends. She told herself that soon enough she would be able to refuse to go anywhere, and her mother, for better or worse, would be on her own.

As if divining her thoughts, Leighton reassured her. "Take heart, for once we are married they will lose interest in us," he whispered to her as they walked into the dining hall.

"Oh, do you think so?" Melissa asked, hardly daring to hope for a future without the constant chitchat and crushing crowds.

"Most definitely, my love," Leighton assured her, slipping a hand around to rest on her back. "I spend a lot of time at Greyhaven, and once we are married I would like to stay there even more often."

Melissa barely heard him as he described his home to her in glowing terms, for her mind was registering only the warmth of his fingers on her back. It seemed as though the man were always touching her, and Melissa, who could never stand to have anyone get too close, suddenly seemed to find this constant contact most agreeable.

As they took their seats, Melissa noted with annoyance that Gloriana had placed Leighton across from her, but she took the opportunity to let her gaze wander over him throughout the meal. She watched him charm the other guests with ease, and she realized it was hard not to like him.

She did like him already, Melissa admitted, even though he could be infuriating at times. It was hard not to fall for him, she thought, mentally rephrasing her words. The viscount was not only handsome, gracious and funny, but he was also always attentive and always…there. It seemed that no matter how many strangers surrounded her, he was always close by, caressing her with his eyes, cushioning her against the world. He seemed so at ease with himself and his surroundings that Melissa wondered if anything ever rattled the man.

She found out soon enough.

The third course had just been served, and Melissa picked at her plate, stifling a huge yawn with one hand. She glanced up to find her mother's quick look of rebuke from the head of the table and then saw Leighton's gentle grin and twinkling gaze across from her. She smiled at him. That was when she heard the commotion.

Melissa cocked her head to one side, wondering vaguely if she were dreaming, for in Gloriana's household there simply was no such thing as a commotion. No one would ever dare provoke a disturbance of any kind in any of Gloriana's residences. It was beyond consideration, yet the noise from the hallway was undeniable.

The voices were quite loud, and one of them, Melissa realized in amazement, was that of Gloriana's staid butler, Brown, who considered it a breach of etiquette to raise his voice above a whisper, as though he managed the house of an invalid.

"But, my lord, my lord… Yes, my lord please, my lord," Brown's voice was saying. Good heavens, he's actually whining, Melissa thought, eyeing the doors of the dining hall with interest. She did not have to wait long. A loud roar erupted outside the walls just before the doors were thrust open with a rattle and a bang.

"Where the hell is my son?" shouted the man who entered. He was a handsome, large middle-aged man, very well dressed in one of the finer cuts of coat, and he might have been distinguished looking if not for his red face and wild behavior. It was obvious, of course. The man was most definitely foxed.

Melissa had no idea how the fellow had managed to get past Gloriana's retinue of footmen, and Brown himself, but as she stared in astonishment, she could only think that this night would surely go down in history as the evening a drunken stranger barged into Gloriana's supper party.

Gloriana. Melissa quickly glanced toward her mother. The lady was white as a sheet, her mouth open slightly, as if she were in shock. While Melissa looked on, concerned, Gloriana sat still as a statue, her only movement the slight quivering of her lip in icy rage at the intrusion.

"Well, where is he?" the man shouted, swaying slightly on his feet.

Leighton stood up smoothly and slipped an arm out to steady the fellow. "Here I am, Father," he said. "How very disappointing that your trip was cut short."

Of course. Melissa saw the resemblance the moment the two men were together. The old gentleman, drunk to the gills, who had bullied his way past the servants, and who was surely the first person ever to shout in this household since the death of Gloriana's husband, was none other than the earl himself—living up to his reputation.

Melissa glanced at her mother; she was still pale and unmoving, and Melissa began to panic at the look on her face, for she realized with a sense of impending doom that this incident did not bode well for her wedding plans. She looked frantically at the other diners, then back at her mother, unsure of how to handle the situation.

The sound of Leighton's soft but firm voice was a balm. Leighton—dear, charming Leighton! He was infallible, and he would take care of it, Melissa thought, nearly sighing aloud with relief. "Father," the viscount began, in a soft but firm voice, "why don't you and I have a word in the study?" Then Leighton, who appeared as calm and collected as usual, gently took the earl's arm, but his grip was shaken off.

"Don't try to get rid of me, boy! What the hell's going on here?" the earl growled. "I come back to find that you've sold yourself to some tradesman's daughter!" The gasps at the table were audible, and Melissa watched in horror as her mother half rose from her seat.

"My lord," Gloriana said, in the iciest tones imaginable. "I'm sure that any social visit that you wish to make would be better conducted tomorrow, when you are in a more sober condition!" Her tone was the kind used to dress down the lowliest of servants, and Melissa's heart sank down to her shoes.

She shrank from the scene, already dreading the consequences, until she saw that Leighton's carefree demeanor was shaken for the first time since she had known him. When she thought of the anger and embarrassment he must be feeling as he tried to appear nonchalant, her heart left its repository to go out to him. She stood up.

"Sit down, Melissa," Gloriana snapped.

"How right you are, Mrs. Hampton. I'm sure that tomorrow will be more suitable for introductions," Leighton said, turning to Gloriana as he took a much firmer hold on the earl's arm. "If you would please excuse us." He bowed her way, then managed to drag his father from the room in a graceful and dignified manner.

No small feat, that, Melissa thought, but then Leighton could manage almost anything. Anything, she suspected, except his father. The thought actually brought a small smile to her lips, for it proved her handsome charmer was human, after all, and somehow that made her positively overflow with warm feelings for him.

"Sit down, Melissa," Gloriana repeated testily, and Melissa realized she was still standing by her chair.

"Excuse me, Mother, I was just going to get you some smelling salts. I know what a strain this unfortunate episode must be," she said. The lie flowed effortlessly from her tongue and succeeded in mollifying Gloriana a slight bit, for as Melissa left the room she could hear her mother bemoaning the bruising of her delicate womanhood by such atrocious behavior—and in her own dining hall.

But Melissa was only postponing the inevitable. She knew that the excuse had only granted her exit from the room and a brief respite. Later, when the other guests were gone, she would be treated to Gloriana's full temper, and she knew that, somehow, she was going to be blamed for this disaster. She shook off the foreboding that thought brought on and hurried into the hallway.

"Leighton?" she called softly. He had the earl nearly to the door, but he stopped, waiting for her to approach. "I'm sorry you have to leave." She turned to his father. "My lord, it is a pleasure to meet you."

"Humph," the man half grunted, half growled at her. His eyes were so red and swollen that Melissa wondered how on earth he could stand with so much liquor in him. She glanced over at Leighton to see him run a hand through his dusty locks and smile quirkily in apology.

"Father's obviously been celebrating ever since he heard the news," Leighton said dryly, and Melissa laughed softly.

"I'm sure everything will look better tomorrow," she said with more conviction than she felt. She did not know the earl, but she knew her mother, and she knew that everything just might be over and done with by tomorrow. She realized that this might very well be the last time she saw Leighton, and she tried valiantly to fend off the feeling of bleakness that threatened to overwhelm her at the thought. Melissa longed to throw herself into his arms, but his father was swaying, her mother was waiting, and the servants were watching.

"Goodbye," she whispered softly. Only years of schooling her emotions enabled her to keep her features under control. Leighton eyed her questioningly, but when she smiled tightly he turned his attention back to his parent.

Only when the door closed behind them did Melissa realize she was wringing her hands in worry. With a sharp gasp of irritation, she pulled her hands apart and pressed the palms against her gown before heading back toward the dining hall. Then she turned around with a groan. She had nearly forgotten the smelling salts.

Leighton leaned over, pulled off his father's left boot with a yank and tossed it aside. Although he had managed to get the earl home and into the sitting room adjoining his bedroom suite, the elder Somerset was obviously not going to bed without a fight. He had dismissed his manservant with a few choice expletives, leaving Leighton the duty of getting his boots off.

"What the hell are you doing?" the earl asked.

"I'm trying to get you to bed," Leighton said, without bothering to glance up at his father.

"Listen to me," the earl ordered with such intensity that Leighton stopped grappling with the other boot and looked up. His father was slouched in his chair, his jacket off, his neckcloth askew and his waistcoat open, glaring at his son. "What the hell are you doing?" he asked again.

"I'm getting married," Leighton answered smoothly, even though his grip on his own temper was slipping. "If you would stay sober long enough to take a look, you would discover that the lady I'm going to wed is a beautiful, clever, caring young woman," Leighton added before turning his attention back to the boot. "I have no idea why you are getting so worked up," he said, pulling off the boot with a grunt and getting to his feet, "but we can discuss it tomorrow, when we both have clearer heads."

"Do you think I don't know what you're doing?"

"Apparently not," Leighton answered, "since you've asked me repeatedly about it." He had already turned toward the door, but stopped to toss a question over his shoulder. "Are you going to sleep in that chair, or do you want me to help you to bed?"

"I can't let you do it." The earl's words were muffled and sounded so strained that Leighton turned around again, a question on his lips, but his own words died in his throat when he saw his father. The earl was bent over, his face buried in his hands as if he were choking back a sob. "I know it's my fault," he whispered. "I know you've had to sell everything—the land, the horses, the paintings you loved—but I never thought you'd have to sell yourself."

Leighton felt as if he had just received a hard blow to the chest, and it threatened to undo him in a way that no boxing bout ever had. Tonight marked the first time in his memory that his father had admitted to his failings, and in truth, it was worse to watch the man suffering his guilt than to see him carelessly perpetrating the deeds.

Leighton took a deep breath to steady himself, and leaned over, sliding his arm around his father's shoulders. "Father, people marry for convenience every day," he said softly. "Estates merge, titles are bestowed, lands are saved. You know as well as I how commonplace it is." Leighton shrugged. "What's the difference if the money is won at cards or at the altar?"

The earl slowly took his hands from his face and looked up at his son. "You really don't understand, do you?"

Something in the words pricked Leighton like the fine point of a blade, and for the first time in years he felt like the child instead of the father.

He couldn't remember just when their positions had reversed; it was something that had developed gradually. Instead of Leighton playing the young rakehell, the earl had taken on that mantle, and since one of them had had to keep a roof over their heads, that task had fallen to the younger Somerset. Leighton had become so used to the reversal of their roles that he didn't resent his position anymore, although there had been a time, when he was younger... He met his father's eyes, and Leighton saw the sadness there, underneath the surface, that he so often did; this time, however, he had the feeling the sadness was for him.

"No, Father, I don't. I don't understand," Leighton said.

"I'm talking about love, boy, love."

Leighton snorted and straightened up. "For God's sake, Father, is that what all this is about?" He nearly laughed aloud at the absurdity of his father's words. "You're a fine one to talk about love! My God, it's harder to keep track of your paramours than your gambling losses," Leighton scoffed, running a hand through his hair.

"But I married for love," the earl said quietly.

Leighton looked at his father's earnest face and sighed. "What a time for you to wax romantic." He paused, considering his words tactfully before glancing over at the earl again.

"Look, Father, maybe I'm just not the type, but this love business has never really worked for me," Leighton said. He shrugged again. "I'm sorry to disappoint you, but I've just never fallen head over heels for someone." He stopped and gazed at his father, who was now regaining his composure, and smiled crookedly. "What you and Mother had was something very special, but I just haven't found it."

"Yet," his father put in.

Leighton ignored the comment. "I appreciate your concern," he said with a smile, "but this marriage really is the best thing for all of us, and I just hope to God you didn't put the screws to it with your little performance tonight."

Leighton raised a finger and rubbed his chin thoughtfully. "I'll have to spend all day tomorrow repairing the damage, and poor Mel! That ogress will probably eat her for breakfast, thanks to you."

"Ogress?"

"Mel's mother," Leighton said.

"Mel? Who's Mel?"

"My wife," Leighton said impatiently.

"You're already married?" the earl asked sharply.

"No, no," Leighton said. "But I'm moving up the date, by God, before you can cause any more trouble. I want Mel away from there as soon as possible. I want her with me."

"Mel? Who the hell is this Mel?" the earl asked irritably. "I thought you were marrying that Hampton chit, the Lady Disdain."

Leighton dropped his hand from his chin and looked at his father, his features suddenly serious. "Don't you ever call her that or mention it to her, even in jest," he warned.

The earl raised his eyebrows and sat back in his chair, a look of wonder on his face.

"Now what?" Leighton asked with a frown.

"Nothing, lad," the earl answered with a smile.

"I mean it, Father. I want your promise right now that you will not mention it to her. She practically winces when she hears it, and I don't want you insulting her, or even teasing her about it."

"I promise," the earl said solemnly.

"It's an idiotic appellation," Leighton added.

"I understand, boy, I understand," the earl said, chuckling softly. "Perhaps a little more than you do yourself." With that cryptic remark, he leaned back in his chair, a big smile on his face, and closed his eyes, signaling an end to the conversation.

Chapter Eight

"**Y**ou simply will have to cry off," Gloriana announced as she paced across the floor of the green drawing room. "I cannot allow this marriage to take place."

Although Melissa had expected such a pronouncement, she felt her heart lurch in her chest at the words. She struggled not to let it show. Seated on the edge of one of the divans, her hands clasped in her lap, she stared steadfastly at the floor, unwilling to look up at her mother for fear that Gloriana might see something in her face. Whatever her feelings were about the marriage, it was best not to reveal them to her mother.

Melissa had been awake half the night planning her strategy, for she knew full well that arguing with her mother would get her nowhere. She would have to be subtle in her attempts to turn her mother's temper. If she failed, she would not be able to marry Leighton, and marrying Leighton had become very important to her, although she didn't care to delve too deeply into the reasons why.

"I refuse to be connected in any way with That Man," Gloriana declared.

"You mean the earl?" Melissa asked mildly.

"Don't mention his name in my presence!" Gloriana gasped, holding a handkerchief to her head. "I have never in my life been subjected to such outrage—and in my own dining hall! I'm sure that Mrs. Marchant has regaled her friends with That Man's very words, and the story of his disgraceful behavior will be all over the city by this afternoon." Gloriana choked out the words, then turned and walked back across the room, her handkerchief fluttering about her like a large moth.

Melissa waited silently for her mother to continue, but when Gloriana said nothing, Melissa decided to play her first card. *Slowly now,* she told herself, hardly daring to breathe. "But, Mother, you were aware of the earl's reputation," she said.

"I knew he was not quite the thing—a gambler, of course—but I had no idea," Gloriana said. "I had no idea that anyone could behave as dreadfully as That Man. We will be the laughingstock of the entire city."

"I don't think so, Mother," Melissa said, her voice smooth and reasonable. "After all, That Man, as you call him, has such a reputation already that the ton is inured to his outrageous exploits. The stories about him are so plentiful that one more will make little difference."

Gloriana paused, as if considering the argument's merits, then sighed as she rejected them. "I just can't countenance it, Melissa," she said. "I had hoped for a position of dignity and respect for you, but now I am not sure the viscount can provide it."

She turned, her handkerchief at her throat. "I will be frank with you. My mother had hopes for my marriage, too, but your father had other plans, dragging his name through the mud with that filthy trade. It debased him," she said coldly. "I will not have that for you."

Outrage for her father and a glimmer of sympathy for her mother warred in Melissa's breast. Poor Gloriana, wanting nothing more than position, had had the ill luck to marry Harlan, who cared nothing for such nonsense. After her husband's death, Gloriana, without his steadying influence, had become obsessed with her hopes of power and privilege, making her daughter's life—and, Melissa suspected, her own—miserable in the process.

Melissa finally looked up at her mother, who had stopped her pacing to stare out the window. "Through all I have maintained my dignity," Gloriana said softly. "Dignity, Melissa. That Man is undignified. He makes sport with his name. I simply cannot approve."

Melissa's heart sank, but she could not give up. She tried not to think of the last time she had done this, that other time, long ago, when she had begged for a man's hand in marriage—and lost. But this time was different, she told herself firmly. The man was different. Leighton was worth fighting for and worth winning, and win she would. Older and wiser, Melissa would not make the mistake of letting her mother know just how much it meant to her. *Don't let emotion cloud the issue. Stay logical,* she told herself.

"This is your chance, Mother," Melissa said calmly. "I can't believe that you would throw it away simply because one of the man's relatives is an embarrassment. Good heavens, if you rejected suitors on those grounds, you would lose half of England."

Gloriana turned and frowned at the jest.

"Mother," Melissa said. "As you said yourself, this is my second season. You're not going to get a better offer." She paused before throwing down the gauntlet. "And consider this. I won't marry Bainbridge," she added, and despite her nervousness, her voice was firm.

"You'll do as I tell you," Gloriana snapped, pursing her lips at her daughter's insolence.

"Perhaps," Melissa said, with just enough mystery to make her mother glance at her sharply.

Gloriana frowned; then she strode across the room again, as though considering Melissa's ultimatum, along with the morning's arguments. Melissa remained seated on the edge of the divan, her back straight, feeling like a barrister fighting for a reprieve from the gallows.

"Very well," Gloriana said suddenly. "I will reconsider my decision. We will see what the viscount has to say today, but I refuse to have anything to do with That Man.

Now, if you will excuse me, I have some correspondence to attend to," she said in cool dismissal.

Melissa rose and walked calmly across the room. She didn't realize until she reached the door that her hands, grasping each other in a death grip, might have given her away. She unclenched them slowly and left, closing the door behind her quietly.

When she stepped into the hallway, Melissa felt as if an enormous weight had lifted from her shoulders, making her light as a feather. She nearly kicked up her heels right there in the hallway at her small victory. Then she looked up and saw that Brown was admitting Leighton.

Her heart soared so at the sight of him that she longed to race across the entrance and fling herself into his arms, servants be damned. He carried a huge bouquet in his arms, and when he turned and grinned at her, Melissa couldn't help quickening her steps. Then she found herself running, and with a sense of wild abandon she threw herself into the viscount's embrace in front of Brown and heaven knew who else. The episode would surely be recounted immediately to her mother, but Melissa didn't care.

Leighton nearly dropped the flowers, but managed to wrap his arms around her, lifting her off the floor so that her toes dangled momentarily in the air as he whispered in her ear. "Has your mother been vile this morning?" he asked. Melissa nodded as he let her slip to the floor again.

He chucked her under the chin. "You really shouldn't have faced her alone, you know," he said softly. "Let me handle it, love. Have you no faith in me?" he chided. Melissa smiled at his conceit, and he feigned affront. "I'll have the whole thing taken care of in but a few minutes. Surely you've realized by now that charm is my stock-in-trade," he said with a quirky grin.

Melissa laughed softly as she took his arm, but she knew he was right. All her fears had been for naught, for she was suddenly certain that Leighton was utterly capable of handling Gloriana. In fact, she was sure that Leighton could handle anything—with the possible exception of his own father.

The earl arrived shortly before tea.

Melissa, who had been reading a book, walked out of the main drawing room just as he was being ushered into the hallway. She had wandered out to see who was arriving and nearly dropped her volume on the floor when she recognized Leighton's father, looking fashionably dressed and sober and cradling an armful of long-stemmed roses.

"What are you doing here?" Melissa squeaked. "My lord," she added as an afterthought.

"Shall I announce you, my lord?" Brown asked in pained accents that suggested he would rather wring the earl's neck—or his own—than tell Gloriana who was here. Melissa couldn't blame him.

She dismissed the butler with a rather panicked wave of her hand, and, only too happy to oblige, he disappeared down the hallway, presumably seeking a task that would place him as far from the earl—and Gloriana—as possible.

"My lord," Melissa said, recovering some of her composure. "It is a pleasure to see you again. What can I do for you today?"

"It's lovely to see you again, too, sweetie," he said, eyeing her from top to toe in a way that was not quite fatherly. "I must admit you are a beauty, just as Leighton said." He winked at her broadly. "I'm afraid I didn't get a good look at you last night."

Melissa smiled at the compliment, and at the dimples, so like his son's, that appeared on the earl's handsome face when he grinned back at her. "You are too kind," she said. "Would you like to join me in the study? We shall have tea soon," she added, looking over her shoulder to make sure the doors to the green drawing room were still closed. "I'm sure we could have a nice visit if you wish."

"No," the earl said, shaking his head. "I'd love to, sweetie, but it's your mother I've come to see. I really must apologize."

Melissa did drop her book then, and the sound of it hitting the floor rattled her already shaky demeanor. "No, my lord, really, you don't have to," she protested as she bent down to retrieve the volume. "Leighton was already here. He's fixed everything."

"I make my own apologies, young lady, although I really can't remember the last time I tendered one," he said with a sly smile. "I'll tell you right now that I'm not going to make a practice of this—it could become quite tedious. Apologies and money," he said, chuckling. "I imagine I owe a bit of both to just about everyone. Now, these flowers are starting to prick me, my girl, so let's get on with it. Where's your mother?"

"My lord, please," Melissa said, reaching out a hand to pull at the sleeve of his coat. "I really think it best if we didn't bother her today. She is...not well. She's taken to her bed."

The earl studied her for a moment, then raised his bushy eyebrows and chuckled. "Don't ever try to make a living at cards, my girl," he advised. "You couldn't bluff your way out of a closet. Now don't fret. I can be just as charming as my son when I put my mind to it," he said.

"Lead me to her," he directed with a grin, and Melissa could only do his bidding, taking him with leaden feet to the doors of Gloriana's sanctum. There she stood for a moment, unable to knock, before she turned and sent the earl a pleading look. He only chuckled and nudged her into action.

With a sense of doom, Melissa knocked, hoping against hope that her mother had suddenly gone deaf or disappeared out the window. No reprieve was granted her, however, for she soon heard her mother saying, "Yes. You may enter."

Melissa opened the doors and stepped over the threshold to see Gloriana seated at her desk. She did not even bother to glance up from her correspondence. Melissa had to swallow hard before she could speak. "Mother," she said, her voice squeaking again. "You'll never guess who's here."

Gloriana looked up, saw her surprise guest, and appeared for all the world as if she had just swallowed a burr. There was an awkward pause while she obviously tried to gain control of herself and Melissa tried to fade into the green silk papering the walls.

The earl stepped in. "My dear Mrs. Hampton, I've come to apologize for my frightful behavior last night," he said with a handsome smile. "I was unaware of my son's plans and returned from abroad to hear the news from a stranger. I'm afraid a little too much imbibing left me imagining all sorts of queer things, when actually I couldn't be more pleased with the news—and with my son's choice," he said smoothly, turning and winking at Melissa.

Melissa couldn't help smiling back at him. His grin, so like Leighton's, was contagious, and his blue eyes twinkled warmly. He was a handsome devil, and obviously had a measure of his son's charm. He moved forward and held out the sumptuous array of roses to Gloriana. "For you, my lovely lady," he said smoothly.

Who could resist such a man? Melissa thought to herself. The answer, unfortunately, was quick in coming.

"Take your flowers and kindly leave my home at once, my lord," Gloriana said, drawing herself up to her full height. She positively sniffed, sticking her nose in the air as though she were the noble and the earl a grubby street urchin trying to pick her pocket.

"At your son's request, I have decided to allow the wedding plans to continue. He has promised me that you will be no further trouble to me, a promise that I obviously cannot rely upon, for you are here being troublesome right now," Gloriana said coldly.

Melissa peeked under her eyelashes at the earl, who was turning as red as a beet. She tried not to wring her hands.

"Although our children may be married, I refuse to be connected in any way to you, my lord. I find your behavior atrocious, your language foul, and your presence undesirable."

Melissa thought surely the man would burst at any moment. She wouldn't blame him if he strangled Gloriana right there at her own desk. She realized she was clenching her hands and shrinking toward the wall when she should be intervening, but it was like watching a cat snarling at a dog. Who wanted to step in? She could only watch helplessly for the bloody conclusion.

As it happened, the earl didn't kill her. He didn't even strike her. He only laughed, and that, of course, was the one response guaranteed to make Gloriana even angrier. Melissa knew that her mother, to whom dignity was everything, couldn't stand the thought of someone laughing at her—and what a belly laugh it was, too. When he had finished, he dropped the roses in a heap on Gloriana's spotless, expensive carpet and turned on his heel before she could speak again.

He stopped before Melissa, leaned over and took her hand, brushing his lips against the skin in an elaborate and formal goodbye. "Farewell for now, sweetie," he said, with a grin that told her he didn't hold her responsible for the debacle. Then he jerked his head toward Gloriana. "Your mother's a fine-looking woman," he said admiringly. "Too bad she's such an ogress."

"It's like oil and vinegar," Leighton told Robert as they watched the earl give Melissa's mother a wide berth. "The two just don't mix."

Privately he dubbed the farce "The Earl and the Ogress," but he kept that title to himself, knowing full well that if his pet name for Mrs. Hampton ever got out, there would be hell to pay.

"I've never seen him so put out," Robert said in an amused tone. And Leighton had to agree as he watched the earl cross in front of them and flop down into a chair nearby, glaring at the furniture as though merely being in the same house with Mrs. Hampton set his teeth on edge.

"Why am I here?" the earl moaned. "I can't gamble, I can't drink, and I have to be in the same building with that witch."

"You're here because you want to show loving support for your son and his future bride," Leighton said smoothly.

"Humph!" grunted the earl. "Thank God she's not her mother's daughter."

"She does appear to be cut from a different cloth," Robert acknowledged. "And she seems quite taken with you, Sheffield. I have a feeling Charles is going to lose his bet."

"Bet? What bet?" the earl asked. He straightened up in his chair, perking up visibly.

"Nothing, Father," Leighton said.

"Well, I'm not convinced that I've lost as yet," Charles said. "And I'd like to know just how you propose to prove that you have won."

"That was never specified in the wager," Robert said.

"Wager? What wager? Waverly, I order you to tell me this instant what you're babbling about," the earl demanded.

"It's Leighton," Charles answered, smiling slyly. "He wagered that he could win the Lady Disdain—not just her hand, but her heart, as well. So far he has the hand, but as to the other, I'm still taking odds," he said hopefully.

But for once the earl did not leap at the chance to take a chance. He frowned at his son instead. "What's this, Leighton?" he asked.

"Just a foolish prank, Father, nothing more," Leighton said, looking a little less self-assured than he usually did. In truth, he was sorry to be reminded of the wager he had made so carelessly weeks ago, for now that he knew Melissa so well, he regretted his cavalier gesture.

She hated the title of Lady Disdain, and he was certain that a bet on her affections would not sit well with her. He could picture the look of betrayal in her eyes, and he did not want to see it. Ever.

Leighton liked things just the way they were. He liked the way she looked at him, with tenderness and admiration in those huge dark eyes, and he liked her tentative displays of affection, such as when she had raced into his arms in her mother's hallway, and he liked the way she responded to his touch, all fire and no ice. As far as Leighton was concerned, the bet was won, so he no longer had any interest in it. "Perhaps we should call it off," he suggested, turning to Charles.

"Oh, so you are not doing as well as it would seem?" Charles asked. He laughed wickedly. "I knew it! Even the great Leighton cannot thaw out this lady. You see, Robert, you should have placed a sum on this. It's still not too late," he urged before turning to Leighton again. "No backing out now, Leighton. I'll have your money on your wedding day," he said, gloating gleefully.

"And just what happens if it's the other way around?" the earl asked.

"What do you mean, my lord?" Charles asked.

"Just who wins if it's Leighton who loses his heart to the lady?"

Charles's peal of laughter made the other guests nearby turn and smile. Leighton, too, laughed softly, but Robert eyed the earl quizzically. "Why, I imagine the lady would win," he said.

"Wrong," said the earl, looking intently at his son. "Leighton would be the winner, if he played his cards right. But one bad hand, my boy," he warned, "and you could lose everything."

"You'll pardon me, my lord, if I view with skepticism any advice that you might dispense on the subject of gambling," Robert said in that dry way of his, and everyone chuckled.

Although Leighton joined in, he couldn't help glancing around the enormous reception room for his bride-to-be. She was standing with some dreadful dull friend of her mother's, the remote look on her pale features only emphasizing her beauty. Her icy green gown was cut low enough to show the swelling curve of her breasts, and Leighton admired the soft curves visible under the smooth silk. Her thick, glossy tresses were drawn up and set with combs studded with sparkling sapphires that matched those set in the heavy necklace she wore.

As Leighton watched her, he longed to reach out and caress her delicate throat and creamy shoulders with a fierceness that made it difficult to listen casually to Charles's blow-by-blow account of the latest boxing match, but listen he did, and not a whit of what he was feeling showed on his relaxed features. He had practiced that art until it was second nature to him.

She looked up, the liquid eyes catching his own across the room, and she smiled. With an almost imperceptible nod, Leighton motioned to her and watched her make her excuses to her neighbors. He returned his attention to Charles until she was nearly at his elbow, then turned to greet her. She had that look of cool composure that made her beauty appear unapproachable—as though she were a work of art come to life—and Leighton could see how that look set her apart.

Among his friends she relaxed a little, but still she had that air about her that warned others not to get too close. Leighton reached down spontaneously and took her hand, pressing a kiss to her fingers, and was warmed by the surprise in the dark eyes. The smile she gave him was his alone, a bestowal that was not granted to anyone else, and Leighton suddenly felt jealous and protective of this unique rapport he had with her. Melissa was his, by God, and soon she would be in name, too, he thought. To hell with his stupid bet—and his father's vague warnings.

* * *

Melissa looked into the mirror and pinched herself to make sure she was awake. The face in the glass looked back at her with big brown eyes wide with wonder at the gauze veil in her hair and the white satin gown that fell gracefully from a high waist cinched in silver.

"Melissa Hampton, you are marrying the handsomest, warmest, brightest, gentlest...funniest man in all of England," she said aloud, and hugged herself with happiness, so glad that the day had finally arrived. It would be a long one, too, for the morning ceremony would be followed by a wedding breakfast at noon that would undoubtedly continue into the evening.

Melissa shook her head as she remembered the thorny negotiations that had been conducted to decide just where everything would be held. Leighton had longed for a wedding at Greyhaven, but the earl had claimed he wouldn't let Gloriana in the house, and Gloriana wanted the celebration in London so that as many notables as possible would attend. In the end, Leighton's town house had been agreed upon, rather reluctantly, by all parties, Melissa being the only one who didn't care a fig for the location of anything.

All Melissa cared about was that, when it was all over, she would go home with the viscount. She would have her freedom—and something more. She would have him. She realized that she was so much happier when she was with Leighton, it was almost like being in love, if she believed in such nonsense, which she didn't. She just had grown to like him a lot, that was all, Melissa told herself. And tonight she would show him just how much, she thought wickedly, blushing and sighing.

Melissa knew what went on in the marriage bed, though certainly not from her mother, who wouldn't even acknowledge the subject. Again, Melissa owed her education to her school friend Betsy Belmont, who had spoken, she suspected, from personal experience. Only now could Melissa share enthusiasm for the act the older girl had described so luridly.

Melissa realized that she really ought to be ashamed of such desires, but she couldn't help it. Every time she looked at Leighton, she saw what a well-made man he was. She remembered every moment spent in his arms and longed to spend a lot more time there.

Tonight, she promised herself as she stood up and whirled around the room in delightful abandon. And today, she decided, she wasn't going to let anything or anyone ruin her lovely mood—not Gloriana, not Gloriana's snippy friends, and certainly not any of the ton snobs. She would give up being the Lady Disdain for a day and revel in her own happiness, just as Leighton seemed to be doing.

She did. Throughout the lengthy ceremony and the enormous wedding breakfast, Melissa smiled. She smiled at her mother's frowns, she smiled at the sometimes haughty faces that eyed her, and she smiled at her husband, who smiled back charmingly, with dimples.

By the time they were standing by the bride's cake, Melissa felt as though she ought to pinch herself again, for she really shouldn't be having such a delightful time.

"You are radiant today," Leighton said, leaning toward her protectively. "And exquisitely beautiful."

"If you keep telling me that often enough, I might start to believe it," Melissa answered smartly. Leighton laughed before looking up to acknowledge some of the guests, who were pressing forward with congratulations. Melissa nodded her greetings to an elderly couple who were taking their leave, but her thoughts were on her husband's voice as he spoke.

"Ah, Duncan," Leighton said, welcoming a ganglylooking fellow with an unruly shock of dark black hair that dropped down into his eyes. "Melissa, this is my cousin, Duncan Rhodes."

"Congratulations, my lady," the man said with a crooked grin as he bowed over her hand. When he straightened, he turned his attention to Leighton, as most did. "Sorry I let the earl slip through my fingers ahead of time, dear boy," Duncan said, "but I see that he hasn't caused any trouble."

"No, not at all," said Leighton wryly. "We're all just one big, happy family, aren't we, dear?" he asked Melissa, putting his hand to the small of her back to draw her into the conversation. Melissa, who had not been paying strict attention, smiled politely as Duncan laughed. It was a dry, coughlike sound.

"Well, he couldn't have interfered with your plans too much, because here you are married, just as you planned," Duncan said as he pulled out an elaborate snuff box, opened it and carefully removed a pinch. "You really should get down on your knees and beg this lovely child for mercy," he chided, pointing his box at Melissa, "knowing that you married her only to support your true mistress."

Melissa was in too good a mood to let his words alarm her, and she had too much practice in appearing aloof to let him see her surprise. He paused dramatically to take his snuff, but when Melissa gave him no reaction, he smiled thinly and snapped closed the lid on his expensive trinket. "I'm referring to Greyhaven, of course. The man's in love with a building, for God's sake," he said derisively, rolling his eyes Melissa's way.

"Despite his often caustic tongue, Duncan is a decent fellow," Leighton said, leaning his head toward his wife.

"Ask him, my lady," Duncan urged, ignoring the gibe. "Is not that mass of stone and mortar, saved in the nick of time by your wife's money, uppermost in your mind today?"

Leighton laughed; it was a carefree, delightful sound that made Melissa smile in spite of the subject matter. "No, it is not," he answered.

"Liar," Duncan said, but Leighton only grinned at him.

"Why don't you make yourself useful and go check on the earl?" Leighton asked.

"Because, contrary to your continuing belief, I am not the man's nursemaid," Duncan said, sniffing. He turned to Melissa. "Good day, my lady," he said, before moving off among the other guests.

"What an odd fellow," Melissa said softly, refusing to let the man's insinuations dampen her spirits. Leighton burst out laughing again. "What is so funny?" she asked.

"How Duncan could be so very wrong," Leighton said.

"Well, then, what are you thinking about?" Melissa asked.

Leighton showed both his dimples, then leaned so close that his breath touched her cheek as he spoke in her ear. "My dear wife, on this my wedding day, the thought uppermost in my mind," he whispered, resting his hand intimately on her lower back, "is getting you into my bed."

Melissa choked back a laugh and leaned away from him to glance at his handsome grin. The look in his hazel eyes made her feel hot all over. "In fact, I think I'll have *you* begging for mercy later tonight," he promised.

This time she couldn't help giggling wickedly, and Leighton chuckled along with her. "I'm afraid I have no experience in these matters, my lord," she whispered back. "How do you know you'll enjoy yourself?"

"Do I look worried?" Leighton countered. His hand slid down to casually take in the curve of her hip. "I'll teach you everything you need to know, and if I've forgotten anything we'll make it up," he said.

Melissa laughed delightedly. "Stop it. You're making me giggle like an idiot. People will talk."

Leighton hooted. "If I cared a whit about what people said about me or my family, I would have wasted away long ago."

"Well, that obviously has not occurred, for you look quite robust to me," she said, smiling even as she began to blush furiously.

He leaned close again. "Oh, I am, dear wife, and I am aching to prove it to you."

"Now stop," Melissa ordered, her face beet red.

"Oh, but I love to tease you," Leighton drawled, his hazel eyes sparkling as he looked down at her.

Across the room, Cecile watched Leighton pay court to his wife, and she found it disgusting. No, it was beyond that. It was revolting. It was... painful.

Cecile swallowed the champagne in her glass quickly. It tasted sour. "See if you can get me something real to drink," she said to her companion, Lord Baltimore. He chuckled at her request and rose to do her bidding. *And get it fast, you idiot,* she thought, smiling archly at him. She scanned the room quickly under lowered lids as she ostensibly watched him depart.

Then her gaze returned, as if pulled by some hideous unseen force, to the newlyweds. She felt a burning in her throat and brought up her glass to drink. Empty. She had forgotten. Bad slip, that.

Usually Cecile was a consummate actress, and no one could see through her. She glanced about again to be sure none of the fools present seemed to be watching her. Presumably nobody remembered her long-ago love affair with the groom; more likely nobody cared.

And she had hidden her feelings well over the years. Who would have thought Leighton was any different from the many who came after? Indeed, who would have guessed that he was the only one she had ever loved?

So engrossed was she in her thoughts of Leighton that she was caught unawares by, of all people, the earl.

"Cecile, my love!" he bellowed, filling the seat next to her and stretching out his arms for an embrace. Cecile put her slim hands on those bulky arms and, holding him at arm's length, presented her cheek.

"Is that the best you can do?" he growled, and kissed her soundly on the lips. He had been drinking, of course, and far more than she had. Idly she wondered why. Perhaps she was not the only one unhappy with this wedding, but why would the earl disapprove? God knows, he could make good use of the girl's money, as would Leighton. Cecile admitted that she always knew he would have to marry money. Was it so hard for her to finally see it happen?

No, Cecile decided, it was not the wedding itself that bothered her; it was the way Leighton was enjoying himself. Let him marry if he must, but he didn't need to look so happy about it! With sudden insight, Cecile realized that because she had always known Leighton would marry for convenience, she had always assumed his marriage would be as miserable and meaningless as her own.

In that split second, Cecile saw far more of herself than she wished to face, and she understood just how different the courses were that they had chosen. She felt a surge of black unhappiness such as she had not known since girlhood, and then, struggling to shake it off, she turned to the only way she knew to lessen the blow—revenge.

Of course, the idea that formed was not a new one. It had been lingering in the back of her mind ever since she had learned of Leighton's little wager. Cecile had stored the information as she did all such tidbits, like a tiny golden nugget for later use. And now... the time had come.

She would shake the happy couple like dice and see how they landed, Cecile decided, and for the first time this day her lips moved slowly into a genuine smile.

Chapter Nine

Cecile raised her eyes, warm with the thrill of the game, to the earl, who was staring bleakly into the crowd. "Do I sense that all is not well with you, Cubby, my love?" she purred.

"Pah! I can't stand the bony witch," he said, pulling a flask from his coat pocket. "This champagne tastes awful," he added, taking her glass and filling it from his vial.

Cecile laughed wickedly as the aroma of brandy wafted to her. "Thank you, Cubby, that is quite enough." She was pleased to be joined in her disapproval of the bride, but bony? Even Cecile could not describe Leighton's little Nobody that way. "I'm afraid I don't see her as bony," she said, eyeing the earl over the rim of her glass.

"Not the girl. The mother," he explained before taking a great swallow from the bottle.

"Oh?" Cecile asked, her brow rising in interest.

"Gloriana Hampton. Pah!" he said again, as though spitting away the foul taste of the name. "I'll not have the woman in my house, Cecile," he warned.

"Well, then, why should you?" Cecile asked innocently.

"And rightly so! Rightly so," the earl agreed. "I'm still the owner of the damn place, aren't I? The cold fish may have bought my son, but she didn't buy my house, and she sure as hell can't buy me!" His voice was loud enough to draw the attention of several nearby guests, but Cecile registered neither surprise nor outrage at the outburst. Instead, she fairly gleamed at this interesting development.

"You are lord and master of your manor, my dear Cubby," she assured him softly. "If you don't want the woman there, forbid her entrance," she advised with a shrug of her slim shoulders.

"You're right, of course," the earl said, his face red with the force of his convictions. "And I will, too. Don't think I won't."

"I have no doubt that you will, my lord," Cecile murmured, reaching out a hand to rest on the earl's arm. "And you are wise to make sure she knows her limits from the beginning. Then there can be no dispute later."

"Right. Right again, Cecile," he said, taking another healthy drink and slipping the flask back into a pocket. "I might as well tell the shrew right now." He got up, none too steadily, from the couch, and straightened up, his most formidable expression on his face.

Cecile, too, stood up and watched him head off in the direction of the blue salon before she turned and began to make her way through the throng to the bride and groom. They were still smiling, apparently in genuine contentment, but Cecile refused to be bothered by the sight.

With a soft look of concern on her features, Cecile leaned close to Leighton, her slim fingers finding his arm. He immediately bent his head to hear her whisper. "Leighton, dear, I fear the earl might be planning some sort of confrontation with your mother-in-law."

"Damn." Leighton's head came up, and a frown stole over his handsome features. He slipped his hands over Cecile's bare arms. "Thank you, Cecile. You are a jewel for keeping an eye on him," he said, smiling tightly. Then he leaned toward his bride.

"I have to check on the earl. Cecile thinks he may be up to something," Leighton said. He touched her arm with a brief movement and then turned to find his father, leaving Melissa alone with the duchess.

"Your Grace," Melissa said, curtsying politely. Privately, she thought it more likely that Cecile was the one up to something, but she suffered a cold kiss on the cheek from the lady.

"My warmest congratulations, dear," Cecile said, a smooth smile on her flawless features.

"Thank you, Your Grace," Melissa said. No matter how polite her words, Cecile still sounded as though she were addressing some loathsome insect, and Melissa realized that the duchess's disdain ran deeper than mere snobbery. She suspected that the duchess harbored a personal dislike for her, although she had no idea as to the cause.

"Please, call me Cecile," the duchess said, as if to countermand Melissa's thoughts. "It was a lovely wedding," she added, opening her fan and beginning to move it rhythmically.

"Thank you," Melissa said softly. Perhaps it was those eyes, or the turn of the mouth, but Melissa knew there was far more to Cecile than met the eye. In fact, the woman was fairly purring. She looked, Melissa decided with a sense of foreboding, an awful lot like the cat who swallowed the canary.

"I believe you may have the wedding of the season here." She looked casually around and returned that blue-green gaze to Melissa. "The guests appear to be enjoying themselves hugely. Of course, Baltimore has drunk far too much," she noted, tilting her head in the direction of Lord Baltimore. To Melissa's horror, his lordship was fast asleep, his head resting on the arm of his chair.

"Good heavens!" Melissa said in shocked surprise.

Cecile laughed. "It is nothing, really. He is frequently in that condition." She fanned herself rapidly. "You should take it as a compliment. It means he has been thoroughly entertained. One might even call it a measure of the day's success. 'Baltimore slept there' is the sign of a good party, dear," she added, glancing about her again. "Yes, everyone seems to be quite taken with the occasion," she said with a slow smile. "Except, of course, Sir Charles Waverly."

"Leighton's friend?" Melissa asked suspiciously. "What is the matter with him?" She glanced about the room, but could not see Charles. If he was sleeping, too, he must be doing it elsewhere.

"Why, the man is disconsolate over the wager, of course. He simply hates to lose—especially to Leighton," Cecile said.

"The wager?"

"Why, my dear, don't you know?" Cecile asked, abruptly stopping her fan.

"Know what?" Melissa asked, dreading the answer.

"Oh, dear, I hope I've not spoken out of turn," Cecile said. She cast her eyes down coyly and snapped her fan closed. "But, no matter. The bet is already won, so what harm could there be?" she asked, her lips curving into the gentlest of smiles as she peeped at Melissa from under lowered lids.

"Leighton wagered Sir Charles that he could win the...what was it they called you? Ah, yes. The Lady Disdain," Cecile said, one eyebrow rising up her forehead.

Melissa flinched at her hated sobriquet, and she realized, too late, that she did not really want to hear what the duchess had to say.

"Leighton bet Charles that he could win not just your hand, but your heart, and here you are, the happy little bride," Cecile said with a sigh, "while poor Charles mopes in the corner, his pockets let." She softly clucked her tongue in reproach.

Melissa stood staring, speechless, as the duchess's words penetrated. And the lady was not yet finished.

"I, on the other hand, am quite pleased with the outcome," Cecile added. She leaned close and tapped Melissa with the very tip of her fan. "I put my money on Leighton."

With another catlike smile, Cecile turned away and moved
gracefully among the other guests. As Melissa watched her,
the sights, the sounds and the smells of her wedding celebration faded, to be drowned out by a buzzing in her ears.
For one desperate moment, she feared she would faint, but
suddenly the murmur of voices, the rattle of glasses and the
rustle of expensive silks returned. It was as if the world had
reeled in some dreadful cataclysm and then returned to its
stationary position, with nothing the worse for wear—except one insignificant bride.

Melissa eased herself down into a chair and reached out
a hand for her glass of water. She felt drained, fragile and
vulnerable—it was a feeling she detested—and she struggled to gather her resources.

So what if Leighton was making bets at her expense? Why
should she care? she asked herself bitterly. It was not as
though she loved the man. She did not. She knew very well
that love was a fantasy, a fiction confined strictly to the
pages of books.

No, she did not love him, but she had trusted him. *More
fool you,* she told herself. Wouldn't she ever learn? Men
were not to be believed. Hadn't Bertie taught her that?

Apparently not, for Melissa had trusted the viscount—
enough to hope that they could build some sort of life together, laugh with one another, enjoy each other's company, make love, raise a family.... She had believed he was
different, and all the while it had been a cruel game to him—
a matter for a wager. And, evidently, the whole ton was in
on the joke. Everyone, that is, except the butt of it.

Melissa took another drink of water, then drained the
glass and called to a passing servant. "Please get me another glass of water," she asked, unsure of her own unsteady legs should she try to stand.

"Yes, my lady," the woman said, bowing her head in
subservience. The address jarred in Melissa's ears, reminding her sharply of just how far the charade had gone. She

could not run and hide from the jeering voices this time, for she was now one of them.

Just as she felt the will nearly leave her body, an odd surge of strength flowed through her, and with it came some sense of calm. Well, it was done, and all the crying in the world would not undo it. She was married to a heartless cad, but better Leighton than some of her other suitors—and at least she was out from under Gloriana's thumb.

She was married now, and that meant freedom, freedom from so many of the strictures that bound an unprotected female, and freedom from the endless nights at Almack's. She was off the marriage market. Gloriana no longer could force her through vile nights surrounded by horrible old hens. She was a viscountess now, and would someday be a countess, so the snobs who looked down on her would have to treat her with respect. No more condescending pap from boors like Grimley!

Melissa felt her backbone stiffen. She would not stand for any more shabby treatment from her husband, either. If he thought she was a mealymouthed mouse who would scurry away to Greyhaven, he was mistaken. She would do as she pleased and please no one but herself. A slow smile played about her mouth as Melissa decided that now would be as good a time as any to let her husband know of her intentions.

She rose to her feet, no longer unsteady, and glided through the ballroom, an icy smile on her face and fire surging through her blood. She caught the sound of Leighton's voice and followed it to find him in the blue salon, where he leaned against a mantelpiece, towering over the earl, who slouched dejectedly on a couch below.

By some lucky happenstance, Leighton was surrounded by just the fellows Melissa had hoped to see: Sir Charles Waverly, Robert Smythe and Lord Cameron Wolsey, his most favored cronies. The devils actually had the nerve to hail her pleasantly as she approached.

"To the bride," Charles gushed, holding up a glass.

"Hear, hear," Robert said, taking a drink.

"Ah, Melissa, love," Leighton said softly, holding out a hand to her. She smiled and moved smoothly to his side.

"Let's drink to the bride and groom," Charles said. Flushed with liquor and not looking the slightest bit disconsolate, he pressed a servant for another glass of champagne and presented it to Melissa with a flourish. "To your marriage," he said.

"To our marriage," Leighton echoed, his hazel eyes caressing her warmly over the rim of the glass he raised in salute.

"To our marriage," Melissa said, holding her own glass aloft. "You have me, and you have my money," she said with a smile, "but you don't have my heart. Sorry, my lord, you lose the bet." Then, to the utter amazement of all who watched, Viscountess Sheffield proceeded to empty the contents of her glass over the head of her new husband.

Barely glancing at her sputtering spouse, she swept by Charles, whose mouth was hanging open with astonishment. For a moment the buzz of conversation stopped as she regally left the room, and then she could plainly hear the loud laughter of the earl, followed by the sound of his voice, raised in a bellow.

"I like the girl! I tell you, I like her," he said.

Still in a state of outraged fury, Melissa stalked upstairs without the slightest thought to her guests, her wedding trip or even her mother. She found her room, which adjoined Leighton's, and stood looking about, tapping her foot in annoyance when she recognized all her personal articles, neatly delivered and unpacked.

Her gowns filled the wardrobes, her collection of watercolors graced one wall, and her books were lodged on the shelves. She strode around the room, which was beautifully decorated in peach, pale green and cream. She hated it.

Her eyes landed on the startlingly thin confections that made up her new set of nightclothes, and she gave a snort of disgust. She rooted in a large cabinet until she found her small trunk, with her most personal items still intact, and threw it on the bed.

She dismissed the gossamer nightdresses that seemed to mock her from their drawers and instead chose a high-necked gown of heavy cotton, which she stuffed into the trunk. She threw a thick robe on top, just for good measure, then stepped out into the hallway, startling a slender young maid.

"Oh, excuse me, my lady," the girl said. "I didn't expect to see you here . . . yet. Ah, beg pardon, my lady," the girl mumbled, turning crimson.

"Your name?" asked Melissa as she watched the maid turn a deeper shade of red.

"Rina, my lady," she said softly, her eyes downcast.

"Rina," Melissa said, "can you help me move some things?"

"Well, yes, but I'm only an upstairs maid. Would you like me to call the housekeeper?" the girl asked, looking more nervous now than frightened.

"No, that won't be necessary," Melissa said. "I know Mrs. Thatcher must be busy downstairs. What other rooms are available here?" she asked, waving a hand down the corridor.

"Here?" Rina echoed, bewildered. "Why, all of them, my lady. The viscount's apartments are here, and his father, the earl, has his rooms down there." She pointed to the end of the corridor, where another set of lavish doors proclaimed a comfortable berth. "All else are guest rooms, my lady, and no one's staying here tonight," she said. Her voice dropped off softly, and she looked down again at the thick carpet under her feet.

"So, all of these are ready for occupancy?" Melissa asked. She turned and began walking toward the opposite end of the hall.

"Why, yes, my lady," Rina said, scurrying to catch up with her. "They are all done up lovely, too, though the blue one on the end is my favorite."

Melissa stopped her steps and smiled at the girl. "The blue one it shall be, then. You can get my gowns, and we shall move them. And Rina—"

"Yes, my lady," the girl said, eyeing her expectantly.

"You've just been promoted. You are now my personal maid."

"Oh, thank you, my lady! Thank you!" the girl said breathlessly as she hurried ahead to lead Melissa to the new room.

The blue room was not large by Melissa's standards, but it was cheerful and cozy, and had the advantage of being located as far from Leighton's suite as possible. Rina helped her with one load, then hurried off to gather more of her clothing, while Melissa put things away.

Melissa was standing with an armful of delicate chemises when her husband appeared in the doorway, toweling his wet hair, presumably cleansed of the champagne with which she had dampened it earlier. "Please go," Melissa requested with only the briefest glance at him. Then she returned to her task and stuffed the undergarments in the nearest drawer.

"Melly," Leighton began, but she cut him off.

"I don't want to hear it," she said without even looking at him. She slammed the drawer loudly.

"Mel—"

"My name is Melissa," she hissed, finally turning to face him. All her anger returned, surging to the surface like a pot boiling over.

"Melissa." Leighton lowered the towel from his hair, which fell perfectly into place even when wet, and held it casually in one hand. "The wager was a mistake. I was arrogant and thoughtless." He put down the towel and reached for her.

"Don't touch me." Melissa drew back her hand as if he would burn her with his touch.

"Come on, Mel, you can't actually mean to move in here," he said with a crooked grin. "We're married now."

"Don't remind me," she snapped.

Leighton looked at her, his demeanor, for once, slipping out of its usual state of unruffled calm to show a combination of both astonishment and annoyance. "What about the wedding trip?" he asked.

"Go by yourself," Melissa answered, her voice cracking. "Have a nice time!" Rina made high marks with her new mistress by daintily slipping past Leighton and going about her duties, giving Melissa the impetus she needed to get rid of her husband.

"And if you want to see me, make an appointment with my secretary," she snapped.

"Who is that?" Leighton asked, suddenly looking weary and very unhappy.

"I don't know. I haven't got one yet, but I will!" Melissa said. She stepped forward, put her hand firmly on his chest and pushed him back out the door before slamming it in his face.

She waited a moment, to see if he would barge back in, but nothing happened, so she simply stood staring at the place where he had been, her hands clenched together in front of her. Apparently she had won, yet her triumph gave her no pleasure, and only Rina's presence kept her from collapsing on the bed in tears.

Rina made several more trips, but Leighton did not return. Finally, when enough had been moved, Melissa called a halt and dismissed her maid for the evening. Bone tired, she crawled into the heavy nightgown herself and slipped into bed alone on her wedding night.

She was too tired to cry, and she expended all her will trying not to think about the last time this had happened—the other time, long ago, when she had believed in a man. She didn't want to remember how she had once fallen in love, only to be betrayed, but she was too weary to fight it, and it all came flowing back like a dam breaking free. Bertie, damn him, returned to her mind with a vengeance.

Melissa stirred in her sleep, moved by the most wonderful dream. In it, Leighton had moved her hair aside and was kissing the back of her neck, his lips warm on her skin, his fingers feather-light along her flesh. He was behind her, his body pressed against her back, and one hand was traveling up her thigh. Her nightgown rode up above her hips, and she could feel his hardness against her.

Melissa moaned softly and turned over. She wanted to touch him. Her face met his chest, and she nuzzled in the soft hairs there as she ran her hands along the lean muscles of his back. How glorious to touch him, to feel his skin under her fingers, she thought dizzily. Then she slipped her arms around his neck, drawing him close, and the kiss that ensued was sweet, hot ... and all too real.

Melissa pulled away, gasped for breath, and opened her eyes to confirm her suspicions. She was not dreaming. The last embers of the fire gave out a soft glow that lit the smooth features of her husband, his lips only inches from her own, his hazel eyes warm with passion.

"How dare you?" Melissa cried in outrage as she scrambled from the bed.

Leighton lay back against the pillows and sighed. He did not look guilty. "I couldn't help myself, Mel."

"Get out! Get out of my bed and get out of my room!" Melissa shouted.

"For God's sake, Mel," Leighton said, slipping out from the covers to stand on the other side of the bed. The dying fire bathed his body in golden light, caressing his wide chest, his bare arms, his naked thighs—and his masculinity.

"Put something on this minute," Melissa shrieked.

Leighton reluctantly picked up the robe he had tossed on a nearby chair and knotted the belt around his waist with a jerk. For once in his life, he couldn't find the words to smooth over the situation, and it was putting him out of sorts. He couldn't seem to cool Melissa's fury, so he tried to calm his own temper, which was snapping to attention at his wife's sudden melodramatic bent.

"For God's sake, Mel. It was only a bet, made in a foolish, conceited moment. I'm sorry. I never meant to hurt you in any way. Now come back to bed, and forget it. It was just a joke."

"Yes, I'm sure it was. I'm sure it all was a joke to you," Melissa said, her voice wavering. "I'm sure you and your friends had a lot of laughs at my expense. Now please go. I don't want to listen to any more of your lies."

So that was it. Leighton ran a hand through his hair and sighed, struggling to figure out just what to do. She thought he had been playing with her all along, even though he hadn't been. He hadn't, God knows, but how the hell was he going to prove it? She didn't trust him now. Every word he had ever spoken was suspect, and now she wouldn't believe anything, no matter what he said. Damn it. How had he gotten himself into this coil? More important, how was he going to get himself out of it?

Leighton wanted things back to the way they were. He wanted his wife. Well, if words wouldn't do, perhaps deeds would. Leighton took a step toward her.

"Leave me alone," she warned.

"I can't, Mel," he whispered, knowing that he truly couldn't. Wasn't that why he was here? He wanted her so desperately that he could taste it, and not just here and now, but for the night and in the morning and every day and every night. Then a horrifying thought struck him, as he wondered suddenly just how far she would take this charade. "I won't let you annul this marriage," he managed to croak out, the words sounding harsh even to his own ears.

Melissa looked at him, incredulous. "So that's why you've come in here, to force yourself on me? You wanted to make sure the marriage was consummated—even if I slept through it—so you would be sure to have my money!"

"Of course not, Mel," Leighton protested.

"Well, you can put your worry aside. I'm not going to annul this marriage," she said coldly. "You can have the money, but you can't have me."

Leighton felt relief wash over him. He had been so panicked at the thought of losing her that it had struck right to the very heart of him. And then he knew. He knew what his father had known all along. He knew what he himself might never have realized if it hadn't come to this.

"Now, are you satisfied?" Melissa asked. "Please leave me alone."

"I can't," Leighton said softly, as the truth blazed itself into his brain. "I truly can't, Mel. You see, I love you."

Far from calming his wife, the words only enraged her further. "How dare you?" she cried. "Get out!" Leighton saw her glance about for something to throw at him, and he started around the bed. "Stay back, or I will scream until everyone in this household comes running," she warned.

Leighton put his head in his hand, the absurdity of the situation hitting him and threatening to render him helpless with laughter. He was in love with his wife, and she didn't believe him.

The consummate charmer, the man who could have his pick of women, uses the three little words for the first time in his life, and what kind of response does he get? The woman threatens to scream the house down. Leighton collapsed into the nearest chair.

"What's so funny?" Melissa asked, her voice as hard as ice.

"Oh, God, Mel, if I don't laugh, I'll cry," Leighton said, rubbing his forehead with his fingers. "It's so damn frustrating. How can I make you believe me?" he asked, looking up her. "Tell me, Mel."

"You can't," she answered. Somehow his earnestness must have showed on his face, though, for she looked at him a long time, the silence broken only by the crackle of the fire. Then she spoke again, softly, gazing not at Leighton but down at the floor.

"When I was sixteen, I fell in love with the squire's son," she whispered, rubbing her arms as though she were cold even in her heavy nightgown. "My mother would have none of it, of course. He was a nobody, and she said he was only after my money. I didn't believe her. I believed Bertie when he whispered all those lovely things in my ear." She laughed humorlessly.

"We planned to run away together until Gloriana bought him off—right in front of me," Melissa said. "She told him she would cut me off, that if he married me he'd get nothing. But she told him that if he dropped his attentions immediately, she would pay him an outrageous sum. He accepted and was gone before nightfall," Melissa said, smiling tightly.

"That's when I learned that my worth could be measured in crowns and pounds. When you have money, everyone wants some of it, and they'll say anything to get it," she said evenly, finally raising her eyes to look at him.

"Oh, so now you're comparing me with that—that fortune hunter," Leighton said, raising his voice angrily.

"You're the fortune hunter!" Melissa shouted back. "You're the fortune hunter," she repeated, nearly choking on unshed tears.

"Oh, Mel," Leighton whispered, his outrage dissolving at the hurt on her lovely face. He stood up and reached for her, longing only to comfort her, but she walked away to the fire and stood with her back toward him, as if to ward him off.

Leighton sighed and ran a hand through his hair, considering his words carefully. "Do you think you're the only one who's ever had a rough time of it?" he asked gently. "I'm sure you've had a lonely life since your father died, with that mother of yours, the tactless wonder, riding roughshod over you. And naturally she had to throw that fellow—What was his name? Bertie. She had to throw that Bertie in your face because she's—'' He paused as several suitable appellations came to mind, none of which he thought he should repeat. "She's mean-spirited," he said simply.

He thought suddenly of his own mother, and how very different she had been, and how lucky he was to have known her. "I wish you could have known my mother," he said softly. "She was vital and full of life, always generous and giving.

"When she died, leaving me with a father who couldn't handle his grief, it was a difficult time. It got worse when he found a way to deal with it—literally—on the gaming tables," he said. "But I didn't run away and hide myself from the world, shamed because my father was acting like a fool," Leighton said, frowning as he spit out the words. "I stood up and took all I could from life, just as Mother did, instead of locking myself away inside."

He looked at Melissa's rigid figure by the fire, wondering if anything he said was getting through to her. He was unable to see her face, and he didn't dare move closer, for fear she would start screaming again. And he had one more thing to say. "Do you think you're the only one to have your heart broken?" he asked wryly.

"When I was young and vulnerable, I fell in love, too. Doesn't everyone? God pity the poor fool who doesn't," he said sincerely. "It's a part of life, Mel.

"In her way, Cecile loved me, too, but she had other things on her mind, and the shaky economy of my household did not suit her needs. She married a doddering old duke with money to burn, then expected me to trot right back to her bed after the wedding, as though nothing had changed," Leighton said, his jaw clenching at the memory.

"She did not accept with good grace my decision to end the affair, and, apparently, still harbors resentment, as evidenced by her calculated efforts to ruin my wedding day—and night." He gave a short laugh. "I suppose hell hath no fury."

"Mel . . ." He took a step toward her. She turned, finally, to look at him, but her features were cool and impassive, her face that of the Lady Disdain.

Leighton felt frustration well up in him again, and he tried not to grimace. "Mel, we have something precious here. Let's not throw it away over a foolish prank or past hurts," he said, holding out his hand.

"I've heard you out. Now please leave, and don't you dare come back," she said icily. "I'm pushing the desk in front of the door just in case, and tomorrow I'll have a stout lock put on."

"And maybe I'll just break down the damn thing," Leighton whispered through clenched teeth. For one moment, she could see how furious he was, but then he turned and left. He did not slam the door.

Melissa watched him go with tired confusion, waiting until the door was closed before sinking down on the bed, her throat convulsed with the pain of holding back her tears. He was so glib, so handsome, and he seemed so sincere that she wanted to believe him, but how could she?

If only she could be rid of the nagging suspicions that his gentle words were all a cruel joke and that he was secretly laughing at her. If only she could trust him again. Melissa realized dimly that it was all too much to consider tonight and, exhausted, she finally slept.

Leighton couldn't even think of sleep. He fumed, stopping only when he found himself actually pacing his own corridor like some thwarted general. Then, without even bothering to dress, he went down to his study, deciding firmly to do something he hadn't done since the night of his mother's funeral. He got out a couple of bottles and proceeded to drink himself into a stupor.

Chapter Ten

Melissa slept late and took her time about going to breakfast. She thought of having something brought to her room, but that smacked of cowardice, so she finally went down, hoping to find the dining hall deserted. It was not. The earl sat nursing a cup of tea and a half-eaten roll as though he were camped there for the day.

"Ah, good morning, my dear," he said, standing when he saw her approach.

"Good morning," she said politely, not quite sure what to expect. She had no idea what repercussions her behavior, including her quick departure, had had on the wedding celebration. The earl seemed to be in a good mood, however, for as she nibbled on a pastry he watched her, a conspiratorial grin on his face.

"Your mother has already sent by a note," he said, pointing to an envelope by her plate.

Melissa frowned and opened the missive, knowing full well what would be inside. It was a summons. Gloriana undoubtedly was in a state over the champagne-dousing Melissa had given her husband and was raring to bring her to book. Melissa did not feel up to it. She smiled across at the earl and tore up the note, leaving the bits neatly on the silver platter where it had awaited her attention.

The earl chuckled. "Not bad news, I hope."

"I'm sure Mother's not pleased with me," Melissa said dryly.

The earl shrugged. "She'll recover."

Years of swinging to her mother's barometer made it difficult for Melissa to be that blasé about Gloriana's wishes. She suddenly felt guilty and selfish for acting on impulse at the wedding ceremony, without considering the effects her actions might have on others.

Melissa realized that Gloriana, who lived and breathed her reputation, might have lost that precious social standing because of her own rash retribution against Leighton. And, although Gloriana would probably suffer the most, they would all be affected. Melissa glanced hesitantly across at the earl. "Are we all social outcasts now?" she asked glumly.

The earl snorted. "Who? Us? My dear girl, it would take a lot more than your little stunt to ruin us. I've been flouting the rules for years, and it hasn't closed any doors. On the contrary, it seems to open them. And, from the reaction I saw last night, you can expect the same."

Melissa gasped and stared at the earl, unable to believe her ears. "You mean . . ."

"I mean," the earl broke in, "that the ton, collectively, was amused. You, my charming little Melissa, just might find yourself the toast of the town," he said, raising his teacup in a mock salute.

Melissa laughed. She lifted her hands to her cheeks and laughed, overcome with a mixture of relief—that the others would suffer no ill effects—and irony. It was so utterly ridiculous. Years of strict propriety, of observing all her mother's rules of polite behavior, had won her little popularity, while one day of being herself and flouting convention utterly had made her a success.

Her giggles died away, finally, as she thought of the other actor in her little play. "What about Leighton?" she asked.

"What about him?" the earl asked, putting down his cup.

"Has he been hurt socially?"

"My dear girl, in case you haven't noticed, the Grey-haven men are a most charming breed," the earl said, his blue eyes twinkling merrily. "And, as I said before, it would take more than one little scene to destroy our reputations. From what I gather, Leighton's stock has gone up, too. After all, he did take the incident with good grace." He paused to eye Melissa closely, giving her a sly grin. "Is he so very despicable?"

"Beg pardon, my lord?" Melissa asked, caught off guard by the question.

"I know the bet was a vile thing," the earl said, reaching out a hand to the sugar bowl. "One should never make light of affairs of the heart, but then, this is all new to the boy."

"What?" Melissa asked.

"Why, being in love, of course," the earl said as he added another lump to his cup.

"He loved Cecile," Melissa blurted out before realizing just how telling her words were.

"Pah. A childish infatuation for the wrong sort of woman. Nothing more than that. A man knows when it is lasting—or doesn't know, if he's not clever enough to figure it out." The earl stirred his tea vigorously.

Melissa looked down at her plate, embarrassed. "I appreciate your interest, but I don't find this a suitable topic for conversation," she said.

"Pah! Now that sounds like your mother," he said, shivering as though the thought frightened him. He pushed away his teacup. "Damned stuff's too cold. Now, don't you start turning out that way, or I'll have to desert the ship."

Melissa, who found it hard to follow the earl's rambling chatter, was beginning to wonder if he had been drinking this early in the day. Perhaps she should forgo her breakfast.

"Melissa," the earl said in a coaxing tone of voice, "now, I agree that you're entitled to your revenge, but don't you think the boy's suffered enough?" The handsome old gentleman looked at her with a roguish smile, his bushy white brows lifted, as if he were awaiting her answer.

Melissa didn't respond and returned her gaze to her plate. The pastry, which tasted like dust in her mouth anyway, was starting to look wholly unappetizing. She was not used to discussing such personal matters, and it made her uncomfortable. Then, suddenly struck by an idea even more disturbing than the conversation had been, she jerked her head upward. "Did Leighton put you up to this?" she asked with a quick frown.

The earl laughed aloud. "My dear girl," he said, looking at her with a jaundiced eye, "no one puts me up to anything."

Melissa believed him. She knew full well how difficult he was to manage, and she had never known him to dissemble. For all his eccentricities, the earl was his own man. His next words, however, were not encouraging.

"But I must admit to an ulterior motive," he said, and Melissa looked over at him curiously. "Of course, I am concerned about the boy's welfare. He's my son, and I do love him dearly," the earl said, gazing down at his silverware. "I am, however, also concerned about my own welfare. You see, my dear," he said, idly toying with his teaspoon, "we need him.

"Someone has to take care of the finances if we are to continue living in the manner to which we—you and I—are accustomed. I'm afraid I've become quite used to Leighton deftly juggling my accounts, and with our new influx of cash—" the earl paused to grin wickedly at her "—we will need someone to make sure everyone is paid. My creditors," he said with a sigh, "can be deuced annoying."

"But—" Melissa began.

He held up his spoon to halt her. "Someone must handle the investments and all that rubbish," he said, flinging out a hand, as if to dismiss such boring tasks, "or we won't find a roof over our head. Having been very close to that prospect, I have no desire to ever reach that point again. If

Leighton is to be reduced to a drunken sot, what are we to do?''

Before Melissa could answer, he continued on another tack. "And, my dear girl, I must add that I take exception to my role being usurped," he declared. "There's room for only one drunk in the family and I believe I have prior claim to the position."

"What on earth are you talking about?" Melissa asked, having totally lost the train of the conversation.

"I'm talking about Leighton! I found him sprawled in his study this morning, in a state of undress and positively reeking of brandy. And, since I haven't ever seen the boy in that condition, I must assume it's a new hobby he's acquiring in response to his, shall we say, marital difficulties?"

Melissa sniffed. "If he wants to get drunk, then let him," she said with a shrug.

"But that's just the thing, dear," the earl said. "We need him. Who's going to keep the creditors from the door?"

"I will," Melissa said simply. She smiled as she looked over at the earl, her face shining with determination.

"What?" he asked.

"I'll do it," Melissa said.

"Do what?"

"Take over the accounts," she said.

"You?" the earl asked, his face showing both surprise and skepticism.

"Why not? I can manage the household accounts," Melissa said defensively. And it was true. Gloriana's disdain for business did not extend to the daily running of several large households, and Melissa had been prepared to do just that. Of course, Gloriana had never let Melissa progress beyond the training itself, but why mention that?

Melissa felt all the excitement of her thwarted ambitions surge through her. Ever since her father's death, she had dreamed of taking charge of his business, of succeeding as he had and watching the investments grow. Being in control of her own holdings would at least be a step in that direction. She tried not to become too excited, but she couldn't help it; here was her chance. She inched toward the edge of her chair. "Where does Leighton keep his accounts?" she asked.

"In the study," the earl answered perfunctorily. Then he raised his head and eyed her more closely. "Good God, you actually mean to have a look, don't you?"

"Why not?" Melissa asked with more boldness than she felt. "Do you think he'd mind?"

"No," the earl said. "I'm sure he wouldn't care. You know as well as I that my son is blessed with an even temperament," he said. "I just never thought a beautiful young thing like you would want to bury yourself in a bunch of musty papers filled with deadly-dull numbers," he explained, shaking his head as though still stupefied.

"I think it would be interesting," Melissa said.

At her words, the earl sat up in his chair, put his chin in his hand, propped his elbow on the table and looked across at her, his sleepy eyes gazing at her calmly. "I know you want me to mind my own business, my dear, but take my word for it, there are more interesting things to do following your wedding than browse through a stack of account books."

Melissa looked down at her plate and blushed furiously. "Perhaps," she whispered, "but I intend to have a look at those books. Would you help me, my lord?" she asked. "I mean, I might need your assistance in finding some things." *And explaining some things,* she thought to herself.

"Me?" snorted the earl. "Why, my girl, I haven't the head for that folderol," he said. "If you must tackle this nonsense, then get Leighton's secretary to help you. Parker's his name."

"Oh, but I couldn't," Melissa said, picturing a know-it-all who would look down his nose at any questions she might raise. "I don't know the fellow, and, well, I really would feel more comfortable, being new to the household, if you would lend a hand," she explained. "Please?"

The earl scowled at her and sighed. "All right. Lord knows I could never resist a beautiful woman, but this has got to be one of the more onerous requests I've ever gotten from one."

Melissa laughed delightedly and rose from her chair. "Now?"

"Why not?" Melissa asked again. The earl, who looked as though he had just lost several hands at cards, had no comment, but rose grumbling from his seat to lead her to the study.

It still reeked of spirits, although all evidence of her husband's alleged drinking spree had been removed by the servants, Melissa assumed. The room itself reminded her of Leighton. The walls weren't paneled in a dark wood, but were covered with bright tapestries that caught the light spilling in from huge windows that looked out over the street.

Melissa put out a hand and ran a finger over the smooth surface of the Louis XV desk, and wished, for one brief moment, that she was in the study under different circumstances. She imagined her husband leading her here to share his work with her, but she dismissed the dream to turn her mind to the task at hand.

"We don't want to be disturbed," she told a passing servant, who then quietly closed the door. She looked across at the earl, who looked pained, then sat down and glanced at the first sheaf of papers. They were the debts.

Out of deference to her older assistant, Melissa tried not to appear too shocked at the enormous bills the earl had single-handedly accumulated. It was all here—the lavish parties, the expensive gifts for his female acquaintances, and the gambling. As one sum followed another, Melissa couldn't help but feel a grudging respect for Leighton, both for putting up with such nonsense and for somehow keeping them both out of debtor's prison.

When the sums were all totted up, Melissa realized that Leighton, like it or not, had been forced by his father to become a fortune hunter, but she managed to squelch the quick surge of sympathy that that knowledge engendered and carry on with her task.

Although the earl only shrugged and smiled at the total, Melissa was unable to return his grin, and that appeared to put him out of sorts. He frowned and grumbled, but found the rest for her—the household accounts, the rents, the mortgages, the income from the sale of land, paintings and valuables. It had all gone out as soon as it had arrived.

They found the report on Melissa's holdings along with the marriage documents, and they called for lunch to be brought in as they pored over the papers. It was a formidable stack, outlining her property, her investments and her shares in her father's businesses, which included a shipping line and several factories.

The debts seemed minor in comparison, and the earl's spirits improved visibly. His son was now, by any reckoning, quite wealthy. The earl practically giggled over his buttered scones, but Melissa was not so easily impressed. She finally threw down the accounts and looked at the earl, her lips pursed tightly. "It's not enough," she said.

He nearly choked on his blueberry tart. "What? Even I'd have a hard time going through that much money in a hurry," he said.

Melissa frowned at him. "You will not go through my money in a hurry, if you please," she retorted, and then paused, looking thoughtful.

"Well, what then?" snapped the earl, miffed at the setdown she'd given him.

"It just seems to me that with all these interests, more money should be coming in."

"Good God, my dear, what more do you want?"

Melissa frowned and looked down at the papers again. "From what's here, I just can't get the complete picture, but it seems as though too many of these businesses are losing money instead of producing it. Papa used to drop such things without a second thought," she said. "If he couldn't turn a profit in good time, then he got rid of it."

"Maybe, but who's in charge now?" the earl asked. "They might do things differently."

"Malcolm Hornsby, Papa's partner, runs all the businesses now, although Mother and I have our shares," Melissa said.

"Well, what does the old girl say about it?" the earl asked.

Melissa laughed. "Oh, Mother would never dirty her hands by taking an interest in the business, my lord. She leaves it all to Hornsby."

"My God, you mean there's something I actually agree with her on?" the earl asked, looking startled. "That's frightening. I must be going dotty after a whole day of poring over figures," he said shaking his head. "And mind you, Melissa, I don't want this getting out. My reputation will be ruined."

"I won't tell a soul that you helped me, my lord," Melissa promised dramatically.

The earl looked at her and grinned. "My dear girl, you are getting too cocky."

They went over the report again, much to the earl's distress, but Melissa was forced to agree with him in the end. She really couldn't find anything wrong, although the odd feeling persisted. The earl suggested, as tactfully as he could, that perhaps she was simply giving her father too much credit.

"Perhaps you are right," Melissa said with a sigh. "Still, I would like Leighton to have a look. Maybe he'll see something we haven't."

"Better him than me," the earl said.

"Oh, dear," Melissa said suddenly. "Look at the time. I've got to dress for dinner," she added, her slight panic evident in her voice.

The earl chuckled softly and reached out a hand to clasp her wrist, stopping her in her tracks. "My dear girl, there is no hurry."

"What?" Melissa asked blankly.

"Melissa," the earl explained, "this is your household. You are mistress here. If you want to be late for dinner, or if you don't want to show up at all ... Pah," he said, snapping his fingers. "There's no harridan here to reprove you."

Melissa's slow smile grew until she positively shone with delight. "Oh, my goodness! How very right you are," she said with a giggle. Her own freedom, forgotten in the gloom of Leighton's defection, rose up to embrace her, and she whirled around the room in happiness.

Then she grabbed the earl's hand, tugging him to his feet to dance around the study with her. Although he laughed, he joined in, and for a large man he was very light on his feet, waltzing her gracefully across the room. "What a wonderful dancer you are," Melissa said sincerely. She glanced up at him and was surprised by the gentle look on his face.

"Oh, you are a wonder, my girl," the earl said softly as he gazed at her. "You remind me of someone I once knew," he added, a wistful smile on his face. "She, too, took pleasure in simple things."

Melissa smiled back and curtsied formally. "I will meet you for dinner at, say, half past the hour," she said before turning to go. She hesitated but a moment on the threshold. "But I really should run and tell the housekeeper we'll be late."

The earl only shook his head and chuckled.

Melissa ignored another summons from her mother, presented to her when she left the study, and ran to tell Mrs. Thatcher to set supper back a half hour. Mrs. Thatcher, in turn, notified the cook and the serving staff, and, of course, the earl was aware of the new time. The only person not informed of the adjustment was Viscount Sheffield.

When Melissa and the earl entered the dining hall, they found him already seated—and scowling. Melissa didn't think she had ever seen him scowl. She smiled politely and took her seat, eyeing him surreptitiously.

"My dear wife," he said, softly but grimly. "In future I would appreciate being notified of any changes in our dining schedule."

"Oh, dear!" Melissa exclaimed. She looked guiltily at the earl. "We forgot to tell Leighton."

The earl shrugged. "Well, from the looks of him, he shouldn't eat anything anyway."

Apparently, the earl had quickly come to the same conclusion that Melissa had: Leighton did not look himself.

His dusty locks were as perfectly tousled as ever, but they seemed to have lost their luster, and his smooth complexion looked sallow, the effect accentuated by the dark circles under his eyes. His usual carefree demeanor was little in evidence—replaced, it seemed, by a rather gloomy and irritable outlook—and his handsome features looked hard and unnatural.

Although her righteous anger of the night before had faded, Melissa could find little sympathy for the man who had betrayed her. "You should really give up dissipation, my lord," she said idly while the first course was being served. "It does not become you."

"She's right, my boy," the earl said. "You just can't carry it off as I can."

"It will ruin your looks," Melissa added.

"I'll try to keep that in mind," Leighton snapped loudly. Then he put a hand to his head and groaned. "It is *so* kind of you to be concerned," he hissed from beneath his fingers.

The earl chuckled, and the sound drew Leighton's head up. "And you, Father, don't you have somewhere else to play? Why are you dining in tonight, if I may ask?"

The earl shrugged. "Why should I go out when I can be entertained right here, free of cost?" he asked. "And the actors, if I may say so, are as engaging as any I've seen in a theater," he added, with a sweeping gesture that took in Leighton and his wife.

Leighton looked as if he were going to say something, but then he scowled and sat looking dismally at his plate.

"Leighton," his wife began, "I'd like you to do me a favor."

"Pardon me?" Leighton asked sarcastically. "Did you say something?"

Obviously his mood was even blacker than his looks, but Melissa persisted. "I'd like you to do me a favor," she repeated coolly. "I'd like you to look over the report that Mother forwarded on my holdings."

"What?" Leighton asked, looking puzzled.

"My holdings," she said. She glanced sideways at the earl, mindful of her agreement not to mention his help. "I looked them over today, and it seems they are not bringing in enough."

"Enough what?" Leighton asked.

"Enough money," Melissa explained.

"It seems they are not bringing in enough *money?*" Leighton repeated.

"I told you he was a clever boy," the earl said.

"My God, do you have any idea how much money that is?" Leighton asked, ignoring his father.

"Yes, of course," Melissa replied testily. "But that's not the point."

Leighton put both hands to his forehead. "Just what is the point?" he asked, eyeing her from beneath his fingers.

"Quick, too," the earl interposed.

"The point is," Melissa said, "are the figures correct or not?"

Leighton sighed and rubbed his temples. "All right, I'll look over the report closely. I'll do you your favor," he said, pausing as he lowered his hands from his face and looked directly at her. "Then I've a favor to ask of you."

"Oh? What's that?" Melissa asked, her eyes narrowing suspiciously.

"I'd like to sleep with my wife tonight."

Melissa's fork clattered onto her plate, and her face turned crimson. "We can discuss this later," she said.

"Don't mind me," the earl said grinning. "Good Lord, but I could make a fortune myself just selling tickets to this show," he moaned, as though lamenting his missed opportunity.

Both participants in the drama ignored his comments, however, for Melissa simply glared at her husband, infuriated that he could bring up the subject in front of his father, while Leighton returned her gaze calmly.

"I'm not going to let this continue, Mel," he said softly.

"I'm not, either," Melissa said, smiling sweetly, but she was referring to the conversation, not the bedroom arrangements. "Leighton, dear, you haven't touched a thing on your plate. You really should eat something," she said. She reached across the table for the most unsavory dish she could see. "Here, do try some of the pickled eggs, or perhaps these bits of tongue. Cook has them positively swimming in fat," she urged maliciously.

It worked. Melissa had never actually seen anyone turn green before, but Leighton took one look at the eggs and the tongue and his pallor changed hue. "If you will excuse me," he said through a tight-lipped smile, and rose from the table.

"Of course," Melissa answered politely. As he left the room, she glanced over at the earl, who raised his bushy eyebrows and grinned at her.

"My dear girl, I do believe you have a mean streak."

The words stayed with her. Although she was certain the earl had not meant to insult her, Melissa found she didn't like the phrase he had used. She thought of Leighton's description of her mother. Mean-spirited, he had called her, and it was true enough. Would Melissa, too, unsatisfied and unhappy with her life, grow so cold and sharp that she would someday deserve the same appellation?

The thought was not a pleasant one, and Melissa tried to rid herself of it as she tossed and turned, alone in her blue bedchamber. Well, at least she had no daughter to take it out on, she thought to herself, but that notion was not comforting, either.

She might never have children, she realized, closing her eyes tightly against that vision. It was not as though she had always longed for them, she told herself. Her life, and her ambitions, had always been so different from those of most other young girls that she had never really expected a "normal" life, but now she found the idea of never having a family of her own painfully sad.

Of course, she might still have babies. She could take a lover; the Lord knew it happened often enough in the ton. They gossiped about one woman, each of whose children, it was said, had been fathered by a different man. But that idea, too, Melissa found distasteful. The future looked bleak as she lay awake in the silence and listened for the turn of the doorknob.

It did not come. She had not requested a lock, as she had threatened, but she had put a heavy chair against the door so that Leighton would not catch her unawares again. But no one jarred the door or the chair as the time ticked away, and Melissa decided that Leighton was not coming tonight.

She was relieved only briefly—until she began to wonder exactly where he was and what he was doing. Was he drowning himself in liquor again, or had he recovered from his marital disappointments? Was he sleeping peacefully, alone in the big bed that they were supposed to be sharing, or had he gone out?

Melissa sat straight up in bed as that thought sank in. As much as she still hurt from his betrayal, she did not care for the idea of her husband seeking comfort elsewhere. She lay down again and tried to get some sleep, but remained awake, her eyes open in the darkness, uncertain which was worse— last night, when he had sneaked into her room, or to- night—when he hadn't.

Chapter Eleven

The dining hall was deserted the next morning, and Melissa felt a twinge of disappointment. Despite all the servants, the place seemed lonely without the company of Leighton and the earl. Melissa sat down, shaking her head at her own foolishness. She had never been lonely in the even larger town house that she had shared with her mother, and God knew Gloriana was poor company.

Perhaps that was the problem. Her expectations of the Sheffield household had been too high. She would have to lower them and find something to do with herself—by herself—to keep busy. She lifted a spoonful of jam onto her biscuit while she mulled over the problem and almost jumped from her seat when she felt a warm breath behind her. She shivered, nearly dropping her spoon, when her husband's lips met the back of her neck.

Oh, my, this was why she would not let him touch her the other night. She could not think straight when he was so near. "Leighton," she croaked.

"Yes, Mel? God, I love to hear my name on your lips," he whispered before his mouth moved along her neck. "Say it again."

"Leighton," she began again, but forgot exactly what it was she had been about to say. As his lips burned a trail down to her shoulder, she couldn't even remember why she was angry with him.

"I'm not going to let this continue, you know," he said softly.

"Good." Melissa noted, from under eyelids that kept threatening to close in sweet bliss, just how rapidly the serving maid exited the room when she saw Leighton nibbling at his wife's neck. She wondered idly if Leighton was in the habit of seducing ladies in his dining hall.

"I'm so glad you agree with me, my love," Leighton whispered. "Let's end this foolish squabble now. I love you, Mel, and I'm not going to give up on you. Admit you love me, too."

Melissa arched her neck, her body turning to liquid under the gentle pressure of his mouth, her skin melting under his smooth fingers as they ran down her arms. She felt drugged by his touch, as though her common sense were slipping away. This was how she had got into trouble in the first place, she thought vaguely, as a vision of the night he had proposed at Vauxhall drifted into her mind.

"Come to bed, Mel," he urged against her ear, his tongue delving into its ridges. Melissa closed her eyes. He was so intoxicating, weaving his spell around her like a—Admit? Admit she loved him? When those words finally sank in, Melissa remembered exactly why they were estranged, and all the mistrust flowed back.

"No!" Melissa said firmly, straightening up. Her jam spoon, which had somehow remained clutched in her hand, finally fell, clanking against her plate.

"Poor Mel, always losing your silverware," Leighton chided smoothly as he moved to take a seat across from her.

This was the old Leighton, lighthearted, charming, devastatingly handsome, and, Melissa suspected, far too sure of himself for his own good—or hers. She tried to frown at him, but her body was slow to function after being turned to pudding by his recent ministrations.

"Don't frown at me, or I won't tell you what I found in your precious report," Leighton said with a sly grin.

"You've looked at it already?" Melissa asked, her eagerness showing.

"Yes, last night, and dull work it was, too," he said as he filled his plate, his appetite having apparently returned with his good humor.

Melissa smiled as she watched him. Then she realized just what his words meant. Last night. He had looked over the accounts last night! While she had been upstairs stewing, he had been down in the study, doing her favor for her. Relief washed over her, followed by a surge of happiness, and she smiled brightly over at him, unable to help herself.

"Don't get too excited," he warned. "I didn't find anything."

"You didn't?" Melissa asked, frowning.

"I don't know why you're so disappointed," Leighton said, shaking his head. "I never would have thought you so enamored of money."

"I'm not," Melissa said. "It just doesn't seem right. I don't know why, Leighton. It's just a feeling, I guess."

"A feeling." Leighton looked skeptical as he began tackling the heaping portions he had served himself.

"Yes," Melissa said. "A feeling. Sometimes I get feelings about things, and, well, I'm usually right," she mumbled, looking down at her plate.

Leighton gazed at her thoughtfully, and she noticed just how much better he looked today. The light caressed his smooth features and shone on his hair, shimmering off the locks as though giving them life. His lips, curving gently, reminded her of just how long it had been since she had kissed them, and she fought an overwhelming desire to press her mouth to his. She told her racing heart to settle down.

"And what does this sixth sense tell you about me?" he asked.

"It told me I would never be rid of you," she snapped, grabbing up her spoon again, "and how true it was!"

"Hmmm," Leighton mused. "Correct so far," he agreed with a grin, "but what does it tell you about me now?" he asked, his voice soft and low and oh, so compelling.

Melissa refused to respond. She already knew what the answer was, and she wasn't about to tell Leighton. She knew that if she ignored the confused thoughts of her brain, her hurt pride and her nagging suspicions and listened to her heart, it was all quite simple. She believed him. She believed he loved her, and she, in return, cared far too much for him.

"Well?"

"My presentiment is that you're going to get fat if you eat the enormous amount of food on that plate," she said, pointing her spoon accusingly at his platter and keeping her other thoughts to herself.

"As I recall, last night you were rather anxious that I eat," Leighton said dryly.

Melissa smiled to herself. It was wonderful to have the old Leighton back, even if she didn't trust him. *How I've missed you,* she thought, peeking at him under lowered lashes.

"From the looks of that report, your father had an amazing head for business, a real talent," Leighton said.

Melissa frowned. "There are those who do not think highly of my father's accomplishments."

"Idiots who already had money." Leighton waved his fork with an air of dismissal. "I applaud him, although it was not his greatest achievement," Leighton said softly. He paused to gaze at her warmly, his hazel eyes sparkling.

"Oh?" Melissa asked, eyeing him questioningly.

"No," Leighton said, revealing one of his gorgeous dimples. "That would be you, my love."

"Really, Leighton," Melissa said with a grimace.

Her husband chuckled at her discomfiture, then shook his head. "God, Mel, you have so little perception of your own worth, it amazes me. Look in the mirror, my love. You are a work of art," he said seriously, and Melissa nearly believed him. Outwardly, though, she only laughed, and

Leighton, still shaking his head, dropped the subject and reached for another biscuit.

For a moment, Melissa watched him eat, but then she realized that her eyes were lingering too long on his mouth. She cleared her throat and shifted in her seat. Perhaps she shouldn't even be here with him, for things were becoming awfully friendly. She really ought to leave, she told herself firmly, but she had missed him, blackguard though he might be.

"Was your father interested in art, too, Mel?" Leighton asked, oblivious to her struggle. "I noticed in the report the sale of some paintings. Was he a collector?"

"Oh, not really on a grand scale," Melissa said. "But he did have some lovely works. The Vermeer you saw me admiring at Waterbury's was one."

"I'm sorry, Mel. I had no idea," Leighton said, his voice gentle. "How did Waterbury get it?"

"Mother," Melissa answered with a sigh. "She seemed to dislike anything that reminded her of father, so when Mr. Hornsby suggested she sell them, she didn't care. You've seen those dreadful things she replaced them with," Melissa added, making a face. "And to think of what we had."

Melissa sighed again at the loss, and then raised her eyes to Leighton's, as if struck by a revelation. She was no longer under Gloriana's thumb, and she had the funds to do what she pleased. She could amass her own collection.

"Leighton, we must buy some paintings of our own," she said excitedly. "We can even try to get some of yours back. Your Rubens," she suggested breathlessly. The easy companionship between them returned so quickly and felt so right that she momentarily forgot she was supposed to be at odds with the man before her.

"My Rubens," Leighton repeated wistfully. "I'm afraid it's gone for good, my love, but it is a beautiful thought." He paused, as if pondering something, and his brows furrowed. "Mel, what else did your mother sell, besides the Vermeer?"

"Oh, there were some lovely Gainsboroughs," Melissa said. "It broke my heart to see them go, Leighton, but now we have enough money to purchase some of our own," she said, smiling. "Oh, I just never thought of creating my own collection. What a joy it must be!" She was so carried away that it took her a moment to notice that Leighton did not seem to share her enthusiasm. He was silent and pensive. "What is it?" she asked, frowning suspiciously.

"The money," Leighton said, tapping his fork on the table as if lost in thought. Then, suddenly, he turned to her. "Mel, you may be right. It just doesn't add up."

"What?"

"The amount quoted in the report for the sale of the collection. It's nowhere near the sum one should get for such works. And I do know my prices," Leighton said dryly.

"So something is wrong with the books?" Melissa asked.

"Perhaps," Leighton said. "The thing to do is to get a more detailed accounting. We can ask your mother for one when she calls today. If she can't provide one, then I'll talk to Hornsby myself."

Melissa's pleasure at being right was chased away by the news of her mother's impending visit. "Mother's coming today?" she asked.

"I would imagine so," Leighton answered, helping himself to more ham. "I'm sure she's positively itching to dress you down. Don't you think so?" he asked with a smile.

"But why today?" Melissa asked.

Leighton grinned at her wickedly. "It's just a feeling." He laughed at Melissa's quick scowl. "Well, I'm assuming she just can't wait another minute, and Father said you ignored two notes from her yesterday." Leighton paused and eyed her with a roguish look. "Actually, I caught him trying to lay bets with the servants as to the exact hour of her arrival."

"You didn't!" Melissa choked.

"Yes," Leighton admitted with a sigh. "But you'll be glad to know that I did not join in when he asked me,"

Leighton said, holding up both hands as if in surrender. "I told him firmly that I have forsworn wagering permanently."

He was so very charming, Melissa thought, that it was going to be awfully hard to keep her heart chilled against him. She felt it warming already to his teasing. *Remain cold,* she told herself. She was trying not to look into his eyes when they were interrupted by the butler, who announced, with the faintest trace of distaste, that her mother had arrived. Leighton chuckled, but Melissa frowned him into silence.

"Just a moment, Garrison," Leighton said, halting the butler with an upraised hand. "Did you win anything?"

Without batting an eye, the man replied calmly, "I'm sorry to say no, my lord. His lordship has fleeced me again. It is a hazard of serving this household, I'm afraid."

Melissa raised her napkin to her lips and refused to look at her husband while the butler managed a dignified exit. "Excuse me," she whispered to Leighton as she tried to stifle her laughter.

"You sound hoarse, my dear," Leighton said sweetly. "I hope you're not coming down with anything."

Melissa glared at him and left, the image of him leaning back in his seat to laugh at her remaining in her mind. She tried to school herself to seriousness as she prepared to meet her mother, but her heart was so very light after bantering with Leighton that even the thought of Gloriana could do little to dampen her mood.

"Good morning, Mother," she said, greeting her mother sweetly. Gloriana was wearing an enormous hat with birds on it that struck Melissa as so ridiculous-looking she found it hard to maintain her composure.

"Melissa," Gloriana said coolly as she stripped off her gloves. "I do not appreciate being kept waiting."

"I'm sorry, Mother," Melissa said. "I came as soon as I found out you were here."

Gloriana made that familiar *tsk* sound in her throat. "Lax servants, I'll warrant," she said, nearly sending Melissa into peals of laughter. "But what can you expect from such a household? Melissa, I expect you to take this place firmly in hand."

"Yes, Mother."

"Don't give me that tone of voice, young lady," Gloriana ordered, eyeing her closely. "And furthermore, when I send for you, I expect you to come. I sent two notes over yesterday, which you either did not receive or ignored. In the future, you will pay prompt attention, Melissa."

"I'm sorry, Mother," Melissa said. "But I'm a married woman now. I have other obligations, and I cannot promise that I will be available to attend you at your convenience."

"Married! Yes, you certainly are married, aren't you?" Gloriana said icily. "I find it difficult to believe that you are able to look so pleased with yourself after your behavior at your own wedding celebration," she spit out.

She paused a moment, obviously trying to rein in her fury. "Please sit down," she said, more calmly, as she walked toward the window. "Melissa, I was shocked and appalled by your actions, which were certainly not those of a lady." She appeared to be working herself up to a real dressing-down until she turned to find Melissa still standing. "Please sit down," she repeated.

"No, thank you, Mother, I'd rather stand," Melissa said calmly.

For a moment, Gloriana looked as though she couldn't believe her ears, but she recovered quickly. "Then I will," she said, and she perched on the edge of one of the medallion-backed gilt chairs as if she were afraid it was not quite clean. "You are forgetting your duties as hostess," she chided, fanning herself delicately.

"I'm sorry, Mother. Would you care for some tea?" Melissa asked with a smile.

"No, thank you," Gloriana said. Melissa gritted her teeth.

A lengthy pause ensued before Gloriana began again. "Well, as much as I was disgusted by your behavior, it appears, thankfully, that my opinion is not shared by everyone," she said, continuing her fanning.

"Apparently, your little escapade is being discussed and embellished in every parlor. Naturally, I loathe gossip and the idea of bringing this sort of attention to the family," Gloriana said with a scowl, "but Mrs. Marchant informs me that there are those who look on your actions as amusing. I, myself, was hailed in the park by none other than the Duchess of Baldwin, who claimed you promise to be a favorite with the ton."

Gloriana looked as though she had a bad case of indigestion, and Melissa tried to hide her smile. "However, there are a few wild rumors going about that hint of a divorce." Gloriana whispered the word as though it were an obscenity. "Therefore, appearances must be maintained. You and your husband should be seen socially. I assume you received an invitation to the Montagues' latest?" she asked.

"I really don't know, Mother," Melissa answered.

Gloriana pursed her lips. "Of course you have. Melissa, you must make yourself aware of these things. I can no longer handle your social engagements for you," she sniffed.

Then why are you here? Melissa thought, but she said nothing.

Gloriana sighed. "I suspected as much, of course. That was one of the reasons I came. Now, I will expect to see you at the Montagues' on Saturday." She stood and picked up her gloves.

"I think not," Melissa said.

Gloriana eyed her coldly. "You will attend, Melissa."

"The Montagues'?" boomed a hearty male voice. "Why, of course, we're all going to the Montagues'. Wouldn't miss it, would we, my dear?" Melissa turned in surprise to see the

earl practically bounding into the room and positively oozing goodwill. She wondered if he had been drinking already.

"Miss Hampton, my dear lady," he said, bowing low over
Gloriana's hand. "I swear you are a vision today. And that
hat, why, it's most fetching."

Melissa's mouth nearly dropped open. She didn't know
what was more unusual—the earl's behavior, or Gloriana's
acceptance of it.

"Please, sit down," the earl urged. "Let me ring for some
refreshments."

"Well, I—" Gloriana looked as though she didn't quite
know what to say to the man she claimed was the vilest
creature she had ever set eyes upon.

"Melissa, dear," the earl said, "I believe Leighton was
asking for you. He's in the morning room." He took her
arm and escorted her to the doorway.

"Are you all right?" Melissa whispered surreptitiously to
her father-in-law.

"Perfectly, my dear. Now, run along," he said. Melissa
stood staring at him in wonder, so he gave her a little push.
"You can catch more flies with honey," he added, winking
broadly at her.

Not quite sure what to make of his behavior, Melissa followed his instructions and went into the morning room,
where she found Leighton standing by the doors to the garden. One of them was swung open, and a warm breeze
wafted in. Melissa walked over to stand beside him and
looked out upon a beautiful day. The sun poured onto the
bright reds and yellows of the flowers, and the light wind
sent a faint perfume into the room.

Melissa admired the view and enjoyed the peaceful silence after her mother's haranguing until she felt Leighton's hand resting lightly on the small of her back. She
stepped away.

Leighton smiled disarmingly. "So this is the thanks I get,"
he chided, "and after I sent Father in to rescue you."

"Did you?" Melissa asked, the earl's odd behavior suddenly clear. "And just how did you manage that?"

Leighton waved a hand, as though the answer were simple. "I threatened him with expulsion from the household. No more free entertainment," he said with a dimpled grin.

Melissa laughed. "Well, as much as I appreciate the effort, we really ought not to leave them in there alone together. They might kill each other."

Leighton chuckled. "Father can be most charming when he puts forth an effort."

"Oh, I know that. I've seen him do it. But Mother can be most . . . obstinate," Melissa said. Her words trailed off as she gazed out over the sunlit grass. The thought of stepping into a squabble between their parents was not the most attractive prospect she could imagine. "It's a beautiful day," she said wistfully.

"Yes, isn't it?" Leighton agreed. He turned to face her, his eyes sparkling mischievously, just as Melissa opened her mouth to speak. "Let's go for a drive," they both said at the same time, and then they fell, laughing, into each other's arms. Melissa would go no further, however, and, although still smiling, she stepped out of his embrace. Mentally, she agreed to a truce between them, but no more than that.

They deserted their parents without a qualm, but Gloriana would have been quite satisfied to see them, for without intending to, they were giving her just what she wanted—they were keeping up appearances. Although it was not the fashionable hour for a drive in the park, there were others of the same mind about, and those people saw the Viscount Sheffield and his bride talking and laughing together like lovers.

Despite the talk of her popularity, Melissa still expected chilly receptions from those they met, so she was astounded when she was greeted with friendly gestures. The earl and Gloriana were correct. Melissa was definitely a new favorite. She found the notion wholly amusing, because the ton, with its fads and foibles, was not her particular worry.

That distinction was reserved for her husband, for as they drove about in Leighton's curricle, Melissa found herself admiring him in a way that was most disconcerting. Seated so close to him, she was alarmingly aware of his lean but muscular frame, and of how nicely his breeches fitted him. When she caught herself watching the way his hands held the reins and remembering their pressure on her own skin, she took a deep breath and concentrated on the scenery.

The truce continued throughout the day, with Melissa treating her husband nicely but keeping a firm distance. Although she enjoyed his company, she was not about to trust him with her heart again.

Later that evening, the earl, in a jovial mood, coaxed them into a game of cards, and Melissa enjoyed the banter that flowed between them, but when the earl excused himself for the night, Melissa felt uncomfortable being alone with Leighton. They had acted as husband and wife all day, yet she did not want the charade to extend into the night hours.

"I'm tired, too," she said nervously as Leighton went to the sideboard for another glass of sherry. "I think I shall retire myself," she added. But, before she could stand, she felt Leighton's warm breath against her neck and his fingers loosening the pins in her hair to send it cascading down her back. "Come to bed, Mel," he whispered, and she felt her body respond right down to her toes.

"No," she said with an effort. His thumb moved along her neck, sending shivers along her spine. "No," she repeated, getting up to move out of his reach. "Stop this at once!"

"Have done with it, Mel, and forgive me," Leighton coaxed, a crooked smile on his handsome features.

"There is nothing to forgive," Melissa answered stiffly. "You married me for certain reasons—money, to be precise—and now you have what you want," she said, unconsciously clenching together her hands.

"No, I don't," Leighton said softly. "I want you," he asserted, taking a step forward.

"That was not part of the bargain," Melissa said, taking a step backward.

"Oh, yes, it was, my love," Leighton said with a smile.

"Well, the bargain has been changed, because you changed it," she answered. "And don't you dare start chasing me around this room as though I were some barmaid."

Holding her head high, Melissa stalked from the room with what she hoped was a great deal of dignity. It took all her effort not to look over her shoulder, and she was nearly to her blue bedroom before she realized her hands were knotted tightly together. Damn that Leighton!

Leighton was not enjoying himself.

As he dressed for the Montagues' ball, he actually ruined his neckcloth; it was an action so unheard-of that his valet, Mr. Morgan, was later heard to curse the master's new bride in no uncertain terms. The valet's complaints fell on deaf ears, however, for most of the household viewed the situation between the master and his wife as vastly entertaining.

Leighton snatched up a new neckcloth and grimaced. He felt more like a man sentenced to purgatory than a new husband—or a man in love. It was not that he minded paying court to his wife. He did not. What he minded was being so close to her luscious body and being denied it.

His mood was not improved when he met her in the hallway as they prepared to leave for the Montagues'. Her long, luxuriant hair was piled high and sparkled with gems, while her exquisite body was draped in a silver gown that bared most of her breasts. Leighton jerked in a breath, ran a hand through his hair and tried to ignore it.

At the Montagues', he tried to ignore the swarm of fee-bleminded young dandies who had clearly decided his wife was all the rage. As he watched her treating them with amused cordiality, he tried to ignore the realization that he no longer had her all to himself. The turtle emerges from her shell, he thought dismally, and then nearly kicked himself. Good God, was he becoming possessive? He ran a hand through his hair and looked away.

"Sheffield!" Robert's voice brought him back to the present. "How is the married life?" his friend asked in a light voice that managed to convey his concern. Leighton shrugged as he looked over at Melissa.

"Your wife seems to have amassed quite a following," Robert said dryly. "One hopes that this does not signal a trend. I dread seeing all the young hopefuls dousing the nearest male head with various brews in an effort to increase their popularity."

Leighton chuckled. "The whims of the ton," he said with an air of dismissal, dragging his gaze away from Melissa long enough to smile at his friend.

"And you?" Robert asked, eyeing Leighton closely. "How are you faring?"

"I've got a beautiful, intelligent and witty wife who has made me a very rich man. What more could I want?" Leighton asked, running a hand through his hair as he smiled casually at his friend.

"You tell me," Robert replied. "Leighton, I've seen you in a thousand tight spots, and you have always extricated yourself with calm and aplomb. It's a talent or a skill of yours, I don't know which, but good God, man, right now you look more nervous than a whore in church," Robert said. "And if you run that hand through your hair any more, you're going to rub yourself bald!"

"If your desire is to cheer me up, Robert," Leighton retorted with a wry grimace, "I'll have you know you're failing miserably."

Robert smiled. "My desire is to help you out, in whatever way I can."

Leighton just shook his head as if there were no way out of his difficulties, and, for once in his life, he was beginning to believe that was the case. A perpetual optimist, he was gradually being worn down by his obstinate wife, who rebuffed all his efforts to win back her trust. Each day he poured on the charm, and she responded with friendliness—and nothing more.

It was not enough. He was becoming heartily sick of the wall between them. He wanted things back the way they were, the way he remembered them. And he remembered holding a passionate woman in his arms. He reached up a hand to run it through his hair and then caught himself, looked at Robert and laughed.

"Those famous Sheffield locks are not long for this world," Robert commented. He glanced over at Leighton's wife. "Is she still angry about the bet?"

"I suppose you could say that," Leighton answered. He sighed ruefully. "Robert, I appreciate your offer, but there's really nothing you can do."

"No, perhaps not, but maybe there is someone who can," Robert said grimly. "Where is that Charles?"

Charles was found near the refreshments, a plate of pastry in his hand. He did not appear happy to be found. "Charles," Robert said, "I've a mission for you."

"What?" Charles said, eyeing his friend cautiously. He knew that look of Robert's, and he suspected the worst.

"I want you to apologize to Sheffield's wife for that wager."

"What?" Charles asked. "I'll not! It was a perfectly good bet, and I happened to win quite fairly."

"No arguments, Charles," Robert warned. "Have you forgotten that I helped you out of that engagement to the tall blond, uh...what would be the polite word?"

"Drat you, Robert, you would bring that up!" Charles snapped, slamming down his plate. "All right, she can have her damned apology," he said, dusting off his hands angrily. "And I hope she chokes on it," he added under his breath, "the cold fish."

Unaware of the struggles going on around her and about her, Melissa finally shook off her group of admirers and made her way to the card room, where she found the Duchess of Baldwin and Sir Percy finishing a game of piquet.

"Percy, you are a wicked player," the duchess teased. "Ah, Melissa, dear, have a seat. I've wanted so to have a few words with you," she said, motioning to a vacant chair. Melissa smiled in genuine pleasure as she sat down beside her grace, a woman she had quickly come to like and respect. She felt at ease with both the duchess and Sir Percy, as she did with very few others.

"I never had a chance to congratulate you, my child," the duchess said.

"Yes," Sir Percy said, clearing his throat. "Congratulations are in order." He appeared to be rather taken with a large portrait adorning the opposite wall, for that was where his gaze was fixed.

"Thank you, Your Grace, Sir Percy," Melissa said, smiling more at Sir Percy's foibles than at the wishes that had been tendered her.

"My dear child," the duchess began. She leaned over to catch Melissa's eyes. "I hesitate to interfere," she said softly, "but I have taken such a liking to you that I feel I simply must say something." She paused a moment before going directly to the point.

"Darling," she said, "I heard you were upset over some silly wager of Leighton's, and I must admit, I was surprised. You're a levelheaded girl. You must know that men are always throwing their money away on such nonsense. It means nothing. Why, the earl and the prince regent once bet on a couple of ants, for heaven's sake—or was it fleas?" She raised a graceful finger absently in the air.

"Ants, I believe," Percy said.

"Well, whatever, darling, boys will be boys, and they will bet on silly things and have their silly pranks. Such is the

breed, but Leighton . . ." She paused. "Look around you,
my child. Look at the dandies, the drunks, the gamblers,
and then look at your husband. You won't find but a few
men among this group to equal Leighton. He is a fine young
man, my dear."

"Damn fine," Percy put in.

"And I think, if you search your heart, you'll find that's
something you already know," the duchess said, reaching
out a hand to clasp Melissa's reassuringly. Melissa looked
down at the fingers encircling her own, and felt the duchess
touching a chord deep within her. She battled against it,
unwilling to discover what was hidden there.

"Now, I suspect Cecile's fine hand in this, and I hate to
speak ill of others, but she is a scheming, coldhearted—"

"Immoral," Percy put in.

"Well," the duchess said, letting that pass. "Cecile has
her own reasons for doing things, and they have nothing to
do with you or what Leighton and you have together," she
said.

"If you intend to live in this world," the duchess said,
lifting her hand to gracefully take in the card room full of
London's elite, "then you must learn to ignore what others
do or say. Who cares what the rest of these fools think?" she
asked.

"What do they know? Lady Disdain or Toast of the
Town? They don't know you," she said, so softly and so
seriously that Melissa felt she could hear her heart pounding in the background. "But there is one here who does,"
the duchess said, leaning close. "And though you may hide
it from yourself, it's obvious to me that you love him."

"Of course she loves him! Plain as the nose on her face,"
Sir Percy chimed in.

Melissa, who was staring straight ahead, unable to face
those who were giving her such sage advice, finally looked
up and glanced around the room. Eudora Beauchamp was
right. The men there, although members of the ton, were a
sorry lot, and when she tried to picture being married to any

one of them she felt a pain in her chest. In fact, the thought of being married to anyone but Leighton made her feel hot and cold and panicked.

Then, as if the duchess had conjured up some magic, or perhaps in answer to her own intense longing, Leighton entered the room. He came just inside the doorway and stood talking with his friends, and when Melissa saw him, she realized they were right.

It was like a revelation—even though she had known it all along. Leighton was above the rest of the crowd. He was different. He was better. And she loved him. Perhaps she always had, but she had let her own pride and fear keep her from admitting it. How could she have let a silly bet come between her and her happiness?

With the admission came a great sense of release, and all the feelings Melissa had locked up inside came surging to the surface. She was free to love Leighton, to trust him again, and, even more than that, she was free to be his wife. Once unleashed, her thoughts continued in that vein, and as Melissa sat there watching her husband, her gaze became so heated that she might well have burned a hole right through him.

Melissa wanted him, and the more she looked at him, the more she wanted him. She wanted to feel his hands on her skin, his lips on hers, and his hard body against her own, but most of all she wanted to listen to the words that had so often tempted her. She could hear them now, as though he were whispering them in her ear: "Come to bed, Mel." Her wedding night was long overdue.

Across the room, Leighton chanced to glance at his wife, and only a lifetime of schooled reactions prevented him from appearing astounded when he caught her hot gaze. Hard on the heels of his surprise came his own response—he relaxed. The edginess that had driven him for days disappeared when he saw the look in her eyes, and he smiled at her, returning her invitation with one of his own. He watched her slowly rise from the chair, and although he was aware of the crowd, he had the ridiculous sensation that they were the only two people in the room.

It lasted until Charles opened his mouth. "All right, I'm going," Charles said with a huff.

"No, now it's too late, you idiot," Robert said, swearing softly. "She will never believe you mean it when we're all standing here together. The lady is not stupid. She's sure to think Leighton put you up to it."

"Good. Then let's forget the whole thing," Charles snapped.

"Don't you try to get out of this," Robert warned, his voice low.

Leighton was hardly aware of the squabble. He was admiring the serene grace with which his wife moved. His eyes caressed her slim white neck, her thick, silky hair and those huge, dark eyes as she approached, and when she smiled at him with that exciting mixture of shyness and sensuality that he remembered so well, he had to restrain himself.

"Ah, Lady Sheffield," Robert said. "What a pleasure to see you again."

Considering that the last time he had seen her she was dousing her husband with champagne, even Leighton found Robert's words a little hard to believe, but Melissa received them quite warmly.

"It is a pleasure, Robert." Leighton decided he liked the way the word *pleasure* sounded on her lips. He wanted to hear her say his name, so he stepped toward her and slipped his hand to her back. She leaned against him ever so slightly and looked up at him, her dark eyes warm and inviting. "Leighton," she said huskily. He wondered fleetingly if this was some new torture she had devised for him.

Then Charles stepped forward, looking for all the world as though he were an errant schoolboy forced by the headmaster to recite. "Lady Sheffield," he said, with a smile that looked more like a grimace, "I would like to apologize—" his voice went up an octave at the word "—for the little misunderstanding over my wager with Leighton."

"Oh, no," Melissa said. She leaned forward and placed a slim hand on his arm. "It is I who must apologize to you, Charles," she said softly. "I'm afraid I misunderstood...gentlemanly wagers and all that." She gave him that sincere, dazzling smile that Leighton knew so well but Charles had never seen. "You will forgive me, won't you?"

"I...I..." Charles mumbled. "Of course I do," he said, looking baffled.

"And now, if you gentlemen will please excuse us..." Melissa said. She tucked her hand into Leighton's arm and sent him a smoldering look that was apparent even to his fellows. "We must go," she said in a soft, husky voice that would have been enough to stir the most coldhearted of men.

Leighton smiled down at Melissa, and then glanced fleetingly at his friends. "Good night, gentlemen," he said. He did not linger to hear their goodbyes, but left, his wife at his side, before Robert and Charles could utter a word.

Both men stared after them, Charles with his mouth sagging open. Finally, he turned to Robert, a quizzical look on his face. "About that wager," he asked stupidly. "I did win, didn't I?"

Chapter Twelve

Leighton slid into the carriage beside his wife. She was seated demurely with her hands in her lap and a Kashmir shawl wrapped around her shoulders against the coolness of the night. Although she no longer burned him with her gaze, she did not scoot away to the corner, as had become her habit. He decided this was a good sign.

"Well?" Leighton asked, curious as to the reasons behind his wife's sudden change in behavior. Since their wedding night, she had been cordial but distant; surely something must have triggered her passionate look in the Montagues' card room.

"Well?" Melissa repeated, glancing at him nervously. She looked down, apparently overcome by shyness, although it seemed to Leighton that her gaze lodged on the bulge in his trousers. She raised her eyes again to his, and even by the dim light in the carriage he could see her blushing.

Leighton smiled. "My dear wife," he drawled, casually putting an arm behind her as he leaned back against the cushions. "Am I imagining things, or are you inviting me to take my pleasure with you?"

Melissa turned crimson, and looked down at her lap. "I don't know what you're talking about," she said, but her gaze drifted over to his thigh.

"Then why do you keep looking at my trousers?"

"Well, if you must know," she said with a frown, "I don't care for them at all." She deliberately looked away.

"Shall I take them off, then?" Leighton asked, leaning toward her.

She gasped and laughed—it was a light, musical sound—then eyed him wickedly. "Don't you dare!"

His face was but inches from hers, and he raised a hand to cup her cheek with his palm. "I'll let you do it, then," he said. He paused to take in the exquisite beauty of her features—the flushed cheeks, the wide, dark eyes gazing at him expectantly, and the mouth that was made to be kissed.

"Do what?" she asked breathlessly.

"Take off my trousers," Leighton said as he leaned closer. Her lips parted ever so slightly in unknowing invitation, and he took them with his own. She didn't demur, but responded with the same inexperienced passion that he remembered so well—and had sorely missed. He slid his fingers behind her neck, forcing her closer, as his mouth explored hers, slowly and deeply.

He couldn't get enough of her. He kissed her again and again, tenderly, then fiercely, his tongue delving and joining with hers, her wild response driving him on until he pushed her back against the cushions of the seat, an action that forced him to remember that they were in a moving carriage, not exactly the best place for what he was doing—or what he would like to do.

In a burst of gallantry, Leighton told himself to call a halt and broke off the kiss, but the desire running riot in his blood would not be denied again, and he found himself simply moving to another location. His mouth traveled along her neck while he took in her own sweet, enticing fragrance—lavender from her bath, mixed with just a hint of Mel's own musky scent.

All thoughts of ending this were forgotten. It was all he could do not to tear the clothes from her body. "God, Mel, do you know how long I've waited for this?" he breathed against her ear.

"Yes," she answered softly. "I'm sorry, but I just didn't trust you."

The words were spoken so sincerely that Leighton pulled back to look at her face. Her dark eyes were sultry now in the lantern light, and her parted lips were ripe for another caress. "And now you do?" he asked.

"Maybe," she whispered. She smiled enigmatically, then raised her hand to his cheek, cupping the smooth palm against his skin, and lifted her lips to his.

Melissa might not be ready to give him all of her heart, but she was prepared to offer the rest of her, and that, for now, was enough, Leighton thought as she kissed him with a slow, sure passion that matched his own. When her mouth left his to blaze a tender trail along his neck, he caught his breath.

"God, Mel," he whispered. He slipped the shawl from her shoulders, his fingertips stealing over her silken skin and then into her hair, sending her gem-studded pins scattering onto the seat and to the floor. He paid no heed, but buried his hands in the luxuriant tresses and sought her mouth with his own.

Melissa sighed when his fingers caught her hair, and all her misgivings disappeared with her shawl as it fell to the floor. She slid her hands underneath his coat to clasp his back, disappointed to feel the rough surface of his embroidered waistcoat and longing to feel the texture of his body instead. Her senses were filled with him, and still she wanted more.

"Do you know how long I've waited for this?" Melissa asked him in her turn, and she heard Leighton's slow intake of breath in response. She arched her throat as his warm, wet lips moved down her cheek and along her neck to her ear, and she gasped when she felt his teeth gently nipping her earlobe.

"No," he whispered. "Tell me."

"Forever." She sighed, sliding her arms around his neck.

"I love you," Leighton said against her hair, and he kissed her again, so slowly and with such heat that she felt as though she would melt away. Then his mouth moved down past her shoulder to the very edge of her gown. He paused, and Melissa, anxious to feel his caress again, opened her eyes to meet his gaze.

"For God's sake, Mel, don't ever wear this again," Leighton said, his voice rough with desire. "It's enough to tempt a saint, let alone the rest of us lesser mortals." He slipped the fabric from her breasts, and dropped her chemise, too, revealing her to him in all her glory.

"You are beautiful," he said, looking directly into her eyes. She wanted to glance away, suddenly shy, but his eyes held hers as his hand slid slowly over her flesh. His fingers moved tantalizingly along her skin, cupping and teasing until she could stand it no longer. She broke away from his gaze and leaned her head back, sighing softly.

Neither of them noticed when the carriage stopped in front of Leighton's town house, but suddenly the cushioned seat no longer rose and fell and the rattle and clatter of horses and vehicle disappeared, making the sound of their own rapid breaths seem very loud indeed.

They looked at each other in surprise, then Melissa struggled to sit up and right her clothes. She pulled at her chemise and gown, feeling rather guilty, like a misbehaving tot, though there was surely nothing wrong with dallying with one's own husband in one's own carriage. She lifted a hand to her hair to find it was beyond repair, the gems that had adorned her locks lost somewhere among the cushions or on the floor.

"Ready, my love?" Leighton asked, and Melissa glanced over to see that her husband, having retrieved her shawl and straightened his coat, was preparing to open the door of the carriage.

She nodded, and he exited the carriage swiftly. Melissa sat a moment, alone in the vehicle, nervously clasping her hands. The time spent in the carriage had been so intimate, so heady, and the ending so abrupt, that she felt awkward. She was far too aware of her own recent sighs and whispers to be comfortable, and although she was still dizzy with desire for her husband, this was all so new and overwhelming that she felt unsure of herself.

"Mel?" She could hear his voice outside, deep and concerned. She put her hands upon her gown, took a deep breath, and moved to the door. He was standing outside reaching up for her, his hair golden in the lamplight, his smile deliciously provocative. Melissa smiled back and surrendered herself to him, warming to the feel of his strong hands around her waist, but instead of setting her on the ground, he simply lifted her into his arms.

"Leighton!" she said in a startled voice when he swung an arm under her knees. He paid her no mind, however, and carried her up the steps, cradled in his embrace. When the butler was slow to swing wide the portal of the town house, he kicked it with his foot and shouted, "Open the door, Garrison!"

It swung open immediately, the butler probably having been at the ready when Leighton yelled, and Melissa noted that the poor man looked quite alarmed to see Leighton carrying his wife. She smiled sheepishly at him in an effort to allay his fears, but it did no good. "What's amiss, my lord?" he asked, his face white.

"Not a damn thing," Leighton answered casually, tossing a smile over his shoulder before bounding up the stairs. Melissa, safely ensconced in his arms, shrieked as the banister flew by beside her.

"Put me down," she demanded, but her husband broke his stride only to lean over the balcony and shout one further instruction to his man.

"We don't want to be disturbed," he ordered.

"Yes, my lord," Garrison answered aloud. To himself he muttered a quiet curse, for he had obviously lost another wager to the earl. He turned on his heel, heading below stairs to report this night's work, his only consolation being that he was not alone in his loss. The outcome of several wagers rode on the date of reconciliation between my lord and his lady, and if this night did not constitute a reconciliation, then he did not know what did.

"You might as well have announced to the world what you intend," Melissa said, trying to frown at her husband as he threw open the bedroom door and then kicked it shut with a bang. Hard as she tried, though, she could only smile when he gave her a dimpled grin. He did not look the slightest bit apologetic.

He let her down gradually, her body sliding against his hard frame as her feet found the floor, and it began again—that delicious heat between them that seemed to turn her to jelly. He wasn't even touching her, but the look in his eye made her breathless.

"Now, where were we?" Leighton asked slyly.

"You've forgotten so quickly, have you?" Melissa chided.

"I'm afraid my mind is all a muddle," he answered with a grin. "Perhaps you can refresh my memory."

"Well, if you're no longer interested—" Melissa began, turning away teasingly.

She felt his hand on her immediately, and in one swift movement he scooped her up into his arms and set her upon the enormous bed draped in red velvet. He sent her a smoldering look before gently slipping off her shoes and sliding a hand up her leg from her ankle to her thigh. Melissa shivered, although the fire in the grate gave out ample heat.

She realized suddenly that the fire glowed, lamps were lit, and the bed hangings were drawn back, allowing in an abundance of light, which it appeared her husband had no intention of extinguishing. Although certain she longed for him in a most wanton manner, Melissa would have preferred a shadowy introduction to the delights of his body. "Leighton," she whispered, intent on asking him to darken the room.

"Yes, my love," he said as he leaned close.

"Leighton," she began again, his fingers on her thigh making her lose her train of thought.

"Yes, Mel? I love to hear my name on your lips. Say it again. Say it all night," he urged before taking full possession of her mouth.

Melissa forgot whatever it was she wanted to say in the sweet, hot bliss of his kiss. Still, his name came to her lips. "Leighton," she whispered when his mouth trailed down her throat. She slid her hands around his neck, but her fingers were frustrated by the soft fabric of his coat, and she tugged at the collar.

"Now I remember," he said, easing away from her.

"What?" Melissa asked, leaning up on an elbow and pushing her hair back over a shoulder.

"Where we were," Leighton said, with a wicked grin. "You had an aversion to my trousers. In fact, I'll swear you promised to remove them."

Melissa laughed softly. "All right," she said, and the smile he gave her both encouraged her and made her too weak to move. She suspected that he could leave her prostrate with a single look, but she gamely rose, scooted to the side of the bed, sat back on her heels and inched upward to slip the coat from his shoulders.

Next came his waistcoat, and she had to drop her gaze from his warm hazel eyes to her own fingers to keep from fumbling with the buttons. The cravat was difficult, too, but Leighton didn't bat an eye at her struggles. He appeared to be enjoying himself immensely, and he did his best to stand still, although his hands had a tendency to wander down her back to her derriere.

"I had no idea these were so intricately tied," she whispered as she finally slid the starched silk from his collar. She looked up at him with a nervous smile, and he pulled her to him with a grin. She gasped when she met his hardness.

The shirt was easy, and when it was gone she looked at him a long while, admiring the smooth, clean lines of his shoulders and the golden hairs on his chest. She ran her hands along his arms, arms that were lean but hard with muscle, and thrilled to feel the texture of his skin for the first time.

When Melissa looked up, her husband was no longer smiling, but was gazing at her with such passionate intensity that she felt as though she might lose her very soul in his eyes. She swallowed hard, her eyes held by his as he slowly reached over to lift her gown gently up over her head. He then did the same with her chemise, throwing the flimsy garment aside while his gaze traveled over her body.

Melissa knew what he was waiting for, and she felt hot and breathless, her heart pounding wildly, as she placed her hands on his hips. She paused for a moment, her fingers lingering against his skin before removing his trousers, as promised, and releasing his hard member. Then she drank in every inch of his lean, muscular body as he stood naked before her.

Her experience with the male form was limited to statues—which Gloriana scorned as scandalous—and, in Melissa's judgment, her husband's body did not fall short of that ideal. A desperate longing to feel his living, breathing perfection made her reach out to touch the hair on his chest. She heard him suck in a breath as her fingers lightly traveled down his chest and ribs. When they reached his stomach, he let out a groan and took her in his arms.

His mouth devoured hers as he held her close, her breasts pressing against his chest. He pushed her gently back onto the bed and followed her there, his hands moving over her skin in a tapestry of movements that left her weak and clinging to his arms. His lips burned a path, wet and hot, down her body from her eyelids to her toes.

"Leighton, Leighton," she whispered as her hands moved through his tousled locks.

"Yes, Mel? Yes, oh, yes," he answered as she moved against his hardness. His every movement was slow, gentle, yet intense, and Melissa felt the heat building inside her as he explored every inch of her body. And then there was that look, the one she had never seen before tonight, the one so at odds with the carefree Viscount Sheffield, a gaze so concentrated and so passionate that she wanted to glance away.

He wouldn't let her. "Look at me, Mel," he breathed against her shoulder, and how could she do otherwise? She met those hazel eyes, half fearing that she would lose herself there, and she watched him press his mouth against her breasts, kissing and suckling until she could stand it no longer and closed her eyes in ecstasy.

"Leighton," she whispered, her hands sliding over his shoulders and into his hair. He parted her thighs, his fingers caressing her with tender urgency until she cried out. "Leighton."

"Yes, love, I hear you," he said, his voice cracking.

Melissa arched against him, her nails digging into his skin. "Leighton," she cried. Just when she thought she could stand it no more, he stopped, his fingers replaced by his own hard body moving slowly against her.

"I love you, Mel. I love you," he repeated as he entered her slowly.

Melissa wanted more. "Leighton," she moaned, but he pulled back, ever so slightly.

"Look at me Mel," he whispered.

Melissa complied. His handsome face was intense above her own. His hazel eyes burned with passion—and something more, but she was too dazed by desire to interpret it. Her fingers felt his shoulder muscles moving under his skin, and she exerted a gentle pressure in an effort to pull him close. But Leighton would not move. "Say it, Mel," he said, his breathing quick and ragged.

"What?" Melissa asked urgently, running her hands down his taut body.

"Say you love me," Leighton said.

Melissa's eyes widened in surprise, and she hesitated a moment, a single heartbeat in which the only sound was their own rapid breathing, before replying. "I love you,"

she said, choking back a sob at the words she had so long
denied.

"Hold on, Mel," Leighton urged, and she did, wrapping
her legs around him. He moved then, sliding into her so
deeply and so quickly that she gasped aloud at the sharp
pain, but as the initial shock faded and their bodies moved
in perfect rhythm, Melissa felt the sweet, hot pressure
building again and taking her with it. She clung to Leighton, oblivious of all else, never realizing what she repeated
over and over as her fingers dug into his flesh.

"I love you. I love you. I love you," she cried in complete abandon, as if the words were life itself.

Melissa awoke early to the strange sensation of hair
against her cheek. She rubbed against it, groggily puzzled,
until she came fully awake. She sat up, surprised to find
herself naked, clutched the blanket to her breast, and then
looked down beside her. Light streamed in the windows and
onto the bed, bathing her husband in the warm glow of
morning.

He was beautiful. The man left Brummel, Byron and all
others in the shade, she decided as she looked down at him.
She gazed in amazement at his golden hair, kissed by the sun
and looking perfectly groomed despite a night of tumbling
around in bed. She raised a hand to her own wild locks and
shook her head. There were dandies who would kill for that
hair, she thought with a smile.

His smooth face, always so flawless, sported stubble this
morning, but it did nothing to mar his features. One arm
was flung back where she had nestled against him. The other
rested casually upon his stomach near the blanket that rode
his hips, and Melissa admired his flat stomach and hard
chest, where she had so recently pillowed her head.

As she watched him, silently sleeping, Melissa felt as light
as the dust motes swirling in the sunshine. The burden of
mistrust she had carried since the wedding was gone with the
night, and so was her own struggle with her feelings, a bat-

tle that had begun the moment she had first set eyes upon the viscount. She loved Leighton, she had told him so, and it felt wonderful.

All the pent-up hurts that had prevented her from admitting the truth appeared to have been exorcised like some demon, and now she was free to care. How foolish she had been to give up on love! She blamed Bertie and herself for that decision, finally realizing that she should not have rejected love itself—just Bertie.

Perhaps her youthful infatuation with him had not been love at all, but simply a frustrated rebellion against Gloriana, for she couldn't help comparing Bertie's quick, hard kisses with the hot, lingering ones that had melted her last night. The memory of her husband's hands on her skin and their wild lovemaking made her heart quicken apace, and she colored as she glanced down at Leighton's naked body, longing to repeat it all again.

Melissa reached out a hand and touched a finger to his lips, not quite sure how to wake him or what to say. When she spoke, she said the first words that came to mind. "I love you," she whispered simply.

Leighton's eyes opened immediately, suggesting that he had been awake for some time while she perused his body. Before she could accuse him of anything, however, he rolled her over, pinning her beneath his body as she laughed and shrieked.

"You meant it, then?" he asked her seriously.

Melissa looked up at him in surprise. His gaze was steady, and no dimpled grin cracked his face. Although the question was obviously important to him, Melissa found her mind wandering. She couldn't help noticing that the shadow of a beard made him look even more provocative than he usually did, and she wondered if he could feel the hammering of her heart against his chest.

"Of course I meant it," she answered. "Did you think I didn't?"

He smiled then, ruefully. "Considering the circumstances, I wasn't certain if you were just saying it to please me or not."

Melissa laughed. "You're right. I probably would have said anything at that point," she said, running her hands over his skin and delighting in its texture. "But it just so happens that it's true. I love you," she repeated huskily. "Care for a demonstration?"

Leighton eyed her wickedly. "Why, yes," he said. He leaned his head down to press his lips against her shoulder, his gaze never leaving hers. "Convince me."

Draped in his robe, Leighton sat at a table by the window, picking at the remains of a healthy breakfast while watching his wife sleep. She was exquisite in face and form, and he wished, not for the first time, that he had some skill with the brush so that he could capture her as she was—among the covers, her hair tossed about her and one slender leg lying free. As he looked on, she stirred, rolled lazily to one side, and opened her eyes.

"Sleeping Beauty awakens," Leighton said, raising his teacup in salute.

He could see her close her eyes again and breathe deeply, as if divining the aroma of the hot brew, mingled with that of the breakfast foods and fresh flowers. He was right. "I suppose you've left nothing for me," she said accusingly.

"A crumb or two."

"I cannot believe the amount of food you eat," she said, rolling onto her stomach and propping her chin in her hand to look at him.

"I'm a man of insatiable appetites." Leighton grinned at her wickedly.

"Thank you for the warning," she answered. Far from looking bemused, however, she rose from the bed smiling delightedly.

Leighton's own grin froze at the sight of her slipping naked from the covers. Her dark mane flowed wildly down her back as she moved, the sunlight catching her graceful form; her breasts were full, her waist was narrow, and her hips curved in gentle perfection. Her long legs were slender—and he remembered just how smooth they were as he eyed them. She stood still for a moment, allowing him to appreciate fully every inch of her lovely form, before she put on one of the thin, lace-edged wraps that lay across the bed.

A knock on the door took Leighton's attention. The servants were there to prepare the bath, and a giant brass tub was toted in and filled with hot water while Melissa quietly ate her breakfast. When the tub was filled, Leighton reiterated his standing order. "We don't want to be disturbed," he said.

"Are you going to keep me a prisoner here?" Melissa asked with a smile.

"No, love, I'm going to give you a bath."

Moments later, when Melissa stepped gingerly into the tub, the water was so hot and soothing that she sighed and slid slowly down, leaning back. She looked at her husband, who had pulled a footstool over to sit beside the brass bath. "Now what?" she asked, feeling a little foolish.

"Wet your hair," Leighton said, and she did. When she came up, she caught the scent of her favorite lavender soap as he began to lather her hair. The man definitely thought of everything. But, then, he was as capable in the boudoir as he was everywhere else, she thought, and smiled to herself.

It was a different sensation to feel a man's hands washing her hair. She often had a maid do the task, but Leighton's fingers were stronger and yet gentler as they swirled through her heavy tresses and massaged her scalp. She leaned back her head and sighed again. Surely this was heaven.

When he finished her hair, he began on the rest of her, and Melissa, who had nearly drifted off in the soothing bath, was nudged from her somnolence by the touch of Leighton's soapy fingers smoothly caressing her toes. She soon felt a warmth that did not emanate from the water covering her, and yet was different from the heat of the night's wild lovemaking. This time she was so utterly relaxed that she could barely rouse herself, and yet she felt the now-familiar fire seeping into her body as Leighton's hands moved in a gentle, lingering rhythm up her legs to her thighs and across her stomach.

When Melissa felt his palms smoothly soaping her breasts, she arched upward in the water. She opened her eyes to see that he had tossed the flower from her hair into the water; rose petals floated on the surface, their fragrance mixing with the lavender to produce a heady perfume.

She wanted to say something, but she wasn't quite sure what. Then, above the sound of the water, she heard a knock on the door, followed by Leighton's swearing under his breath. "We are not to be disturbed," he said between gritted teeth.

The butler spoke up bravely. "I'm sorry, my lord, but my lady's mother is here, and she is most insistent."

Melissa finally found her voice. "My mother?" she said with a groan, and slowly slipped below the water.

"Set the earl upon her," Leighton ordered his man. Then he looked at his wife, now rising again to the surface. "Shall I have them put her off or put her out?"

"Neither," Melissa said with a frown. "I'll see her, or I'll never hear the end of it."

She stepped from the bath and leaned over to kiss him softly, trying not to drip upon his robe. "Promise you'll give me a bath again?" she asked huskily.

Leighton nodded mutely, looking so disappointed that she nearly laughed. "You have the rest of my life to give me all the baths you want," she said with a grin before grabbing a towel. "And I'll hold you to it."

Leighton did not appear comforted by her words, but stared glumly at the tub. "The rest of your life," he echoed.

* * *

By the time Melissa reached the massive staircase, she had worked herself up into a righteous fury over her mother's demanding visits. Her plan to tell Gloriana in no uncertain terms that she would no longer tolerate these unannounced calls was foiled, however, when Garrison told her that her mother had left.

"She went for a drive with the earl, my lady," he explained.

"She what?"

Even after Garrison repeated his words, Melissa could not believe them. She rushed back upstairs, surprising her husband and his man, who was slipping on Leighton's coat. She must have looked odd, for Leighton immediately asked her what was wrong.

"Nothing, I suppose," Melissa said uncertainly, leaning back against the door. "My mother's gone."

"Oh?" Leighton adjusted his sleeves without a glance.

"Yes. According to Garrison, she went for a drive with the earl."

Leighton dismissed both his man and the notion that Gloriana and the earl had left together with a wave of his hand. "I don't believe it," he said.

"Well, it's true," Melissa said. A fantastic notion was taking root in her mind, and she couldn't shake it off. "My God, Leighton, you don't suppose he's going to drive her into the Thames, do you?" she asked, half-seriously.

Leighton put his arm around her. "Garrison must be trying to take you in. I'm afraid my father has a tendency to turn even the most normal of households into a hotbed of lunacy."

When summoned, however, Garrison repeated the same phrase to Leighton, and swore it was true. Leighton could only shrug and shake his head, for, as Melissa had discovered, when it came to the earl, no one could be sure of what he would do next.

Melissa, still vaguely troubled about Gloriana, insisted that they take a drive themselves, and a lovely afternoon in the park chased away her worries. The sunshine had drawn lots of others outside, a dazzling array of the ton's sparkling set that kept the viscount and his lady too busy to really look for the earl, and as Melissa assured herself, Gloriana certainly had never required anyone's concern before, and probably didn't now.

They returned home for tea, but, reluctant to quit the sunshine, they took advantage of its last glowing rays by adjourning to the garden. By the time the earl returned home, Melissa was nearly asleep, seated under a tree with one of her books, while Leighton looked over some correspondence Mr. Parker had pressed on him as he passed through the town house.

It was a warm, still day, full of the sweet aroma of summer grass and beds of flowers, and although the sounds of the city were not far away, the walled garden was quiet and peaceful. Melissa nearly jumped out of her skin when the earl's voice boomed out a greeting.

The volume that had been lying open on her chest slipped to her stomach as she leaned up to look at the earl. "My dear, you do look lovely today," he said, nodding and smiling at her as he found a seat. He was obviously in a jovial mood. He could not have been with Gloriana. Melissa leaned back against the tree.

"I missed you at breakfast," the earl said, winking broadly at Leighton, who shot him a quelling glance. Melissa smiled and closed her eyes again.

"You seem to be in fine spirits, Father," Leighton commented.

"I am, I am," the earl said. "I've a plump purse I won last night, which makes me a happy man."

"You've been gambling," Leighton said.

"Now, don't get yourself in a fuss. It's just the results of a few small wagers, judiciously made," the earl said.

"Father, you've got to stop robbing the servants or soon we won't be able to hire anyone," Leighton said dryly.

"Pah, I'm not robbing them. If the idiots want to take a risk with me, well, let them," the earl said, but he sounded disgruntled.

"Well, I don't want to know a thing about it," Leighton said, looking meaningfully at his wife, who opened one eye and smiled lazily at him. "We're going to be leaving for Greyhaven in a few days, Father. You will join us, I assume?"

"Humph. I don't know," the earl hedged.

"We wouldn't think of leaving you here," Leighton's tone left no doubt that he expected the earl to come along.

"Meaning you don't trust me in London," the earl groused. "I've behaved myself, haven't I?" he asked. "Speak up for me, Melissa dear."

"What?" Melissa finally roused herself and sat up. The sun, as it sank lower in the sky, was casting long shadows across the grass.

"I've behaved myself, haven't I, sweetie?" the earl asked, his eyes twinkling.

"Well, I..." Melissa began. She felt awkward. "Of course you have, but we would love for you to come with us," she answered judiciously. "I'm so eager to see Greyhaven. I've heard so much about it."

"I don't doubt it," the earl said, scowling. "Leighton worships the place. It's a nice house, but too quiet. Nothing going on there, though perhaps you two could keep it lively," he said, suddenly grinning.

"We'll try," Leighton said dryly, and Melissa smiled at them both. She decided then and there that she loved both of them just as they were, with their own little flaws and foibles. As she listened to them trade barbs, the fading light of the sunset glowing on their handsome faces, she realized that she was surely the happiest female on earth. The thought made her shiver; it was as though life were not meant to be so easy, and she felt a tiny shadow of foreboding.

"Are you cold, my love?" Leighton asked, and Melissa looked up suddenly, surprised out of her reverie by the sound of his voice.

"Yes," she said softly, convincing herself with the words. Yes, that was it. The cool of the twilight had crept into the garden, giving her a chill. That was all.

Chapter Thirteen

"I'm not going," the earl announced.

Melissa nearly dropped the book she was carrying to look up at her father-in-law, who was poised calmly at the top of the stairway as though making a proclamation from a mountaintop. They were all to leave for Greyhaven in just a few minutes. The trunks were packed, and the new coach, along with two others for servants and baggage, was waiting at the door. The earl's announcement could not have come at a more annoying time.

But it was all the more dramatic for its timing, and the earl was nothing if not dramatic. Melissa glanced across at her husband, standing near her at the bottom of the staircase. He was eyeing his father with an expression that came as close to annoyance as one would ever find on Leighton's handsome features.

"What?" he asked in a weary tone, as though he had played this scene with his father many times.

"I'm not going," the earl repeated.

"And why not, if I may inquire?" Leighton asked patiently.

"Because I'll be bored to death, that's why," the earl barked. "Are you hoping to do me in before my time?"

"Quit shouting the house down and come down, will you?" Leighton asked.

The earl grinned and complied, taking each step with a jaunty air, as though he knew the argument was already won. When he reached the bottom, he slapped his son on the back. "Son, I must congratulate you again on your choice of a bride. She is lovely, and I am glad you are both happy as clams, but, good God—" he cleared his throat "—there is nothing more deadly dull than a pair of love birds.

"It struck me last night," the earl explained, shaking his head rather sadly as he slipped an arm around his son. "Supper was a pleasant enough affair, but hardly worth staying for. And the cards," he said with a shudder. "It takes quite a lot to put me off my game—"

"It takes nothing to put you off your game," Leighton cut in.

The earl gave him a scathing glance, dropped his arm, and turned to Melissa. "As I was saying, it takes quite a lot to put me off my game, but you two," he said, putting a hand to his brow as though pained by the very memory. "How either of you won a hand is beyond me. You never looked at your cards, for God's sake. You were too busy eyeing each other. And the *way* you looked at each other would make a parson run in shame. I'm a man of the world, and I'll tell you—"

"All right, Father. You've made your point," Leighton said, cutting him off with a quelling look. "You don't have to come with us, but I would like a word with you alone in the study before we leave," he added, eyeing his father meaningfully.

"Certainly, my boy," the earl said with a grin. "I'll await you at your leisure."

"I'm sorry that you're not coming with us," Melissa said, smiling sincerely at the earl. "You will be missed."

"God bless you, my dear, but I doubt that," he said. He kissed her soundly, and she threw her arms impulsively around this man who had become so dear to her. Then she watched him swagger off, obviously pleased at having thwarted his son's wishes. She glanced over at Leighton, who shook his head, though he was grinning, too, as he leaned against the banister.

"Are you ready to go?" he asked, stepping toward her.

"Almost," Melissa said. "I'm collecting some books to take along."

"Do you think you'll have time to read them?" Leighton asked, casually running a finger down her cheek.

"Without your father along to chaperon us, probably not," Melissa answered, her voice sinking to a whisper as his thumb traced her lips.

"My advice is this—don't take them," he said softly, his hazel eyes warm with desire. "I have plans for you."

Melissa felt her knees buckle. A few days spent in and out of bed with her husband had not lessened his effect on her. He could still turn her to pudding in an instant, and he proceeded to do just that. He smiled at her intimately, tipped her chin up with his finger, and lowered his mouth to hers.

"Well? Are you coming or not?" the earl bellowed from down the hallway.

Leighton stepped away from her and smiled, both dimples making their appearance as he gazed down at her. "Don't let me forget exactly where we were," he said, before turning away to meet his father in the study.

Melissa smiled as she watched him walk away. She slid the volume that she still clutched in her hands onto a nearby table, then picked it up again. She stood for a moment, undecided, before finally packing it away with a few others. She sent them out to be stowed in the new coach, although she suspected Leighton was right. She probably would not have a chance to open them.

Leighton found his sire in the study, looking pleased with himself and pouring a large glass of brandy. It was not a good sign. Leighton frowned.

"If you've come in some effort to sway me," the earl said with a sidelong glance, "you're wasting your time. I'm not going."

"All right, Father," Leighton said. The last thing he wanted right now was an argument. He finally had his house in order, and he wanted to keep it that way. His father, however, was not known for maintaining an even keel.

The earl turned and raised a bushy eyebrow, as though a little surprised by his son's easy acquiescence. He paused, as if to digest this development. "Then you've come to deliver a last-minute lecture on proper behavior?"

"Would it do any good?" Leighton asked, sliding smoothly into a medallion-backed chair.

"Pah. Not the least bit of good," the earl said, grinning at his son.

"Well, then, I won't waste my breath," Leighton said with a smile of his own. "I will tell you this, though, Father. I won't be ruined again. It may seem as if my wife has unlimited funds, but I know how quickly you can go through money. Don't do it," he warned, giving his father a serious look. "It's my money, and I'll not throw it away on your opera dancers and gambling sprees. I'm leaving Parker here to keep an eye on you, and—"

The earl cut him off with a groan. "Parker!"

"And," Leighton went on, "if I hear even the vaguest rumor of costly behavior on your part, from him or anyone else, I'll hire a group of thugs to pack you up and bring you home."

"Pah!" the earl grunted. "You've nothing to fret about, my boy. I'm a new man, can't you see? Your marriage has turned me around."

Leighton laughed aloud. "You must think my marriage has left me addlepated."

The earl's reply was cut short by a knock on the door. It was Mr. Parker, who looked even unhappier than he had when he was told to watch the earl.

"Well, good traveling, my boy," the earl said, taking the opportunity to make his exit. He smacked Leighton heartily on the arm and was gone in a twinkling, leaving Leighton, who was well used to such tactics, to shake his head.

Short of locking the man up, as Robert had suggested, Leighton could only wait and see if the earl's reasonable behavior continued. If not, he would have to turn to stronger measures. He was not going to lose Greyhaven now that he had saved it; nor was he about to see his new fortune squandered in a few games of cards.

Leighton sighed and turned his attention to his secretary, who stood before him looking extremely agitated. Parker was devoted to his duties, efficient, and could be counted on to rise to nearly every request—no matter how unusual—without batting an eye. He was also sometimes difficult; it was a trait that Leighton had learned to accept, for he genuinely liked his secretary. However, today he was sure that his father already had produced enough theatrics to do for the entire household.

"Yes, Mr. Parker?" Leighton asked.

"It's that Mr. Hornsby," Parker said, in a voice that revealed his feelings in no uncertain terms. Leighton's secretary was plainly outraged.

"The fellow who handles the Hampton businesses?"

"Yes," Parker said. "He won't give me the accounts. He won't even let me look at them. He had the audacity to question our right to see them!" Although Parker had been forced, owing to the earl's penchant for wild behavior, to deal with unscrupulous solicitors, irate creditors and even the occasional unsavory female, this unpleasant encounter had clearly topped all.

"I'm sure it was no fault of yours, Mr. Parker," Leighton said smoothly.

"I'm sorry, my lord, it is just that I am not used to being treated with such...contempt," Parker said. "To be frank, one of the advantages of my position is that a noble name, such as your own, opens many doors. Apparently, titles mean nothing to this fellow, but then he's nothing more than a tradesman," he said, spitting out the word with disgust.

Leighton tried not to smile. Personally, he was grateful to the tradesman—or his partner—for saving Greyhaven with some of that tainted money made in business. "Well, I'll take care of it myself," he said, rising to his feet, "when I return from Greyhaven."

Parker looked positively pickled. Leighton sighed. He knew that look. "Well?" he asked.

"Well," Parker said, "I feel a strong word of support from you would not be amiss, and waiting that long, why, to be frank, my lord, it makes me look bad."

"Oh, for heaven's sake, Parker," Leighton said, but his secretary did not change his expression. Leighton frowned. All was prepared for the trip, and he had an almost physical longing to see his home. But, he decided, this errand shouldn't be a long one. He could pull the accounts, turn them over to Parker and still be on the road in good time. "All right, Parker, I'll take care of it before I leave," he said.

"Thank you, my lord," Parker said, his tightly pursed mouth finally relaxing, his temper soothed. Leighton patted his arm as he passed, and left to break the news to his wife.

Melissa was standing outside talking to Rina, who had never left London before and was looking forward to great adventure on the road. Although loath to disappoint her maid, Melissa tried to discourage her from expecting too much excitement. As far as Melissa was concerned, traveling by coach was a boring way to spend a day.

"Melissa." She turned at the sound of her husband's voice calling her name and amended her own thoughts. Today's trip might be much more entertaining than usual, she reminded herself as she watched Leighton approach. His blond hair was ruffled by the breeze, and he gave her a dazzling, dimpled grin as he stepped close.

Putting a hand on her back, Leighton urged her away from the servants, and they walked together toward the new coach. "I'm sorry I took so long, Mel, but Parker caught me," he said. "Something has come up. Apparently, Hornsby gave Parker some trouble over the books. Hornsby wouldn't let him see them, which has Parker in a lather, so I'll have to run over there today."

Melissa felt the gentle stab of disappointment, but tried not to let it show. "Oh, that's too bad. But we can go at any time," she said.

"No, I want you to go on ahead," Leighton said. "Everything's arranged, and the horses are at the ready. I'll be along just as soon as I can. I'll ride, so I'll probably catch up with you before you get very far," he added.

They had reached the new coach, and Melissa stopped to look at him, surprised that he wanted her to leave without him. She shook her head in disagreement. "I'll wait for you," she said. "Or, better yet, I'll come with you. I'd like an opportunity to talk to Mr. Hornsby without Mother shushing me."

Leighton paused, as if considering the suggestion, then reached a hand to tuck back an errant lock of her hair, a gentle smile tugging at his lips. "If you are bound and determined to accompany me, then you are welcome to, but I would just as soon handle the fellow myself. I don't want him to get the idea that this a social call, or that he can treat my people shabbily."

Melissa frowned. She supposed Leighton was right; she was sure Mr. Hornsby would not want her as witness if Leighton gave him a real set-down. Still, she wasn't eager to spend a few hours alone in the coach, either.

"We could wait to leave tomorrow," Leighton suggested, and Melissa could see the disappointment in his face. She was reminded sharply that his true passion was Greyhaven, and she felt a twinge of jealousy.

"No, no," she said softly. "I know you're eager to get there. I'll go on alone." She was rewarded with a dimpled grin. He was obviously pleased at her decision, and he helped her into the coach, slipping in himself to say good-bye in comparative privacy.

"Soon, my love," Leighton whispered, taking her hands in his and leaning over to kiss her. She melted into the cushions under the ministrations of his skilled fingers on the nape of her neck and his mouth on her own. She was still dazed with desire when he left her, her head back and her eyes closed until she heard the door shut behind him and his shout to the driver.

She poked her head out the window and waved, watching his tall blond form, hand raised in farewell, until she could see him no more. Then, she slipped back against the cushions, trying to fight the odd sense of melancholy that overtook her. Honestly, the man was barely out of her sight, and already she was pining for him!

Melissa shook her head at her own foolishness. Leighton had not married a clinging vine, but rather a woman with a mind of her own. How could she, so fond of her own independence, suddenly become so dependent? Melissa chided herself for her possessiveness, and then, more or less resigned, picked up her books, thankful, after all, that she had packed them.

Although the dusk was gathering outside, the air was still warm, and the rocking of the coach lulled Melissa to sleep. She had dozed for much of the trip, blaming her husband's habit of keeping her up half the night for her daytime tiredness. She had no complaints in that regard, however, and she drifted in and out of dreams with a smile on her face.

It wasn't the pistol shot that woke her, but rather the sudden jolting of the coach. Melissa opened her eyes to twilight, only to be thrown off her seat as the coach slammed into something. She heard the crack of crumbling stone, followed by the odd sensation of being suspended in the air, and she clung to the seat while the floor under her teetered and swayed before finally coming to a stop, one side nearly upended.

Outside, the coachman was shouting above other voices, someone was screaming, and the horses were snorting and stamping in fright. Melissa pulled herself up, inching her way toward the door, which was tilted upward. She stretched out a hand to push it open just as the horses jerked forward, sending her backward as the coach rocked ahead. Then the tongue broke loose, and the carriage, minus the horses, fell through the air, throwing Melissa against the roof.

The blow didn't knock her out, but it hurt, and she cried out, a sound that was drowned out by the splash as the coach hit water. Although her eyes were closed against the pain in her head, she soon felt, rather than saw, the water rushing in around her, and its sharp chill woke her from her stupor.

Melissa opened her eyes, but it made little difference. She was surrounded by darkness, and she knew in an instant that her life was in jeopardy. She took a deep breath, braced herself and kicked open the door, pushing herself into the cold blackness, then up and up for what seemed like forever, before she came gasping to the surface.

Melissa had not been swimming in a long, long time, and she could feel the unfamiliar pull of the current, yet she struggled on, trying to break away. Her throbbing head made it difficult to open her eyes, and when she did she saw only the dark surface of the water or the black shapes of trees against the twilight sky. Blindly she swam toward the shouts she could hear coming from shore, and finally she made it to a rocky shelf, where strong hands pulled her out.

She sputtered, coughed and shivered as someone thumped her on the back, then threw a cloak around her. Her energy spent, she willingly let herself be carried to one of the coaches amid a din of solicitous voices. Melissa was too tired to divine their questions, let alone answer them, so she silently blessed Rina when the maid took control.

Rina shushed the other voices that pressed in upon her, and came straight to the point in her own practical manner. "Do you need a doctor, my lady?" she asked calmly and clearly.

"No," Melissa answered. "I just need to rest, and I'm cold."

"Back away now, all of you," Rina told the coachmen, the postilions and the servants. Melissa was seated in the second coach, where, in privacy, Rina helped her into dry clothing. Wrapped up warmly in a soft shawl and tucked away on the cushioned seat, she began to feel better.

"Here, my lady," Rina said, producing a bit of brandy, presumably from Mr. Morgan's supply. Melissa took a sip and felt the warmth immediately begin seeping into her bones.

"Are we to stop at the next inn or go on ahead?" she heard a voice ask from outside, and a man's grizzled face appeared at the door.

"How far is it to Greyhaven?" Melissa asked weakly.

"An hour, maybe two, my lady," the man answered. "I know the Boar's Head's but a piece down the road."

"How is Henry, the coachman?" Rina asked. She turned to Melissa and explained, "He took a nasty fall when the carriage broke loose."

"Nothing broken, but he's not up to driving, that's for sure."

"Does he need a doctor?" Melissa asked.

"Won't have one," the man snorted.

Melissa smiled. She was of a like mind with Henry in thinking that doctors seemed to cause more problems than they cured. "Then let us go home, to Greyhaven, my man. What is your name?" Melissa asked.

"Bill, my lady," he said, doffing his hat. "I was driving the second coach when the mishap occurred, and I'd like to see nothing like in my life," he said. "As nasty a piece of work as ever I've seen," he added, shaking his head.

"Why is that, Bill?" Melissa asked.

"Well, it looked to me—and Clarence, there, my post boy—that someone purposely shot at the coach," he said. "I thought for sure it was one of those cursed highwaymen, but we never caught sight of anyone."

"Maybe it was," Rina said. "Perhaps the spineless knave ran when he saw the mischief he had caused."

Bill paused to chew on that for a moment. "Maybe," he finally answered. "One guess is as good as another, I always say. But I'll tell you one thing, that bridge railing was mighty quick to go, and so was the tongue."

Even though she was not at her best, Melissa was alert enough to catch an odd tone in his voice, and she looked at him intently. "What are you saying, Bill?"

"I'm not saying nothing, my lady," he said, suddenly looking down at the hat in his hand. Then he glanced nervously over his shoulder. "Just thank be to God, my lady, that you're a swimmer," he said, nodding his head, "or else they'd be searching for you on the bottom." He turned to go, and Melissa could hear him mounting to his perch. She leaned back against the cushions and closed her eyes.

"Don't pay any attention to his nonsense, my lady," Rina said. "Those fellows are always spinning stories just to raise their own hairs. It gave me quite a scare, and that's no mistake, when the horses started going wild after that gunshot, and there you were sitting on the edge of the bridge."

Rina paused as though shuddering at the memory. "But you're safe and sound, with hardly a scratch on you, so there's no sense dwelling on it. And I'm sure that even if you couldn't swim, one of the men would have rescued you," Rina reasoned.

But Melissa had felt the pull of that cold, rushing water, and she knew that Bill was probably right. If she hadn't gotten herself out of that river, she would never have come out alive. Even if one of the men had gone in after her, how soon would he have found the coach, and just how fast could he have pulled her out? Not fast enough, she was certain.

Since none of them were in the water when she dragged herself out, she strongly suspected that none of them could swim. Certainly, she had never imagined that her ability to swim would save her life. And who would have guessed she could swim? Who would have pictured the pampered, wealthy Lady Disdain paddling about in the water? Melissa smiled to herself at the notion. She had never told anyone.

With her eyes still closed and the brandy relaxing her, Melissa let her mind drift away from the coach and her brush with death, back to her youth and those warm afternoons when Gloriana was gone, visiting somewhere, and her father would take her out to the lake. "Now, don't tell your mother," he always said, and it had become a delightful secret to be shared.

"Everyone should know how to swim when they live on an island," Harlan had told her seriously. But then he had rolled onto his back to float, spouting like a whale while she giggled, and Melissa had had the feeling the purpose of the lessons was not solely instructional.

Melissa kept her eyes closed and her thoughts centered in the past as the horses covered the miles to her new home. She did not want to think about the river, or the awful moment before she had kicked the door open—a moment when she had thought the coach might be her tomb. She did not care to hear Rina's practical comments, either, so she remembered her father's face, the hot sun and the cool water, and the secret they had kept, until the coach stopped.

It was dark by then, and Greyhaven looked cold and forbidding under a thin moon veiled by clouds. All her dreams of seeing Leighton's home through his eyes were long gone as she struggled, tired and bedraggled, up the stone stairs.

Melissa took supper in her bed, alone, and sat propped up against the pillows waiting for Leighton until she finally fell asleep. She spent a fitful night in the strange bed, without the warmth of her husband beside her, and dreamed that she was drowning in the river as something cold and dark pulled her down.

When she awoke, still alone, Melissa felt heavy-eyed and as sore as if she had been pummeled by a gang of cutthroats. Every muscle in her body hurt, either from being knocked about in the coach or from the effort of swimming to shore, and on her forehead she sported a large bump, which promised to become quite colorful.

Despite her aches and pains, Melissa felt physically well, and she discarded the idea of a day in bed as too lazy for her taste. She rose and explored her new home. The tour seemed rather forlorn without her husband, but the house was lovely. She noticed, with sadness, the blank spaces on the walls where paintings had been, yet there was still much to admire, especially the lovely room, with its walls, by Verrio, still intact, that Melissa knew must be Leighton's favorite.

Although she decided not to walk the grounds because the day was damp, Melissa did venture outside to view the building and was pleased to find it not at all forbidding by daylight. She breathed a sigh of relief that Leighton's love was not a moldy old castle, but a warm home of recent construction. Not as huge as many of the ton's country homes, Greyhaven was breathtaking because of its beauty. The wings blended seamlessly in with the main block, and the splendid classical facade of stone was lined with rows of windows that flooded the interior with light.

She could see why Leighton loved it. Greyhaven was graceful and tasteful, Melissa decided with a smile, an appropriate home for an art lover. She stood, for a moment, simply admiring the building itself, its lines and its stonework, then went back inside to the Verrio room, where she curled up on the coach to read.

Melissa was still there when Leighton appeared in the doorway, the dust of the road still on his clothes. She looked up and smiled, the sudden burst of joy she felt at the sight of her husband taking her breath away.

He grinned back at her, one dimple creasing his cheek, as he stepped forward. "I didn't mean to rush in on you like this," he said, gesturing toward his travel-stained clothes, "but I couldn't wait to see you."

Melissa, who thought only how wonderful he looked, rose at his words and was in his arms in an instant. "I missed you," she whispered in his ear.

"I missed you, too, Mel," he said softly. "I should have been here yesterday, but I spent half the day chasing after that annoying Hornsby, who has supposedly gone to Scotland for a month, and the rest of the day trying to rein in my father." He sighed, then leaned back to look at her. "You've grown more beautiful," he said.

Melissa laughed. "I doubt that. In fact, it's quite the opposite. Look at my wounds," she said, lifting a lock of hair to expose the large, swollen spot on her brow.

"My God, what happened?" Leighton asked, smoothing aside her hair with his fingers to examine the bruise, which was beginning to discolor and promised to look this bad, or worse, for days.

"Didn't you hear?" Melissa asked.

"Hear what?"

"About the accident we had on the way," she said, realizing that he must have come straight from the stables to find her.

"What kind of accident?" Leighton asked, his brows furrowed in concern.

"Well, the coach fell off a bridge into the Thames," Melissa answered lightly.

"What?" Leighton paused and looked at her, as though unable to believe his ears.

"Not the horses, mind you," Melissa explained. "Just the coach."

"With you inside?" Leighton asked, his voice rising. She felt his hands on her arms, gripping her tightly.

"Well, yes," Melissa said. "The coachman fell, too, but onto the bridge, not into the water."

"Who dragged you out?" Leighton asked, and Melissa heard the catch in his voice.

"No one," Melissa said. "Actually, I did. I managed to get out of the coach and swim to shore, though I hope that some brave soul would have come in after me, had I not."

"You swam to shore?" Leighton asked, eyeing her skeptically.

"And why shouldn't I?" Melissa said haughtily. "I'm not a fashion-loving halfwit like my mother, you know."

"No," Leighton said, smiling at her ire. "You are not. I never believed you were. I did not suspect you were a child of nature, either, but thank God you are. Thank God you can swim," he said, and he pulled her to him. For a long while they stood together, Leighton holding her tightly, stroking her hair as it flowed down her back.

"So you can swim," he whispered. "You are full of surprises, my Mel."

Chapter Fourteen

~~~~~~~~~~~~~~~~~~~~~~~~~

Melissa felt herself being pulled down, dragged under the cold, dark water by something slippery and evil. Struggling to reach the surface for a breath, she gulped for air and choked as she took in liquid instead. Then, as she fought, the water suddenly grew hot, close to boiling, and the creature that grasped her fiery and red, for she could see his form under the shimmering orange surface. She gasped, sat straight up in bed, and saw the demon before her, a mass of flames.

She was awake now, but it was no comfort, for the sight that met her eyes was more horrifying than any nightmare. Fire, real and hot, consumed the bed hangings that surrounded her. Melissa closed her eyes against the heat and smoke, raised one hand to her throat as she coughed, and put the other down beside her, feeling in the darkness for her husband. He was not there.

She screamed then, a cry of pure terror, and opened her eyes wide in the hope that she would see something other than the blaze, but this was reality, not a dream, and she saw, in a split second, that the bed was nearly engulfed. Only one corner hung free of flames, and without a pause, Melissa clutched her mouth and dived for the opening. She went through it and onto the floor, rolling as the acrid smell of her own singed hair entered her nose and the frightening crackle and hiss of the fire filled her ears.

Melissa hugged the floor as if it were a loved one and gulped in the air that lingered there while she looked back at the bed, and as she watched, the wooden structure caved in upon itself. She moaned—it was the only sound her parched throat could make—for she realized that if she had hesitated but one minute longer, she would have been crushed beneath the burning wood.

Melissa felt faint at the thought, but had no desire to be caught by the flames again, so she struggled to roll over and crawl to the door. She raised herself up and pulled on it several times without success. For one brief, horrifying moment, she thought it was locked, but suddenly the handle turned and she was in the cool, dark hallway. She ran then, taking great, glorious breaths that hurt her irritated throat, and tried to scream, but nothing came out. Finally, she heard shouts from down the hall, and her husband's voice calling her name. She fell into his arms and clung to him as he shouted directions to the servants who surrounded them.

"You're all right?" he asked, his voice a tense whisper.

Melissa nodded against his chest, still clutching him, but he pried her arms away, transferring her to Rina, who stood nearby. Melissa whimpered in protest as the maid helped her down the hall. "My lord has to help put the fire out, my lady," Rina explained. In her mind, Melissa understood, but she still longed for Leighton to hold her, and Rina was cold comfort.

"Come downstairs, into the main part of the house, and I'll get you some brandy," the maid said, practical as ever. Brandy. Rina was always filling her with brandy, Melissa thought, a little light-headed, before being deposited in a chair like so much excess baggage. She sat, staring unseeing, until the liquor was placed in her fingers, and then she took a sip, relaxing slightly under its soothing warmth.

"Let me get you a cloak, my lady," Rina said, and Melissa nodded mutely. When Rina left, Melissa glanced up at the main staircase, her eye caught by the massive mirror that graced the entrance of Greyhaven. She got up shakily and walked over to stand before it, extended a hand to touch the cold glass and shuddered.

Her thin, lacy white gown was black and torn and looked utterly indecent. Her hair was sticking out at odd angles and she could see where it had been scorched, leaving short tufts behind. The familiar lump on her forehead was now either smudged with dirt or had started to turn purple. Without a doubt, she had never looked—or smelled—worse.

Melissa put a hand up to her hair in an effort to smooth it, and then closed her eyes at the sight, running her hands futilely over the damaged locks while she tried not to cry. She slipped her hands to her face, choking back a sigh as she fought the tears and won, but when she opened her eyes again, she had great sooty marks on her face. It was not an improvement.

A little strength seemed to ease back into her bones with the brandy and the thought that her husband might need her. Rina returned to slip the cloak around her shoulders, and Melissa realized she had been shivering, her bare feet cold upon the stones of the entrance. She wrapped the mantle around herself and started up the stairs.

"Don't go back that way, my lady. It might be dangerous," Rina cautioned, and Melissa laughed aloud. It was a high, wavering sound.

"After what I've been through, I think I can safely greet any misfortune," she assured her maid. She had only to walk a short way down the hallway, however, before meeting her husband.

"It's out," he said with a grim smile.

"Oh, thank God," Melissa said, throwing her arms around him and resting her head against his chest.

"Yes," Leighton said. "Thank God it was confined to our suite. There's some damage below, of course, but nothing like what could have happened if it had spread." He paused, his chin against her hair, as if in thought. "Were you up reading?"

"No," Melissa said, shuddering at the memory. "I was fast asleep."

"Oh," Leighton said, as though considering her answer. "I thought you might have left a lamp burning by the bed, because the fire appeared to be centered there. Luckily, it didn't spread very far."

"It was centered there. I can attest to that," Melissa said. She leaned her head back to look at him. "Where were you?"

"I was in the study. I couldn't sleep and thought of some things I should be doing," Leighton explained.

"In the middle of the night?"

He shrugged. "I couldn't sleep."

Melissa returned her head to his chest, pressing her cheek against the softness of his robe. "Perhaps you left a lamp burning when you got up," she suggested. Suddenly overwhelmed with fatigue, she stifled a yawn.

"Perhaps," Leighton answered. "Perhaps."

The next day Melissa felt nearly back to normal. Rina had cut her hair quite artfully, snipping out the singed parts, and had pulled back the shorter locks with combs, so that they were hardly noticeable.

Physically, Melissa actually felt better than the day before, when her muscles had ached from the coach mishap. Of course, diving onto the floor had done her no good, but it didn't appear to have created any new bruises. A look at the desolation that had been their room was a sobering sight, and, amazed that she had escaped without burns, Melissa counted herself lucky as she faced the new day.

She was plagued, however, by a lingering sense of foreboding. Misfortunes usually came in threes, she thought superstitiously, then chided herself for crediting such nonsense. Still, she found it difficult to believe that she had nearly lost her life twice in as many days, when nothing untoward had occurred in the previous eighteen years.

Of course, she had never been the adventurous sort, and she could lay the blame upon her bold new ventures into the world, but for the fact that she had not really undertaken anything new, except her marriage. And her mishaps had happened in the tamest of places. She certainly had taken many a coach trip and had slept in many a bed before without incident. It was odd, but she just couldn't shake the eerie apprehension that something was tugging at her thoughts, just out of reach—something she did not want to face.

Leighton was busy directing repairs, and Melissa was restless. She found the house stifling, perhaps because of a lingering feeling that she couldn't get enough air. Although the sky threatened rain, she decided to explore the grounds. She packed a bag with some apples and books and slipped out the back of the house.

Melissa was heartened immediately, and entranced by the surrounding park, which was refreshingly natural. No formal gardens stretched out in endless symmetry, but, like a pastoral painting, the surrounding countryside provided its own delightful view.

Melissa hiked up a green hill behind the house to a lovely open-air pavilion with gleaming white columns that reminded her of a Grecian temple. A wide, cushioned seat curved around a fountain, whose waters were now still, where Pan cavorted with his flute in marble splendor.

It was a charming and peaceful spot, and Melissa sank into the cushions, admiring the beeches and the white and mauve of the candytuft that dotted the hills. Compared to her country home, with its carefully sculptured greenery and perfectly manicured gardens, Greyhaven was wild and free, and Melissa felt a kinship with it.

She drank in fresh air that was scented with wildflowers and the musk of the forest that stood at the rear of the structure, giving it a sense of privacy. From her secluded perch, Melissa could look down upon the house, its roof and chimneys rising below the hill where it was nestled, or she could look elsewhere, to the green hills and tenant fields, crisscrossed with low stone fences, that surrounded her.

It was a beautiful view, and Melissa simply sat quietly for a long while, letting the songs of the birds and the rustle of the leaves envelop her in peace. Then, finally, she opened the bag she had brought along containing her books. She picked up one and leaned back, but suddenly the drama of her Gothic, *The Castle Marne,* seemed distasteful. She chose a different volume, a collection of poems, and was soon nodding over the lines.

She was swimming again, the water cool and refreshing before her, with great lily pads and flower petals that made it resemble her bathwater when Leighton had tossed in the roses. Her hair trailed behind her, and she could hear the gentle trickle of a hidden waterfall. She was gliding through the water, serenely, until she felt it, a familiar tug, pulling at her leg.

The water demon, as Melissa had come to think of him— the cold creature that tried to pull her down and deprive her of breath—clutched at her again, but she fought against him and slipped from his grasp. Then she was thrown back, gasping, as he reared his head. Up from the water he came, billowing smoke, and she coughed and choked, backing away. She wanted to close her eyes against the hideous apparition, but she couldn't. It held her transfixed until, through the swirl of darkness, she saw his face. The shock of it sent her reeling, for no fiery, horned demon was he.

It was Leighton.

Melissa screamed. She sat up so fast that the book fell from her lap, landing with a thud on the tiled floor. For a moment, she had a dizzying feeling of disorientation as she struggled to awaken and recognize her surroundings. Then the pavilion took form around her, peaceful and white and gleaming. She leaned back against a soft cushion, her hand to her throat, and sighed.

It must have rained while she slept, for she could hear the trickle of lingering water from the roof, a reality that had obviously found its way into her nightmare. Melissa watched a drop travel down one of the columns and tried to make sense of the rest of her dream, afraid even to consider what the vision had implied. She *refused* to consider it. It was unthinkable.

Melissa knew, in her heart, that Leighton had nothing to do with her accidents. They were accidents, that was all. It was merely coincidence that Leighton had not been in the coach with her, as planned, when it careened off the bridge, just as it was merely coincidence that Leighton had not been in the bed with her when it turned into an inferno.

Leighton loved her, and she loved him. What reason would he have to kill her? She clenched her hands together tightly in her lap as that old specter she had thought she had vanquished reappeared to answer her question: Money.

Her money. The money that had tempted Bertie. The money that had made her prey to all the fortune hunters and had wed her to one in particular. The money that Leighton had needed to keep his precious home.

No, Melissa told herself. She laughed aloud; it was a cold, forced sound in the stillness. It was too ridiculous. Leighton was a warm, loving, charming man, not a cold-blooded murderer. She shook her head. Reading too many Gothics had fired her own imagination. She picked up *The Castle Marne* and chuckled.

"What's so funny?"

Melissa nearly jumped out of her skin. She had been so deep in contemplation that she had not heard his approach. She glanced up at her husband guiltily, as if he had divined her thoughts.

Something must have shown on her face, for the smile left his features. "What is it, love?" Leighton asked in concerned tones as he stepped up into the pavilion.

"Nothing," Melissa said, too hastily. "You startled me, that was all," she explained. She placed the volume down beside her on the cushions. "I was merely laughing at my book."

Leighton sat down beside her and picked up the discarded volume. "*The Castle Marne.* Hardly a humorous text," he mused with a dimpled grin. "More of a romance, I would imagine. Personally, I don't care for 'em," he added, tossing the book aside.

"Leighton!" Melissa scolded, frowning at him.

"Too dusty and dry—and all those pages," he complained, inching closer to her, and sliding his arm behind her. "I like my romance alive and breathing—or should I say breathless?" he asked, a wicked gleam in his hazel eyes. Melissa couldn't help smiling, her unease slipping away.

"If it's romance you crave, my Mel..." he said softly, and suddenly she was in his arms, her being centered on Leighton as he took her mouth and pulled her close. Back against the cushions they went, barely pausing to breathe as they kissed each other hungrily.

Leighton's hands pulled at her gown, exposing her breasts and running his hands over her flesh until Melissa weakly called his name. "Leighton, not here," she whispered as he loomed above her.

"And why not?" he asked her huskily, his hand moving up under her gown to slide along her thigh. "Who will notice?"

Melissa looked past him, beyond the pavilion, but all she saw were black clouds racing across the sky. In the silence, she heard the rustling of the trees overhead and the first sprinkling of raindrops, and, as if to still her protests, the rain soon formed a curtain around the pavilion, creating a world of privacy for two.

"How did you manage that?" Melissa asked.

Leighton dropped his head to her chest, laughing softly, then raised up to look at her again. "As much as I would like to take credit for the weather, I'm afraid we'll have to put that one down to... romance," he said with a provocative smile.

Melissa felt herself melting at the look in his eyes, at his smooth lips curving gently as he teased her. Her heart raced and her breath came quickly just from watching him. She raised a hand to his jacket and pulled him downward. "Then kiss me," she said.

He did. He kissed her mouth and her shoulders and her breasts while his hands sought her thighs. Melissa struggled with his jacket and shirt, throwing them open to run her hands over the muscles of his bare chest.

A fevered desire was upon them, and neither could wait, Melissa arching against him until his fingers found the secrets underneath her skirts. She pulled at his trousers, even as he caressed her, impatient for his body, as if only the heat of their union could erase any doubts she felt about him. "Leighton, Leighton," she whispered.

"Yes, love," he answered. "Yes," he repeated as he finally slid her gown up to her hips and thrust himself inside her.

"Leighton," she cried aloud, clutching at his shirt. Their remaining clothes only heightened their passion, for the day's love was sweeter for being stolen in the pavilion. Outside, the rain poured down around them, a cool breeze casting a few drops inside the building, yet far from their cushioned bower. Inside, they were bathed in the twilight of the storm until a streak of lighting illuminated their bodies with its eerie glow.

"Yes, Mel, yes," Leighton cried as he pounded into her. They urged each other on until their shouts of joy and release were drowned out by the crash of thunder. Spent, they lay entwined, listening to the rain on the roof.

Melissa surrendered to a sweet lethargy that kept her curled in her husband's arms, savoring the passion they had shared. How could she feel anything but love for the man who was even now whispering how much he cared for her?

She felt guilty and foolish for her suspicions. Although she was sure Leighton had no idea that she doubted him, she still longed to make it up to him, as though she had wronged him with her imaginings. She leaned up and pressed a kiss to his ear.

"Mel," he said, his voice soft and surprised. "I thought you were sleeping." He looked down at her, his hazel eyes tender and his mouth curving gently.

Melissa smiled ruefully. "I can't. Like a little child, I've been plagued with nightmares."

"Oh, my poor Mel," Leighton said, his arms tightening around her. "After what's happened to you in the past few days, it's no wonder you're having bad dreams. First to be thrown in the river, and then nearly burned in your bed," he said, shaking his head, as his hand gently caressed her cheek.

He paused, as though considering these events. "So far, it's been a pretty exciting marriage, I would say," he commented.

"For me, at least," Melissa said. "You missed the dunking and the toasting. I'll try to include you in the next mishap," she promised, matching his light tone.

"Oh, are you planning another?" Leighton asked. "I can't imagine anything worse than what's already happened to you."

"Don't say that," Melissa said, feeling again that dreadful sense of foreboding. "That's just the sort of phrase that tempts fate."

"So, you're superstitious, are you? Well, let's see," Leighton drawled, running a hand down her arm. "You've been through fire and flood. It sounds like some sort of biblical testing to me. What's next? Is it plague or pestilence?"

"For God's sake, don't wish any kind of illness on me," Melissa said with a shudder.

Leighton squeezed her tighter even as he teased her. "All right then. Plague it is. Are you expecting a swarm of locusts? I hardly think that worse than what you've already been through." He chuckled at her serious face until she was shamed out of her bleak mood and smiled back at him.

"That's my Mel, my lovely, precious Mel," Leighton said, and she dismissed all her frightening fantasies at the sound

of his warm words. He leaned down to kiss her and she
melted against him, her eerie disquiet forgotten.

Time slipped by effortlessly as they watched the raindrops and spoke in hushed whispers of their reverence for
the beauty of the land. They ate the apples Melissa had
brought with her, licking the sweet juice from each other's
chins, and lost themselves in long, wet kisses until finally the
rain began to ebb.

"It's barely a drizzle now," Leighton said. "Shall we
make a dash for it?"

Melissa looked down at the long, grassy slope ahead of
them and, without giving a thought to the expensive slip-
pers on her feet, agreed. Together they ran laughing down
the hill, the gentle, cool drops splashing on their faces as
they went, and Melissa felt as fresh as the breeze.

They slipped in the French doors of the library, a little
wet, but none the worse for their outing, and Melissa
thought again just how silly and superstitious she had been.
Leighton was right. What could be worse than what had already happened?

She regretted the thought in an instant, for as soon as they
entered the hallway, it was obvious a plague was upon them.

"Leighton! What a pleasant surprise. Why, we had no
idea you were here," purred the low, sultry voice of the
Duchess of Pontabeigh.

Melissa's mouth nearly dropped open when she saw her.
The duchess, as beautiful as ever, was dressed in the flim-
siest of gowns, in a dazzling green that matched her eyes. It
was cut so low over her breasts that the creamy mounds appeared ready to escape their confinement at any moment.

Melissa glanced down at her own attire in horror. The
simple day dress that she had donned this morning could no
longer be termed presentable. It was rumpled, wrinkled and
spotted with rain from her romp with Leighton. Her slip-
pers were soaking wet and ruined, and only a great amount
of self-discipline prevented her from raising a hand to her

hair, which must look just as bad as the rest of her, if not worse.

"I thought you were to be on a tour of the lakes with your wife. Ah, there she is," Cecile said, as though suddenly discovering Melissa, although she had been standing at Leighton's side. "I couldn't quite see you taking the tour without her," Cecile said with a low laugh.

"Look who's here," she called over her shoulder, and Melissa, to her mortification, realized that more people were going to view her disheveled state.

Leighton must have felt her tense, because he spoke up quickly. "We're not dressed for visitors," he said. "If you'll excuse us for a moment."

"Oh, but I wouldn't hear of it," Cecile said. "Duncan, Salvatore, Charlotte, look who's here." Melissa recognized Leighton's less-than-friendly cousin, Duncan Rhodes, who came ambling out of the salon along with a tall, dark gentleman and a short, round woman. "Cubby," she called then, and to Melissa's surprise, the earl, looking extremely drunk and smiling guiltily, tottered out behind them.

Melissa hadn't seen him in such a state since the night he'd barged into Gloriana's dining hall, and she was saddened by the sight.

"Cubby," Cecile teased, slapping him playfully with her ever-present fan. "You really should have let us know Leighton was here before inviting us down for the house party."

House party? Melissa would have shrieked aloud if she could have found her voice. Unfortunately, the polite dictates of society and years of training from Gloriana told her that one did not run away from one's guests, whether invited or no. She tried to be as graceful as possible in greeting the visitors, while trying not to glance down at her hem to see just how muddy it was.

Duncan Rhodes nodded and gave her a scathing glance, which did not surprise her. Leighton's cousin always looked at her as though she were responsible for causing him indigestion. Melissa presented him with a cool smile. The dark stranger the duchess addressed as Salvatore was Count Viscali, an Italian nobleman most effusive in his greeting, while the other woman, Charlotte Osgood, was more than likely a henwit, since she giggled over the introductions.

Melissa was thankful for the calm demeanor of her polished husband, who smoothly acknowledged the guests and then turned back to the duchess. "Cecile, it is a pleasure to see you, as always," Leighton said lightly, "but you really must excuse us now."

Just grab that fan and crack her over the head with it, Melissa urged silently. *Or maybe I will.*

As if guessing her evil intent, Cecile pounced on Melissa as a cat would a mouse. "But my dear, what has happened to you?" she said. "You look positively frightful. Has Leighton been beating you?" she asked, her voice oozing lurid innuendo. Just in case the others had, by some miracle, missed the evidence of Melissa's woeful state, the duchess pointed her fan directly to the lump on her forehead.

Melissa almost swore aloud, for in all her concern for her appearance she had forgotten the hideous bump, which was by now quite colorful.

"Shame on you, Leighton," Cecile purred, smiling coyly.

"Really, Cecile," Leighton began, but he was cut off by a booming voice.

"What's that?" the earl asked. "My God, sweetie, what happened to you?" He sidled up close to inspect the bruise thoroughly, although Melissa suspected his eyesight was hindered by too much liquor. She stepped back. "Of course he doesn't beat her, do you, Leighton? My God, you better not, or you'll have me to answer to, young man."

Melissa felt hysterical laughter welling up in her throat.

"Father, I'd like to see you in the study immediately, please," Leighton said. "Melissa has had an accident," he explained to the others, "and she needs to rest." Melissa took her opportunity. Without waiting for Cecile to find some other excuse to make her linger, she scooted up the stairs with almost indelicate haste.

"Cecile, if you will please excuse us. I'm sure you can entertain the guests yourself, but then, you've already been doing that, haven't you?" Leighton asked.

Melissa missed the venomous exchange; if she had not, she might have felt a little vindicated. As it was, she felt utterly humiliated, and about as attractive as a leper. All her fears for Leighton's affections returned, and with them, her own feelings of doom. The plague, in the person of the Duchess of Pontabeigh, had arrived on cue, and as far as Melissa was concerned, a swarm of locusts would have been preferable.

Chapter Fifteen

After a long bath, Melissa felt calmer—until Rina informed her that more coaches full of guests, invited by the earl, had arrived. Melissa told herself the news was not necessarily bad, for this second group might well include friends who would provide a welcome escape from the stifling presence of Cecile. When Rina rattled off the list of names, however, Melissa's hopes were dashed; she knew none of the new arrivals.

Melissa longed to strangle the earl, but Greyhaven was still his home, no matter how much he professed to dislike it, and he was entitled to use it as he desired. She tried to push aside the sense of betrayal that his actions engendered, for she knew what he was and she knew that he was not going to change simply because he had developed a fondness for her.

If the earl was to be left unmolested, then, her next wish was to return to the city, take the aborted wedding trip to the Lake District, or travel to any of her mother's country homes—except Lynley Court, where Gloriana was supposed to be staying. She wanted to leave Greyhaven now and stay away until this unplanned party was over. Wish as she might for escape, however, duty decreed that, although she had not invited these people, she must gracefully act as their hostess. To that end, she finally descended below, conferring with the housekeeper and the cook and making arrangements for rooms and meals and divertissements, while retreating further and further into herself.

Feeling like an outsider in her own home was nothing new to Melissa, who had never been at ease with her mother's friends, so she simply slipped back into her role as the Lady Disdain—the better to protect herself from the stings and barbs of Cecile and her cronies. With many years of practice behind her, Melissa took a deep breath and walked out to greet her guests.

It was worse than a plague. After a few hours with her visitors, Melissa felt as though she were undergoing some kind of medieval torture. What she disliked most about the ton was displayed in full force, reminding her of the worst events that her mother had forced her to attend—only this time there was no going home, for the party was in her own house.

No one seemed to be sincere or friendly to Melissa, yet the duchess sparkled like a diamond in the boisterous and fast set. She flirted outrageously with all the men, taking a particular interest in her old beau, Leighton. Every time Cecile sidled up to her husband, practically spilling her breasts into his lap, Melissa didn't know whether to laugh or vomit, but she steered clear, having no desire to be publicly ridiculed again.

Although Melissa found it an easy task to avoid Cecile, one of the other guests, the Italian, Count Viscali, was much more difficult to evade. It seemed that every time she turned around, the count was at her elbow, smiling lasciviously. He was rather handsome in a swarthy sort of way, but not at all to Melissa's liking, and she had no desire for his company. Still, he pressed her, pushing the very boundaries of propriety by constantly kissing her hand, brushing against her, or leaning close. Each time, Melissa coolly yet graciously extricated herself from his presence, and each time he returned.

Finally, Melissa escaped outside, enjoying a breath of the still-damp air while she watched the party through the long windows. Cecile was the center of a large group, and Melissa could not see Leighton. She sighed softly, longing for his presence at her side.

"Ah, she doesn't hold a candle to you, lovely lady. I care not for yellow hair, but crave the dark," a deep voice whispered. Melissa nearly jumped a foot at the sound. "Oh, I've startled you! But that I could take away that moment, for I wish only to give you...pleasure," the count said softly. He was but inches from her in the darkness, and Melissa felt a tremor of trepidation, but she would not let it show. Instead, she put on her coldest face.

"Please go find someone else to compliment," she said stiffly. "I have had enough." Turning to enter the house, she missed the snarl of anger that passed across the count's features, belying his handsome words.

Back inside, Melissa breathed a ragged sigh and put a hand to her throbbing temples, promising herself that she would go to bed soon, even though the night was still young. She could surely not take much more. Spying Leighton in the clutches of several giddy women, with the duchess nowhere in sight, Melissa, bent on making her excuses, took a step toward her husband. She did not get far.

"Ah, the happy little wife," purred a silky voice, and Melissa turned to find the duchess right behind her. "And Leighton is keeping you happy, isn't he?" Cecile asked, pausing to fan herself slowly. "Perhaps with a little love in the pavilion?" She smiled like a cat at Melissa's startled look.

"Oh, yes, I've been there many times," Cecile said smugly. "Why do you think the god of the fountain is Pan?" She laughed musically, but the sound was brittle and sharp to Melissa's ears.

"A word of warning, my dear," the duchess advised, tapping Melissa lightly with her fan. "You may think that you have his full devotion right now, but he will move on. Leighton is a collector. He loves beautiful things, and surrounds himself with objects of art, including women. You are just one in a long line of beauties, and you, too, will be replaced when he searches for a new . . . piece."

Melissa stood staring, dumbfounded by the duchess's little speech. If Cecile was hoping to reduce her rival to tears, she was to be disappointed, for Melissa did not turn pale and run away like a fearful mouse, nor did she rage and tear her hair, another reaction that undoubtedly would have suited the duchess. Instead, Melissa calculated exactly what would deflate the overblown duchess, and then she did it. She laughed.

"You are really something, aren't you?" Melissa asked, and then she laughed again. The sound, sweet and tinkling in the hot air of the salon, drew several glances. It also drew the duchess's ire.

"No one laughs at me," Cecile said, incensed, "especially not you. You'll be sorry you did, I promise you that. I am a powerful woman with many friends and resources that you could not even imagine. You are a nothing, a nobody!" she hissed.

"And you, Your Grace, are a bitch," Melissa retorted before turning on her heel and leaving the astonished duchess behind.

Melissa's head throbbed, and she felt herself shaking in the aftermath of the confrontation with Cecile. She couldn't face Leighton just yet, fearful that her agitation would show or, worse, that some of what Cecile said might be true.

Instead, she escaped out into the entranceway, with its cool stone floor, and slipped into a chair in a dim corner to gather her resources. When she heard footsteps, she felt a twinge of panic, fearful that the count was still pursuing her, for she knew this was not a place to be caught alone. But the steps passed her by, and she relaxed once again.

Her reverie was soon interrupted, though, by more footsteps, and then the sound of conversation not far away. "I'm disappointed in you, Rhodes," said a low voice Melissa did not know. "I came here expecting to play faro, not billiards. I don't trifle with such paltry sums."

"I'm sorry, my lord, but you know that the viscount doesn't approve of the gambling," came the answer, and Melissa recognized the bored accents of Leighton's cousin, Duncan Rhodes. She sat unmoving, listening intently, for she suspected that the two men were up to no good. Why sneak away out into the hallway to speak, unless one did not want to be overheard?

"I don't give a damn about Sheffield. Why is he here? More to the point, why am I here? You're the one who came to me, Rhodes, and to Montgomery and Priestley, I'll warrant, promising some deep play. The earl's got a fat new purse to let, you said. Well, here I am, and I've yet to see a bit of coin worth trifling with."

"I'm sorry, my lord, but I had no idea Sheffield was here. I thought he was off to the lakes with his new bride," Duncan said with a note of disgust.

"Well, he's here, with his bride, and the earl swears he's given up gambling. I'm leaving in the morning, and my guess is the others will, too. Don't bother me again," the voice ordered, and the sound of retreating footsteps echoed down the hallway.

Melissa remained where she was, anger welling up in her chest at what she had just heard. Leighton's cousin was pushing the earl to gamble again, and promising some fancy sharps that they could pick his purse, full of her money!

Perhaps this hideous house party had been Duncan's doing; that alone was enough to make Melissa long to strangle him. She tried to recall all that she had heard about the man, but her information was pitifully slim. He was wealthy, she knew, and Leighton liked him; that thought made her cringe at his betrayal.

If she remembered correctly, Leighton had often sent Duncan to watch over the earl in his absence—apparently a case of the fox guarding the henhouse. In fact, the earl had been in Duncan's keeping when he had rushed home early from the Continent and barged into Gloriana's dining hall to disrupt the wedding plans.

Melissa wondered if Duncan had urged the earl into that debacle, although she couldn't imagine why Duncan would want to interfere with Leighton's engagement. But then, she couldn't imagine why Duncan was setting up the earl now, either. Obviously, he had done it before, too, encouraging the earl's gambling, and presumably his drinking.

Melissa felt her face color with fury at the thought of someone preying on the gentle earl, pushing him to be his worst. And the cost! Melissa had seen the accounts. Just how much money and how many paintings and family heirlooms had been lost because of Duncan's mischief? What on earth was his motive?

Melissa was determined to find out—and to put an end to Duncan's filthy schemes, as well. In this case, knowledge was power. Once his tactics were known, Duncan could no longer operate; his influence would end. Melissa rose from her chair, resolved to find Leighton's cousin immediately. She did not have to look very far.

"I thought you might be asleep," he said.

Melissa nearly jumped from her skin when Duncan stepped out from behind a massive chimneypiece. He walked casually over to the huge mirror that flanked the entrance, and waved a hand at it, as though pointing out a simple problem to a child. When Melissa looked at the spot she saw herself, a shadowy figure, reflected in the glass.

So, he had seen her at some point, but hoped that she had heard nothing. She would have to disabuse him of that notion. "I'm afraid I'm wide awake," Melissa said coolly, walking toward him. She stopped then and paused to assess the man before her. He was tall and gangly, with a shock of dark hair that hung down across his forehead, and he betrayed not a bit of remorse or nervousness. "Why?" Melissa asked.

"I beg your pardon?" Duncan said, eyeing her skeptically.

"Why do you do it—betray your family, sell your own uncle for pieces of silver, sabotage the trust and friendship of a man who likes and respects you—"

Duncan held up a hand to halt her. "Spare me the pious speeches, please. I'm not a villain from one of your Gothics," he said. "All I ever did was give him a little nudge, perhaps provide the means on occasion. The earl did all the gambling—and losing—himself."

"Why?" Melissa repeated, unmoved.

Duncan tossed the lock of hair back in place. "I want the house."

"Greyhaven?" Melissa asked in surprise.

"Yes," he answered simply. "I've always, shall we say, coveted her with a lustful eye. And, I might add, I would have her right now, if it weren't for you."

Melissa was appalled. "You pretend to be Leighton's friend, when all the while you're scheming to rob him of the thing most dear to his heart?" she asked.

"Oh, please," Duncan sniffed. "You know nothing of the world, you poor little thing. Everyone does what he has to do, as does Leighton," he said with an air of dismissal.

"Perhaps I am ignorant, of such deceit and villainy as you are proficient in," Melissa said, lifting her head.

"So superior," Duncan said with a sneer, his hair slipping back down over his forehead. "Look to thine own house, my dear. I've never taken one coin from the earl, but your father won half the man's fortune."

Even the Lady Disdain could not hear that out unmoved, and Melissa gasped, stunned by his words. "I don't believe you," she said simply.

"So Leighton didn't mention it?" Duncan asked. "I've often thought it odd that he chose you, considering all the other women he could have had, but perhaps he has some intricate revenge in mind." He chuckled at his own suggestion.

"I don't believe you," Melissa repeated, her voice rising.

"And I don't care," Duncan said with another toss of his hair. "Believe what you will. And as for your eavesdropping, tell Leighton what you wish. As they say, the game is yours, darling. Play it as you see fit. I'm for more lively company." He gave her a scathing glance and then moved away, reminding her of a snake that had left its poison in her veins.

Melissa tried to shrug away his words, but, as with so many of the bizarre events of the last few days, they wouldn't be so easily shunted aside. They lingered like venom pumping into her heart, and she knew this new suspicion would only add fuel to her nightmares.

She sighed, putting a hand to her head. It was throbbing again, and no wonder. It seemed that everyone was trying to make her believe the worst of her husband. She longed to slip up to bed and close her eyes, but she had one more task ahead of her, so she dropped her hands, raised her chin, and went looking for the earl.

She found him in the billiard room, alone, drunkenly knocking balls one against another. Melissa walked in silently and stood by the table, waiting for him to acknowledge her. He continued his play for some time while she watched, until finally he glanced up long enough to note her presence, then returned to his game.

"If you've come to scold me," he said, "don't bother. I've already scolded myself." He leaned over the table to make his shot, the ball cracking loudly in the silence that followed his words.

"As long as you did a good job," Melissa said softly.

"What?" the earl asked, straightening up to eye her closely.

"At scolding yourself. You did do a thorough job of it, I trust?" she asked, putting on her most serious expression.

The earl gazed at her warmly. "You are a dear, aren't you?" He sat down in a chair, his shoulders slumping. "I guess I'm beyond reformation."

"Oh, I'm sure that's not true," Melissa said, sitting down beside him. "May I speak frankly?" she asked. It was a bad choice of words, for Melissa could almost see the shutters closing around him as he reached out for his drink.

"Go ahead, dear. If I don't like the conversation, I'll walk out on you," he answered brusquely.

Melissa looked down at her hands, firmly clenched together in her lap. Things were going poorly already. She took a deep breath and decided to try anew. "Sir," she began.

"Oh, call me Cubby, for God's sake," the earl said.

"Cubby." Melissa repeated the word with a frown.

"All right, then, call me Cuthbert, if you must," he growled over his glass.

Melissa smiled down at her lap. "Cuthbert, then. I like it," she added. The earl grunted, but Melissa plunged right on with her speech. "By no design of my own, I overheard a conversation of your nephew, Duncan Rhodes, that I found most disturbing. When I confronted him, he admitted that he's been pushing you to gamble in the hope that you'll lose everything and he can buy Greyhaven."

The earl turned pale, took a gulp from his glass, but said nothing. He glanced over at the windows a long while, as if digesting the information. "Ah, the joys of familial devotion," he finally said. If he had been wounded by the news, he didn't show it, but then, Melissa knew how very carefree the Greyhaven men could act. Was he acting?

The earl leaned back in his chair, grunted in disbelief, and then placed a hand over hers. "Well, all's well that end's well, eh?" he asked, eyeing her. "If I hadn't lost my fortune, Leighton wouldn't have married you. And I'm glad he did."

Melissa felt a lump in her throat. For all his bravado and eccentricities, she sensed that the earl was a very lonely man. "So, now, there," he said, patting her clenched hands as if it were she who needed comforting. "You see, it's all been to the good, and what fun I've had losing it, too," he said with a chuckle. "Now, of course, I have endless funds to work with," he added, giving her a wink, "so Duncan's plans will come to naught."

Melissa tried to appear stern at his last words, but she couldn't help the smile that touched her lips. It was banished, though, by the other question that nagged at her. "Did you gamble with my father?" she asked softly.

"I don't know. Who was he?" The earl laughed at his own jest, but stopped when he saw Melissa's sober features. He sighed. "Harlan Hampton. Yes, I lost to him, but don't tell your mother. She would have a fit," the earl said, shaking his head.

He looked down into his glass, his face thoughtful, as though he were remembering. Finally, he spoke. "Your father loved to win," he said. "Power and money were important to him." The earl finished his drink with a swallow. "Sometimes a man doesn't realize what's really important. Believe me, I know," he added sullenly.

"You don't harbor any resentment toward him?" Melissa asked.

The earl laughed. "My God, if that were the case, I'd hate half the people I know," he said. Then, pausing to reconsider he said, "I *do* hate half the people I know, but not necessarily those who have won my money."

Melissa felt relief wash away the poison in her veins. "What of Leighton?" she asked suddenly. "Is he bitter toward those people . . . toward my father?"

"That I can't say. Never speak for another man, my dear, even your son," the earl advised. "Although I can't imagine Leighton bitter about anything, the boy is a man unto himself."

Melissa frowned. The answer was not as clear or as comforting as she would have wished.

The earl set down his empty glass with a grunt. "God, I hate it here," he said. "Wouldn't mind if Duncan took the place, but I suppose Leighton would be heartbroken."

"I can't understand why you don't like it," Melissa said. "It's so beautiful."

"Too many memories," he said softly. "Too many ghosts that won't rest." He sighed and rose from the chair. "Well, I'm away from these shades and back to London, where I'll have a go at reforming myself again," the earl said, disarming Melissa with his dimpled grin.

He was a handsome, charming devil, she thought as he took her hands in his and raised them to his lips, kissing them gallantly. "Now, don't worry your pretty head about my bad habits, my dear. Go on and enjoy the party."

Melissa nearly laughed aloud at his advice. Between that shrew Cecile, the intrigues of cousin Duncan, and the overall nature of her guests, the word *enjoyment* simply did not apply. But now was not the time to rebuke her errant father-in-law for his failings. Melissa leaned up to kiss his cheek instead. "Take care," she whispered.

"I always do, my dear," he said with a wink, "for if I didn't, who would?"

Melissa watched him go, his step jaunty once more, and she was struck again by the realization that the earl was a very lonely man. He needs some grandchildren to play with, she mused, and then checked her own thoughts. She was too unsure of her relationship with her husband to contemplate such things, even though she was well aware that she might be carrying a babe right now. She shoved the idea aside, fearful somehow for such a child's future, and raised a hand again to her painful head.

Melissa decided she had simply had enough for one evening, and, leaving the billiards room, she rejoined the party only long enough to find her husband and give her headache as an excuse for an early good-night.

She slept briefly, grateful that no nightmares haunted her dreams, but awoke when Leighton came to bed, although he slipped in next to her silently. As she lay sleepless beside him, the evening's conversations returned, and with them some nagging questions.

Should she tell Leighton about Duncan, or leave well enough alone, as the earl had put it? Should she share the reason for the earl's distaste for Greyhaven, or did Leighton already know how much his father missed his mother? And what about Cecile's words? Truth to tell, they were the most troublesome and hard to forget.

"Leighton," Melissa said suddenly in the quiet.

"Hmmm?" he answered sleepily.

"Did you ever—" Melissa began, hesitating, half-fearful of the answer. "Did you ever meet anyone in the pavilion before? A lover, I mean?"

Leighton roused himself enough to turn toward her. "No. Mel, my love. What is it?" he asked softly.

"Nothing," Melissa whispered against his chest. "I just hoped that this afternoon was special."

"It was special," he said, lifting her face to his. She nearly lost herself in the shadows of his eyes and in the heady desire of his kiss, but even as she felt her blood sing surrender, another question lingered, unasked. *Did you know my father? Did you hate him for taking the fortune that should have been yours?*

Morning brought no answers. Melissa, tired and cranky from another night with little rest, was not even sure what the questions were any longer, and even if she had known, she would hardly have had the time to ask them. There were menus to be planned and entertainments to be arranged, and Mrs. Osgood couldn't stand the air from the west wing—all that lingering smoke!—and must be moved.

While Melissa was giving a tour of the grounds to several ladies who appeared quite uninterested, the earl abruptly made his departure, leaving the guests he had invited behind. Although Duncan and his sharp friends followed suit, the rest of the party seemed content to stay, much to Melissa's dismay.

By late afternoon, the remaining guests were restless, and Count Viscali suggested an excursion into Haven's End.

Leighton declined to join the group, but once Melissa realized that the count was staying behind, she allowed herself to be cajoled into going along. Her hopes that fresh air and a change of scenery might improve her spirits were soon dashed, however, for she was seated beside the giggling Mrs. Osgood, and the arrangement made the ride to the village seem endless.

Melissa stepped from the coach with relief and, insisting that she had some purchases to make, managed to extricate herself from her fellow travelers. She watched Cecile gather her retinue, then took the opportunity to explore the village herself.

She found a cozy little milliner's shop and bought her mother an outrageous-looking piece adorned with enormous pink bows and sporting a large net veil. She knew Gloriana would love it. For herself, Melissa bought a lovely little straw bonnet, which she decided to wear home; then she considered every other hat in the place, even though she normally hated to pass the time in such a fashion. Finally, she realized that she was hiding in the shop, and, scolding herself for neglecting her duties, she regretfully left the quiet shop and stepped outside.

The sun was already going down, but her group was nowhere in sight. She decided to head toward the coach, and was crossing the street when, above the normal village sounds of talk and clatter and carts, a small boy's voice arose. "My lady, look out!" he yelled.

Melissa turned toward the voice, and where there had been nothing before, a team of horses was now coming straight toward her. They must be runaways, she thought, for they were not even slowing, but then she saw the shadowy figure of a cloaked driver—and she knew. He was trying to kill her.

She didn't run. It was too late for that. She dived out of the way, just as she had thrown herself from the burning bed, rolling as soon as she hit the ground. And as she turned she heard the thunder of the horses, massive beasts that could easily trample her to death with their sharp hooves. They pounded so close that she felt the air move with their passing and was choked by the dust the lethal hooves kicked up as they went by.

She didn't stop rolling until she heard the wheels whirl past her, and then she lay, shivering in the dirt, while shouts of concern and exclamations of outrage rose around her. This time she didn't cry.

"Are you all right, my lady?" asked a man who leaned over her. He was eyeing her warily, as though he expected her to be dead.

"Yes," Melissa answered. She was shaking, but she got to her feet and feebly tried to dust herself off. She was covered from head to foot with grime, of course, and her new hat was smashed beyond recognition. She imagined there would be new bruises to add to her old ones, perhaps even an additional lump for Cecile to taunt her about.

Cecile. As soon as the name came to mind, Melissa looked up, searching for the duchess in the small crowd that was gathering. She finally found her, tall, golden-haired and serene, among the other members of the house party. They were making their way forward, and from their comments, it appeared that they had viewed the incident from farther down the street.

When they approached, Mrs. Osgood took one look at Melissa and fell into a swoon, from which she was revived only by the swift administration of smelling salts. Apparently, Melissa herself was not sufficiently distraught to be offered the remedy. If the situation had not been so grave, she would have laughed aloud, for Mrs. Osgood was found a chair from a nearby bakery, and was seated, and a village child was given a coin to fan her vigorously in the event of any further spells.

Melissa, meanwhile, stood, covered with dust, her gown torn by rocks that had probably cut her legs, as well, and watched the proceedings. "Perhaps you should get her a cup of water, too," Melissa put in. Her suggestion was met with much nodding from Mrs. Osgood, who was obviously too overcome to speak; it was a condition that Melissa could only hope would continue.

Finally, with Mrs. Osgood sufficiently recovered, the group turned its attention to their hostess, but Melissa was hardly overwhelmed by their sympathy. She listened while they all voiced their concern, and she wondered just which of them actually meant their words.

Someone was trying to kill her, and Melissa could ill afford to trust anyone. She looked directly at Cecile, who had said nothing. Was the duchess pleased by the day's work, or disappointed that Melissa was not dead? The green eyes and cat's smile told her nothing, and Melissa felt her emotions rage to the surface so wildly that she had to ball her hands into fists to prevent herself from scratching the woman's eyes out.

"Let's go," Melissa said.

"Well," she heard someone say, "she's a cool one, I'll give her that."

"Probably comes from being in trade," another voice whispered, but Melissa paid no heed. She just wanted to be rid of these people and to think. She had to think.

She ignored Mrs. Osgood's fussing and summoned the coaches, stepping in without ceremony and sitting in a corner. Since she was so dreadfully dirty, no one cared to sit close, and that suited perfectly, but still it was difficult to concentrate, because their voices intruded on her thoughts.

Oh, if only she could think clearly! Motives and suspicions and opportunities all became tangled up in her head, but one thing was obvious. She could no longer continue as she had, or she would not live much longer.

The closer they came to Greyhaven, the more Melissa hoped that Leighton would be there to greet the coach, to help her down, and to chase away the demons that were daunting her. When the door was opened, she realized she was actually holding her breath, her hands tightly gripping

ne another, but when she stepped from the carriage, he was
ot there.

As soon as they walked into the house, the other guests
illed around, and her mishap, along with Mrs. Osgood's
ibsequent collapse, was recounted at length to the group.
eighton, however, was conspicuously absent.

Melissa's heart fell, and she was grateful only that the
ver-present Count Viscali was not at her elbow, offering his
wn type of consolation. She excused herself and ran up-
:airs.

She took a bath, cleansing away the grime of the street,
ut her mind remained dark and muddy. She let Rina dress
er, not knowing quite what else to do, for her heart re-
used to accept the conclusions she had reached, and so
orbade her to act upon them.

She went down to the study, awaiting Leighton's arrival,
nsure what would happen when he did, but knowing that
ie could do nothing without seeing him, if only for the last
me. As she sat at his desk, she looked idly through the
rawers, as if some clue might be waiting there.

Melissa slammed the last one shut when she heard the
oor open, and there he was, as handsome as ever. "Mel,
ly love," said her husband, his voice warm and tender, his
yes caressing her as he walked across the room to take her
i his arms. She returned his embrace, and, to her horror,
ound herself sobbing against the softness of his buff coat.

"Oh, Mel, I'm sorry I wasn't here to meet you, but a few
f us went hunting after you left," he said, his fingers gen-
e against her hair. "My God, I just can't believe what
appened! That someone would drive so carelessly in Ha-
en's End. It's always been such a quiet little place." Melis-
a pulled away, trying not to look disgusted by his words.

"You're tired, Mel, my love. Here, let me get you some
randy," he said, turning away from her to step to the side
ible and pour a glass.

Melissa took it from him and looked down into the am-
er liquid. Brandy. Wasn't it Rina's job to fill her full of the

vile stuff? She stopped with the glass halfway to her lips, then she lowered it slowly, staring at her husband all the while, the blood leaving her face as another suspicion took root.

Of course, she knew that it was Leighton. Who else but her husband would want her dead? She had suspected since the beginning, and now she was sure that he was responsible for all the accidents that had nearly claimed her. Still, it was one thing to know he was trying to kill her and quite another to look at him, face-to-face, while he tried to end her life.

"What is it, Mel?" Leighton asked, his handsome face soft with concern.

"How dare you?" Melissa hissed. "How dare you do this to me? Whatever made you believe that you could do this?"

"What?" Leighton looked disarmingly puzzled.

"I suppose there's a reason for it," Melissa said. She put a hand to her throbbing temples and walked away from him. "I know there's a reason for it, but what?" She spoke to the room at large as she paced, never getting too close to her husband.

"I've heard that the Duke of Pontabeigh is ailing. Is that it? Perhaps he won't live much longer, and you would like to marry his wife. Is that it?" Melissa threw the words across the room at Leighton, who betrayed nothing but confusion and concern. But then, that was his vocation, wasn't it? Hadn't he admitted to her that charm was his stock-in-trade?

"Or is it the grudge you bear my father?" she asked, turning suddenly, her hand still methodically rubbing her forehead. "He took a large portion of your birthright, did he not?"

"What are you talking about?" Leighton asked, his eyes wide. Melissa laughed; it was a cold, eerie sound that seemed to echo in the dim room. "Mel, sit down, love," Leighton said, stepping toward her. "Have a sip of brandy."

"You have it," Melissa said. She stood still for a moment, deathly still, and then tossed the contents of her glass into his face.

Chapter Sixteen

Melissa didn't stop to gather anything from her rooms. She didn't summon Rina. She didn't even take a trunk. She grabbed her cloak, spoke to no one, slipped out of the house through the garden, and walked down to the stables, where she ordered one of the coaches made ready.

"Where is Bill? I want him to drive me," Melissa said, unsure of whom to trust, when she could not even trust her own husband.

"Here I be, my lady," said a voice, and Melissa saw a man raise his hand in the dimness of the stable interior. He was seated at a barrel, where his supper was balanced, and as she watched, he dropped his fork and stood up.

"But, my lady," protested the stablemaster. "It's a bit late to be heading into the village by yourself."

"I won't be alone. Bill will be with me," Melissa said, glancing at the man who came to stand beside her. She recognized the grizzled face as indeed that of Bill, the driver who had first planted the seed of suspicion in her mind after her coach went into the river. *If only I had kept a wary watch after your warning,* she thought. But then, who would believe she could be the object of a killer?

"But, the viscount—" the stablemaster began.

Melissa cut off his words with the cold gaze that had made the Lady Disdain famous. "Are you refusing to obey my wishes?" she asked.

"No, my lady, of course not, but it's dark," the stable-master said, rubbing his nose nervously. "At least take some outriders."

"No, thank you," she said.

"But, my lady!"

Melissa looked at Bill. "You have a post boy?" she asked.

He nodded to her. "Clarence," he yelled, and a scrawny youth scurried from the inner recesses of the stables.

"Yes, sir?"

"Get your jacket on. We're driving the viscountess into Haven's End," Bill said firmly, and Melissa thanked God that someone was helping her. Perhaps she really could escape; she dared to hope, yet her whole body remained taut and tense. Although used to hiding her emotions, Melissa pushed her acting abilities to the limit as she tried to appear outwardly cool while her insides boiled wildly. *Don't look over your shoulder,* she told herself.

The stablemaster shrugged, giving up his objections, and Clarence ran back into the stable. He returned with his livery on; the coat was slightly small for his growing frame.

The coach and horses were duly brought out, while Melissa tried not to look impatient. She turned slightly, so as to have a better view of the house, but saw no one following in her footsteps. And what would she do if he came after her? There was nowhere to run, nowhere to hide.

If he caught her trying to leave, what would he do? A wife was her husband's property to do with as he willed, and Melissa knew that his servants would obey his commands. Even someone like Bill, who appeared sympathetic toward her, could hardly stand against his master. No, Melissa decided, if he found her, Leighton certainly could prevent her from leaving, and then what?

Surely he would not try to kill her here at his home while there were still guests in the house, Melissa thought, but then she scoffed at her hopeful reasoning. Such trifles had not stopped him but a few minutes before. *Nothing will stop him.* The words formed in her mind against her will. Unfortunately, she knew, her husband could and did handle almost anything with ease. Did that skill extend to murdering his wife?

"Are you ready, my lady?" Bill asked.

"Yes," Melissa choked out, her thoughts having carried her away. She straightened her shoulders and eyed the stablemaster. "Thank you, my good man," she said, willing the fellow to stay put and not run to his master with the tale that she was taking an unescorted trip into the village.

She got into the coach and sat back against the cushions, hoping that long service to the eccentric earl had inured the man to odd comings and goings. She knew, too, that some estateholders took their duties very seriously, and were known to go out at night to minister to a sick or troubled tenant. *Let him think that's my mission,* she prayed silently. "Drive on then, Bill," she said aloud, and they were off.

Hardly daring to breathe, Melissa kept still, staring straight ahead, her hands resting on her lap, until she was fairly sure they had left the grounds. Then, giving in to her impulse, she turned around and looked back. Nothing met her eyes but the darkness of the forest and field under a nearly full moon and the points of light that were the windows of Greyhaven, rapidly fading away.

She fought a fleeting desire to fly to Lynley Court and her mother, who suddenly seemed desirable company, but she cast that notion aside. What good would it do her to hide there? Leighton would only find her, sooner or later, and she couldn't spend the rest of her life in fear, wondering where he would strike next.

Melissa waited until she could no longer see the lights of the house before she knocked on the coach roof. The vehicle slowed and stopped, and then Bill's face appeared in the window. "This is not a good place to stop, my lady," he said, eyeing her solemnly.

"There's been a change of plans, Bill," Melissa said as briskly as she could muster. "I've decided to go to London."

Bill's worn features did not even register surprise. Perhaps he had suspected something from the moment she asked for him in the stables, or maybe he simply was used to unorthodox orders from the earl and his family. "Yes, my lady," he answered, without question, and returned to his chore with all speed.

Melissa breathed a sigh of relief. At least she was safe for now. As long as Leighton didn't guess where she was going. As long as he didn't catch up with her. Melissa took a deep, ragged breath and realized that her life was balanced on a very delicate set of circumstances. But for now, she told herself again, she was safe. And if she got to London—when she got to London—she would take care of this business once and for all.

Leighton poured water into a bowl and leaned over to splash his face clean. As he dried off, he wondered how many times his wife planned to douse him with liquor throughout their marriage. He was struck with a sense of déjà vu as he remembered his champagne bath at their wedding reception. Unfortunately, her aim was becoming more lethal; his eyes still stung from the brandy. He tossed down the towel on a nearby table in the room that was now serving as his own and ran a hand through his wet locks. At least, on the previous occasion, Mel had given him a reason for her temper, but today he was utterly in the dark. He could make no sense of the ranting and raving she had done in the study. It reminded him more of his great-aunt Ethel—after she had lost her senses—than of his wife.

The notion made Leighton's brow knot with worry. Mel was definitely not herself. God knew she had been through enough lately to upset anyone, but there was more to it than that. She had been complaining of nightmares and sleeplessness; perhaps she simply needed some rest. Or was it something else entirely?

Leighton had longed for them to spend a quiet fortnight or two at Greyhaven, spending the hours in long walks and lingering lovemaking. Instead, he had dealt with one disaster after another, culminating in this ridiculous house party. His father's behavior in arranging the event was unfortunate, but the earl's behavior usually was. There was little help for that, and one could only become accustomed to it.

Leighton sighed. For once in his life, he actually wanted to leave his treasured home, and if Melissa was not feeling better soon, he would, by God, and the guests be damned! He knew the odd assortment of visitors were an added strain on her. Perhaps he should suggest she return to London alone, although he dreaded the notion. Still, if it would make Melissa happy, he was willing to part with her—but only for a little while.

Unsure of what kind of reception he would receive from his wife, Leighton slowly opened the door to her suite, which adjoined his own. The room was dark.

"Mel?" he asked softly. He raised a hand to the bed curtains, but she was not resting among the pillows. He could hardly believe she was with the guests, for she had not seemed in the mood for superficial social chatter. Then a vision of his tigress attacking Cecile sent him out the door.

It was already rumored that she had called the duchess a bitch to her face. The tale had made Leighton smile. He liked to see his wife stand up for herself—as long as he was not the object of her fury, he noted ruefully. But, considering the state Melissa had been in when she'd left him, she could be capable of a lot more than name-calling, and the prospect of the duchess and his viscountess brawling like schoolboys was not very pleasing.

When he did not find Melissa with Cecile or the other guests, however, Leighton pinned his hopes on the Verrio room. It was empty. He looked in the billiard room and the state drawing room, where most of the house party could be found, but Melissa was not there. His concern was growing. Where could she be? And why? Her behavior had been so agitated that he kept turning ideas over in his head, trying to find a reason for the change.

And then it struck him. Leighton stopped in his steps as he realized that Melissa might have hit her head in the cart mishap this evening. Some sort of injury, unnoticeable to the eye, might be causing her odd behavior. Leighton felt a tingle of fear now, stronger and sharper than his simple concern. A doctor. He should send for one, just in case. But what good would a physician be when he had no patient?

Leighton forced his thoughts back in order as he continued his search. Stepping into the library, he paused just a moment, his eyes scanning the room for his wife. She was not to be seen.

"Sheffield, my dear fellow." Leighton nearly swore under his breath at the sound of Mr. Nearhood calling him. Leighton turned, a cordial expression on his face, and nodded his head in acknowledgment; if the man so much as lifted that idiotic quizzing glass of his... "Your bride is quite the cool one, I must say," Nearhood commented.

"Oh?" Leighton said, giving the man a daunting glance. "What could you possibly mean?"

Nearhood had the grace to look a little flustered. "I simply meant that she barely blinked an eye today when she was nearly run down. Got up, dusted herself off, and that was that," Nearhood said with a wave of his hand.

"Perhaps too much is being made of this incident," Leighton said, couching his remarks with a smile. "I know

how you fellows like a good story, but let's not blow it out
of proportion.''

"Out of proportion?'' Nearhood scoffed. ''My God,
man, the woman was but a hairsbreadth from death. That
fellow meant to kill her, make no mistake about it. I swear,
there's not a safe place on the roads today, what with the
highwaymen, the wild bucks who race everywhere, the lu-
natics who set out to trample people for the sheer sport of
it,'' he said, shivering visibly at the frightful condition of the
country's roadways.

Leighton's head jerked up, and his eyes narrowed. ''What
do you mean, the fellow meant to kill her? I thought it was
an accident.''

Nearhood snorted loudly. ''A hooded driver making
straight for her? Not bloody likely. A boy shouted her a
warning, and the horses never swerved from her direction.''

"But Cecile said . . .'' Leighton's words trailed off as he
recognized his folly in listening to anything from that quarter.

"What's that?'' Nearhood asked. He was looking pleased
with himself for being the first to give the viscount the true
tale. When Leighton didn't answer him, he continued the
conversation himself. ''I suppose your wife made light of it
to you, too, just as she did to us, but don't you believe a
word of it,'' he advised familiarly.

"What?'' Leighton asked, suddenly turning his attention toward his guest again. ''Oh, yes, certainly,'' he answered, still distracted, his thoughts racing ahead. ''Excuse
me, Nearhood, but I must look in on her. You understand.''

"Yes, of course,'' Nearhood answered, smiling smugly.

Leighton left the room and bounded back up the stairs,
still reeling from the shock of the truth. Someone was trying to kill his wife. It was all coming together now. Someone had tried to run her down today, and she had narrowly

escaped death, just as she had escaped the fire and had nearly drowned. Leighton slapped himself in the forehead at his own slow-wittedness; he felt more like beating his head against the wall.

"You idiot, you stupid idiot," he ranted as he flung open the doors to their rooms. Melissa had not returned, and Leighton felt the slam of panic in his chest for the first time in his life. Whoever it was who wanted his wife dead might be succeeding this very minute.

Leighton didn't stand on ceremony. He shouted for the housekeeper. "Have you seen my wife?" he bellowed, his heart hammering in his chest, as he met her on the stairs.

"No, my lord, I've been—"

Leighton cut her off. "Tell the staff I want her found. Drop everything else. Do you understand?"

"Yes, my lord," Mrs. Hawkins said. Red-faced and flustered, she obviously didn't understand the reasons for such a request, nor why her normally gentle employer was growling wildly.

Leighton took no time to explain, nor did he care what she thought, as long as she did his bidding. He didn't stand idly by, but set out through the house, cursing it for being too large as he went through all the rooms, heedless of who was occupying them. He had made it through the main section and the damaged wing, even searching the dark ruins of their former rooms, when they found him.

One of the footmen hailed him, and the stablemaster was dragging his feet behind, sending Leighton's heart plummeting to the floor. From the looks on their faces he thought for one desperate moment that they had found her body, and he couldn't stand it. "Well?" he snapped.

"It appears, my lord," said the footman, "that my lady has gone to the village."

"What?" Leighton asked.

"I'm sorry, my lord, it's my fault," said the stablemaster. "I tried to stop her, but, my lord, she does have a mind of her own," he explained. He eyed Leighton nervously, as though his words might draw forth another outburst. "When I saw that she was sure and determined to go, my lord, I tried to get her to take some outriders along, but she would have none of it."

Leighton's voice, which neither man had heretofore heard rise above a cordial shout, could only be described as a roar. "You let her go out at night alone?"

The stablemaster stepped back, rubbing his nose. "Well, she wasn't entirely alone, my lord. Bill was driving her, and he took his post boy along with him."

"A driver and a post boy?" *Someone's trying to kill her, for God's sake!* Leighton wanted to scream, but he wasn't sure who the culprit was, and until he did, he thought it best to keep his own counsel. If the villain did not pursue her, the road to the village was usually safe. Nevertheless, a driver and a post boy would offer no protection against any serious threat, as Leighton well knew. The road to the village... Why had she gone the village? "The village. You're sure she said the village?" Leighton asked.

"Yes, my lord."

Leighton ran a hand through his hair. "All right, then, saddle my horse. I'll go after them."

"Yes, my lord," said the stablemaster, and he backed away, apparently glad to have his job still. The footman followed quickly behind, looking none too eager to be left alone with his master when he was in such a taking.

Leighton paid no attention, but ran to grab a cloak and his pistols. Why the village? Had Mel gone looking for some clue, or to confront her tormentor? No answers came to him, only more questions, and one loomed above all others. Would he know if he looked his enemy in the face? Leighton had his suspicions, but he was not sure, so he flew from the house alone, hoping against hope that he could reach Melissa before another attempt was made to take her life.

* * *

Melissa leaned her head back against the cushions and closed her eyes, exhausted. With no strength left to fight them, visions of her husband flitted through her mind. She recalled with vivid clarity the moment she had first seen him, really seen him, at Almack's. She remembered sparring with him and laughing with him and longing for him. She remembered the night in the pantry when she had nearly torn his clothes from his body, and she recalled their wedding night, full of recriminations and grief.

She sobbed aloud. If Leighton were going to do this, planned to do it all along, why couldn't he have done it then, before she had fallen so desperately in love with him? Instead, he had waited until she had begged for the pleasures he could give her, waited until she had lost herself in his eyes, and now the knowledge of what he had attempted was like a knife plunging into her heart.

When, among all their moments together, had Leighton decided to kill her? Melissa wondered suddenly if she had given him the idea. She had once asked him, half-seriously, if he thought the earl would drive Gloriana to her death in the Thames, and then, a few days later, she had been driven into the river herself. Had he taken her suggestion to heart, or was it only another bizarre coincidence in the incredible chain of events that had followed?

Melissa shook her head, trying to cast away the memories that haunted her, and finally, overcome by their poignancy, she sobbed herself to sleep.

By the time they arrived in London, her tears were done, and Melissa swore silently to herself that she had just spent the last drop she ever would on Viscount Sheffield. He was worth no more. Feeling a measure of her strength return, she directed Bill to Gloriana's town house.

Melissa expected the place to be quiet, since Gloriana usually took her most favored servants along with her to Lynley, leaving only a skeleton staff behind. Still, Melissa was surprised at how long she stood at the door, awaiting a response. Finally, a young maid whom she didn't recognize opened the door.

"Yes?" she said pertly.

"I'm Mrs. Hampton's daughter," Melissa explained as she walked in. "I've decided to stay here for a few days. Is there someone I can send to get my trunks?" Having left Greyhaven with nothing but the clothes on her back, Melissa wanted some of her things brought from Leighton's town house, but she had no intention of going there herself ever again.

Before the maid could answer, Melissa heard steps on the stairs and glanced up in surprise to see her mother. "Melissa," Gloriana said, looking startled.

"Mother," Melissa said with a nod. "I thought you'd gone to Lynley."

"Yes, I was prepared to go, but then, additional engagements... were pressed upon me," Gloriana said, her voice sounding decidedly odd.

"Mother? Are you all right?" Melissa asked, stepping closer. As Gloriana came down the steps, Melissa could see that her mother's cheeks were flushed. In fact, the woman was positively blooming with health. Perhaps Gloriana fared much better on her own, when she wasn't butting heads constantly with her daughter, Melissa thought guiltily.

"I'm fine," Gloriana answered, putting a hand up to her hair to pat it into place. "But what are you doing here? Where is Leighton?"

Melissa sighed. She had so hoped to avoid this. With Gloriana at Lynley Court, Melissa could have taken care of matters without interference, or could at least have begun her task, but now... She could hardly fob her mother off with excuses, only to have her learn the truth from one of her gossipy friends. There was nothing for it but to tell Gloriana what she intended to do.

Melissa looked significantly at the maid waiting patiently at her side, surprised that her mother had forgotten the girl's presence. "Shall we go into the green drawing room?" Melissa asked.

"Why, yes, of course," Gloriana answered. Her voice was so uneven that Melissa glanced back curiously, just in time to see her mother gaze anxiously up at the staircase. Melissa eyed her mother in amazement. For want of a better word, Gloriana looked flustered, and Gloriana *never* looked flustered. Melissa shook her head as if she were dreaming, then followed her mother into the green drawing room.

Gloriana actually sat down instead of pacing the room in her usual manner, and Melissa took a position next to her on the enormous couch. She was surprised at how calm she felt. For once, her hands were resting comfortable at her sides. After four attempts on her life, arguing with Gloriana seemed tame, if not positively homey.

"Mother, I'm sorry to bother you, but I need to stay here for a few days."

"Why? Where's Leighton?" Gloriana asked again. She was wearing her hair differently, Melissa noticed. The curls were softer, and made her look much younger.

"He's staying at Greyhaven," Melissa answered.

"You've had another falling-out," Gloriana said accusingly.

Well, I suppose you could call it that, Melissa thought, but she said nothing while trying to choose her words. This was not going to be easy.

Gloriana took her silence as confirmation of her suspicions and launched into a lecture. "Melissa, you cannot come running home to me every time you have an argument. Really, I'm surprised at you," she added, regaining some of her old huffiness. "A woman belongs with her husband, for good or ill."

Melissa held up her hand, calling a halt to what looked to be a lengthy reproof, for she knew it was best to get the deed over with as quickly as possible. "But he won't be my husband much longer, Mother," she said softly. "I'm going to get a divorce."

Melissa braced herself for the tirade that would surely ensue, but Gloriana's short gasp was followed by silence, the news apparently striking her dumb. Her eyes widened in horror, and her rosy cheeks turned as pale as a ghost's, but it was her speechless state that began to concern Melissa. Although she had spent a lifetime fetching hartshorn for her supposedly delicate mother, she was totally unprepared for what happened next. Stolid Gloriana, the terror of six households, fainted dead away.

Melissa gasped in astonishment, rushed to her mother's side and took her hands. "Mother, Mother," she cried frantically, but Gloriana remained still. Finally, Melissa dropped her mother's hands to run for the smelling salts.

It took her forever to find a servant and even longer to revive Gloriana, and all the while Melissa was plagued by guilt, because her words had sent her mother into a swoon. Melissa wanted to wring her hands in frustration, for since her arrival nothing had gone as she anticipated.

Melissa had expected her mother to chastise, harangue and threaten her—in short, to treat Melissa as she always had—but perhaps this news was just too jarring. After all, what could be worse for a woman who valued social position above all else than a daughter who was divorced, a pariah, a social outcast?

When Gloriana's eyes fluttered open again, she still didn't scold. In fact, she nearly pleaded with her daughter. "A divorce," she whispered, aghast. "Melissa, you cannot mean it! Have you lost your mind? Marriage is not always what we expect," she said, "but it is for life." Gloriana pursed her lips in her familiar fashion, reassuring Melissa that the woman before her was, indeed, her mother, and not some impostor. "A woman's lot is to persevere."

Oh, Mother, if you only knew how I'm persevering, Melissa thought.

Gloriana took a deep breath and changed her tactics. "Of course, you may stay here, as long as you wish, but promise me you will abandon this ridiculous notion of yours."

"I can't, Mother," Melissa said, softly but firmly.

Gloriana looked positively panicked. "Promise me you will think about it," she said.

Melissa glanced down at the floor, then nodded slowly to calm her mother for the moment. "All right," she said.

Gloriana's bosom heaved with her relief, and Melissa's heart went out to her mother, for this once-formidable woman was practically reduced to begging because of Leighton's treachery. The effects of his actions would be felt by so many, and for most, the results would be devastating.

"Well," Gloriana said briskly, regaining some of her color. "Since you are here, you may come with me to an engagement tonight."

Melissa would have laughed, if she could have mustered up a smile. "Mother, the last thing I want to do is to go to one of your parties," she said.

"It's not one of my parties," Gloriana retorted, looking a little annoyed. "It's being given by a friend of your father's," she said, as though the very words were rather unsavory. Gloriana seemed to be returning to her old self, Melissa noted. Obviously, the change of topic did her good. "An invitation I felt obliged to accept," she explained.

"No matter, Mother, I'm just not up to it," Melissa said.

"Of course, you know best, but since you are a guest in his household, I naturally assumed you would feel obligated to accompany me...." Gloriana broke off and eyed Melissa meaningfully.

Good God, how many strings was she going to attach to her town house, Melissa thought irritably. *If I had the money, I'd go to an inn.* "All right, Mother, but I can't promise to stay long. I've spent the night in the coach, and I'm exhausted.''

"Of course, Melissa dear. I'll send for some things from the town house, but I'm sure you left a few gowns here that would be suitable. I'll have the maid lay something out, and I'll have a light dinner sent up, for I'm sure the supper will be late."

Melissa listened to Gloriana's now-crisp voice as she took control, organizing the evening and arranging her daughter's life, but for once Melissa did not argue. She leaned back her head, sighed and nodded, grateful to simply follow along.

Leighton rode from Greyhaven as though the very hounds of hell were at his heels, but his efforts yielded him nothing. The village was quiet, the coach nowhere to be found. No guests were lodged at the inn, and those locals who were left in the common room after an evening of drinking reported no traffic along the main street. Haven's End offered no clues. Of course, Melissa might have been waylaid along the road, but Leighton had seen nothing to suggest that.

What now? He could go back to Greyhaven and send out all his men, trusting them to search for her in the dark. Leighton closed his eyes as he envisioned her body, far off the road, perhaps in a creek or under some bush, where it wouldn't be found for days.

He rejected that vivid image, however, forcing himself to believe that she was still alive. But where? He slammed a palm against his forehead in frustration. Think, Leighton! His normally clear mind was not working at its best. If she had not gone to the village, where had she gone? And why tell the stablemaster she was going to the village? Leighton ran a hand through his hair, then paused as he was struck by a thought. Why say she was going to the village...unless she wished to throw her pursuer off the track.

Leighton realized with a start that his wife must be aware of her own danger and was trying to escape it. No. He shook his head, mentally tossing that theory aside, for if Melissa knew someone was trying to kill her, why hadn't she come to him? The answer came to him in the space of a heartbeat, and he let out an anguished groan.

He knew with blinding certainty that Melissa had purposely fled Greyhaven, and he knew why she had left without telling him. Her words in the study came back to him, the strange rambling about her father and Cecile making sense in a sickening way.

Leighton raised his head with a sigh. He even understood now why Melissa had tossed the brandy in his face. She had thought he was poisoning her.

Chapter Seventeen

Determined not to be late, Melissa dressed hurriedly and rushed out into the hallway, only to nearly crash into Gloriana. "Oh, excuse me, Mother," Melissa said, falling in beside her.

"There is no need for haste, Melissa. It is unladylike and unseemly," Gloriana said, pursing her lips reprovingly.

Melissa tried to nod soberly instead of chuckling at the now familiar axiom. She suddenly remembered the hat she had purchased for her mother and wished she had brought it. Melissa smiled to herself. There was nothing like adversity to drive a family together, she thought wryly.

As they walked together, Melissa kept glancing over at her mother, surprised at how nice Gloriana looked. Melissa couldn't decide whether the change owed itself to her own reassessment of her mother or some unexplained phenomenon. She noted that Gloriana was dressed more austerely than usual, and that in itself was a definite improvement. Although the blush gown she wore was heavily embroidered, it lacked the ribbons and bows that always made her look rather like an overdressed doll, and Melissa admired the change.

It was unusual, too, to see Gloriana without her usual retinue of servants. No throng of maids and footmen awaited them at the doorway, only a single manservant who did double duty by escorting them from the house to the carriage. In fact, the town house seemed positively deserted, and Melissa felt a twinge of foreboding before she stepped out the door. It was probably just her own nervousness, but, for once, she was glad to be going to a party and leaving the silent rooms behind.

Her unease followed her outside, however, and Melissa looked over her shoulder, still not sure of her safety. Her eyes searched the shadows until she was seated inside the carriage; then she raised a hand to the curtained window to peek out, her face pale and still as a statue carved from stone. No one lingered in the lamplight, but the darkness held many hiding places. She sighed softly, uncertain even of what she was looking for.

How long would it take Leighton to discover that she was gone? To guess she was at the town house and come looking for her? Melissa knew she would not feel really safe until she was divorced—and Leighton no longer had reason to kill her.

Melissa soon regretted her decision to attend the party, for even the eerie silence of the town house seemed preferable to this superficial socializing. She tried to smile, but the events of the past few days had worn away her composure, and she couldn't help glancing over her shoulder, as if she expected Leighton to come barging in to drag her off, even though he had no way of finding out where she was.

Her fellow guests were an odd mix, and Melissa could not find anyone she cared to talk to. Those who were "in trade" gave her the cold shoulder, because Gloriana had never let her associate with them. Undoubtedly, they saw her as a snob, like her mother, and Melissa was too tired to try to prove them wrong.

Those who sported bluer blood commented coyly, and none too discreetly, on the absence of her husband. Mrs. Marchant's remark, uttered just loud enough for Melissa to overhear, was typical. "I told you it wasn't a love match. A question of money that's all it was," the matron sniffed.

Melissa felt like turning around and confirming the rumor to the old crow's face. *No, it certainly wasn't a love match,* she thought bitterly. *Anything but that.*

Melissa slipped away from the crowd and caught herself frowning at thin air when she heard a friendly greeting behind her. "Why, if it isn't Harlan's lovely daughter," said a familiar voice, and Melissa turned to see her father's old business partner.

"Mr. Hornsby, what a lovely surprise," Melissa said with sincerity as the older gentleman took her hand in his own and patted it gently. She felt herself relax at the pleasure of seeing a kind face.

"Leighton said you were in Scotland," Melissa said, but she wondered immediately if Leighton had lied about that, too. She now considered every word her husband had ever spoken suspect, every action, every look, every touch....

"Yes, I was," Hornsby said. "I hope nothing's amiss?" he asked quietly, his brows furrowed with concern.

"No, I—" Melissa closed her mouth upon her own words. Although she longed to unburden herself to her father's friend and partner, she knew it was better not to mention the divorce until she presented her petition.

She hesitated then, unsure of what to say, as she recalled the reason Leighton had wanted to see her father's partner. Just what of the supposed discrepancies in Mr. Hornsby's reports? Melissa nearly laughed. It all seemed so long ago and so unimportant now. As the earl said, why quibble over money when you have so much? And perhaps Leighton had been lying about that, too, to appease her.

"I know he wanted to talk to you," Melissa simply said, "but he's not here tonight, so business will have to wait. I must admit I'm glad to see you out enjoying yourself, instead of working too hard," she added with a smile.

Hornsby laughed; it was a dry, soft sound. "All work and no play makes for a dull life, eh?" he asked. "But I see you have no refreshment, my child. Let me get you a lemonade."

"Thank you. That would be nice," Melissa said. She waited patiently for his return, glad to have found someone whom she could talk to without fear of repercussions. She couldn't imagine Mr. Hornsby ever gossiping, let alone saying anything bad about her. Her father's partner had always treated her like a favored niece.

"Here you are, my dear," he said, handing her a glass. "I've some for myself, too. These summer gatherings are always hot and thirsty."

Melissa nodded and drank some of the lemonade. "I imagine the weather in Scotland was cooler."

"Yes, it was lovely. You must have Leighton take you there. It is especially beautiful this time of year. Lovely woodlands, heathered moors, and the red grouse are numerous."

"You were hunting, then?" Melissa asked politely. Hornsby nodded, and the conversation turned toward game and sporting. Melissa was content to listen to his soft voice, kind and calming, but soon she couldn't stop herself from yawning.

"I'm afraid I'm boring you, my dear," Hornsby said with a self-deprecating smile.

"Oh, no, not at all," Melissa said. "I assure you, my rudeness is due to my own lack of sleep."

"Now, my dear, don't stand on ceremony with me. If you're tired, let me take you home," Hornsby said.

Melissa was sorely tempted. Hours in the coach had done her little good, following as it did many fitful, dream-filled nights, and she realized that she hadn't slept well in weeks. All those nights that she lay awake, worried or fearful of nightmares, were finally catching up with her, for she could hardly keep her eyes open. Melissa drank her lemonade, hoping that it might revive her, but, cool and soothing as it was, it did not have the power to refresh her exhausted mind and body.

"I was going to leave soon anyway. Why don't you let me see you home?" Hornsby asked, and his kind words finally swayed her.

"All right, Mr. Hornsby, thank you. That would be nice," Melissa said.

"Here, sit down, my dear, and I'll just tell your mother that you're leaving with me," he said, giving her a sage nod, "so she won't worry."

Melissa smiled her agreement and sank into the chair to wait. She was so comfortable there, though, that she resented his quick return and his gentle urging to the coach. She struggled to stay alert during the ride home, reminding herself that a lady never rested in public, or so Gloriana said. *But as soon as I get home,* she promised herself, *I'll drop into bed with my clothes on.*

Melissa was to be disappointed, however, for when they arrived at Gloriana's town house, Hornsby insisted on seeing her in, and Melissa could hardly refuse, when he was so concerned about her well-being. And, of course, politeness dictated that she invite him to sit down. Although she expected him to refuse, he accepted quite cordially, forcing her to call for refreshments.

She sank down onto a couch in the main drawing room, feeling suddenly dizzy, and put a hand to her forehead. When she closed her eyes, the room swam sickeningly around her.

"I'm sorry, my dear. I suppose I put a little too much sleeping powder in your lemonade," Mr. Hornsby said softly.

If you knew what I'd been through lately, you wouldn't make jokes like that, Melissa thought. She tried to smile at the jest, but her head slipped back against the back of the couch.

"I really must apologize for all the trouble I've caused you," Mr. Hornsby said. "I had hoped to finish this all neatly and quickly, but it is so difficult to find good help, for any line of business." Hornsby spoke so sincerely that Melissa forced her eyes open in confusion.

It was no use. Her vision swam until her eyes closed again, but still she heard him speaking. "The ineptness of the fellows I hired to do a simple job has forced me to take matters into my own hands," he explained. "And now, I, too, am not mastering my task very well. I was afraid you were not going to make it home."

Melissa felt her heart sluggishly coming to life in her chest as his words sank in and her confusion turned to panic. "You've poisoned me!" she croaked out hoarsely.

"Oh, my, no. That would never do," Hornsby said. "This must look like an accident, my dear. We don't want the authorities sniffing around suspiciously. Of course, if you and your husband had cooperated and drowned in the Thames, we would have been spared this distressing conversation," he noted. "But, your husband *would* decide to stay home at the last minute, wouldn't he? And who would have thought that such a delicate child could swim so well?"

Melissa didn't answer. She could no longer move her lips.

"Definitely too much sleeping powder. And it worked so fast! But I'm not at all familiar with this sort of thing," Hornsby said with a sigh. "And, of course, the fire was a dreadful failure. After that, I decided to forget about trying to take care of both of you at once. Much too difficult.

"You will appreciate, my dear, that after careful consideration, I then decided to eliminate you first, to spare you the grief of losing your husband. Let him do the mourning—until his time also comes." Hornsby paused, and Melissa wondered painfully if he was getting up. If he rose to kill her now, she did not have the strength to struggle. But he only sighed again.

"I do regret this, you know. Your father and I were well suited for business. We were equally ruthless," he said, as Melissa strained to listen. "But, after his death, I resented giving away his share. I found better uses for the money. No one would have known, but your husband, greedy fortune hunter that he is, had to nose around.

"Ah, well, I can see that you are asleep, my dear. Forgive me, but I'm afraid I must deal you a fatal blow with something. This must look like a robbery, you see. All the tongues will wag, and the neighbors will be outraged, and everyone will clamor for protection from the low thieves that plague these fine neighborhoods. And no one will be the wiser."

Melissa was past hearing him now; his voice was nothing more than a soft buzz in her ears as she drifted off to sleep. She never heard what happened next. She never saw Hornsby grab a hefty candlestick from the mantelpiece, never saw him raise his hand for the fatal blow.

But someone else did, and he heaved himself forward with a strength he hadn't known in years, his hand reaching for the wrist that wielded the deadly brass. The Earl of Greyhaven grunted as his fingers closed on the assailant's arm, but Hornsby's looks were deceiving. Although small, he was wiry and fast, while the earl carried too many extra pounds and much too much extra liquor.

He had been drinking again, and in his inebriated state had wandered here to look for her. Finding the place deserted, the earl had decided to wait, eventually doing so horizontally. He had been sleeping off the drink in the far recesses of the room when he had heard voices, and, rousing himself sufficiently to listen, he had soon been tensely alert.

Hornsby's words had wakened him, but unfortunately they could not dissolve the liquor that lingered in his body. Even one of the city's wild young bucks could hardly be expected to put away several bottles and then fight a good fight; at his age, the earl was definitely not up to it. But he gave the best he could, using his larger size to his advantage. A younger man than Hornsby would have ended it immediately; as it was, the two men strained together, neither gaining the upper hand.

Unable to wrest the candlestick from the smaller man, the earl finally threw himself at the fellow. They both hit the floor, as did the candlestick, rolling harmlessly away while the struggle continued. It was a valiant effort on the earl's part, but it failed nonetheless, for the fall made him dizzy and his reflexes were too slow.

Hornsby managed to get his hands around the earl's neck and apply pressure, sending the earl's world swimming. Already savoring his victory, Hornsby let go with one hand to reach for the fallen candlestick. It was a mistake, for the earl threw himself upon the smaller man again, breaking Hornsby's hold and landing him a facer. Hornsby was only stunned, though, and wriggled away to stand up, blood oozing from his mouth, the candlestick clutched in his fist.

"Really, my lord, I'm sorry to involve you in this," Hornsby said, panting for breath, "but I've a fortune to protect. I had hoped that your son would simply take his bridal booty at face value and be happy, but he had to meddle in my affairs. I can't have that," the man added, raising his arm to strike. "My apologies."

They both heard the knocking, faint but clear, from the front of the townhouse, and the sound made Hornsby pause. The earl seized that moment, kicking out with his foot and knocking Hornsby off balance while noise erupted from the front of the house. The candlestick swung down with deadly force then, and the earl felt the blow as it slammed into his head. Help, in the form of whoever was breaking down the doors, was a little too late in arriving.

The first thing Leighton saw as he entered the room was his wife, slumped lifeless on the coach, and his world stood still. Then he saw her chest rise slowly and fall back gently in even breaths, and the earth swung back into motion as he rushed toward her, reaching out for her, his own breath painful in a throat tight with emotion. Through the corner of his eye, he saw a man slipping through the rear windows, but he did not change his course. Pursuit would have to wait until he made sure Melissa was all right.

"Mel, Mel," Leighton said softly, as he sank to his knees beside her. He grasped her hands in his own, then touched her face lovingly. "Mel," he said, more insistently now, but she gave no reply.

Leighton could find no sign of injury upon her; she must be in a faint—or drugged. He rose to get some water to try to revive her—and smelling salts, he thought suddenly, certain that Mrs. Hampton's household would have them somewhere. But where? He cursed the lack of servants, and abandoned all thoughts of pursuing the retreating figure.

Leighton glanced around the room for any signs the man had left behind, and it was then that he saw his father lying in a pool of blood. He took a step forward, his heart racketing in his chest again. He heard pounding on the doors of the town house, but ignored it to kneel beside the earl.

His sire still breathed, too, but a large gash on his head was still bleeding. Leighton took out a handkerchief and wrapped the wound tightly as the doors slammed.

"Mary! Mary! You lazy girl, where are you?" shouted Gloriana. "What's happened here?"

Leighton had never thought he would be glad to see his mother-in-law, but he could use her help tonight. He dared not leave his father, yet he was still worried about Melissa. Torn between his two patients, he would welcome Gloriana's clearheaded assistance.

"In here, Mrs. Hampton, quickly," he called.

"Leighton?" Gloriana asked as she stepped into the room. Leighton saw her take in the scene in a glance: Melissa propped, unmoving, on the couch, and he himself bending over his father, who was awash with blood. Before

e could utter a word in explanation, however, the stoical
Gloriana let out a scream that would have wakened the
ead, and she kept it up while Leighton, unable to move
rom his father, tried to calm her down.

Although perhaps ineffective against the dead, her vio-
ent shrieks did manage to rouse her daughter, and Leigh-
on nearly shouted himself when he saw Melissa stir. She
moved but a little, yet it was enough to arrest Gloriana's at-
ention—and halt her wails.

"Melissa?" she said hoarsely, sinking down beside her
daughter. "Melissa? Are you all right?" she asked, surpris-
ng Leighton with the tenderness in her voice.

He was not close enough to catch the whispered reply, but
e heard Gloriana's sigh of relief. "Mel, did he poison
ou?" Leighton asked.

"Who? Cuthbert?" Gloriana screeched, raising her head
o glare at Leighton in outrage.

Leighton shook his head impatiently. "Did Hornsby poi-
on you, Mel?" he asked again.

"Hornsby?" Gloriana repeated in shocked tones.

"For God's sake, pay attention," Leighton said to his
mother-in-law, waving a hand toward Melissa, whose eyes
had fluttered open. To his surprise, instead of arguing or
aking exception to his language, Gloriana did as he bid,
eaning close to listen to her daughter's answer.

"No, only sleeping powder," Gloriana told Leighton, re-
eating Melissa's words.

"Still, we'll have a physician look at her, too," Leighton
aid as he checked the bandage on his father. "Too much
leeping powder can be just as fatal as poison." The bleed-
ng had stopped, so he loosened the wrap a little. "I've
topped the bleeding, but I hesitate to leave him. You'll have
o go for help," Leighton said.

"I'll do no such thing," Gloriana said, her voice crack-
ng. "You go for help. I'll stay with your father," she ex-
lained. Then she stood up, walked to the earl, and dropped

to her knees beside him. While Leighton and his wife
watched in amazement, the oh-so-prim and always perfectly groomed Gloriana picked up the earl's bloodied head
and cradled it in her lap.

"Cuthbert, you old fool," she said quietly. "What have
you done now?"

Leighton stayed only long enough to hear the earl moan;
it was a good sign that he would be fine. Then he stood up
to send for a physician. He wondered if the earl would faint
dead away again at the sight of Gloriana's face bending over
his own, but the woman looked as though she would not
budge from his side, so Leighton could only hope for the
best.

He stopped for a moment to gaze at his wife, who had
closed her eyes again, and he felt a tug on his heart. "I'm
going to get help, Mel," he said, the words sticking in his
throat. There was so much else he longed to say, but he
dared not linger. "I love you," he whispered, pressing a
fleeting kiss to her forehead before leaving her side.

Melissa rolled over in bed and snuggled against her pillow, sighing serenely. Her eyes fluttered open to see the afternoon sun peeking through her curtains. She smiled, rolled
onto her back and stretched luxuriously. For the first time
in weeks, she had slept peacefully and soundly.

Wrapped up in one of her old nightgowns, tucked into the
bed she had slept in for many years, and aided by the lingering effects of a sleeping draft, she had spent the night
dead to the world and free of the hideous nightmares that
had plagued her. No more water demon.

Melissa sat straight up in bed. Leighton! She vaguely remembered apologizing to her husband last night, when he
was trying to make her drink innumerable cups of tea, but
how could she adequately express her regret at thinking him
a killer? Recalling the warmth of his arms as he carried her

to bed, and her whispered pleas for him to love her, she
lored with embarrassment.

"Tomorrow," he had said, "when you're awake." But
1at if he was only putting her off? What if she had totally
enated him with her accusations? All her old doubts came
shing back, along with a desperate determination to re-
lve any estrangement. She loved Leighton, now more than
er, and she was going to get him back, even if she had to
ovel.

Anxious to look her best, Melissa picked up the bell to
1g for her maid, but then she realized that, unless Glo-
1na had retained someone this morning, the house was
arly devoid of help. The main body of servants were pre-
mably still at Lynley, while several of those who re-
ained had conveniently disappeared last night, un-
ubtedly bribed by Hornsby.

Left to her own devices, Melissa dragged out the brass tub
herself and ran down to the kitchen to heat some water.
fter lugging the water upstairs a couple of times, she had
new appreciation for the servants. Her bath was not as
xurious as usual, but her own efforts somehow contrib-
ed to her sense of well-being when she finished. She
essed herself, enjoying the peace and quiet to be had
thout a maid's constant chatter, and was rather pleased
th the results.

She even turned around in front of the mirror, admiring
e bright green gown that had been tucked away in a
ardrobe since she had bought it a year before. Gloriana
d claimed it was too glaring, but Melissa thought the color
ite flattering. It was cut low over her breasts, and was a
tle tighter than when she had had it made—all points in
r favor if she was trying to woo her husband, she de-
led. Refusing to fuss with her hair, she let it fall unfash-
nably down her back to her waist, knowing full well that
is just the way that Leighton liked it.

Finally, Melissa presented herself downstairs, only to discover that the husband she was so eager to see was gone, the new maid she questioned claiming to have no knowledge of him or his whereabouts.

Disappointed, Melissa made her way to the main drawing room, where she found the earl ensconced on a coach, his head neatly wrapped in a clean bandage. His feet were propped up on Gloriana's best tufted footstool, and around him were littered the remains of some sort of repast, along with several newspapers.

Melissa couldn't decide what was more astonishing, the sight of such a mess in Gloriana's best receiving room, or the fact that Gloriana, sitting nearby with some needlework, was allowing it. Melissa decided it was best not to comment. Instead, she smiled at their greetings and walked over to the earl.

"My hero," she said, leaning over to place a kiss on his cheek. "How are you feeling today?"

"Fine, perfectly fine," he said. "I haven't been cosseted like this in years," he added with a grin, nodding at Gloriana.

"The doctor said he needed rest, so he's staying right here for now," Gloriana explained.

"Pah! Do you think that idiot knows anything? He wanted to bleed me, for God's sake," the earl groused. "Don't know a man who wasn't worse off for a doctor's care," he concluded. "And, anyway, he didn't mean for me not to move from this exact spot. How long would you have me stay here?" the earl asked, winking broadly at Gloriana.

"Until you are quite well," she responded stiffly.

The earl winked at Melissa then. "It'll be a long convalescence."

Gloriana frowned, and Melissa tried not to laugh. "Where's Leighton?" she asked.

"He's gone after Hornsby," the earl said, his face darkening. "He went out last night, as soon as you were in bed, ough I knew he'd never catch up with him. He sent word und this morning that he and Parker were at the villain's fice, going through what's left."

"He's escaped, then?" Melissa asked.

"Yes," the earl answered. "Leighton sent the authorities ter him, but my guess is the fellow's on his way to some reign port by now."

Gloriana sniffed. "A fine place for the man. I never liked m."

The earl grunted in response. "A better place would be tting in prison or hanging from the nearest tree for what tried to do to our Melissa." The earl gave Gloriana a lelong glance. "Well, enough of that for now. Here, ar," he said to Melissa. "Have a muffin. Blueberry, mind u, and simply the best I've ever tasted."

Melissa reached out for one in disbelief. Here was Glo- na with a man she had always claimed to despise, yet she as urging him to lie about on the couch, toss his newspa- rs around and scatter crumbs all over the best furniture. was beyond anything. "So you found a new cook?" elissa asked, taking a bite.

"Pah! Who needs one, when we've the finest cook in all gland right here?" the earl asked, nudging Melissa. Your mother made those."

Melissa swallowed so hard that a blueberry nearly stuck her throat, and she had to put a hand to her mouth to event crumbs from spewing out in a decidedly unladylike shion. She hardly dared to meet Gloriana's eyes, and when e did, she received a glare that warned her she had better t choke on the homemade delicacies. "When I was a girl, learned all the duties of running a household," Glo- na said, insinuating by her tone that her daughter's edu- tion had been woefully lax.

"They are delicious, Mother," Melissa said with a smile
"It appears you've been keeping some secrets from me." /
her words, the earl's cup clattered into his saucer, and Gl
riana blushed furiously.

Melissa was saved from Gloriana's retort by Leighton
entrance. Looking up at him, she was suddenly struck b
how very handsome he was. He was dressed in a claret coa
that fitted nicely along his wide shoulders, and buff breeche
that hugged his thighs before disappearing into his to
boots. As usual, he moved with a lithe grace, his golden ha
shining. No one would ever have suspected that he had no
closed his eyes throughout the night.

"At last, my boy," the earl said. He moved as if to ris
from his couch, but Gloriana held out a hand, warning hi
against it. The earl sank back into the cushions, lookin
thoroughly chastised, but clearly loving every minute of i
"You must be exhausted after chasing after that devil a
night," he said to Leighton.

"I'm fine," his son answered casually. "How are yo
feeling?"

"Never better," the earl said with a grin. "I'm bein
thoroughly cosseted, thanks to Gloriana and your lovel
wife."

Leighton smiled at Melissa, a warm light in his eyes as h
stepped toward her. "And you, my love? How are you?"

Melissa returned his tender gaze. "I'm happy to be aliv
thanks to my hero, here," she said, patting the earl, wh
grinned even wider. "I'm glad it's all over. It is over, isn't i
Leighton?" she asked, a worried frown puckering her for
head. She didn't really care to see Hornsby swinging fro
the nearest tree, as the earl had suggested, but she didn
fancy having to spend the rest of her life looking over he
shoulder, either.

Leighton sat on the edge of her chair, one muscular le
swinging free. "Well, yes and no," he said, running a han
through his dusty locks. "You're safe now, and I'm su

at's been everyone's main concern," he said firmly, ancing around the room as if daring anyone to disagree.

His odd tone caught the attention of their parents, for Melissa saw Gloriana look up sharply from her needlework, and the earl shifted his weight, as if he were uncomfortable. "Well, let's have it," the older man said.

"Hornsby's gone," Leighton said simply. "My guess is at he's out of the country by now. I've done what I can to e him tracked down, but he's a clever character, and he bviously planned his escape carefully—and for some me." When Melissa gazed at him wide-eyed, Leighton ressured her. "You don't have to worry about him anymore, ve. He won't be back."

"How do you know that?" Gloriana asked sharply.

"Because he has no reason to return. He took everything ith him. Everything," Leighton said.

"What do you mean?" Gloriana asked, her face turning ale. She looked over at the earl helplessly. "What does he ean, Cuthbert?"

"He means, my dear," the earl drawled, crossing his legs, that we are all done up, out at the heels, in dun territory." loriana gasped aloud, and Melissa shot her a glance, ondering if she would need the hartshorn.

"You mean we're penniless, all of us?" Melissa asked.

"No, we're not exactly penniless," Leighton said. "Mrs. ampton has her estates, I have the town house, and Faer has Greyhaven, and there are a few things Hornsby left ehind."

"Besides debts?" the earl asked sardonically.

"It will take some time to sort it out," Leighton said. loriana looked ill. "Mrs. Hampton, it's not as bad as it ounds. We won't be tossed into debtor's prison or into the reets. It's just a change of circumstances."

"Well put, my boy," the earl said with a grin. "We're well miliar with that, aren't we?" Although Leighton did not turn the smile, the earl's spirits seemed high. "Well, I, for

one, see this as a rare opportunity," he said. "I've bee
wanting to ask a certain lady to marry me, but I didn't wa
to appear to be a fortune hunter." He winked at Meliss;
who stared at him stupidly.

"Oh, Cuthbert," Gloriana said, dabbing at her eyes wit
her handkerchief.

Melissa, still confused, glanced up at Leighton, wh
looked as if he were struggling with a bad bout of indiges
tion.

"Yes, oh, yes, I would thank heaven to have your com
fort during these trying times," Gloriana said, reaching he
hand out to the earl.

Feeling as though she were at a play that was too com
plex for her understanding, Melissa turned to her husban
questioningly. "I believe," Leighton whispered, leanin
close, "that you're about to become my stepsister."

"What?" asked Melissa, her voice rising with her sur
prise. Her eyes flew from her husband back to her mothe
just in time to see that lady disappear into the earl's em
brace. Only Leighton's presence on the side of her cha
prevented her from falling out of it.

"I don't believe it," Melissa whispered dazedly to he
husband. Leaving the lovebirds in the drawing room, the
had repaired to the blue parlor to marvel over the ton's un
likeliest couple.

Leighton shrugged casually, his usual carefree smile re
placing any surprise he might have felt over the union o
their parents. "Who can predict where Cupid's arrow wi
strike?" he asked.

"Arrow? He must have used a sledgehammer to get thos
two together," Melissa said. Leighton laughed, and th
sound melted her heart, bringing her mind back to her ow
brush with Cupid. She threw her arms around her hus
band, hugging his chest in a tight embrace.

Leighton smiled against her hair, warmed by her sponta-neous show of affection, but the next thing he knew she was weeping into his waistcoat. He gently smoothed the ma-hogany locks back from her forehead. "What is it, Mel?"

"How can you ever forgive me, Leighton, for all the hor-rible things I thought? All the terrible things I said—" Melissa's words ended in a sob. She raised her head to look at him, her dark eyes brimming with tears. "I didn't want to believe that you were a killer. I tried not to believe it, but there were so many coincidences."

For the first time, Leighton realized how much his wife had gone through, beyond the physical threats. She had had to struggle through the emotional upheaval, as well, with no one to turn to, no one to trust, and her suspicions tearing her in two. "My poor Mel," he whispered, his arms tightening around her.

"Can you forgive me?" she asked again.

"If you can forgive me for being so busy with business and Greyhaven that I didn't realize what was happening until it was nearly too late," Leighton answered, his own voice thick with feeling. "Having won you, I was blind to the need to keep you," he whispered.

"It's not your fault. I didn't realize someone was trying kill me until it was nearly too late myself," Melissa said, shivering in his arms. Then she looked up at him, a warm smile on her lips. "Thank you, Leighton."

"For what?" he asked, softly cupping her face with his hand.

"For choosing me from all the heiresses you could have married, for loving me, for never giving up on me, and for never, ever, letting me turn you away."

Leighton grinned away her praise as he rubbed his thumb along a teardrop that trailed down her cheek. "Why let a little matter of suspicion of murder stand between us?"

Melissa laughed and turned her head to kiss the finger that traveled along her skin. "I do believe I am the luckiest of females," she said. "It seems that, no matter what I do, you won't leave me."

"Let's not test the point," Leighton warned, gently outlining her full lip. "And you may not think you're so lucky when we have to move in with our parents."

Melissa's eyes flew up to his, wide with surprise. "Are things that bad?"

Leighton sighed, letting his hand fall from her face. "We'll see, but I imagine we'll have to sell all the property and get something a little smaller than we're all used to."

What Melissa was used to now were vast estates with several wings, scores of servants, and more than enough rooms to entertain enormous house parties. A slightly less lavish existence did not hold any terrors for her, although she was not too eager to live with Gloriana. Then, suddenly, she was struck by a thought that drove all else from her mind. "What of Greyhaven?" she asked.

"We'll sell it, too," Leighton said.

"What?"

"We'll sell it to Duncan, just as he's always wanted," Leighton said, matter-of-factly.

"But, Leighton, it's your love, your passion," Melissa protested, stepping back, shocked, to look into his face.

"No," Leighton said softly, pulling her close again. "It's just a building. You're my love, my passion."

Melissa, who had often been jealous of his deep-rooted love for his home, felt tears prick her eyes. "A fine fortune hunter you turned out to be," she said shakily.

"I think so, too," Leighton agreed. "I've done very well for myself, indeed. Far better than I'd ever dreamed."

*   *   *   *   *

BIG SUMMER READ

Summer Reading At Its Best

In July, Harlequin and Silhouette bring readers the Big Summer Read Program. Heat up your summer with these four exciting new novels by top Harlequin and Silhouette authors.

SOMEWHERE IN TIME by Barbara Bretton
YESTERDAY COMES TOMORROW by Rebecca Flanders
A DAY IN APRIL by Mary Lynn Baxter
LOVE CHILD by Patricia Coughlin

From time travel to fame and fortune, this program offers something for everyone.

Available at your favorite retail outlet.

BSR

OFFICIAL RULES • MILLION DOLLAR MATCH 3 SWEEPSTAKES
NO PURCHASE OR OBLIGATION NECESSARY TO ENTER

To enter, follow the directions published. If the "Match 3" Game Card is missing, hand print your name and address on a 3"×5" card and mail to either: Harlequin "Match 3," 3010 Walden Ave., P.O. Box 1867, Buffalo, NY 14269-1867 or Harlequin "Match 3," P.O. Box 609, Fort Erie, Ontario L2A 5X3, and we will assign your Sweepstakes numbers. (Limit: one entry per envelope.) For eligibility, entries must be received no later than March 31, 1994 and be sent via first-class mail. No liability is assumed for printing errors, lost, late or misdirected entries.

Upon receipt of entry, Sweepstakes numbers will be assigned. To determine winners, Sweepstakes numbers will be compared against a list of randomly preselected prizewinning numbers. In the event all prizes are not claimed via the return of prizewinning numbers, random drawings will be held from among all other entries received to award unclaimed prizes.

Prizewinners will be determined no later than May 30, 1994. Selection of winning numbers and random drawings are under the supervision of D.L. Blair, Inc., an independent judging organization, whose decisions are final. One prize to a family or organization. No substitution will be made for any prize, except as offered. Taxes and duties on all prizes are the sole responsibility of winners. Winners will be notified by mail. Chances of winning are determined by the number of entries distributed and received.

Sweepstakes open to persons 18 years of age or older, except employees and immediate family members of Torstar Corporation, D.L. Blair, Inc., their affiliates, subsidiaries and all other agencies, entities and persons connected with the use, marketing or conduct of this Sweepstakes. All applicable laws and regulations apply. Sweepstakes offer void wherever prohibited by law. Any litigation within the province of Quebec respecting the conduct and awarding of a prize in this Sweepstakes must be submitted to the Régies des Loteries et Courses du Quebec. In order to win a prize, residents of Canada will be required to correctly answer a time-limited arithmetical skill-testing question. Values of all prizes are in U.S. currency.

Winners of major prizes will be obligated to sign and return an affidavit of eligibility and release of liability within 30 days of notification. In the event of non-compliance within this time period, prize may be awarded to an alternate winner. Any prize or prize notification returned as undeliverable will result in the awarding of that prize to an alternate winner. By acceptance of their prize, winners consent to use of their names, photographs or other likenesses for purposes of advertising, trade and promotion on behalf of Torstar Corporation without further compensation, unless prohibited by law.

This Sweepstakes is presented by Torstar Corporation, its subsidiaries and affiliates in conjunction with book, merchandise and/or product offerings. Prizes are as follows: Grand Prize—$1,000,000 (payable at $33,333.33 a year for 30 years). First through Sixth Prizes may be presented in different creative executions, each with the following approximate values: First Prize—$35,000; Second Prize—$10,000; 2 Third Prizes—$5,000 each; 5 Fourth Prizes—$1,000 each; 10 Fifth Prizes—$250 each; 1,000 Sixth Prizes—$100 each. Prizewinners will have the opportunity of selecting any prize offered for that level. A travel-prize option, if offered and selected by winner, must be completed within 12 months of selection and is subject to hotel and flight accommodations availability. Torstar Corporation may present this Sweepstakes utilizing names other than Million Dollar Sweepstakes. For a current list of all prize options offered within prize levels and all names the Sweepstakes may utilize, send a self-addressed, stamped envelope (WA residents need not affix return postage) to: Million Dollar Sweepstakes Prize Options/Names, P.O. Box 4710, Blair, NE 68009.

For a list of prizewinners (available after July 31, 1994) send a separate, stamped, self-addressed envelope to: Million Dollar Sweepstakes Winners, P.O. Box 4728, Blair, NE 68009.   MSW7-92

WELCOME TO

The quintessential small town where everyone knows everybody else!

Finally, books that capture the pleasure of tuning in to your favorite
TV show!

GREAT READING... GREAT SAVINGS... AND A FABULOUS FREE GIFT!

Each book set in Tyler is a self-contained love story; together, the
twelve novels stitch the fabric of the community. The covers honor
the old American tradition of quilting; each cover depicts
a patch of the large Tyler quilt.

With Tyler you can receive a fabulous gift ABSOLUTELY FREE by
collecting proofs-of-purchase found in each Tyler book. And use our
special Tyler coupons to save on your next TYLER book purchase.

Join your friends at Tyler for the sixth book, SUNSHINE
by Pat Warren, available in August.

*When Janice Eber becomes a widow, does her husband's friend
David provide more than just friendship?*

If you missed *Whirlwind* (March), *Bright Hopes* (April), *Wisconsin Wedding* (May), *Monkey Wrench* (June) or *Blazing Star* (July) and would like to order them, send your name, address, zip or postal code, along with a check or money order for $3.99 (please do not send cash), plus 75¢ postage and handling ($1.00 in Canada) for each book ordered, payable to Harlequin Reader Service to:

In the U.S.	In Canada
3010 Walden Avenue	P.O. Box 609
P.O. Box 1325	Fort Erie, Ontario
Buffalo, NY 14269-1325	L2A 5X3

Please specify book title(s) with your order.
Canadian residents add applicable federal and provincial taxes.   TYLER-6

COMING IN JULY
FROM HARLEQUIN HISTORICALS

TEMPTATION'S PRICE
by Dallas Schulze

Dallas Schulze's sensuous, sparkling love stories have made her a favorite of both Harlequin American Romance and Silhouette Intimate Moments readers. Now she has created some of her most memorable characters ever for Harlequin Historicals....

Liberty Ballard...who traveled across America's Great Plains to start a new life.

Matt Prescott...a man of the Wild West, tamed only by his love for Liberty.

Would they have to pay the price of giving in to temptation?

AVAILABLE IN JULY WHEREVER HARLEQUIN BOOKS ARE SOLD